BIGGER FISH

THE **SECOND** EDITION

ANNA BOWMAN THRILLERS
BOOK THREE

Westley Enterprises Publishing
Helena, Montana
www.westleyenterprises.com

SECOND EDITION
ISBN 979-8-9916308-1-8 (Paperback)
ISBN 979-8-9916308-2-5 (eBook)

Dedicated to the final boss.

ALSO BY AK WELLER

Enemy Closer
House on Fire
Bigger Fish
No Port in a Storm
The Lost Portrait

CONTENTS

BIGGER
FISH

I sat with pencil poised over the blank answer sheet, battling the double vision that threatened to make my writing illegible. After a few seconds, I realized no one was providing me with an answer to write. I looked up from the paper and saw my four companions watching me expectantly.

"You guys think *I* know?" I asked.

It was a dismal realization, but not the end of the world. After all, bar trivia at the Hamilton in Washington, DC wasn't exactly the Paris Peace Conference. Thinking this, I zeroed in on Sharen directly across the table from me. She'd pulled "Paris Peace Conference" out of the hat in the last round, so why not this?

"Fear of being happy," I prompted. She shrugged. My ears began to seek out telling whispers from nearby tables in the packed bar, but no one was blabbing.

Dominique Danes, my neighbor in life if not at our booth, startled everyone by smacking Sharen on the arm and urgently, silently, motioning with both hands for me to pass her the pencil and paper. I complied, taking the opportunity to sip at my fourth—fifth?—something-th martini. If I played it right, Dom would keep the answer sheet and I'd be off the hook. I had no idea how I'd been elected the smart one in the group, anyway.

While Dom scribbled, erasing and correcting a couple times, I gazed serenely around at the bar in general and my four companions specifically. Speaking of being happy. The atmosphere was drunkenly exuberant, I was among friends, and as far as I knew, no one wanted to kill me.

One short week had passed since FBI Agent James Camposanto and I had returned to Washington, DC after rescuing a lost Renaissance masterpiece, Raphael's *Portrait of a Young Man*, from a hidden estate in Argentina. The painting was back in Poland now, where a welcome-back exhibition was in the early planning stages. We did that. For all the screw ups and cataclysms and downright unconscionable behavior that got us there, we did it.

Three days ago, I'd returned to my long-forsaken Krav Maga class, which ended in an invite to bar trivia. I'd asked Dom to join me, even though she knew none of my classmates, because she was the only person with whom I could imagine enjoying a night out. My three classmates were nice enough, but I only remembered Sharen's name because her job as an OPM Accountant was the inspiration for a long ago lie that no longer mattered. I couldn't even remember the other two people's names.

Again Dom smacked Sharen, who didn't seem to mind the attention at all, which yanked me out of my reverie. She slid the paper back to me, and I silently mouthed, "Cherophobia."

"I'm ninety percent sure that's it," Dom explained. She took a drink of her scotch—I do admire a woman who drinks scotch—and amended, "One hundred percent. How I know, I don't know, but I know."

"Good enough for me," announced the woman to Sharen's right, whose name might have started with a K. She grabbed the answer sheet and took it to the emcee, sashaying just enough that the man sitting to my right became unnaturally still as he appreciated the view.

Sharen and Dom were getting along like peanut butter and jelly, and intuition told me my other two classmates would be leaving together. They were cute. K Something and M Something. They'd met at class, and the two had been orbiting one another like satellites for as long as I was aware of them.

You'd think being a fifth wheel would upset the apple cart of contentment I had going, but it only made me more comfortable. Once our team was finished losing trivia, I'd find my way back to Jim's house in Arlington, Virginia where rested my dog, Dude, and my Jim, whatever he was.

James Camposanto. If he were the answer to a trivia question, that question would probably be, "Who does this guy think he is?" A mastermind. An intriguing if infuriating romantic partner. The reason my life wasn't boring. The gleeful control freak who'd had the absolute gall to suggest the clothes I wore tonight might be too skimpy. Because the weather may turn, he'd insisted. But he'd had that spark in his eye, and I knew he'd only said it to provoke me. It had worked, which meant I'd been a few minutes late to trivia.

Lost in the pursuant memories, I scoffed aloud, "Fear of being happy. How is that even possible?"

"It's when you think something bad is about to happen because you can't be happy forever," Dom sagely explained. "Take you, for instance."

"Me?" I squeaked.

"Yeah, you, Space Force. You had to sit at the end of the booth facing the door. What'd you think is gonna happen that you need to be guarding the door?"

M Something piped up in my defense. "No one thinks something is going to happen. Doesn't hurt to be cautious."

"Oh okay mhm," Dom mumbled. "So you didn't snap up that seat to be next to our girl Anna. You just wanted to be on deck in queso emergency."

I distinctly heard her say "queso." Maybe I'd had a bit too vodka much.

M Something glanced unwillingly at me, then caught K Something's eye as she meandered back to us through the crowd.

"I plead the fifth," he concluded.

While we waited for the scores from the last round to be announced, Sharen and Dom folded together into a whispered conversation. M and K made awkward small talk across the table. I sat back and enjoyed the entertainment, sipping at martini number who-the-heck-cared and wondering how I was going to get from DC to Arlington without ending up in a ditch.

Jim had dropped me off, insisting he'd be happy to come get me no matter how late I stayed out; but he was probably asleep by now, and I didn't want to wake him up. I could ride the Orange Line almost all the way to Jim's house, but I'd still have to walk about a mile, and I really didn't care to.

I decided to take an Uber, recalling my mostly unused salary as an FBI Intelligence Analyst that had been piling up for months and months. Might as well spend some of it. I opened the app on my phone, then glanced toward the door, wondering if it had started raining again.

My curiosity could not have been timed worse, because I locked eyes with a man walking into the bar. Automatic embarrassment shifted at once to recognition. I knew him, and he knew me, and he wasn't supposed to be there. He wasn't even supposed to be on this side of the Atlantic Ocean. Was I seeing things?

Too drunk to look away, I stared brazenly at the familiar face with a mixture of puzzlement and discomfort. He matched my gaze for what felt like an eternity, then settled into a seat at the bar with clear line-of-sight to me, took off his coat, and ordered a drink. I tried to ignore him, part of me hoping I was seeing things, that he'd disappear if I played it cool.

For a few minutes I feigned interest in the others' conversation, but soon my eyes drifted back to the bar. The man was still there. He'd received a pint of beer and was, unfortunately, solid and real enough to pick it up and drink it.

I watched him sip his beer and only snapped out of it when the emcee turned down the music to announce the winners. Our team took the round, but we didn't even place in the overall scores.

"Anna, why don't you go claim our prize?" Sharen suggested. "You look like you could use a free beer."

"Yeah, Anna, let's see the legs that launched a thousand ships," Dom put in, causing Sharen to erupt with laughter.

I was too focused on the man at the bar to appreciate her assessment, but I did slide out of my seat. Knowing I wouldn't be back, I dropped some cash on the table and waved a half-hearted farewell to my confused companions.

"Say hi to Jim for me," Dom called after me.

At the name, the man at the bar glanced up and saw me walking toward him. As I passed his seat, I heard his mostly-empty glass clink as he sat it down and knew I had about eight seconds to form some kind of plan. Eight hours wouldn't have been enough, not in my state of advanced inebriation. I turned a corner, reached the door to the women's restroom, stopped, and turned around.

David Marchand stood in front of me, too close, his face passing in and out of focus in the poor lighting as I tried to decide if I was the kind of person who saw things when she drank too much.

David couldn't be here. He was the youngest brother of Marcel Marchand, a French crime boss whose clutches I'd escaped back in December in London. David may have turned traitor to help me escape, but that didn't mean I was happy to see him.

"I'm sorry to surprise you like this, Anna," he said in a low voice, his accent more apparent than ever in the sea of American conversations providing background noise. "Are you all right?"

"I'm very drunk. Very, very, very."

"I can see that. However, I need to talk to you, and it can't wait." He pushed open the door to the family restroom and waved me inside.

"Ew," I complained. "Can't we go outside?"

"Oui, if that suits you better."

He offered me his arm and I sputtered with laughter, demurring, until I took a wrong step and nearly broke my ankle. I grabbed his arm and mumbled, "Friends are gonna think you picked me up."

"They can't be dumb enough to make such an obvious error in judgment."

"You're a funny little French guy, you know that?"

He waited until we were outside on the sidewalk to reply, "I worry you might not be able to understand what I'm saying in your current state."

"No, no, being drunk makes me normal smart."

"You are flirting with alcohol poisoning."

"I flirt with everything. Just say what you came here to say."

He started to, but before he could get the first word out his gaze shifted to a spot over my right shoulder. I turned around, not even considering whether that was his intention, and found myself looking up at all six feet, seven inches of James Camposanto.

I backed up, dizzy with indignation and liquor, and saw my dog, Dude, tethered to Jim's right hand by a slackened leash. Dude's tail began to wag as soon as I noticed him, but I was too surprised to greet him properly.

"Did you *follow* me here?" I demanded of Jim.

"I was at your apartment and wondered why you hadn't called yet." He smiled at me and then looked over my head, narrowing his eyes at David to ask, "Is this guy bothering you?"

Over my own fit of laughter at this, I heard David ask, "Are you James Camposanto?"

"Jim, Jim," I gasped, turning again and backing into Jim's non-dog side for support. "This is David Marchand. This is Marcel's baby brother. He helped me escape from the house with all the dogs!"

Of course, Jim already knew this, as he'd masterminded said escape; but again, I was very drunk. Shoulder-to-shoulder with Jim, I felt him tense up. David took a half-step back.

"I'm not here to cause trouble," David preempted. "I need your help."

Jim's arm slipped protectively around my waist anyway. I rested my head on his shoulder, as it seemed to have suddenly doubled in weight, and closed my eyes as Jim asked, "With?"

My eyes popped open at David's low answer of, "Luke."

Luke Jackson. Had it really been less than a month since we said goodbye in Chile? The intervening weeks had seen Jim lavish me with affection and distractions, all to heal the wounds caused by his own Machiavellian hand. Luke was out of my life and down on his luck. His former boss, David's brother Marcel, wouldn't take him back. Luke was supposed to have found safe harbor in Italy with a new benefactor, but if Jim knew whether he'd made it there safely, he wasn't telling me.

It seemed to me that Jim took several minutes to answer, "Luke who?"

"Don't be a jerk, Jim," I snapped. "What happened?"

"Anna," Jim said sharply, fingers digging into my side. "Maybe it's best if you don't talk right now."

"Ugh. You're so bossy."

"Let's go to Anna's apartment," he bossed, adding most reluctantly, "If that's okay with you, Anna."

"It's closer," I agreed. "Why'd you bring Dude? Not that I'm complaining."

Jim didn't answer, but as we fell into step on the sidewalk heading toward my apartment on Dupont Circle, David asked, "This is your dog, Anna?"

"That's my boy."

"He's magnificent. The largest Alsatian shepherd I've ever seen."

"I like you, David. How's Penelope doing?"

"She grows less like a Malinois and more like a person each day."

"Next time you see her, please inform her that I love her."

David chuckled, and I thought I heard Jim force a reluctant breath of laughter. I knew I'd be getting a lecture soon enough, some hogwash about being careful and whatnot.

The ten-minute walk helped me sober up enough to realize it was way too cold outside for the ten-minute walk, and I was shivering miserably by the time the three of us and Dude slipped into the warm shelter of my apartment building's lobby. Jim, comfortable in his light jacket, was kind enough not to say, "I told you so."

We climbed into an elevator, I swiped my key card to get us moving, and Jim judged the time was right to ask David, "So what does Luke want? What happened to him?"

"I don't know what happened. He won't tell me. Marcel sent

me to Atlanta to take care of some business at our international office. I then traveled to Denver to meet Luke, at Luke's request, and we rented a car and drove down to Alquer—Alqubur—uh—"

"Albuquerque," I supplied.

"Yes, New Mexico. He wanted to speak to you but was wary of contacting you directly, so he sent me. He mentioned a leak at the FBI."

"So he wants to chat," Jim concluded. "Is that all he told you?"

Jim's carefully-worded question elicited information without giving it, unlike what I wanted to ask David ("Did Paolo find out he didn't kill Marisol?"). I decided to follow Jim's advice and shut up, though my feathers were still a little ruffled about it.

Before David could answer, the elevator doors opened on my floor and we filed out, not speaking again until I'd locked my apartment door behind us. I invited the men to make themselves at home while I took a quick detour to the bathroom, calling, "Don't talk, I don't want to miss anything!"

I hurriedly did my business, washed my hands, and returned to the living room to plop down on the floor, leaning against Jim's long legs.

"As to why Luke didn't come here himself. He doesn't know who to trust," David explained. "He thinks Marcel wants to kill him, and he might not be wrong about that.

"He told me Marcel asked him to kill Fernando and Marisol Serna on Paolo Barbato's request, then to kill Barbato himself. I have no idea why Marcel would ask for this, but for Luke it was a way back in after helping Anna escape.

"Luke told me he planned to seek refuge with Paolo in Italy rather than returning to Marcel in London, but he no longer believed it was safe to do so."

"So why not go back to Marcel?" Jim asked. "Bridge too burned?"

"I haven't discussed any of this with Marcel, obviously. I'm not an imbecile."

If it was clear to me that David was losing patience with us, it must have been clear to Jim, but he pressed, "If Luke's so worried about a leak, he can get over it. We stop the leaks we want to stop. If he wants to talk, he knows how to reach me."

"Why do I feel I have wasted my time coming here?"

Jim didn't answer. I squirmed, wondering if he were going to ignore David's news. When I couldn't keep it in any longer, I asked, "What are you gonna do, Jim? You can't do nothing."

"I guess it can't hurt to humor him," he answered, plainly unhappy about it. "Where is he?"

"I don't know," David admitted. "Probably still in Al— uh—New Mexico. He told me Anna would be able to find him."

Jim asked something that made so little sense to me I didn't even hear real words. That convinced me I was going to be missing the rest of this conversation. I excused myself to the kitchen to make coffee, brought three steaming mugs back to the living room, and tried my best to tune in. After the tenth time I nodded off and almost struck my head on the coffee table, Jim sent me to bed with a bottle of water and a trashcan.

2

Sunday, March 14, 2021

At some point during my restless sleep, "Take Me to Church" popped into my head and got stuck, a ten-second snippet playing on repeat, over and over and over until I woke up just to make it stop.

It was light outside, but Jim had pulled my bedroom curtains closed so only the suggestion of it penetrated the room. I struggled out of the sheet wrapped around me and dashed to the bathroom, barely making it to the toilet before my stomach contents were rejected into it with gusto. I got it all out, popped slightly too much aspirin, brushed my teeth, and took a shower. All the tap water I chugged, not to mention the painkillers, refused to stay down. It was going to be a long day.

I staggered out of the bedroom to face whatever level of sanctimonious disapproval Jim felt like bestowing on me. He was watching TV, looking tired but otherwise no worse for wear.

Dude and David weren't immediately visible, and I wasn't

certain either had actually spent the night at my apartment. The previous night was something of a blur. I sank down onto the couch and rested my pounding head in Jim's lap.

"Okay, lecture me already," I moaned.

"Me? I would never."

"Where's David? Did he leave?"

"He's on the patio."

I sat up with a groan and looked through the patio door. David was sitting on the concrete, Dude in front of him. The Frenchman appeared to be teaching the German Shepherd how to high-five.

"I think it's love," Jim said, a smile in his voice.

I collapsed back down. "I'm never drinking again."

"Uh huh."

I remembered his appearance last night and asked sharply, "Why did you follow me to the bar? Stalker much?"

"You told me you'd call me if you needed a ride. I got worried. Rightfully so, it turned out."

"Ugh, I'm not a child. You're unbelievable."

"Don't kid yourself. If David had wanted to hurt you, he could have."

"With Dom and three kravists right inside with their noses pressed to the glass? I don't think so."

"I don't see us reaching a consensus here. Do you want some breakfast?"

I thought about it, then dashed to the bathroom again.

Jim called after me, taunting, "Is that a no, or...?"

After praying to the porcelain god once more, I felt mostly

normal, even shooting Dom a quick text to make sure she'd gotten home okay. She asked me who the cutie in the trench coat was (referring to David, I assumed), and I left her on Read.

I emerged from the bathroom to find David had brought Dude back inside and was industriously working away in my kitchen with Dude watching his every move. It was an odd sight, to be sure, but I was too hungover to comment on it.

I sat next to Jim again and whispered, "So what are we doing?"

"David is making breakfast, and I'm watching the news."

"Why are you being more sarcastic than normal? Are you mad at me?"

His nostrils flared, the only physical sign of angst he seemed willing to give. "You're irresponsible. David could have been there to—"

"To kill me?" I cut across him, letting my incredulity out in a burst of laughter. "David isn't an assassin. Why would anyone want to kill me, anyway?" I purred, nuzzling at his neck. "I'm delightful."

"You're the bane of my existence," he corrected. His quick kiss planted on my cheek somewhat softened the news. "There's not much left to do, anyway. David and I got it all sorted after you passed out. He's waiting for his flight back to London."

"Are you driving him?"

"No, he's taking the Metro."

"Ah." I slipped into a cozy contemplation of the grey hairs at Jim's temple. He didn't let me rest for long.

"So what's the rent on this place, anyway?" he asked, too casually.

"I'm gonna go help David," I said in a rush.

I fled, not bothering to disguise my aversion to the topic around which Jim was dancing. He wanted me to move in with him, and I was too attached to my independence to make that leap. Sure, his home in the 'burbs was a palace compared to my shoebox on Dupont Circle, but it was *my* shoebox. I wasn't even ready to start a physical relationship with him, let alone merge my life with his. We were at an impasse.

Never mind that I'd hardly stepped foot in my apartment since we got back from Chile. Despite my resolve to keep calling Dupont Circle home, I'd lingered at Jim's house for a full week. We both had to report to his boss, Richard Beauchamp (pronounced 'Beecham' for God only knew what reason) tomorrow, and Jim had insisted I stay with him under the guise of preparing me. He didn't have a hard time convincing me, but I now realized he wasn't only concerned with preparing me. He was genuinely worried for my safety. He could be such a mother hen.

Over a breakfast of scrambled eggs, bacon, and store-bought croissants which kept drawing disapproval-laden glances from David, the men were kind enough to fill me in on the discussion I'd missed. The gist of it was, David had not convinced Jim that the leak to which he referred was a cause for concern, but he had enlisted our help in tracking Luke down and hearing what he had to say.

His favor to Luke thus completed, David planned to return to his brothers in London and carry on as though no meeting with Luke, let alone Jim and me, had ever taken place. I hoped he was right to be so sanguine about the whole thing, knowing

Marcel's love for his youngest brother might not cover over a betrayal of such magnitude.

David was an MI5 asset since partnering with them and the FBI to spirit me away from Marcel, and he was still passing bits and pieces to the British intelligence service through Mary, the MI5 operative who'd personally rescued me.

David departed shortly after breakfast, once Jim was satisfied that all their ducks were in a row. Jim, Dude, and I returned to Arlington, where Jim compelled me to practice, *again*, what I was going to say in our meeting tomorrow.

Jim was justifiably nervous: None of our shenanigans in South America had been officially sanctioned. He hadn't even told anyone I was down there. Officially, I had slipped my passport, laptop, and phone into Jim's luggage in Berlin on New Year's Eve and split, and by the time he realized I was AWOL he was already on his way home. I purportedly stayed in Berlin until a week ago, only returning to the States when my father came to get me.

Jim, meanwhile, had allegedly paid a routine visit to his cousin in Argentina, Fernando Serna, which ended in disaster. Jim would claim to have demanded the Raphael from Fernando, whose reaction escalated into violence. Jim couldn't very well pretend the Raphael hadn't been recovered, as it was all over the news.

But here's what really happened:

Just over a year ago, I was on assignment in Houston with my partner, Tommy Holladay, working undercover to infiltrate the Colombia-based Tres Islas Cartel. Our boss, Philip Levin, blew our cover. I barely made it home alive; Tommy wasn't so lucky. I was no closer to proving Philip's misdeeds today than I was two years ago.

I had Jim to thank for that, as I had him to thank for every good and bad event since he'd shattered my dream of becoming an agent by pulling the strings that got Tommy and me, lowly intelligence analysts, into Levin's undercover operation in the first place.

That's where Luke Jackson came in. Luke was an assassin on Marcel Marchand's payroll. That night in Houston, Luke had been there to kill cartel heavyweight Francisco Lira. Once that job was done, he'd fled into hiding in Colorado until it was time to get his next assignment from Marcel.

Luke and I officially met when Jim sent me to Colorado to find him and question him about that night. And by question, I mean befriend him and gain his trust. I did my sordid job and earned myself an invitation from Luke to join him in London, if I cared to. I did care to, not only because I'd become attached to Luke but because I still wanted answers. Jim told me Luke might have them. He didn't.

At that point, I had no inkling of Jim's larger goals. I didn't know most of this charade had been choreographed by Jim to get me closer to the man who'd asked Marcel to sic Luke on Francisco Lira: Paolo Barbato. Jim wanted me to get closer to Barbato to put to rest the cold case Jim was supposed to be solving, and Jim wanted me to get the Raphael away from Fernando without arousing suspicion.

Luke had killed Fernando, spared Fernando's kid sister

Marisol in exchange for the painting, and lost his last chance to get back into Marcel's good graces. Fernando deserved what he got, but I didn't believe Luke deserved to be left holding the bag. He'd elected to join forces with Paolo instead, or so we'd thought. Luke was supposed to be in Italy with Paolo now, safe and sound. If David were to be believed, Luke hadn't even made it out of the States.

I assumed I'd find out why, because I knew I'd be able to find Luke. We just had to get through this meeting with Beauchamp first.

3

Monday, March 15, 2021

The thing about falling deeply in love with Jim was, I was technically dating my boss.

I had been for months, but it never occurred to me in such bleak, black-and-white terms until I was getting dressed on the morning of our meeting with the big boss. Beauchamp was of course my boss too, even though I'd never met him and had only learned his name in the last month. In his typically infuriating style, Jim hadn't told me anything about Beauchamp but his name.

The big boss didn't need to know Jim had partnered with an international assassin to recover the Raphael, so I had to convince Beauchamp I'd never been in Argentina. Sorting out all the details was a nightmare, but fortunately for me Jim did all the thinking. I simply had to memorize the cover story and then get suspended or fired for supposedly going haywire in Berlin.

While dutifully memorizing and practicing my lines to Jim's

satisfaction, I hadn't given any thought to what I was going to wear, so I found myself panicking when I threw on the first items of clothing I found, looked in the mirror, and saw a delicious little office scandal staring back at me.

I examined myself with a judgmental eye. I was wearing my favorite outfit: black pencil skirt ending right at the knee, conservative black pumps, figure-hugging blue tank top mostly concealed by a tailored black jacket. I'd done my hair for the first time in who knew how long, my waist-length, bottle blonde locks set in gently spiraling waves that almost distracted from the inch-wide, ginger stripe along the crown of my head. I'd even slapped some makeup on my face for that I-haven't-been-getting-kicked-around-for-most-of-my-life look.

"Why do I feel like this sends the wrong message?" I asked when Jim walked into the bedroom tapping his watch. He looked me over, taking his time even though I was certain he'd been on the cusp of telling me to hurry up. He didn't insult me by pretending not to understand.

"Blue?" he ventured, leaving it at that.

I shared a dubious glance with my reflection. "A Lewinski reference? Really?"

"I think you look—uh…" He gave me an apologetic smile. "I want to tell you you don't look sexy, but I can't make myself do it."

"Think he'll buy it?"

"If you don't go to pieces on me."

"When have I ever?" I demanded, adding hastily, "Don't answer that. Let's just go, I don't want to be late on top of everything else."

We bid farewell to Dude, jumped in Jim's car, and squeezed ourselves into the press of traffic wending its way up from Arlington, Virginia into the heart of the nation's capital.

Jim held my hand across the center console for most of the ride, casually releasing it when the shadow of the J. Edgar Hoover Building passed over us. He slid into a reserved underground parking space, and we rode the elevator up to his floor.

I'd been working for Jim, neither officially nor voluntarily, since the beginning of last year, but I'd never set foot in his office—our office. Neither had I met a single one of his coworkers, subordinates, or superiors, the noteworthy exception being my neighbor, Dominique. That's a whole story.

I wasn't even certain what either of them did, only that Jim's office was called the Continuous Evaluation Unit. When Jim had first appeared on my radar, I'd looked him up in the FBI directory and found him listed only as an agent, which I'd known even then was a meaningless moniker. Dom worked for Jim and was consistently mum about what she or anyone else in her office did.

When I stepped off the elevator and followed Jim through a pair of unlocked, glass entry doors, I was sorely disappointed to find myself in the most aggressively non-descript office I'd ever seen.

The solid wall behind the entry doors, which blocked the rest of the office from view, was featureless but for a comically small placard bearing only the suite number. No office name, no official seal, not so much as a token American flag. Following Jim around this wall, I saw maybe 30 cubicles, all with extra-high walls that shielded their occupants from direct sight.

I could hear muted conversations, the gentle tap of key-boards, an unseen laser printer humming warmly. Behind and to the left of the cubes, a dozen closed office doors were arranged in an L-shape. Jim led me toward the office at the far end on the left, opened the door with a wave of his badge and a press of his thumbprint to a scanner, and ushered me inside.

"Okay, *this* is more like what I pictured," I said.

Gazing around at the standard desk-bookshelf-filing cab-inet arrangement, the dark colors, the photo of our current Commander in Chief dutifully hanging on the wall amongst degrees, awards, and photos, my eyes fell on an out-of-place looking poster. He'd hung it on the wall right next to the door, making it invisible when the door was open.

Roughly two feet wide by three feet tall, the black-and-white image was dominated by photographs of three children—a pre-teen girl and a younger boy and girl. Above the photos was the plea, "MISSING," and below each was a name, age, and physical description. The poster had seen better days, its edges torn and curling behind protective glass.

Jim noticed me staring and asked, "Had you never seen it before?"

"No. They look so serious. For children."

Etta, Emilio, and Regina Barber started back at me, frozen in time, until I forced myself to look around for something less depressing to focus on.

Jim's window overlooked E Street and its classical, uniform façades that stretched as far as the eye could see in either direc-tion. At the entrance to the parking garage across the street, a homeless man was meekly accepting a handful of change from a besuited woman trying to walk east, toward Ninth Street. Jim appeared in my peripheral vision, gazing down at the street with me.

"Want to know what I pictured?" he asked suggestively.

"I can guess. Can you do it in—" I checked my watch "—four minutes?"

"Not properly."

"Then how about a cup of coffee, tiger?"

He shook with laughter. "It's in the breakroom. I'll be back. Don't touch anything."

"As if," I mumbled to the door that closed behind him.

The very moment I was alone, I started opening drawers in search of the scotch I knew he'd have hidden somewhere. I needed something to help get me through this meeting. Sadly, I hadn't turned up any alcohol by the time Jim returned with two cups of coffee and a mistrustful expression. I leaned against the filing cabinet drawer I'd just closed.

"You really can't help yourself, can you?" he asked lightly.

"I don't know, I've never tried."

"Come on, time to meet the big guy."

"God?"

"As far as you're concerned."

We walked over to the next office. Jim knocked once on the door, which opened from the inside far too quickly.

"Jim—good—just on my way to get you." Beauchamp looked at me briefly, then back at Jim. "Come in, sit down."

As I was apparently a non-entity, I felt free to stare at this Richard Beauchamp person and take my time sizing him up.

He was about six feet tall, white hair cropped close, maybe a decade older than Jim's 42. He had the broad shoulders of an athlete and the beer belly of a former athlete, and he carried the extra weight well enough in an expensive suit befitting his position. Overall he wasn't unattractive, but his nose was a little too round, and his cheeks bore the unmistakable, permanent flush of someone who has a love-hate relationship with liquor. I thought I'd detected a mostly-quelled Louisiana accent when he first spoke, but when he'd seated himself behind his desk and got down to business, it was gone.

"Well. It's a pleasure to finally meet you in person, Miss Bowman," he said, waving us both into chairs in front of his desk. Based on what I'd already observed, it was a nice surprise not to be addressed as Little Lady.

"Likewise," I said, leaving it at that. Jim had encouraged me to stick to one-word answers where possible.

"Jim, I spent all weekend with the report you turned in at the last possible second on Friday, and I've got to say: It carries the distinct odor of horse manure."

"Please elaborate," Jim offered, unimpressed by this accusation.

"In a minute. First, I'd like to spend some time alone with Anna. Why don't you go back to your office and I'll send her over when I'm ready for you."

I met Jim's eyes, willing him not to panic, but it was too late.

"Is that going to be a problem?" Beauchamp asked.

"No," I answered for both of us, flashing him a bland smile.

"You heard the lady," he said, making me wince. "Beat it. Go

"Y understand, Miss Bowman?"

"So,

For sleeping with him?"

brown, slig mable reason, as I looked into his muddy insane impu ot eyes, I was briefly possessed of the ruth. Maybe he was part cobra.

take that cybersecurity training before I have to write you up."

As Jim stood, grudgingly compliant, I thought I heard him breathe a sigh that sounded like several curse words strung together. Either Beauchamp missed it, or he let it go. I may have been able to conceal my panic faster than Jim had, but it was no less acute, especially as Jim departed and the door snapped shut, leaving me alone with Beauchamp.

I didn't know this man at all, let alone trust him. I didn't even know why Jim was so intent on obfuscating my involvement in recovering the painting. Was he simply trying to cover his tracks, or did he have some reason not to trust Beauchamp? First Philip, then Jim, had lied to me and used me, and by then I'd have been a fool to expect anything better from the next guy.

My insides writhed madly, as though trying to rip themselves from my body and flee the room behind Jim, as Beauchamp fixed a beady eye on me.

He opened up the discussion mildly enough, asking, "How's that coffee? Drinkable?"

"Barely."

"You drove in with Jim this morning, huh?"

"Yes."

"Why?"

He coaxed me out of single-word responses with that one.

"We're supposed to be dating," I said.

"That's against Bureau policy."

"What, salacious and hackneyed cover stories?" I shot back, pressing my lips together, immediately regretting my sarcasm. His eyebrows shot up.

"No, inter-office roma—"

"I know that. It's a cover, Mister Beauchamp—"

"Rich."

"—Richard. And it was Jim's idea, so I'd prefer not to take flack for it. Sir."

"So you're telling me it's a cover?"

"Yes. I thought you knew—"

"You're not in a relationship?"

My composure slipped. "*That's* why you wanted to talk to me alone? I prefer younger men," I lied, sitting back and crossing my legs to make sure he felt disappointment rather than suspicion. His gaze darted down to my thighs, then back to my face.

"I really don't give a hoot what consenting adults do, policy or no, but you've got to understand where I'm coming from. Jim's been elbows-deep in one doozy of a side hustle for years now. I've got a boss too, and at some point I'll have to explain what he's been doing. That day seems to be looming, and here I sit flipping through Jim's forty-one page report and it dawns on me I don't actually *know* what he's been doing, not all of it. If it turns out he's been ploughing his operative, pearls will be clutched and I will eat crow. Understand?"

"Wow, that was a lot of different metaphors."

"Do you understand, Miss Bowman?"

"*Yes.*"

"So, are you sleeping with him?"

For some unfathomable reason, as I looked into his muddy brown, slightly bloodshot eyes, I was briefly possessed of the insane impulse to tell the truth. Maybe he was part cobra.

wonder if he'd returned to the cabin in Hesperus, Colorado, where we'd met.

Fortunately, I wasn't a woman anyone would describe as wise, and my two weeks were up. Either I'd be able to go to Albuquerque because Beauchamp's travel ban was lifted, or I'd be free to do whatever I wanted because I'd be unemployed. In either case, if I didn't find Luke in New Mexico, I could head up to Colorado for some déjà vu.

Jim would have to take some time off, but he wouldn't hear of me going alone. I didn't know whether he'd brought Beauchamp up to speed on the latest from Luke via David, so I decided to play dumb if it came up.

I girded my loins and appeared at Beauchamp's office as ordered at 9:00 a.m. on March 29, bereft even of the comfort of Jim's presence. Instead of Jim in the left-hand chair, I found a round little woman with a fluffy, mouse-brown topknot and a stretchy pink dress that was no match for her curves. She smiled politely at me as I took my seat, and she waited for the nod from Beauchamp to introduce herself.

"I'm Mattie, from Human Resources. I'll be sitting in on this meeting as a matter of policy. You feel free to ask me any questions. I'm here for you."

Lord, she sounded like she was bearing witness to my dismissal. That didn't bode well. I slid into the second chair and gave her a tight smile in return for her courtesy. My full attention moved to Beauchamp, who looked grave.

"Miss Bowman." I noted the shift from Anna with dismay. "We've decided the best thing to do will be to suspend you without pay for three months."

Mattie clicked her tongue in barely audible disapproval. Beauchamp's eyes slid over to her with a baleful glint.

"Mister Bowchamp," she said confidently, "I think it would be beneficial to Miss Bowman to hear a little context, given the impact this decision will have on her. Don't you think?"

"I don't really care," I said across Beauchamp's answer. "Do I still have to stay in the area?"

"No, you can travel freely," he said. "That's your only question?"

"… Yep."

"Okay, great. Sign this." He pushed a piece of paper across his desk toward me. I read over it quickly, not caring what it said, and signed at the bottom. "Need a copy? No? All right then. Thank you for coming up, Mattie. Meeting adjourned."

She shot him a sour look and departed in high dudgeon, my signed whatever clutched in one cute little chubby hand. I fled Beauchamp's office right behind her and didn't look back.

I longed to know if Beauchamp's evident dissatisfaction with the whole thing was because my punishment was too harsh, or too lenient. I felt I'd gotten off pretty light and was battling a disconcerting sensation of euphoria as I left the FBI and returned to Arlington.

Jim, who'd been ordered to stay away, was waiting there for me. I told him about my suspension, and he gave Beauchamp a verbal lashing that would've taken the varnish off a sailboat. I sat on the couch and listened happily, my heart bounding with affection for this man who had gotten me into all of this and somehow couldn't accept that I was being metaphorically flogged for it.

Since Jim's side of the story left no wrongdoing at his feet, even Fernando's death going down as justifiable self-defense about which no law enforcement entity outside the FBI would even know, no disciplinary meeting awaited him. Nevertheless, Jim had to go into the office now that my meeting was over. I caught a ray of hope as he was leaving.

"Beauchamp mentioned something about our next move, said he wants to talk it over with me. I think he assumes you'll be involved."

"So I'm not getting punted back to King's office after my suspension?" I asked, referring to my boss in the Organized Crime Unit from which Jim had stolen me.

"I don't know—Did you not ask about that?"

"Uh… no."

"I'll find out for sure. You'll be here tonight?"

I nodded. "Bring Thai food."

"Yes, ma'am." He kissed me, ruffled Dude's ears, and left.

I looked down at Dude, mirroring his thoughtful gaze. "You know, I should be furious that I'm getting slapped around for something that wasn't even my fault. Shouldn't I?"

He stared at me, eager to understand what I wanted and supply it as soon as possible. God, I loved him. I bent down and kissed him right between his big, velvety ears.

"Whatever. No time like the present to call that darn casino again."

According to my recollection, this was the billionth time I'd called the casino in Albuquerque to ask about Luke. By then, every front desk employee knew my number, and half of them wouldn't pick up. I got lucky and reached one of the more long-suffering associates, a shift supervisor no less.

"Sandia Resort and Casino, this is Staci, how can I help you?"

"Hi Staci, it's Anna Bowman."

She took half a beat to catch up to my familiar tone and answered brightly, "Oh, hi Anna. I was hoping you'd call. I have news for you."

"You're kidding."

"Got time for a short story?"

"I'm all yours."

"So, last night a lady got pick-pocketed in the lobby and no one seen nothing, so I had to write a report and look at the security camera footage, like to refresh my memory, and I seen that guy walking into the hotel."

She wrapped it up so abruptly that I was speechless for a moment. "You—you saw him?"

"I think, yeah. He looked like you said, tall dark and handsome with a large side of scruffy. And he was wearing what you told me—" I felt a spasm of triumph. Luke hadn't expanded his wardrobe since leaving Chile, which to me meant he wanted to be found. "—and he looked right at the camera when he walked past. Get me your email address and I'll send you a screenshot."

"Can you make it a text?" I asked. She agreed, I thanked her profusely, we hung up, and I stared at my phone until a text from a 505 number came through. I opened the attached jpeg, trying not to get my hopes up too much.

Even through the mess of confused pixels and fish-eye distortion, I picked Luke out of a jumble of other people immediately. Just as Staci had said, he was looking right at the camera. Her text included a little blurb of extra information:

"Also he isn't staying here. He never came up to the front desk and I haven't seen him in the hotel. I think he gone into the casino and I never seen him leave. Good luck!"

I had to take a moment to marvel at her version of the English language. It made her sound ditzy, but I'd talked to her enough to know she was exceptionally sharp. Must be a dialect thing.

I found a flight to Albuquerque that left Thursday—April Fool's Day—booked two tickets, texted Jim to tell him when we were leaving, and then started packing.

6

Thursday, April 1, 2021

Our bags were packed when we went to sleep Wednesday night. Since our flight would leave from Reagan International at 6:00 a.m., I was prepared for the natural disorientation of waking up to a zero dark thirty alarm. When it erupted from Jim's phone, I was already awake, and I sprang out of bed and ran to the bathroom.

I came back out to find Jim on the phone, an unusually sulky look on his face. I saw no visible evidence of him getting ready to go. The clock by his side of the bed read 2:08. Jim's alarm wasn't supposed to go off until three.

Several seconds passed in thick silence while I tried to figure out why it was 2:08, and Jim listened to whoever he was on the phone with.

His eyes darted to me, and he said, "Okay."

"Oh, it was your phone ringing," I answered myself. "Duh."

Jim gave me a look, putting his finger to his lips, and I inferred he was on the phone with someone who oughtn't know I was there. Beauchamp?

"I'm tempted to say that's none of your business," Jim said, his voice bitter with barely suppressed dislike. Maybe it wasn't Beauchamp.

Overcome by curiosity, I stepped toward him to eavesdrop. He backed away from me, and I crossed my arms, pouting.

"Fine," I mouthed. I started getting dressed, trying to ignore the super secret conversation. It was pretty easy to do, since his voice sank lower and lower until he was whispering into the phone like a sweaty teenager.

I yanked on a comfortable flying outfit (perhaps a bit too roughly) and emerged from the neck hole of my hoodie to see Jim sitting at the foot of the bed, staring down at his now-dark phone screen.

"Are you going to tell me who that was?" I asked.

"Paolo."

"Oh, crap." I sat down next to him. "What did he want?"

"Me. To come to Italy."

"Why?"

"Why indeed."

"So he didn't say?" I prodded, not giving him any time to answer before I demanded, "Did you tell him you can't go?"

"I don't have a choice."

He sounded exhausted, as though he'd already mentally endured the argument I was building up steam to start. If it was emotional blackmail, it worked. My temper retreated as quickly as it had flared.

I slid a hand onto his back, pleading, "Do you have to go *now?*"

Turning to me, he hit me with the strangest combination of profound mistrust and open appeal I'd ever been subjected to. He almost didn't have to say, "Please wait for me to get back before you go to New Mexico. Please."

"Jim…"

"I know you want to help Luke, but you can't go alone." At my frown, he corrected himself by saying, "You *shouldn't* go alone."

"I probably won't find him right away," I reasoned. "You can meet me there after Italy. I'll get a head start on the search. Do the grunt work. It'll be fine. How long do you think Paolo will—"

Jim cut across me to say, "He's never kept me there more than a day. You can wait for me here."

"Just like you can tell Paolo to go bite lead."

"Not as easily as you can wait five minutes," he fired back, his composure slipping.

I shot to my feet. My sympathy evaporated that quickly, and I snarled, "You put us *both* in this situation, you know. Remember?"

"It's not my fault Luke didn't go to Italy. That's probably why Paolo wants to talk to me, so I'd say it was Luke who—"

"Bull. Don't even try that on me." I fumed for a moment, then asked, "If he wants to talk, why doesn't he talk? Weren't you just talking?"

"You know why I have to go."

"Right back at you, Jim," I spat.

Before he could answer, I left the bedroom in search of a reason to not be in the bedroom anymore. All my luggage was in there, and what I needed to do was drag it out to Jim's car so we could get to the airport on time. In lieu of that, I grabbed his keys off the hook by the garage door and stuffed them in my pocket. Either I was going to the airport, or neither of us was.

Dude scratched at the back door, asking for a potty break, and I turned to let him out. I was halfway across the living room when Jim came out of the bedroom, let Dude out, and—to my puzzlement—stepped outside right after him. The back door snapped shut with a clap, and as I peered into the darkness, wondering what he was doing, I saw a rectangle of light floating in the air for a split second. Was he calling Paolo back, safely outside the reach of my prying ears?

I used the opportunity to load my luggage into Jim's Suburban, then went ahead and loaded Jim's too. I was finished loading, dressed, holding a thermos of to-go coffee, and beginning to get worried when Jim and Dude finally came back inside.

Without looking at me, he ducked back into the bedroom. When he emerged a few seconds later, his jaw was set as he whisked past on his way to the garage door. I sipped at my coffee, almost eager for the coming battle. I knew I was right. Luke needed us, and he'd waited long enough. Paolo Barbato was just going to have to wait his turn.

Jim sighed loudly, then walked up behind me.

"Don't attack me, okay?"

Reluctantly, I muttered, "Fine."

He wrapped me in a bear hug from behind, squeezed me rather hard, and whispered into my ear, "Luke will be okay for a few more days without you. I'm not telling you, Anna. I'm asking you."

Wilting, I argued, "I didn't buy refundable tickets."

"Why not?"

"Because they're more expensive, and I'm not rich or a government employee." I felt him laughing silently against me and asked, "What's so funny?"

"You opened your mouth, and your dad came out."

Scoffing, I asked, "So you two are like buds now, huh?"

"Oh, no," Jim said, still laughing. "He hates me. A lot."

I smiled to myself, wondering if Jim's assessment were right. People tended to assume my dad disliked them, because he was a curmudgeonly old fart. He was actually pretty good at seeing the best in people, a trait he'd failed to pass along to his youngest daughter.

"Let go already," I whined. Jim released me, and I set my thermos on the coffee table before turning to face him. "I want you to tell me exactly why Paolo is making you go to Italy, and exactly why you don't want me to go to Albuquerque alone."

"And then you'll cooperate?"

"Don't get greedy."

Sighing, he wrapped me in his arms again. This time it was more of an embrace than a submission hold. "Paolo didn't say why. I expect he'll want to drill me about Luke on his home turf where he thinks I feel vulnerable. And he likes to play these power games with me. He's living on the run, in hiding—I've never met him in the same place twice—and pushing me around makes him feel like he's still got control over something. He'll ask me where Luke is, I'll tell him I don't know, and he'll pat himself on the back for getting me to come all the way to Italy for a five-minute conversation."

"And you'll preserve your relationship with him," I concluded.

"Exactly."

"And as to the second question…?"

"I know you can look after yourself better than most. But if something were to happen to you, I'd always believe it was because I wasn't there."

"I don't understand why you think this is so dangerous."

"That's funny. I can't understand why you think it isn't."

I felt him check his watch behind my back.

"Will you at least let me drive you to the airport?" I asked.

"I'd love that, but my keys seem to have gone missing."

"You should keep better track of your stuff."

He released me again and reached toward the pockets of my hoodie with both hands, but I skipped away. This initiated a brief, low-speed chase around the sofa that ended when Dude stepped between Jim and me, sat down, and barked once, a sound which translated roughly to, "I love you, but I will kill you."

"You're such a hall monitor," I said to Dude. I fished the keys out of my pocket and tossed them to Jim. "Let's get you to Italy."

▼

Mentally, I was holding my breath all the way to Dulles International Airport, through the line to purchase a ticket for Jim to Rome (from where he'd receive further instructions from Paolo on where to go), up to the line for security, through our parting kiss, and finally to the moment when Jim turned on his way toward the terminal and waved goodbye to me.

I exhaled so loudly after he disappeared from view that a woman standing next to me jumped in surprise.

"Sorry," I mumbled as I fled toward the exit.

I couldn't believe it. I hadn't told Jim I'd wait in Virginia, and he hadn't pressed the issue. I hadn't even removed my luggage from the back of the Suburban. It was so out of character for Jim to leave something as wildly impulsive as my own behavior to chance that I almost convinced myself he knew what I was going to do and had resigned himself to it.

After all, this wasn't like the last time I'd gone searching for Luke in London. It was even less like the first time, when I'd gone to Hesperus to find him. I'd undertaken both of those tasks alone and dealt with the danger quite effectively, thank you very much. Any danger now existed entirely in Jim's head, and the longer I sat around twiddling my thumbs, the greater the odds I'd never find Luke.

I dashed back to short-term parking, fired up Jim's Suburban, and broke every speed limit between Dulles and Reagan. Traffic was a nightmare, but I made it to my gate with seconds to spare and boarded my flight to Albuquerque, New Mexico.

7

Thursday, April 1 to Friday, April 2, 2021

The trip was uneventful but mind-numbingly long. After multi-hour layovers in Chicago and Dallas, I made it to Albuquerque in time to take a cab to the casino and arrive before Staci the Shift Supervisor got off work.

I rolled up to the front desk, picking Staci out immediately. She looked exactly like she sounded, an elf-sized Latina no older than 20, long dark hair French braided down her back, silver nametag advertising her enviable supervisory position. I decided to thank her in person for being such an absolute paydirt factory and possibly leverage our loose association to get access to more security camera footage.

Sadly, I only got half of my wish. I told Staci who I was, thanked her for her help, and asked if Luke had showed up since we last spoke. She hadn't seen him since he'd showed up on the security camera. A man I assumed was Staci's own supervisor was hovering over her shoulder, looking hawklike and suspicious, so I didn't bother asking about the security footage. That concluded the finely-tuned portion of my plan.

I lingered at the casino's bar for a few drinks, hoping I'd get lucky and Luke would show up before I had to go looking for him. After an hour, I realized it wasn't going to be that easy. There were a lot of other places in Albuquerque Luke might be, so I had to start pounding the pavement.

I left the hotel and called a cab, waiting on the curb for about a quarter hour. The evening air was chilly but pleasant, perfumed by decorative sage and rosemary shrubs basking in the high desert sunset.

While I waited, I turned off my phone. Either Jim had a layover before his transatlantic flight, or he'd decided to risk the ire of the flight crew by turning on his phone. I'd begun racking up angry little red notifications on the text, email, and phone apps, and I didn't have the guts to face them yet. Better to live in denial of their existence for as long as possible. I didn't need my phone anymore, anyway.

The casino hotel sat in the far northeast quadrant of Albuquerque, the Sandias looming large behind it and I-25 roaring past the other side. If I went south, I'd reach downtown Albuquerque in eleven miles. A certain cabin in Hesperus, Colorado, was about 220 miles northwest of me.

I'd considered going to Hesperus, and why not? It was as good a place as any to look for Luke. But it was so far, and leaving Albuquerque without a genuine effort to find him here would be silly. He'd been at the casino recently, and he'd so obviously wanted to be seen. Maybe he even knew, somehow, that I'd been calling the casino looking for him.

I had a list of other places to search for him, though unfortunately it was not as well-informed as the list I'd assembled during my search of London last year. On the good news side of things, Albuquerque was about fifteen times smaller than London. I could check every building in the city, given enough time. My only barriers were having nowhere to lay my head and store my stuff, and a boss-slash-boyfriend who was probably letting me goof around just to see what I would do.

My cab pulled up, and I directed the driver to a motel near the intersection of I-25 and I-40. This motel accepted cash, which meant I wouldn't have to use the credit card through which I knew Jim could track me down if he cared to. Judging by his attempts to contact me, I could no longer pretend he was okay with this.

I paid for two nights, hid my luggage in the bathtub, peeled back the disgusting coverlet, and considered taking a nap. Instead I took a shower to wake myself up, outfitted myself in a low-brow night out ensemble, and stuffed my wallet and phone into the pockets of my jeans. I set out on foot for the westernmost establishment on my A-List of places where Luke might have shown his face.

If Luke were loitering around, waiting for me to ferret him out, where would he be loitering? My first and only guess was at a bar. There's nothing like a bar to hang out for hours without the inconvenience of any particular activity or children screaming at the next table.

A one-and-a-half-mile walk west from my motel brought me to a small brewery halfway between the Rio Grande and the interstate. I let myself inside and looked around at the early evening crowd. No Luke. I sidled up to the bar and asked the compact redhead manning it for a pilsner and a favor.

The security camera photo from Staci would have been helpful, but I wasn't ready to turn my phone back on yet, so I described Luke to her and asked if he'd been around. He hadn't, but I opened a tab anyway. People filtered in gradually until the place filled up, but none of them was Luke.

Around eight, I closed out my tab and moved on to a string of bars on Central Avenue. I wended my way back east, getting a pint at each establishment and asking every employee about Luke with nary a glimmer of recognition. I kept it up until the bright lights of bars and breweries twinkled out about half a mile from the interstate. This abyss seemed like a natural stopping point, as did the eight pints of light beer I'd pounded over the last six hours.

I set my feet toward my motel, temporarily defeated and entirely boozed up. The neon lights and laughing clusters of merrymakers faded away behind me as I walked quickly enough to look like I had somewhere to be.

I was aware of the danger long before it came to a head. Footsteps behind me on the otherwise deserted sidewalk were my first clue that someone had taken an interest in the drunk girl trotting along by herself at midnight. The look and feel of the buildings around me gave me no reason to suspect I was in a bad part of town, but my gut told me that didn't matter right now.

I paused at a side street, using the pretense of checking for oncoming traffic to take a swift look over my shoulder. There was definitely someone keeping pace with me about twenty yards back. With a belly full of liquid courage, I elected to turn around and plant myself there while he passed. He took his time, giving me ample opportunity to study the thin face, unkempt hair and clothes, and baleful glare of a gangly white guy who could've been 25 or 55. I didn't know him from Adam.

As he passed me, he snarled, "Wha'you lookin' at, skank?"

I decided he was being rhetorical and didn't answer, keeping my gaze fixed stonily on him until he had to turn away to step off the curb and cross the side street. Beneath my automatic indignation at being spoken to that way, I felt a whisper of curiosity. The vagrants in Washington were so much more polite. I was willing to bet they did better, too. I'd have given him the tenner in my pocket if he'd asked, but instead he'd called me a skank. Maybe he wasn't hurting for cash at the moment.

I let him get about fifty yards ahead, then carried on. I passed between another motel on my left and a nicer hotel on my right, my gaze riveted to each successive pool of light under the street lights he passed. He turned twice to see if I was still behind him. Given my luck today in general, he was probably headed for the same motel I was, right on the other side of the interstate.

He disappeared into the deep shadows of the highway overpass, and I soldiered on, watching the other side for his reappearance. My soggy wits realized too late that he had stopped, and I was under the overpass with him. Was he waiting for me?

I stopped and looked around, nerves stretched tight. He stepped out from behind a pylon a few yards in front of me.

"You following me, skank?" he demanded.

"I'm just trying to get home," I sighed.

"Take the long way. This is my spot."

I checked behind me. No one. I turned back to him. "Or I could just walk past you like a normal human being."

My powers of de-escalation had never been great. They appeared to have deserted me altogether. He bristled, taking two steps toward me.

"Beat it, skank."

Without conscious thought, I raised my hands in front of me, palms out. This was why I trained Krav Maga. I didn't make a habit of seeking out physical altercations, but somehow my innocent, well-meaning choices led me there time and again. The least I could do was learn how to win.

"Please let me pass. I don't want any trouble."

"Too late. Shoulda thoughta that before you eyeballed me."

"I wasn't eyeballing you! I thought *you* were following *me!*"

"Yeah, fancy lady thinks I want something from her?" He stepped forward again, and I slid back half a step. Rage was rapidly overpowering my already handicapped other emotions.

"I'm just being cautious," I hedged.

"Be cautious somewhere else, skank."

That was one skank too many. "Get out of my way, you moron!"

He charged, and I landed a solid kick to his chest that forced him to stumble backward, huffing in rage. He came again, and

I kicked him again, executing in my drunken confidence the most flawless side kick-spinning back kick-roundhouse combo I'd ever managed. It made me so dizzy I almost kissed the concrete, but he was hardly phased. He clung to the pylon for brief support before springing back, this time with something shiny in his right hand.

Uh-oh.

Before I could panic too much, I went on the offense and barreled into him, blocking a sweep of the knife with my left forearm and punching him in the throat at the same time. While he hacked and gasped and reached blindly for me with his free hand, I jerked him forward by the knife hand and stripped the weapon away, backing up to give him some room to think.

He looked me up and down, wiped a hand across his mouth, and dashed across Central to the other side of the overpass. I sprinted the rest of the way to my motel, threw myself through the door, set the safety chain, and fell apart in a fit of hysterical laughter.

"Ho-ho-ho-lee crap," I crowed at the empty room. "That was so much fun. I'm so stupid. Whoa."

I whirled and pressed my face to the peephole to verify I hadn't been followed. I laughed again, adrenaline still surging through me like fire. I was barely sober enough not to head back out to look for some other trouble to start.

I showered yet again to shed the bouquet of cigarette and weed smoke I'd picked up (I wasn't paying by the gallon after all) and passed out on the rock-hard bed, my shiny new knife displayed on the nightstand like a trophy.

8
Friday, April 2, 2021

The previous evening came back to me in bits and pieces, in no particular order. My most cogent memories were of the first brewery and the first two bars on Central. After that things started to get fuzzy. I went through my pockets and verified my phone and wallet were still there.

In the back pocket of my jeans, I found a credit card receipt with a phone number scrawled on the back. The name and card number belonged to someone else; I'd been paying cash all night. I'd gotten the receipt at someplace called The Library, apparently. I had no memory of it.

I plopped back into bed, stared at the ceiling, and replayed the fight in my head. My purring ego was undaunted by the passage of time and the addition of a hangover. I had kicked that guy's butt and taken his stupid knife. Maybe that would teach him not to treat random women like garbage.

It occurred to me that I might have imagined the whole

thing, at least until I found the switchblade on my nightstand. I stared at the knife, marveling at how little encouragement my inner hooligan needed to emerge as the dominant personality. I decided to switch to soda for tonight's search.

"But your inner hooligan isn't the problem, is it?" I asked the knife. A rare moment of genuine self-reflection had snuck up on me, and I had to get through it to move on.

Why hadn't I told Jim I was coming here? How immature was I, convincing myself I could get away with this simply because I hadn't explicitly told him I'd wait for him to get back? Was I an adult man's adult girlfriend, or an idiot teenager sneaking out of the house for the thrill of making mischief?

Okay, so I was predisposed to mild to moderate, well-meaning skullduggery. On the other hand, Jim had almost certainly lied by omission about why he didn't want me here alone. He was genuinely worried about me, but there was another reason. A bigger one.

Had I subconsciously set out to punish Jim for lying to me again, or was I so desperate for a do-over of that bitter farewell with Luke in Chile that I'd reduced Jim and his bad habits to mere pretext?

Never mind all that. I stuffed the knife in my pocket and set my thoughts toward real problems I could really solve. I hadn't found Luke after one day of searching, so I'd keep at it until Jim stormed down here to rail at me and then help me like he'd intended to all along.

While I assessed my physical state and tried to decide on the best way to use my time until the bars started opening again, I watched the news and puttered around alternating between motel coffee and tap water, neither of which tasted better than my beer-flavored morning breath. I brushed my teeth once the last of the coffee was gone, then sat down at the foot of the bed to take in an end-of-the-news-cycle blurb about my Raphael.

The tale of its recovery had finally filtered down to the local news channels, the original details distilled into a depressingly concise announcement that, "The Federal Bureau of Investigation confirmed yesterday that an agent, whose name is being withheld, was instrumental in locating and securing this painting…"

A photo of the Raphael appeared on the screen, and my heart thumped at the sight of his coy little smile.

"… A portrait painted by Raphael in the sixteenth century and missing from Poland since World War Two. The FBI won't say how it was found or where, only that the investigation into its former owners remains active. Fans of Raphael will have to start saving up now for a ticket to the exhibition in Kraków…"

I tuned out, feeling wretched. If the agent were ever named, it wasn't going to be my name. At best I'd get to be Jim's arm candy for the exhibition.

I nearly jumped out of my skin as a knock at the door jerked me from my reverie. I stalked to the window, twitching the curtain aside. My shoulders slumped as a breath of pure relief left me. It was housekeeping, not my vagrant friend here to demand his knife back. I opened the door, leaving the chain latched.

"Hi, I'm good, sorry. Forgot to put out the little sign."

"Okay, have a good day," the woman intoned, already walking away.

I suddenly felt so desperately lonely that without pausing to second guess myself I plugged in my phone and powered it up to face the music. The Camposanto Concerto, as it were.

I waited on tenterhooks while the messages rolled in: a voicemail from my dad, three texts from my mom, and eleven texts and three voicemails from Jim. I had also picked up an Instagram message from Dom and eight emails. Not a bad haul, all things considered.

I decided to take them from best to worst, reading Dom's message first. She had sent me a meme and a brief request to enjoy my time off. The emails were all spam. My mom had texted to inform me Jim was calling her to ask where I was and she wasn't telling because she didn't know. Interesting.

My dad's voicemail contained only a solemn request to let him know if I was dead or not, if it wasn't too much trouble. I chugged another glass of tap water before tackling the messages from Jim, forewarned that he had evidently decided to take this as badly as possible.

His first text was the predictable question, "Home yet?" It spiraled from there quite dramatically.

"Hello, you alive?"

"Ashley just texted to tell me she checked on Dude. You're not in Arlington. Where are you."

"If you're not dead, you're going to be."

Ten minutes later, the texts started again. "Okay, I'm mad. If I have to come down there and get you you're going to be in a world of hurt."

"CALL ME."

Nearly two hours passed.

"I'm so worried about you please answer me."

"You know what, you better hope I don't find you."

"Why couldn't you just wait for me?"

"Headed to Albuquerque now. You asked for it."

"Please please please call me."

I checked the voicemails next. His tone was measured, his words careful. "Anna. I know you went to Albuquerque. I'm not mad. Call me, okay?"

A second voicemail, saying only, "Why is your phone still off."

By the last voicemail, I was barely holding back laughter, so amused at his meltdown that I didn't have a thought to spare for how much stress he was going through. It was self-induced anyway. He knew I could take care of myself.

His tone was gentle, contrite. "Anna, I'm sorry for freaking out. I honestly expected something like this, so I don't know why I'm surprised. Try not to run away from me when I find you, okay? I love you."

I guessed he was in Albuquerque already, or would be soon. The last voicemail had been sent this morning, and it was nearly noon now. I took a deep breath, squared my shoulders, and called him back. It didn't even ring once before his voice, cold and hard as steel, answered, "Anna."

"Jim."

"What are you doing."

"I changed my mind. I assumed you knew. Also I forgot to turn on my phone."

"Are you kidding me?"

"… No."

"Where are you?"

Why lie? I was too weak. "Big Eye Motor Inn. Room fourteen."

"Wow, real classy. Guess that explains why I couldn't find you."

"Not my first goat rodeo."

"Stay. Put. I mean it."

"Or?"

"Or nothing. Obviously threatening you has no more effect than appealing to your better nature. I got to Saint Paul and had to call Paolo and cancel our meeting and fly here instead."

I squirmed guiltily. "Really?"

"He's not happy."

"… Oh?"

There was silence on the other end of the line for so long that I wondered if he'd hung up. At length he said, "Well. I'm headed there now. Don't go anywhere."

"I won't."

I resisted the urge to spruce up, furious at myself and riddled with anxiety about the consequences of Jim snubbing Paolo to come "rescue" me. I watched TV and pretended not to listen for a car pulling up outside, leaping to my feet at a series of booming knocks at the door about ten minutes later. I opened the door, but not fast enough for Jim, who pushed his way inside and slammed it closed behind him. I backed away, not sure what to say.

"Wow… I don't think I've ever seen you this mad," I finally breathed, not sure whether to laugh or lock myself in the bathroom.

"I'm not mad," he said slowly, his tone disagreeing. "Why would you do this to me?"

"I didn't know you'd stand Paolo up over it. I'm sorry."

"Once again you've managed to screw up things you don't understand. You're like a toddler with a lighter."

I flared up, nearly screaming, "Don't you take that tone with me! I don't understand because you don't tell me anything! You'd think by now a smart guy like you could figure out I'm not going to blindly obey you!"

"Are you trying to see how mad I can get before I have an aneurism?"

"You said you weren't mad."

"I'm mad!"

"Because you know this wouldn't have happened if you'd been honest with me." I crossed my arms and waited in vain for an answer. "Fine, don't admit it, but you know I'm right. Feel free to sit around being butthurt. I have a job to do."

I tried to walk past him, but he caught me by the upper arm and yanked me to a stop. I twisted out of his grip and shoved him backward before my brain could even process what was happening. He stumbled, hitting the wall beside the TV so hard I felt a spasm of physical pain.

Someone in the next room pounded on the wall, a muffled, "Keep it down in there!" filtering through the thin partition.

"Oh my God I'm so sorry," I gasped, reaching instinctively

for Jim. He swatted my hands away and righted himself, looking equal parts embarrassed and enraged.

"Forget it. I shouldn't have grabbed you."

"Jim…" He allowed me to wrap my arms around his neck and pull him against me, where I breathed, "How bad is it?"

"All right, Anna, I'm not made out of glass—"

"No, I mean what I screwed up. Is it just that you offended Paolo, or is there more?"

"There's more."

"Why didn't you tell me?"

"Rich. He told me not to read you in to anything until your suspension is up. To treat you like an uncleared civilian."

"Is that who you called when you went outside with Dude?"

I felt his nod. "He wouldn't budge. Technically, he's right. You're locked out for a while."

"So you still can't tell me?"

"I can't." Finally he returned my embrace, burying his face in my hair to add, "And… it seemed like you were running away from me… for him. No one would blame you… The suspension, on top of everything else… Anna, I thought…"

"You dummy," I whispered fondly. "I don't want to get away from you." Pulling away, I tried to force out those last three words, but I couldn't do it. Instead I pressed one hand to his face and smiled, hoping he understood.

Frustrated, he asked, "Why not?"

"Same reason you don't run screaming from me," I said. I kissed him quickly, concluding, "I have absolutely no idea."

Though he gave me an unwilling laugh, he said wearily,

"Your independent streak and my controlling nature are going to cause sparks a lot."

"I like sparks."

"Oh yeah?" He grinned, mood shifting on a dime. "Let's get out of this crummy motel, and I'll show you some real sparks."

I had no objection, and Jim had a rental car parked outside as well as a room at the very hotel that seemed to be the locus of my relationship with Albuquerque. He drove us back to the casino while I wistfully related all that had happened since I landed. I edited the knife out of my encounter last night, pushing my trophy deeper into my pocket even as I described my decisive victory.

To my astonishment, Jim accepted my story calmly and even congratulated me on the richly-deserved beat down I'd delivered. I segued into the news story I'd seen, hoping he knew more than the copy editors at KOAT. He cut right to the heart of what I really wanted to know.

"Rich got a packet of tickets to the exhibition yesterday. Four of them. He claimed two for him and his wife, and gave me the other two. So, yeah, if you know anyone who likes art and wouldn't mind taking a trip to Poland with me…"

Ignoring the bait, I complained, "Beauchamp didn't do anything! Why does he get half the tickets?"

"You've got to give him some credit for letting me operate pretty much unsupervised."

"No, I don't. I bet the Art Crime guys are having kittens. When is this thing, anyway?"

"May third. Apparently there's some significance to that date, some collaborator getting arrested for the theft or something."

"Hans Frank," I recited promptly. "He wasn't a Polish collaborator, he was German. He was the last person who had the painting before it disappeared in nineteen forty-five."

"Auspicious year."

"Jeez, I don't know if one month is enough time to sort all this out… What if Luke really is in serious trouble?"

"Then we'll go to Poland some other time."

I beamed at him and blurted, "I seriously love you."

He parked the car at the casino hotel, turning to fix me with an inscrutable expression. "That's the first time you've admitted that out loud."

"That can't be right."

"I'm quite certain."

I rolled my eyes and hopped out of the car, leading the way inside.

Jim had secured a large room on the top floor, the Sandias looking close enough to reach out and touch on the other side of a lush, green golf course. While Jim ordered room service for lunch, I wondered where Luke had gone from here. It wasn't hard to imagine him waiting until the early morning hours when the casino closed, ducking outside, skirting the golf course, and disappearing up into the Sandia Mountains. With the right equipment, which I knew he could get, a smart man could stay hidden up there indefinitely. I just couldn't fathom why.

"Do you think he's gone back to working for Marcel?" I asked the window, assuming Jim would hear me and jump aboard my runaway train of thought.

"That doesn't seem very likely, but we can't rule it out. Let's not talk about Luke for a while," Jim requested, goading me away from the view to look at him. He sat down on the bed and beckoned me over.

I asked, "What do you want to talk about, then?"

"I don't want to talk about anything. I want to tie you to this bed and make love to you until you can't walk."

Laughing nervously, I stopped just outside arms' reach and asked, "What's your second choice?"

"It's a distant second, but… lunch."

The word made my stomach gurgle in anticipation. "I've got to vote for lunch. Sorry."

9

Friday, April 2 to
Saturday, April 3, 2021

A few minutes later, I was taking yet another shower—enjoying it this time—when I heard lunch being delivered and caught a whiff of something spicy that made me groan with sudden-onset, acute starvation.

I heard a breathy laugh through the bathroom door, followed by Jim's low, "Better hurry up or you'll be licking the plate."

"Yeah, right."

Jim didn't look up to polishing off an entire New Mexican-sized plate of fajitas for two, but I hurried through the rest of the shower anyway to stake my claim. Once I'd hoovered up more than my fair share of the food, I felt a wave of exhaustion wash over me. It had been a long night, and I was looking at more of the same tonight. I had no trouble convincing Jim to delay the start of our search by a couple more hours.

Jim turned on the TV and adjusted the volume down until all I could hear was a muffled hum of voices and music that lulled me right to sleep. I was gently lured back into consciousness sometime later by fingers combing through my hair. The combination of Jim, shower, and food had made for a short but heavy sleep. I was nearly comatose, mind blank and body so deliciously numb that I was sure I'd been reduced to nothing but an impossibly alive head. I feigned sleep for a few seconds, not wanting Jim to stop.

"It's six," he said at length. "You want to head out soon?"

Oh, right. We were still looking for Luke. I mumbled my assent, staggered out of bed, and got ready to go out. Since I still felt like I'd been roused from a twenty-year coma, Jim suggested I start at the casino bar with an energy drink.

I followed Jim to the elevator, where I leaned against him and nearly fell asleep standing up. At the ground floor, the doors opened on the casino's central bar and a scene of fevered weekend revelry.

The good looking bartender, loud music, dense crowd, and UFC prize fight on most of the flat-screen TVs all served to enhance that flighty, addictive weekend feeling. I could have sworn someone had turned up the sound effects on the nearby gambling machines to near-deafening volume.

Jim nursed a scotch on the rocks while I choked down an energy drink, and we sat and people-watched while I waited for the caffeine and other stimulants to artificially revive me.

I accidentally locked eyes with the bartender, a Black woman about my age with recently-buzzed hair who was wearing the heck out of a Canadian tuxedo. Our eyes met six or seven more times before I realized she was regarding me with something akin to recognition. I didn't know her. I drained my energy drink and made eye contact again, and she finished up cashing out an older couple before walking over to me.

"Another?" she asked, leaving it to me to ask the question.

"Yes, please. Do I know you?"

"Don't think so. Another scotch, Slim?"

Jim arched one eyebrow at the nickname but let it slide. "Sure, thanks. What was that about?" he asked once she'd slid away.

"I don't know. It's like she knows me from somewhere."

"Evidently not."

While we waited for our refills, I looked around aimlessly, wondering if I'd missed a similar attitude in any of the other bar patrons. None of them so much as glanced my way. Two drinks appeared on the bar in front of us, and as I turned to her to thank her, she pointedly looked behind herself at a row of miscellaneous tchotchkes under the liquor bottles. I followed her gaze, irritated at her circumspect behavior.

I let out a low gasp. She smiled and drifted away.

Jim stared at me. "What?"

"Look."

I pointed at a 4x6 photograph displayed in a plain black frame and propped against the mirror that formed the wall behind the bar. It was a selfie of the bartender and *Luke*. Had it been there when I arrived on Thursday? I sincerely hoped not, as that would have meant my self-guided tour of the bars on Central and subsequent hobo fight were a massive waste of time.

Jim took a hearty draught of scotch before asking, "Is that…?"

"Yeah, it is. What the…?"

Not nearly as interested as I was, Jim quipped, "That's what we at the FBI call a clue."

I was vibrating with impatience by the time Tuxedo came back.

She smiled gravely at me. "Seen it now?" she asked.

"Yes, how long has that been there?"

"A week."

"Dang it. Can I see it?"

"Got to throw me a password first. He insisted."

"A password?" I repeated stupidly. "I don't know any—oh! Uh… Kevin Bacon?"

She nodded once and handed me the framed photo before returning to her other customers. I squinted at the high-contrast photo, gleaning nothing from its contents. Luke wasn't pointing at anything or gesturing at all. Neither was holding anything (except the phone that took the photo), and both were smiling blandly. There weren't even any words on their shirts.

I handed the framed picture to Jim, sighing, "I don't get it."

He turned the frame over and removed the cardboard backing. He whipped out the photo, glowered at the back of it, and passed it to me, grousing, "You miserable, high and mighty, multilingual show offs."

The photo had been printed on an inkjet printer on regular printer paper, and the back bore a short message written in sloppy cursive, in French: "San Gregorio Lake Trail, April first.

If Gumby's with you, ditch him. Next message at trailhead if I miss you."

I laid the photo face-down on the bar, sighing in defeat. I was a day late. Jim leaned over and glared at it again, as though trying to interpret the words in a language he didn't know.

"What does it say?" he asked. "Does that say 'Gumby'? He better not be talking about me."

"Um…" I hesitated, staring into abstraction for inspiration.

He scoffed, messed around with his phone for a moment, and then held it up over the message as though about to take a picture of it. I realized too late what he was doing. By the time I'd snatched the photo away, he was reading the translation off his phone. A crease appeared between his eyebrows.

"He only wants to see you? Too dang bad. Where's this trail, anyway?"

"Look it up, I have no idea."

He already was. "About eighty-five miles north, near Cuba."

"We might as well go now if we're going at all. We already missed him."

Jim didn't bother arguing with me. He paid the tab, including a generous tip, and we jumped in his rental car for the hour-and-a-half drive. I drove while Jim navigated, guiding me north on I-25 for ten miles before we headed northwest on Highway 550. It was the same route I would've taken to Hesperus. Night fell almost as soon as we got on the road. Except for Jim's sporadic directions, we drove in silence, lost in our own separate thoughts.

I didn't know what to make of Luke's behavior. If he didn't want to go to Italy to be near his new boss, Paolo Barbato, why avoid Jim as well? I couldn't do anything for Luke without involving Jim, and he knew it. He had to have figured out by now that even if I tried to come alone, Jim wouldn't have it. I knew I should ask Jim what he was thinking, but for the moment I didn't care to know.

We found the trailhead in Cuba, and I parked in front of the covered bulletin board that bore the standard warnings, maps, infographics, and random additions by hikers. I left the headlights on so we could look around the trailhead for Luke's next clue. While Jim prowled around at the limit of the light's beams, I focused on the bulletin board. This time, knowing there was something to find, I didn't need anyone glancing significantly at Luke's message.

Near the top of the board, where no one shorter than Luke could have placed it, was a piece of paper attached to the cork with an open safety pin. It was blank but for a poorly depicted, vaguely phallic cartoon that I guessed was a non-artist's attempt at a bishop chess piece. It was the same thing I'd drawn on my mailbox in London to send Luke a message—though my bishop was much better.

I made sure Jim was distracted, then leapt up and made a grab for the paper. It was several feet over my head, and I was no shorty. I missed, jumped again, missed again, and sighed too loudly.

"What?" Jim called from several yards away. He could reach it without even jumping, but I had no idea what the message contained in addition to the bishop drawing, if anything.

"Nothing—spider," I called. "See anything?"

A gusty sigh. "Nope."

I peeked out from behind the board. Jim was standing in half-darkness, facing the woods with his hands on his hips, silently advertising how totally over this charade he was. I took a running start, jumped, and finally got a good enough grip on the paper to tear it away from the bulletin board. I winced as the safety pin bounced off my head and was lost in the pine needles under my feet.

I unfolded the paper and nearly laughed aloud at how extraordinarily boring my discovery was: a phone number. Committing it to memory, I stuffed the paper in my back pocket and walked around the board to where Jim was still standing.

Wherever Luke was now, and whyever he'd gone to such lengths to keep Jim out of the loop, I decided to play along at least until after I'd called the number and conferred with him.

"Maybe he never made it here, or maybe he decided not to leave another clue," I suggested.

"Maybe he's lurking five feet away, pouting because you let me tag along," Jim shot back, directing his next words into the woods. "You're a sore loser, Jackson!"

"I don't think he's here, Jim."

"Waste of a tank of gas…"

"Do you even want to find him?"

He half-sighed, half-growled, "Yes."

"Then let's go back to the casino. Maybe the bartender can give us more information."

As Jim headed back toward the car, I slipped the paper out of my pocket and let it fall to the ground, reciting the number to myself to make sure I really had memorized it. At a whispering rustle of underbrush just outside the headlight's glow, I scampered quickly along after Jim without looking left, right, or back. He had taken the driver's seat and had turned on the passenger seat warmer for me.

If it hadn't been for the nap and the energy drinks, I would've fallen asleep on the ride back to the hotel. As it was, I was fighting to keep my eyes open when we finally arrived, returned to our room, and climbed into bed.

▼

Curse my fat, drunk fingers to hell and back.

I was jerked awake at seven in the morning, responding unconsciously to the insect-like buzzing of my phone on the nightstand. I reached for its glowing face, accidentally slapped it to the floor, and stretched out of bed toward the floor to pick it up.

When I finally got the screen close enough to my sleep-blurred eyes to see what all the buzzing was about, I saw an alarm. I silenced it, opened my alarm app, and realized that after my beer-and-adrenaline cocktail Thursday night I had set the alarm for Saturday, not Friday. Maybe that had made sense to me at the time.

I replaced the phone on the nightstand and turned toward Jim to see if I'd woken him up, but he was still breathing the shallow, infrequent breaths of deep sleep. I picked up my phone again.

"Found your wiener drawing," I texted to the number I'd found on the bulletin board, getting a quick laugh at the thought of how my message would be received if I had the wrong number.

The response was quick. "You know perfectly well that was a bishop."

"Were you there?"

"I waited all day and you never showed," he non-answered.

"We got there last night."

"We?"

"Don't act surprised. Where are you now?"

"Ditch Gumby and I might tell you."

"Why?"

"I don't trust him."

I sent back only a surprise emoji, annoyed by his attitude. He didn't respond for so long I almost fell back asleep.

"Meet me at El Bruno for lunch. Noon."

I Googled it, seeing two locations for El Bruno: one right there in Albuquerque, and one in Cuba, near the trailhead. I texted back, "Please tell me you mean the one in Albuquerque."

"Nope."

Annoyed, I began typing too fast and stumbled over several dozen typos in a row before finally hacking out, "You were there, weren't you!"

"Gumby's a sore winner. That's worse."

"You're both losers. How am I supposed to get there without Jim? It's his rental car."

"Guess you'll have to figure it out."

"See you."

I deleted all the text messages and returned my phone to the nightstand. There was no way I was getting back to sleep after that. I glared at the ceiling, fuming, unable to believe it. Luke didn't trust Jim. What a crock. Jim was right, Luke was a sore loser.

By the time Jim woke up at half-past nine, I was dressed and ready to go, my mind made up.

10
Saturday, April 3, 2021

"I need the car."

I presented Jim with a steaming cup of coffee to sweeten the deal. While he drank it, sitting up in bed and regarding me with increasing dubiousness, I explained the bishop drawing, the texts from Luke, and what I planned to do.

"At least let me come to Cuba with you," he insisted. "I can wait in the car."

"To what end?"

"I don't know. I don't like him trying to separate us like this."

"He's not going to do anything to me."

He glared at me.

"Nothing I won't like," I dug, trying to rile him up.

"I'm coming with you."

"No," I groaned. "I promise, I'll have lunch with him, see what he wants, and come right back. Maybe I can convince him to let you help."

"Yeah? Maybe he can convince you to run off again."

I sat down next to him on the bed and squeezed his leg through the blanket. "You're not that insecure. Quit faking."

"What's to be insecure about?" He took a slow drink of coffee, giving me time to ignore his rhetorical question, and answered himself, "I wake up in a nice hotel room with my girlfriend to find her dressed and ready to drive ninety minutes to meet her ex, alone. A mere mortal might be worried by this behavior, but I'm enlightened enough to know that since I'm to blame for your current suspension without pay situation, there's no reason in the world to believe you might be feeling nostalgic about Lu—"

"All *right.*" I sighed. "I get it. What do I have to say to convince you?"

He considered this briefly and concluded, "Help me understand why you have to go alone."

The short answer, that Luke told me to, would only deepen his mistrust, so I said, "The sooner we find out what he wants, the sooner we can get back to Virginia and you can go see Paolo. If you come with me, like you did last night, he won't show his face. I just want to get this done."

I thought that was all very reasonable and airtight, so Jim's narrowed eyes caught me off guard.

"What?" I asked.

"The tips of your ears are turning red."

I resisted an impulse to clap my hands over my ears and argued, "No, they're not!"

"Let's make a deal: I let you go alone, and you promise to

move in with me."

After a moment to process his words, I grumbled, "Oh, that's low."

He shrugged. "And yet."

"I can't move in with you. Rich told me to leave you alone. Our cover isn't a thing anymore. You'll get in trouble, and I'll probably get fired."

"If you get fired, the point will be moot," he pointed out. I simply stared at him. "I don't expect you to move in right away. I only want a promise. Just two little words."

I studied his innocent, open expression. "I really can't tell how serious you are about this."

"You asked me how you could convince me. But we both know you'll do whatever you want." Jim leaned forward and tugged my t-shirt up a few inches, exposing the waistband of my jeans. "You're unarmed."

"I left my Glock in your safe. I don't like the rigamarole of checking a firearm. So what?"

"Will you take mine?"

"If it'll ease your mind, sure."

He carried a Kimber 1911 9mm, a full-sized, unwieldy weapon in my hand. I dutifully holstered it to my belt where I ordinarily carried my Glock 29.

"This is ridiculous," I groused, adjusting my jacket in front of the mirror and turning back and forth to make sure the weapon was concealed. "My Glock carries one round more, and not this weak sauce nine millimeter stuff. The nineteen eleven is such a fetish gun."

"I don't want to hear it."

We'd already had this argument half a dozen times, and neither of us would be giving up ground anytime soon. I gave him a farewell kiss, promised again that I'd be careful, and set out for Cuba.

▼

Luke was already at the restaurant when I arrived, hulking in a corner of the patio dining area and looking positively feral. He saw me before I saw him, and I approached him cautiously.

"Where's Jim?" he asked by way of greeting.

"Back at the hotel."

"Sit down, you're making me nervous."

I laughed, settling into a seat across from him. "I'm making *you* nervous? Have you seen you?"

"I haven't spent the last couple months in the lap of luxury like you. You look good."

"Thanks."

We stared at each other, silence settling between us. I wondered if he was recalling our conversation in Chile with the same vivid clarity I was. He must have seen this on my face, because his tense posture suddenly relaxed and his gaze fell to the bowl of tortilla chips in the middle of the table.

"You really hurt my feelings," I whispered, not meaning to sound so petulant.

His lips pressed together in a hard line. "Thought it would

be better that way."

"Maybe it was." I looked up as a waiter appeared at my elbow. I ordered a margarita on the rocks and Luke followed suit, eyes tracking the young man as he meandered around the tables taking other orders.

"Nice roots," he said, finally smiling. "Pepé Le Pew chasing you around?"

I pushed my hair back behind my ears self-consciously. "It's fried. I wish Jim hadn't made me bleach it."

"That monster."

"What is going on? David ambushed me at a bar in DC and told me you couldn't go to Paolo. Why? Did Paolo find out you left Marisol alive?"

"If he did, he hasn't mentioned it. He told me not to come to Italy without that painting. How'd he find out about the Raphael?"

"You're asking me? How should I know? Maybe he saw it on the news and figured out Fernando had it. Not exactly a big leap of logic when they're telling the whole world an FBI agent recovered it."

"He knew immediately. While I was still getting out of Chile. It hadn't hit the news yet. I checked."

"Oh…"

"I had to see you, Anna. To warn you he knows more than he should. That leak's still trickling."

"I think Jim's on top of it."

"I don't know what you see in that guy."

Our drinks arrived, and rather than shotgunning mine as I'd

been planning to do, I rested my elbows on the table and covered my face with my hands.

"*Please* tell me that's not what this is about."

"Not entirely. Have you gone back to work?"

"For about five minutes. I'm one month into a three-month suspension at the moment. Why?"

"I know who the leak is. It's your boss, Richard Bowchamp."

"It's pronounced 'Beecham'," I corrected automatically, already shaking my head. "Wait. How do *you* know about Beauchamp? I've barely learned his name. It's like Jim was hiding him from me—or me from him."

"Marcel."

Luke's one-word answer needled at me, making me want to reach across the table and smack him. I took a huge gulp of my drink to keep my hands and mouth occupied while my brain caught up.

"Marcel *what?*"

"He—" He paused, thought for a moment, and decided. "If you're not keeping Jim out of this, that's your choice. But I don't want to have this conversation twice. Where is he, anyway? Peeking through the bushes?"

"He's in Albuquerque." I started to explain further, but something stopped me. Luke didn't need to be privy to our drama, and something told me Jim would prefer I keep those details to myself.

"He let you come here alone?"

"Yes and no." Before he could reply to that, I sputtered, "It's just not possible. Beauchamp knew the whole plan, start to finish. He's the only one besides Jim."

"I'm telling you, Barbato's been talking to him. Bow—Beauchamp may not be telling him everything for whatever reason, but he's feeding him bits and pieces for sure. He must have told him about the Raphael."

"Why would he do that?"

"You're the G-man. You figure it out."

I still didn't believe him, but I forfeited the argument for the time being. "You couldn't have told me this over the phone? Or told David and had him tell me?"

"With Jim talking about phone taps right and left? That would've been suicide. I didn't want David mixed up in all this, anyway. Way easier to get you here."

"It's not Beauchamp. It can't be."

"Sure, Anna." He sipped at his margarita, made a face, and took a large gulp of water. "That's not all."

"Oh? Don't be such a woman. Spit it out."

We both paused to chuckle with immature delight. Luke took a steadying breath and said, "You're going to be so mad."

"That explains everything."

"Shush. Remember in London, when you asked me if I saw Tommy in Houston?"

"Sure," I said with a nod. Back then I'd still believed Luke might have information about what happened the night Tommy's and my cover was blown with the Tres Islas Cartel. It was a simpler time.

Luke interrupted my thoughts by saying, "I didn't realize at the time that a certain detail would end up being this important."

I had just taken a huge bite of chips and salsa and had to tuck it into my cheek like a hamster to respond eagerly, "What? What detail?"

"*Where* I saw him."

"What are you, getting paid by the minute?"

"I want you to know I didn't deliberately withhold this. I didn't know it mattered."

"Fine. Acknowledged."

"You assumed I saw him at the warehouse. But I didn't see either of you there. I heard when the bullets started flying and ducked out the back way to get out of the crossfire. I came back later and took care of Lira, and then I left. I nearly bumped into the rest of the TIC guys at the fleabag motel where I was staying.

"That's where I saw your boy Tommy. He was with them."

11

Saturday, April 3, 2021

I swallowed partially masticated shards of tortilla chip and heard myself ask, "What do you mean, 'with them'? Tommy… You mean they were holding him captive?"

"It didn't look that way. You told me the two of you were undercover, so it didn't seem that odd."

"This… I don't understand… He was *alive?*"

"Well, yeah."

"I don't understand," I repeated.

"You're shorting out. Take a minute."

I took a long drink from my margarita, waiting until the tequila poked me in the brain stem before I asked, "What exactly made you realize this was important? Now after all this time?"

"I was thinking back over what we talked about in Chile. How cagey you and Gumby were about this Tommy kid. I thought maybe… I realized you two might not know. You thought he was dead."

"This is a lot to process."

I already knew there was a chance Tommy survived that night, but it was too slim to contemplate. He never showed up back at the FBI or anywhere else, so I'd decided he was dead. Jim had agreed. The end.

Maybe Lira was the only one of the TIC who knew our dirty little secret. Maybe Tommy had thrown me under the bus and wangled his way back into the cartel's good (or at least tolerant) graces. Maybe this whole time, he'd been too afraid of me and Philip to show his face. Whatever had happened that night, Luke's news had shaken loose all my certainty that the Tommy chapter of my life was over. I wasn't even sure if I wanted him to be alive or dead.

"You mad?" Luke asked.

"What? No. No… I'm glad you told me. I just don't really know what to do about it. Have you told anyone else?"

"Nope. Speaking of anyone else, how long's your hall pass good for?"

I smirked at the implication. "I need to be back in time for dinner, or else. Come with me."

"You can't be serious."

"Of course I'm serious. You said you wanted to tell us both at the same time, right? You need to learn to trust Jim. Nothing's gonna get done without his help, and you know it."

He actually looked like he was considering it. He took another drink of his margarita and seemed to have adjusted to the taste. He glanced over the menu to stall for time. "What are you getting?"

"Bored."

"For lunch, dork."

"Carne adovada."

Our waiter returned to take our orders, and while we waited for our food I indulged Luke with a synopsis of events since we parted in Chile. No other diners were seated within a couple yards of us, but I kept my voice down anyway. I avoided the question of whether or not he was coming back to Albuquerque with me until the check came and I snapped it up.

"Well?" I asked.

"I…" He trailed off, thinking. "I like being in the wind. It's safe. Don't have to worry about anyone but myself."

"You won't worry about me, just because I'm not with you?"

He met my eyes, looking tender for half a beat before frowning at me.

"I'm sure Jim has been and will continue to take very good care of you."

Touché. "Fine, leave it to him," I relented. "I'll be sure to pass along your high regards."

I dropped some cash on the table and turned to go, making it all the way to the rental car before I heard footsteps crunching along the gravel parking lot behind me. I pretended not to notice and climbed into the driver's seat, not locking the doors behind me as I usually would. Luke settled himself in the passenger seat and stared straight ahead for several seconds before turning to me.

"You're gonna get me killed," he concluded.

"At least you'll die happy," I shot back.

The closer we got to Albuquerque, the more anxious I became. Whatever Jim had been expecting upon my return, I was sure it wasn't a plus one. I didn't want to have to deal with Luke and Jim's deep-seated, mutual dislike. This was going to be awkward.

At the casino, I asked Luke to wait at a bank of nickel slots while I went upstairs to ease Jim gently into his new reality. I let myself into the room and found him sitting at the desk, industriously typing away on his laptop. He smiled at me in greeting, an expression that faltered as he took in my anxious demeanor.

"What happened?" he asked, closing his laptop.

"Luke came back with me." Okay, not so gently. Since Jim already looked like I'd ruined his day, I added, "He thinks Beauchamp is the leak, and Tommy might still be alive."

"… Is that all?"

"Um… he said he can't go back to Paolo because Paolo told him not to show his face without the Raphael. He doesn't know how Paolo found out about it."

"By watching the news, I assume," Jim proffered, uninterested.

"That's what I thought, but he said Paolo knew immediately. Before any of the news stories hit."

"Okay. Is there more?"

I shook my head.

"Paolo hasn't mentioned Marisol?" he pressed.

"No."

"All right." He reopened his laptop. "Tell Luke I said thanks for the information."

"Jim!"

"Yes?"

"You need to hear him out. Don't brush this off just because you don't like him."

He held up a finger and said, "One, Rich isn't the leak. Two, Tommy's body never showed up, so obviously he *might* still be alive, and three, if Paolo wants to give Luke the cold shoulder over a painting, I can no more change his mind than I can put that painting in his hands."

I crossed my arms. "So suddenly the master of the universe can't be bothered to collect some information that he might be able to use later. I'm not buying it. You just want to be difficult."

Unruffled, he ordered, "Send him packing, Anna."

"Won't."

"Fine. But don't expect me to roll out the welcome wagon. I'll hear him out, and then he's gone."

"Whatever."

Feeling like a wartime courier ping-ponging from one general to another in search of a truce, I rode the elevator back down to the casino to find Luke again.

"He's not happy," I announced.

Luke laughed. "No kidding."

"Come on up. He's eager to be horrible to you."

"Is he gonna shoot me?"

I casually flashed my expensive piece on loan from Jim. "Not without this."

"Clever girl."

But Jim wasn't in the room when we got there. He'd left behind a childish clue as to his whereabouts: a bed completely covered in luggage with my swimsuit perched on top.

"Wow, he's taking this well," Luke observed, smiling. He was clearly warming up to the arrangement.

I grabbed my swimsuit. "I'm gonna go try to cheer him up a little. You… uh…"

"I'm taking a three-hour shower."

I waited until he was shut in the bathroom to change into my swimsuit, then I secured Jim's gun in the hotel safe and found my way to the pool. Jim wasn't in the swimming pool or the hot tub, so I peeked into the sauna and found him supine on one of the lower benches. He looked like a Pharaoh lying in state, waiting to be mummified. As I shut the sauna door behind me, he opened one eye and quickly shut it.

"These histrionics are most unbecoming," I said haughtily. We were alone in the sauna, the temperature cranked up above 140 degrees Fahrenheit.

"Felt like a steam. Sue me."

He sat up as I took a seat next to him. Since there was no point in revisiting my previous arguments, I decided to take another approach.

"Keep your enemies close, they say," I tried. "What's closer than the same hotel room?"

"By 'a steam' I meant 'not thinking or talking about this'."

"Fine." I kissed him, biting his lip when he didn't immediately put his hands on me. "It's not like I need privacy to enjoy your company."

"Well, I do," he said; I moaned in answer. He shook with silent laughter, but when he spoke again his tone was serious. "I'm going to need some iron-clad proof before I believe Rich is up to anything."

"Now you know how I felt when you told me about Philip. I thought you didn't want to talk about it?"

He was about to respond when the sauna door opened. I scooted away as though Jim's body had suddenly been charged with an electric current. Without a trace of chagrin or disapproval, a tiny old woman tottered in, checked the temperature, and settled onto a bench across from us with a sigh of deep contentment.

"Don't mind me," she quavered.

"I need to cool off anyway," Jim mumbled, beating a hasty retreat. I followed him, sputtering with barely contained giggles.

I paddled around aimlessly in the pool while Jim swam laps, and after half an hour he was ready to act his age. We returned to the room, where Luke was, as promised, still in the shower. Jim got dressed, cleared off the bed, and sat down at the desk to disappear behind his laptop.

Ignored for once, I flipped on the TV and sat on the floor to watch it, the better to keep my wet hair and swimsuit from soaking into the bed. It was nearly five o'clock before Luke emerged, fully dressed and looking and smelling so good my heart sank with a thud right into my stomach.

He sat down at the foot of the bed next to me, saying, "Shower's all yours. Might be some hot water left."

"Are you two going to be okay while I…?" I started to ask.

From behind his laptop, Jim said, "We're all adults here, aren't we?"

I wasn't so sure about that, but I could practically feel the chlorine turning my hair green. Rushing through a shower, I was surprised to leave the bathroom and find Luke still there, stretched out on the bed and watching TV without the slightest trace of disgruntlement.

"What's for dinner?" he asked tonelessly.

I sat down next to him. "I dunno. We need to take care of some business first, don't you think?"

He grunted his assent. Jim's response was to stand up, close his laptop, and disappear into the bathroom. I turned to Luke, who shrugged.

I sighed, "I guess it can wait a few more minutes."

Jim took his time and came out of the bathroom towel drying his hair. The look that passed between him and Luke, while as brief as a flash of lightning, was just as charged. I stood up, no longer interested in taking care of business.

"I'm going down to the casino buffet," I announced. "Be back in an hour or so."

"Let me get dressed and I'll come with you," Jim said, but I shook my head firmly.

"Sorry, I guess I wasn't clear: I'm going down to the buffet, and you're both staying here."

"Says who?" Luke argued.

"Says me. If I come back and you two haven't achieved some kind of understanding, I'm gonna make a new friend at the bar and spend the night with one woman instead of two."

12

Saturday, April 3 to Sunday, April 4, 2021

I grabbed my wallet and a room key and departed, not even half as ashamed of my behavior as I should have been. Two grown men were letting everything go to crap because they didn't like each other, leaving someone like me to scrape things back together. How did that make sense?

On the way down to the ground floor, I reconsidered my choice of dining. I'd been to a caino buffet in Vegas, and it was about as cheerful as a potluck at a wake. I doubted the one here would be any more lively. Instead I found a booth at the bar and ordered beer and hot wings, watching a replay of last night's UFC fight on a TV over the bar.

Tuxedo was back, now wearing a backless tank top and camo leggings instead of the eponymous denim ensemble. I caught her eye a couple of times before she found the time to wander over. She leaned against the opposite side of the booth and crossed her arms.

"So, how'd your little scavenger hunt go?" she asked.

"Great. In a manner of speaking…"

"Can I sit? My break just started, and I'm not tryna spend it talking to my coworkers."

"Be my guest. Want some wings?"

"I'm vegetarian."

"I'm Anna. Nice to meet you."

She smirked, helping herself to one of the carrot sticks I had no intention of eating. "I'm May, but my friends all call me Mayday."

I considered her age. "Do you know why?"

"I'm dying to know what all that business yesterday was about."

"Oh… uh… my ex—the guy in the picture—was playing mind games with me and my boyfriend. They… they used to be friends." I silently congratulated myself; that almost made sense.

"That gangly dude with you is your boyfriend?"

"He's not… gangly…"

"The ex is *way* hotter."

I privately disagreed, laughing instead of arguing. "They're both unbearable. I've kind of been wondering, though… What exactly did Luke say to you when you took that selfie?"

"Mm," she mused, snapping up a stick of celery. "Luke, huh? He told me his name was Brian. Should've known that was a lie—He doesn't look like a Brian. He flirted with me for a while, bought me a couple of shots, then told me he needed help with a little practical joke. Told me you'd be coming in and he wanted to leave you a message. For your information, he described you as 'bleach blonde hair down to her waist, big brown eyes, and a body that'll make you weep.' I played along. He couldn't slip me a big tip, so he slipped me something better," she finished, chuckling, then presented a respectable attempt at an apologetic smile.

I was a lot of things, but I wasn't a hypocrite, at least not when I was feeling self-aware. I grinned at her. "He's something else, isn't he?"

"Girl, he's in his prime. You made a bad deal. No offense. You do you. Thanks for the break—you want another Shiner?"

"Yes, please."

May grabbed my empty pint glass and returned to work, leaving me laughing to myself. Rather than sending my refill over with the server, May brought it back herself. I was glad she did, because I'd thought of something else to ask her.

"How'd you know it was me, though? That description probably fits hundreds of women in Albuquerque."

"Fewer than you'd think. He told me you'd probably be with Slenderman, actually. I get that now."

"Wow." I took a drink of beer so I didn't have to try to think of a response. For all I knew, the negotiations were proceeding amicably upstairs, so I did my best not to dwell on Luke's unnecessary meanness.

I finished my wings and polished off my second pint, paid my tab, and wandered around the casino for a while, unwilling to go back to the room so soon. Luke and Jim been alone less than an hour, and I figured they needed more time to get anything done. I flushed $28 down a couple of slot machines, loitered next to the blackjack tables to watch real gamblers at work, and eventually ambled back to the elevators and rode up to the top floor.

I hadn't consumed nearly enough beer to be anything but buzzed, and that buzz had worn off when I stepped off the elevator and found my door. I leaned close to the door frame and listened, but no sound came through. There might have been nothing but an empty room waiting for me. I squared my shoulders and prepared for the worst, opened the door, and stepped inside.

Jim was lying on the bed, his precious laptop open on his chest, and Luke was at the desk eating dinner. Among the various plates and utensils delivered with room service, there was a half-empty bottle of Glenlivet 18, an empty tumbler upside down next to it. I found two more tumblers quickly, like playing a 3D, adults-only game of Where's Waldo: one at Luke's elbow, and one on the nightstand next to Jim. The latter muted the TV when he noticed me.

"Look who decided to join us," Jim said, plainly drunk. I looked from him to Luke, torn between laughter and annoyance.

"Maybe she couldn't make any friends," Luke suggested seriously.

"May and I were getting along just fine. Turns out we've been to a lot of the same places," I said, watching Luke's face until he discerned my meaning. He laughed once, popped a nacho into his mouth, and poured a healthy measure of scotch into the third tumbler.

"I'll drink to that," he said, offering me the glass. I crossed the room to take it out of his hand.

After a delicate sip, I asked the room at large, "So, what did I miss?"

"Well—" Luke started, but Jim cut across him.

"No, she flounced away, she doesn't get to know what she missed. It's only fair. Spoiled rotten little brat."

"Yeah, I'm gonna have to agree with Jim." Luke shrugged. "I guess you'll never know."

"So you're both definitely too far gone to accomplish anything tonight, huh?" I received two inarticulate grunts of agreement. "Will you even remember this tomorrow?" That went unanswered. I attempted one more question. "Have we come to an agreement on sleeping arrangements at least?"

"It didn't come up," Jim mumbled, focused on his laptop again. Based on the movements of his finger on the touchpad, I suspected he was playing Solitaire. I also suspected he was lying.

Rather than challenging him, I retreated to the bathroom to get ready for bed. Leaving Luke to his late dinner and Jim to his puerile card game, I burrowed underneath the covers and tried to fall asleep. All the business we had to attend to would have to wait until tomorrow.

I drifted off in a brightly-lit room with the TV squawking and conversation cutting in and out between Luke and Jim. I absorbed none of their words.

▼

Jim's voice was the first sound I was aware of the next morning. His tone was serious, his words too muted to make out. I turned my head slightly and saw him silhouetted against the open window, sunrise tinting the Sandias the color of orange sherbet beyond.

I had to take issue with May's choice of the word 'gangly' to describe him. He was as lithe as a jaguar. I was distracted for hardly a second before his voice grabbed my attention again.

I held my breath and listened.

"… not like she's under indictment or something… Look, I don't know. I'm still looking for her." A long stretch of silence followed, then Jim said, "Obviously, so we don't miss the opening in Poland… Forget the cover story, she's earned it and you know it."

I assumed 'she' was me. Which cover story were they talking about, though? Jim's and my office dalliance, or me being in Berlin while Jim found the Raphael in Argentina? The context didn't rule either out. I closed my eyes, trying to block out the rest of the conversation. I wasn't in an intelligence gathering mood.

My movement roused Luke, who sleepily dragged me closer to him and started kissing my neck. Weighted down by his heavy arm across my chest, I let him carry on while I tried to figure out why he was still here. I had been sure Jim would kick him out at some point, leaving him to find his own room or sleep on the street; but apparently he'd spent the night with us.

Though I didn't dislike the feeling of his lips on my skin, I whispered, "You know Jim is standing right there, don't you?"

"He doesn't care," Luke answered.

Jim didn't care? Since when? I was afraid to ask Luke what he meant and didn't realize Jim's phone call had ended until he asked with rich sarcasm, "You two having fun?"

"Yep," Luke said at once, unabashed.

Embarrassed beyond words, I started worming out of Luke's arms as Jim said, "I'm getting coffee. Be right back."

He let himself out of the room, leaving me more confused than I'd ever been. If this had something to do with whatever he and Luke had decided over that bottle of Glenlivet, I wasn't getting it. I stopped trying to escape from Luke, who soon fell back asleep. While the sun rising over the mountains pushed more and more sunlight and heat into the room, I waited for Jim to get back and start acting the way any normal man would.

As soon as Jim let himself back into the room, I left Luke snoozing on the bed and followed Jim into the bathroom. Rather than venting any reasonable indignation, he smiled fondly at me and passed me a paper cup of hotel lobby coffee. Whatever he'd been intending to do in the bathroom, he put it off to talk to me.

"Confused?" he asked, taking in my expression. I nodded, and he said with a very mature sigh, "I guess we're all savages now. I figured you'd be pleased."

"Savages?"

"We decided not to compete with each other, because we've all got bigger things to worry about. You don't belong to either of us, so we're not going to pretend like you do. Isn't that enlightened? The scotch was a helpful lubricant."

I tried to take a drink of coffee, but it was too hot. Glaring at the inaccessible beverage, I asked, "So… are we savages, or are we enlightened?"

"I don't know, Anna. I'm just trying to keep the peace."

"I am so confused," I breathed.

Jim gave me a bracing pat on the back and started shaving. Since he wasn't kicking me out of the bathroom, I took the opportunity to start working a handful of conditioner into my dry hair.

With a sidelong glance, he asked, "Aren't you supposed to do that in the shower?"

"I have to let it soak. It's this desert air… Thanks a lot for making me bleach it, by the way."

"Rich and I agreed you needed to change your appearance," he said, unapologetic. He paused to concentrate on a particularly difficult spot, then added, "It was either that, or cut it. I like it long."

"Oh yeah?"

"So does he, by the way. Turns out we have a lot in common."

"Wonderful. Did you two talk about anything… I don't know… important last night?"

"If by important, you mean Luke's so-called news, no."

That, it transpired, was a topic reserved for breakfast. While Luke and I destroyed bacon and eggs, bagel and lox, milk and cereal, toast and jam, and orange juice and coffee, Jim was satisfied with a suspiciously light breakfast of coffee and yogurt and took it upon himself to chair our little meeting.

He kicked things off with, "First of all, I want to know how you decided Rich is the leak. Not that you need to know this, but we already know who it is and it's being managed accordingly."

"It's like this," Luke started, and I could tell he'd rehearsed this in anticipation of explaining himself. "Paolo had Marcel send me to Houston to do Lira. Once I agreed to the job, Marcel put Paolo and me in touch so he could stay out of it. So I went to Houston, did my business, kept my nose out of the cluster that went on while I was waiting to make my move, killed Lira, and disappeared to Colorado to wait for my next assignment."

"Why Colorado?" I interrupted.

He shrugged. "I like this part of the country. It's sparse, temperate, people aren't too friendly, don't ask a lot of questions. Unlike you."

"Well why'd you lie to me in London?" I pressed.

Something like pain flashed across Luke's face, and he asked hesitantly, "Can you… narrow that down a bit?"

"When I brought up Paolo. By name. You said you'd never heard of him."

"Did I?"

I crossed my arms and shot a glance at Jim, who was supposed to be moderating. He was too busy peering suspiciously at Luke to notice my irritation.

"I didn't think you should know yet. I wasn't sure how much you already knew…" Luke halfway explained, his voice fading to a quiet, "Sorry."

"It's okay," I said with a shrug. "I love being lied to. It's such a turn-on."

"Really?" Luke and Jim asked in perfect unison.

"*No!*"

Chuckling, Luke went on with his story. "Anyway, I was out

of touch with everyone from the time I left the warehouse and told Paolo it was done until July, when I called Marcel and told him I needed to come back to London before my next job. He was against it—doesn't like me hanging around. I told him everything that had happened, all the stuff with Philip and Anna, and I convinced him to make an exception. He decided to put me to work in his office in London, trying to figure out how the FBI tracked me to Colorado. Now I know he suspected Paolo was working with you, and I guess he was half right.

"Marcel keeps the operation in London as small as possible, prefers not to poop where he eats so to speak. It's mostly storage. It was a skeleton crew at the office, me and a receptionist who didn't know what was going on and a couple of teenagers Marcel farms out all the cyber junk to. One of them got into Paolo's computer, don't ask me how.

"He had encrypted emails from some DIY home server with an IP address in Maryland. We couldn't read the emails, but by then teenager number two had worked out Abigail was really Anna, and we figured the server guy was your boss. Meaning Jim."

"I live in Virginia," Jim put in.

"Yeah, and where does your boss live?"

"Maryland. But so do millions of other people."

"Sure. Marcel wasn't in too much of a hurry to pin that part down. He just wanted me to kill Anna. I told him to go pound sand, so he asked me to kill Fernando and Marisol Serna for Barbato instead. Aside from wondering if Paolo had some kind of problem with Latin Americans, I didn't think much of it. I started trying to find Serna.

"Fast forward to that information dump in Chile, and I realized the emails might not have come from Jim because you kept saying you lived in Virginia and had for about a decade. For all I knew you had a place in Maryland you used just for the email server, but it made me curious all the same.

"So I reached out to David and he asked the kid in London to find out more about that IP address, and he found us a physical address to go with it along with a name and a full credit report—data gold mine. Can't be that many Richard Beauchamps tied up in all this. We decided we'd better let you know, so David went to DC and you know the rest."

"Why didn't David tell me all this himself?" I asked.

"He didn't want to. Ever since he helped you escape, he's scared to death Marcel will find out he's two-timing with MI5. He had to go to Atlanta anyway, so he said he'd make a detour to DC, give you the message, and then wash his hands of us. We knew you'd come running, and you'd try to do it on the sly. Sorry, baby, you're pretty predictable."

"I'm getting that," I said.

"You're not buying it," Luke guessed, studying Jim's face.

"All the information David got came from Marcel's people."

"David's in MI5's pocket, you saw to that."

"Doesn't mean he's not in his brother's pocket, too. Blood is thicker than water after all."

Shaking his head, Luke argued, "The deal with the Italians was it for David. I guess he draws the line at human trafficking. He's fed up."

"Marcel is still thinking about partnering with the Italians?"

I asked, astounded. The Frenchman had all but a signed confession from Barbato that he was in bed with the FBI.

"Yeah, the Italians, not Barbato. He wants Paolo dead, remember? He's not thinking about partnering, he *is* partnering. All he sees is dollar signs."

"Say Rich is talking to Paolo, too," Jim mused. "For what purpose? Why are you assuming it's nefarious? I'm talking to Paolo, and there's nothing underhanded about it."

"You don't need Paolo's money, and you're not giving him the information he wants," Luke summarized, challenging, "What else do you need to know?"

"How about why Rich hasn't spilled the beans about Anna?"

"Why are you so sure he hasn't?" Luke shot back. "How'd Marcel's nerd find out her real name and everything else in that dossier?"

I put my hand up as a stop sign, curtailing Jim's heated response. "We're not getting anywhere like this. You both need to stop and take a breath."

Jim took a drink of coffee instead, his gaze drifting away into abstraction somewhere in the vicinity of my left hand on the table. Luke took a bite of toast as though it had personally offended him.

Waiting until their proverbial feathers had de-ruffled, I ventured, "We're going to Poland with Beauchamp and his wife anyway." I allowed a full second for arguments before continuing. "Why don't we just... see what Beauchamp does? It's all information at this point, as long as we don't let on that we suspect him. Right, Jim?"

"*We* don't suspect him," Jim grumbled. "But, yeah, I'm willing to keep an open mind. But I'm not flying you back to Washington with us. You'll have to get there on your own power."

Jim tore a piece off the room service receipt, wrote something on it, and passed it to Luke. I took a peek as Luke read it: Jim's address, gate code, and phone number.

"Try not to scare us to death when you show up," Jim said.

13

Sunday, April 4 to
Wednesday, April 21, 2021

After my brief but eventful stint in the Wild West, I bid Luke goodbye and good luck and hopped on a flight back to DC with Jim. Sometime between taking off from the Albuquerque Sunport and touching down at Dulles Sunday night, I contracted the flu for the first time in my entire life.

The best part was Jim's sanctimonious declaration that I'd picked the bug up when I was bar hopping in Albuquerque, and it served me right. I was so infuriated I had half a mind to refuse his demand that I convalesce at his house rather than going home to Dupont Circle. He won me over with a brief, but surprisingly imaginative, hypothetical description of me taking Dude for a walk between bouts of puking my guts out.

The next three days were unmitigated hell. It was the first time I'd been sick in nearly a decade, and I'd give the experience one out of five stars. It was fun being waited on hand and foot.

Unfortunately, I had too much spare time in which I could do nothing but worry about Luke. By the time I woke up Thursday morning, fever broken and appetite rekindled, I was half-mad with anxiety and wild theories about why he still wasn't safe and sound in Arlington with us.

Jim didn't seem too concerned, frankly.

To distract myself, I invited Dom to join me at Krav Maga the following Wednesday, and I spent the next few days focused on regaining my strength. Dom enjoyed the class so much that she joined me the following Wednesday, but by then I'd pivoted to a fresh, new problem.

On my way out the door to go to Krav, Jim had given me his credit card and asked me to find something to wear to the Raphael exhibit, along with a matching tie for him. The warm and fuzzy feelings this had engendered stayed with me all the way to the class in Columbia Heights and up to the moment when Dom came in, spotted me, and joined me on the mat to stretch before class started.

"Didn't you see my text?" she asked lightly instead of saying hello.

Her usual smile and cheery tone were not in place, and though she didn't exactly seem angry, there was something about her tonight that warned me something was up.

"I didn't. Sorry."

"Just thought we could ride the Metro together," she said with a shrug, moving seamlessly into a hamstring stretch as she reached toward her ankles.

"I came from Jim's house anyway," I said. She finally smiled, probably because I'd stumbled directly into her trap.

"Right, of course. You two seriously crack me up. I mean you're too much."

"Oh?"

She sat up straight, actually wiggling her feet in delight. "You're together, pretending to be together, and pretending *not* to be together—all at the same time. You haven't been back to your apartment in months. Quit playing. Like anyone cares."

"Beauchamp does," I mumbled.

"And so what? If Jim walked right into Rich's office, threw a water balloon at his head, knocked over his Ficus, and flipped him off, Rich might—*might*—consider giving him a slap on the wrist."

"So Jim's the Teflon Don. Good for him. I could still get in deep trouble for flouting Beauchamp's orders."

"He won't mess with you if he knows it'll make his favorite employee angry at him. Jim can see that. Why can't you?"

I took two beats to finish stretching my wrists before asking tartly, "So you and Jim have been discussing this?"

"This? This being that you and he are a foregone conclusion, and you're just delaying the inevitable because the last time you committed to someone it was a complete disaster?"

I nodded.

"Nope. He and I only talk about work. But if you don't agree, why let the man suffer?" With a serene smile, she stretched her arms over her head and nodded toward another group of students stretching in the opposite corner. "Go start something with that guy, and cut Jim loose."

I followed her nod, understanding neither her forced off-handness nor her gesture.

"Cut Jim loose? Why in the world would I do that?"

"Because you can be with whoever you want to be with, and not letting Jim lock you in is torturing him. It's not fair."

Still staring at the cluster of students, I saw one man glance toward us and then quickly look away, focusing on the ceiling instead. I didn't recognize him, but the awkward moment only made Dom's words ring truer.

"What you just did? It's called creating a false dichotomy," I said, causing her to scoff so loudly that several more people turned toward us.

The instructor called the class to order before Dom could answer back, and when class ended an hour and a half later, neither of us chose to resume the discussion.

Sharen, who'd warmed so quickly to Dom at our trivia night last month, pounced on her the moment class ended, so I waved goodbye to them both and left alone. I wasn't ready to go home, but I did have the errand attached to Jim's credit card yet to complete.

I walked a couple miles to an upscale shopping center where I occasionally window-shopped but had never dared to set foot in any of the stores. After I was chased out of three different establishments by nothing more than the disbelieving stares of the salespeople, I admitted defeat and headed to Macy's to shop in peace with the rest of the proletariat.

After an hour of tedium, I ended up with three dresses, three pairs of shoes, and three ties for Jim, all of it far more expensive than I was comfortable with. Since shopping hadn't eaten up nearly enough time (it was only 8:30), I wandered on foot in a generally westward direction until I spotted a bar that struck my fancy.

As I settled into a corner booth, I had to smile to myself at the absurdity of my behavior. I used to drive around at night in my quiet home town of Manchester, Texas, to avoid being at my house with my then-husband, Aaron. Being around him when he was drunk was hazardous to my health, and he was pretty much always drunk, so I'd stay out until I figured he was asleep and it was safe to go home again.

Now there I was in Washington, DC, doing pretty much the same thing to avoid a man who loved me so much he wanted to share his home with me, who trusted me so much that he was letting another man shoot his shot—simply because I was too chicken to have a conversation. I yearned for another knife-wielding transient to fight. That was easy. That I could do.

Jim called me right after I ordered a drink, and I left my coat and shopping bags behind and stepped outside to take the call.

"Almost two thousand dollars at Macy's," he greeted, a smile evident in his voice. "I'm curious on so many levels."

"I tried to go somewhere fancier, but they spotted my red neck from a mile every time."

"Are you on your way home?"

I pictured him sitting on his couch, glass of wine in hand, ready to lecture me the moment I walked in. Dom had probably already warned him I was on my guard, which meant he was now eight or twelve steps ahead of me. He interpreted my protracted silence as a 'no.'

"Where are you now?" he asked. He was trying not to smile again, I could hear it. Was he enjoying this silly game I'd concocted?

I confessed, "The Old Ebbitt Grill. Cool place."

"Are you alone?"

I suppressed an actual growl. "Yes, but don't worry, I've been walking around drunk with headphones in, staring at my phone and jaywalking and asking strangers for directions while flashing your fancy black credit card—"

"All right, all right, I get it. Dare I ask where you intend to sleep tonight?"

Somewhere beneath the attitude, I detected a whisper of hurt feelings. Heart softening, I sighed, "No, I'll be home soon. I need you to decide on a dress for me, since I couldn't."

"I can help with that. By the way, I've got our tickets to Kraków. We leave next Wednesday."

"Well, that's something to look forward to."

We said goodbye and hung up, and as I turned back toward the restaurant to go inside, my own reflection in the window caught my eye. A vaguely familiar man was passing behind me, and my reflection locked eyes with his for a split second. I turned toward the real man and watched him walk away, my palms itching slightly. He'd given me a rather menacing look, but he hadn't done anything. He didn't look back at me as he turned west on G Street.

I hurried back inside and found my beer waiting for me. Now that my game of cat-and-mouse had ended in a predictable victory for the cat, my enthusiasm for drinking alone had evaporated. I chugged my beer, dropped some cash on the table, and left.

Outside, I turned right without really thinking and started toward G Street. When I turned west toward Metro Station I paused, realizing this was the same direction that the staring man had gone. I also remembered why he was familiar: He'd been at Krav Maga. He was the man Dom had pointed out when we were stretching, a new face which had been turned toward me more often than I liked.

I didn't know or care what his problem was, but the mere suggestion that I'd been followed made me so angry I wanted to chase him down and interrogate him. Deciding for once that discretion was the better part of valor, I turned around and headed southeast for the Federal Triangle station instead. It would set me back a stop, but at least I was less likely to encounter the same man again.

Late as it was, the metro was still so crowded I could hardly squeeze myself into a car at Federal Triangle. Amongst the government employees in grave business attire with their hangdog expressions and all-consuming smartphone addictions, I felt as painfully out of place as I had at the clothing store where everything was some shade of white.

I stood near one of the doors, clutching a vertical pole for support as the train lurched from one stop to the next. Since I had one arm full of shopping bags, I swayed back and forth nauseatingly with only one hand for support while my beer toyed with the idea of making a reappearance.

Oh yeah, this was way better than having a serious conversation with my boyfriend.

How would that go, anyway? How long could Jim and I beat around the bush before we reached the obvious conclusion? I was in Jim's chain of command, and the flimsy pretext that had allowed us free rein was now spelled out in a clinical, black-and-white report on an operation that was concluded.

For us to be together the way Jim imagined—the way I wanted as badly as he did—one of us had to find a new place in the FBI or leave it altogether. I couldn't ask Jim to do that, and I knew he wouldn't ask it of me.

Could I go back to Christopher King's office? Would I be happy there? I doubted it. I'd never been thrilled by a life standing still, let alone one that moved backward.

Fully zoned out, I forgot which side the doors opened on at the Rosslyn station. Before I could do more than gasp in surprise, I had been yanked off the train by my shirt and herded away with the press of people disembarking. I didn't see who'd manhandled me and didn't try very hard to pick them out. It was probably just some impatient jerk who spent way too much time on the Metro.

I joined the queue waiting to get back on the train, meeting one passenger's puzzled expression through the window and rolling my eyes as though to say, "What can you do?"

I was in no rush to get home, anyway. Jim was a night owl, but if I dawdled long enough, I might find him asleep when I got home.

Plopping down on a concrete bench, I watched the train slide out of the underground station and settled in for a quarter-hour wait. The crowd that had disembarked with me filtered away, leaving only a handful of people on the platform. They all boarded the Blue Line car that arrived a few minutes later, leaving me alone at Rosslyn station. That was a first.

I checked my watch: 9:16. About ten more minutes until the next train. After texting that same information to Jim and waiting in vain for the message to go through, I looked around aimlessly, trying to decide if it would be better to wait at street level in case Jim tried to call again. At least my text message would get sent. On the verge of standing up, I spotted movement at the far end of the station.

I wasn't the only person on the platform.

14

Wednesday, April 21, 2021

At the far end of the station, where the tracks disappeared into the southbound tunnel, a sign hung on the concrete wall bearing the message "Welcome to Virginia" with a big, red heart. Virginia was for lovers. Why had that popped into my head?

A few feet nearer me sat a hulking, black cube of metal, some kind of electrical hub or secure storage. I spotted him lurking in the space between the wall and the cube, half his body leaning around the obstruction. I caught a flash of his face before he turned away, looking at nothing.

It was that *same* guy. If this were some kind of clumsy attempt to strike up a conversation…

He turned, met my gaze, scanned the empty station with obvious intent, and started walking toward me. Irritation shifted immediately to panic. This was not about chatting me up.

Fight, flee, fight, flee, fight—I couldn't decide fast enough. I sure didn't want to get shot or stabbed or bludgeoned in the back, so I set my shopping bags down and squared up to him, raising my hands when he was about three yards away.

"Whoa, stop," I challenged, forcing my voice to a volume that felt deafening in the underground space.

He stopped, hands shoved deep into the pockets of a bulky grey jacket.

"What do you want?" I snapped. There was a time to be polite to strangers, and this wasn't it.

"Anna?" he asked.

I studied his face for some clue to his intentions. He was white, about my age, stocky and balding with round glasses perched above a thick, brown beard. The determined glint in his eyes didn't give me a single reason to speak kindly to him.

I snarled, "Never heard of her."

He walked closer, closing the distance to two yards. "Weren't you at class earlier?"

Mentally, my guard dropped for a moment. He'd recognized me from class, as I'd recognized him. But I hadn't introduced myself or even spoken to him, which brought my hackles right back up.

Shouting now, I warned, "Come any closer and we're gonna have a problem."

I glanced behind me at the escalators, thinking surely someone, anyone, would be coming along at any moment. Someone would hear me. But still, no one appeared. Anyone coming to the Rosslyn station would probably show up right in time to catch the next train. I assumed I'd be on my own for no more than three minutes. Way too long.

In the split second that my eyes left him, he closed the distance to one yard.

At this distance, I was forced to accept he was not only the guy from Krav Maga, but certainly the same person who'd passed me in front of the bar. He'd been shadowing me all night, and I'd been so distracted by my stupid Jim troubles that I'd let it happen.

Both his hands left his pockets at the same time, and my gaze was automatically drawn to the one that rose the highest, almost directly in front of his face.

He was holding up a small square of paper—a photo, I guessed—to compare the picture to me? It was just a distraction. His left hand rose right behind it, a small handgun directed at my chest. I jerked to my left as he fired twice in quick succession, the first round grazing my arm and the second missing me completely. I was lucky his draw to first shot wasn't faster. I slammed into him with all my weight, my right hand closing blindly over the top of the weapon, my left grabbing for his face as though his eyes and mouth were the fingerholds of a squishy, complaining bowling ball.

The gunshots echoed painfully, but none followed. My palm had prevented the second casing from being ejected, but I didn't get the weapon away from him fast enough. He twisted out of my grip before I could get two hands on him, and he started clearing the malfunction. I rushed him, he tried to grab me, and I ducked under his arm to lock both of mine around his knees. Just like Luke taught me, I launched myself upward and let the man's weight carry us back down, all the way to the ground where I probably had the advantage. I wasn't wrong, but the ground was unforgivingly hard.

After some grappling that had us both winded and gasping, I ended up on his back, one hand twisted into his hair as I bashed his face against the concrete five or six times. As soon as he went slightly limp, I dove for the gun still clutched in his left hand and was able to get it away. I stood and backed away from him, clearing the malfunction, and pointed the unfamiliar weapon at him as he started to pick himself up.

"Don't you dare move," I commanded, meaning to sound fierce and undaunted and only managing a hoarse half-whisper. My hands were shaking like two tiny chihuahuas. Finally my brain got a word in edgewise and I screamed, "Help! Someone please help me, I'm being attacked!"

The shots had already captured the attention of the woman in the ticketing station one level up. She appeared at the top of the escalator and called down, "Cops are on the way. You hurt?"

Forgetting about the first bullet, I called back, "No. Be cool if you could help me restrain this guy, though."

I could almost hear her ardent desire not to do so, but she started down the escalator anyway. Hardly had she reached the ground at my level before three police officers appeared at the top of the escalator, bristling like tines of a fork. I lowered the weapon and waited like a good little citizen for them to give me commands: Put the weapon on the ground, lie face down, put your hands behind your head. They didn't know who started this.

My bewildered attacker received the same treatment, and then we were each handcuffed, patted down, and forced to sit and cool our heels on benches at opposite ends of the station. Though one officer stood near me, hand on his radio, I was ignored while the other officers talked to the man who'd attacked me.

As adrenaline drained from my body and my pulse stopped pounding in my ears, eventually I could hear their conversation. I couldn't make out their words, but the man's tone made it quite clear my intentions, if not my very character, were being fiercely impugned. I looked around and spotted three different security cameras that might have captured the incident. He could say what he wanted.

Apparently they'd left someone at the top to stop people coming down to rubberneck, because after ten or so minutes only one more person put in an appearance. I looked up and saw Jim descending the frozen escalator three steps at a time. So my text *had* gone through… or Jim was tracking my phone.

"What happened?" he demanded, directing the question at the ticket agent who was pressed against the wall looking like she'd like to be anywhere else.

"I heard two shots. I don't know anything," she babbled.

The officer babysitting me physically blocked Jim on his way to my side, extending one hand and barking, "Hold up. Sir, you need to tell me who you are and how you got down here."

With far more restraint than I would've demonstrated, Jim stopped, showed the officer his credentials, and explained that the officer at the station entrance had allowed him to come down to check on me. That done, Jim hurried over to me. He knelt on the ground between my knees and pressed his hands to my face.

"Are you oaky? Were you hit?"

"Yes, no," I intoned. His gaze moved from my face to my right bicep, forcing me to amend, "Maybe a little."

"Anna…"

"Don't start lecturing me. Don't you dare."

"Fine. I can wait."

He sat beside me, one hand resting protectively on my knee, while the officers continued sorting things out. I tried my best to do the same, but my brain felt heavy and stupid and I couldn't even hazard a guess as to why someone would put so much effort into killing me. Since Jim was probably thinking along the same lines, I decided to let him handle it.

An officer came down the escalator, collected the ticketing agent, and returned to the upper level with her. After about a quarter hour more, the officer with us radioed his fellows to ask what was going on. Jim stood up and hovered over the shorter man, listening unchallenged to the response. I could hear it from my seat. The officers upstairs had reviewed the security camera footage. It was quite obvious I'd been the victim, however briefly.

Though my brain was telling me two or three hours had passed since the attack, when my handcuffs were removed and I automatically glanced at my watch, it wasn't even 10:00. How could that be possible? The one officer stayed with Jim and me while two more dragged my foe up the escalator, hopefully into a squad car headed to a jail somewhere. I glowered after the would-be assassin, wishing I'd shot him.

Once they were out of sight, the officer with us asked me, "Are you ready to give your statement?"

Before I could answer, Jim said, "She's not ready to, and she doesn't have to."

The officer shrugged. "Suit yourselves. Sure would be helpful to know your side of it, though."

"He tried to shoot me. I stopped him," I recited. "And he's right, I'm not ready to make a statement. Can I just go home?"

"Yes, soon," the officer assured me, asking, "Want something for that?" He answered my wordless confusion with a nod at my bleeding arm.

"I'll rub some dirt on it," I sighed. He didn't seem to catch on that I was joking, but he let the matter drop.

The officer and Jim exchanged business cards and a very civilized handshake, and we were finally allowed to leave. At the same time, the snarl in the Metro system was released, and the escalators came back on with an echoing groan. The people who'd been queueing up outside piled onto the downward escalator, and not a single one of them missed the opportunity to stare at Jim and me as we rode up. One enterprising young man even asked us what happened, but we both ignored him.

As Jim and I climbed into his car, which was parked illegally in a bus lane, I had to ask, "Why'd you come to the station? Not that I wasn't happy to see you…"

"I got your text," he said softly, leaving it at that.

Since my text hadn't included a plea for help, or even a hint that I was in trouble, I knew this was barely half an answer. I was too tired to press him, so I melted into the passenger seat warmer, Jim's hand gripping mine over the center console, and allowed deep exhaustion to pull me under.

The drive from Rosslyn Station to Arlington Heights took less than ten minutes, so I was only mostly asleep when the passenger door opened and someone unbuckled my seatbelt. It wasn't Jim, because his hand tightened around mine as someone else tried to pull me out of the car.

"Give her a second to wake up," Jim chided.

Luke's voice returned a gruff, "Forget that."

Tired as I was, my heart soared. Luke was okay. He was finally here.

He hoisted me out of the car and carried me inside, depositing me gently on the sofa and sitting down next to me. I shook my head, trying to wake up.

"What happened?" Luke asked.

From behind and above me, Jim countered, "Will you take care of that first?"

Luke grunted, "Huh? Oh. Sure."

They'd lost me. I leaned my head back and closed my eyes, barely stirring as Luke swiped something wet over the cut on my arm, which began to sting and burn.

"Is this—is this from a *bullet?*" he demanded.

"Get me a glass of wine and a German Shepherd and I'll tell you all about it."

Luke finished cleaning the wound and slapped a bandage on it. Jim poured the wine, Luke let Dude inside, and I curled up on the sofa with Dude halfway in my lap to recite a clinical version of the story from the time I spotted the guy at my Krav class to the time the last officer left us at Rosslyn Station. When I was finished, Luke and Jim wore matching expressions devoid of shock or confusion.

Luke surprised me by saying, "Well. At least your guy's alive and hopefully talking. Mine's on a slab in Cleveland."

I looked from Luke to Jim and back, not realizing my mouth was hanging open until Luke reached over and tapped me gently under the chin. While I was still trying to think of something to say, my stomach grumbled so loudly both men looked down at my torso in puzzlement.

Finally I asked, "Do you think I could get some tacos or something?"

15

Wednesday, April 21, 2021

Luke was quick to second my motion to acquire tacos, and Jim set off at once to find some. On his way out the door, he turned to Luke and barked, "Tell her about Cleveland."

"Yes, sir, right away, sir," Luke grumbled.

"Is he mad?" I asked. I honestly couldn't tell. Something more was going on, and I suspected it was my fault somehow.

Luke read my expression too easily and assured me, "Not at you."

"So what happened in Cleveland?"

"Well, I knew it was a matter of time before something happened."

He pulled me against him and ruffled Dude's ears fondly before launching into the tale.

"I decided to take a roundabout route here, not make it too obvious where I was going in case someone was following me, you know. I went straight north, all the way up to Wyoming, and then east to Cleveland. I hitchhiked, stole cars, rode a Greyhound bus. Whatever worked. I got there last night.

"I was exhausted. Tried to make the cash you gave me hold out as long as possible, so once I got to Cleveland I had plenty leftover to buy an Amtrak ticket to DC. I even got a private compartment, felt like a real high roller. I had to stay one night in Cleveland, though, so I found the closest motel that didn't demand a credit card for 'incidentals'—I hate that they do that—and got woken up in the middle of the night by someone coming through my door."

I choked on my wine, gasping, "What? Who?"

"No idea. I don't even know how I woke up, he was so quiet about it. He tried to shoot me, I got the gun, and I killed him. Stupid. I should've figured out why he was trying to kill me before I returned the favor. But, you know, heat of the moment."

"Did anyone hear?"

"Nope. Silencer."

"Suppressor," I corrected.

He chuckled. "Whatever."

"You think Marcel sent him…?"

"Him or Barbato. They both want me dead. So I took the guy's phone, left him and the gun in the room, and went to the train station to wait. Man I was nervous… but I guess no one found the body until I was long gone."

I pictured where I'd been during this incident (taking a leisurely bubble bath, if memory served) and asked, "Why didn't you call us? Didn't Jim give you his number?"

"I did. He did some voodoo with the phone and figured out

it was a burner purchased in Chicago on Sunday. Nothing useful."

"I can't believe Jim didn't tell me. I've been worried sick about you."

"Don't decide how mad you are at him yet," Luke urged, a smile in his voice. "It gets worse."

"Oh?"

"I told you I grabbed the guy's phone, right? Well he started getting texts about the time I got on the train, so I started answering them."

"Texts from whoever hired him?"

"Bingo."

He passed a cheap flip phone into my free hand, open and displaying a list of text messages. I scrolled through them one by one.

+13126486725 (21/04/2021 07:49): wheres my delivery conf
+17865002323 (21/04/2021 07:55): right here. got anything else? omw to dc.

"Oooh, hitman jargon," I murmured. Assuming Luke was the 786 number, I asked, "You were asking for another target, right? To see where?"

"Yep. Might've worked, but they wanted proof I was dead first."

+13126486725 (21/04/2021 07:56): conf
+17865002323 (21/04/2021 07:56): didnt you get the photo? left the package at the front door. heading out of town already.

There were no other texts. I checked the call log and saw an incoming call from the 312 number right after Luke's last text, but it went unanswered. A subsequent outgoing call to Jim's cell had gone through, so I asked, "Jim knew about all of this?"

"Sure did."

"That doesn't make sense. He would've warned me. He would have locked me in the basement!"

"Yeah, he would have, if he thought your number was up. But he figured they'd go after him."

"So he's mad at himself," I concluded. "Well, he should be."

Happily, Luke went on, "I got here a little after eight, wanted to know where you were, so Jim called you. When he called you again later and you didn't answer, he jumped on his white horse and took off, and you know the rest."

"He *tricked* me into avoiding him! Who does that?"

"Yeah, he really is terrible," Luke agreed. "Just a garbage human being."

"I wouldn't go that far…"

"Of course you wouldn't."

"… And now he's off by himself getting *tacos?* What the heck was he thinking!"

My raised voice spooked Dude, who leapt off the sofa and nearly knocked my wine out of my hand in the process. I yanked my phone from my pocket and called Jim.

Jim answered, "Please tell me you don't want sushi instead."

"You get your narrow butt back here right now!" I hissed.

I listened to a few seconds of road noise while Jim pondered my tone. At length he said, "I didn't realize how hungry you were. I'm almost to the taco place."

"Just because I was the target doesn't mean you aren't *also* a target!"

"If I were, they would've hit us both at the same time."

"Oh, you think you know *everything*—"

"I prefer to, yes."

"Just—hurry up!" I hung up before he could answer.

I tossed my phone on the sofa, locking eyes with Luke. He was looking a bit too smug for my liking.

"Are you seriously that happy that I'm mad at Jim?"

"Mostly I'm happy that you're okay. But yeah, this is fun for me."

"I'm happy you're okay, too." Resuming my seat next to Luke, I rested my head on his shoulder and sighed. "Gun to your head, who's behind it: Paolo or Marcel?"

"Gun to my head… Paolo."

"Why?"

"Because Jim thinks so. He told me."

"Must be nice. Jim telling you stuff."

Luke's hand slid up my arm, stopping short of the minor wound I'd incurred. "He doesn't feel the need to protect me."

I had no answer to that. I sipped at my wine, enjoying a comfortable silence and the absence of that low-level anxiety about Luke that had been ruining my life for two and a half weeks. More like two months, if I were being honest. My wine glass was empty and my eyelids drooping again when Dude perked up, his ears standing at attention. Half a second later I heard the garage door cranking open, and I was standing in the kitchen pouring myself a refill when Jim came inside.

He took in my steely expression and, without a word, set two brown paper bags on the counter. He pulled a foil-wrapped taco from one bag, unwrapped it, and brought it over to me.

"These are the best tacos in Northern Virginia. Please eat one before you start in."

It was the least I could do. My hunger had somewhat subsided, however, and I was only able to force down a couple bites before setting the taco down on the counter. Dude brushed past my legs like a fluffy shark, but I was too distracted by Jim's less than contrite expression.

I said, "True or false: You used Dom and this moving in business to trick me into avoiding you all day."

His eyebrows pushed together briefly, and he fought back a smile. "False. I understand why you'd suspect as much, but it was a happy coincidence, nothing more. I wasn't even that worried about myself, or I'd have taken serious measures. Do you believe me?"

While I deliberated, I reached for the discarded taco and found nothing but a grease spot on the kitchen counter. Jim and I turned to Dude, who was sitting a cautious yard away. He licked his chops innocently, his eyes alight. I tried to summon up some kind of chastisement for him, but I could only laugh. Luckily, Jim had secured a surfeit of tacos and we had more than enough to spare one for Dude. We left the grease spot for Dude to attend to and took the rest into the living room where Luke was waiting.

As I passed Jim a couple tacos, I belatedly answered, "Yes,

I believe you. But just so you know, that jerk at Rosslyn never would've gotten me alone if I'd been on my guard."

"So?" he challenged.

"So don't gossip about me with Dom!"

"Who's Dom?" Luke asked, his mouth already full of carnitas.

"Colleague," Jim answered. He shot me a nervous side-eye and added, "Maybe she'd want to go to Kraków."

"What do you mean?" I squeaked. "You're not taking me to Poland?"

He blinked owlishly at me. "Is that a joke? Someone just tried to kill you."

"I'm not missing the exhibition!" I erupted, throwing another half-eaten taco down on the coffee table with a wet *splat*. Dude hurried over to do his duty. "If you don't take me, I'll— I'll—*crap*, I don't even know. I'll shave my head."

"Anna," Luke piped up. "He's right, just—"

"No!" I stood up, grabbed my shopping bags, and carried them into Jim's bedroom, calling, "End of discussion!"

I slammed the door behind me and dumped my entire haul onto the bed, then selected a dress and forced myself to calm down before I started wriggling into it. Wouldn't want to make it a casualty of my temper tantrum. I was rotating this way and that in front of a full-length mirror when Jim mustered up the courage to enter.

"Nice dress," he offered blandly.

I glared at it in the mirror, a floor-length, long-sleeved, navy blue dress with exactly one point of interest: a keyhole slit at the sternum, letting my cleavage get a little bit of screen time. It had looked boring on the hanger, but I bought it a size too small and thought the effect was quite titillating.

"Thanks. I guess I'll wear it to the *next* once-in-a-lifetime, history-making, lost Renaissance masterpiece exhibition opening I'm invited to."

"Do you not understand there's a price on your head? Do you think they'll give up just because that idiot failed?"

"Jim, I would literally die to see that painting hanging up where it belongs."

"So you see what I'm worried about."

"I am not missing this. I'll just have to watch my back, like I did today with definitive success, thank you very much. I mean, how am I safer here than in Poland? I might be safer in Poland, actually."

Rather than answering back, he crossed his arms and looked me over. I could tell he'd descended deep into thought, but about what I had no idea.

He stepped closer to me, arms outstretched, and I pressed my face to his chest. The flood gates opened as he wound me up into a suffocatingly tight embrace. I had just brushed closer to death than I ever had before, with the possible exception of getting stabbed in the abdomen when I was 17. I'd take a professional gunman over a knife-wielding teenage psychopath any day of the week; still, it was jarring. I didn't cry, but my self-defensive anger drained away, leaving me raw and frightened enough that I actually considered following Jim's advice and skipping the Poland trip.

"I hope you didn't bother getting a tie to match this one," Jim whispered seriously. "My closet is lousy with navy blue ties."

"What am I, an infant?" I shot back. I wormed out of his arms, rooted around in the pile on the bed, and presented him with a ruby red, silk tie. "When you said 'matching,' I chose to interpret it as 'coordinating.' I hope it's the right length."

While he was considering the tie, I slipped on the stilettos I'd bought to go with this dress and stood in front of him, grinning as he realized we were nearly eye-to-eye.

He looked down at my feet and said, "Those are a tactical nightmare."

"Well, I bought flats to go with the other two." I paused, one shoe already off. "Do you… want to see the other two?"

He understood what I was really asking and took his time answering, winding the tie around one hand while he thought. Finally, "You got shot. It's late. Let's save the fashion show for tomorrow."

"I wasn't shot. I was grazed."

"I have an idea about Poland. I don't think you'll like it, but if you're determined to be so blasé about your own life, we might as well use it to our advantage, since you saw fit to nuke my plan for Albuquerque."

"That's… an interesting collision of your two dominant instincts."

"Do you want to hear the plan or not?"

Luke came in before I could answer, holding out a taco.

"Last one, either of you—hey. Wow."

He tossed the taco at Jim, who caught it reflexively, and gave me a much more pointed inspection than Jim had.

"Holy crap, you're sexy."

"That's more like it," I said with a grin. I gave him a twirl, he whistled, and Jim rolled his eyes so hard I could almost hear it.

"Can we help you, Jackson?"

Ignoring him, Luke bundled me into his arms and gave me a hungry kiss. "You taste like tacos. And here I thought you couldn't get any more delicious."

"Thanks, Casanova," I said. "You should write love poems."

"Anna and I were discussing the trip to Kraków," Jim reminded me.

Luke let me go and took the taco back from Jim, wolfing it down in two bites before weighing in. "Are you gonna shave your head if I tell you how stupid it is to go?"

"Yes." My tone dared him to argue, but he didn't.

"Then you're going to have to figure out a way to get me over there, too. Next time someone comes after you, I want the pleasure of personally ending them."

"You should've seen me," I said, brightening. "I took him right to the ground and he couldn't do a thing about it. You'd think Paolo would've sent someone with a broader skill set."

He didn't answer, leaving me to wonder if he was asking himself how anyone could be so recklessly self-satisfied, or maybe if the hitmen hadn't even been sent by Paolo. Personally, I believed they were. I thought the vagrant in Albuquerque was a possible first attempt, a testing of the waters. I didn't voice my theory.

"So what's this grand plan of yours, Jim?" I asked.

"I'll tell you tomorrow. I'm tired." He tossed me the tie, adding with bitter defeat, "Bring them all. We can choose when we get there."

Flush with victory, I changed into PJs, stowed all my purchases in Jim's closet, and followed Jim and Luke back out into the living room. Jim disappeared into the kitchen to refill my wine and pour himself a glass. Luke demurred. I sank down onto the couch next to him.

"Speaking of the incompetent idiot who let you ground and pound him," he started in. "Are you in any kind of trouble with the police?"

"I don't think so. I'm sure I'll have to give a statement before we leave."

Jim reappeared, adding, "I'll see if I can get a crack at him tomorrow. Until we know more, you both stay here. Period."

Neither Luke nor I cared to argue the point. I preferred to snuggle down next to Luke and engage in the much more pleasant discussion of what to watch on TV. Jim planted himself on the other side of me and draped one arm over my leg. Luke's answer was to claim my other leg, his massive paw resting heavy on my thigh. If humans could purr, they would've had to turn the TV all the way up to drown me out.

16

Wednesday, April 28 to
Saturday, May 1, 2021

I was up at 2:00 a.m. the following Wednesday morning, dumping all my carefully packed suitcases into a pile in the middle of the living room.

Our flight from Washington to Kraków, with stops in New York and London, was scheduled to depart in four hours. Jim was exactly the sort to drag me to the airport two hours before boarding, so that left me two more hours to channel all my stress into reorganizing and repacking. Between my renewed worry for Luke, who'd left for his own flights two days ago, and my brand new anxiety about Jim's plan, I wasn't in the best of mental states as I stood over my tiny mountain of clothes, shoes, and toiletries.

I dove in and eviscerated all my carefully rolled clothes and bagged liquids in search of knives, ammo, magazines, especially pointy ballpoint pens, or anything else that might make a TSA agent lose their mind. Satisfied, I repacked it all and barely got myself dressed and caffeinated in time to leave the house at the pre-appointed time of 4:00 a.m.

Richard Beauchamp and his wife were already waiting at the gate when Jim and I rolled up, one of us a tad ruffled by a random extra screening he'd had to endure. They were sitting in a half-full waiting area at the end of a row of seats, the better to allow Beauchamp to manspread comfortably into the concourse. His wife stood when she spotted Jim and waved us over, though she was so short it hardly made a difference.

She was precisely as I imagined her from name alone, Betty Beauchamp: a 50-something-year-old former cheerleader who was definitely always at the top of the pyramid. She was probably 80 pounds soaking wet, not an inch over five feet tall, with lively green eyes and shoulder-length, reddish brown curls that were no more God-given than my own red hair. In her case it was probably greys that forced her to turn to the bottle, whereas I was trying to get back from blonde to my real hair color.

She was dressed to shame. I felt like a monster in my baggy sweats, long-sleeved t-shirt, and messy braid that I definitely hadn't slept in, towering over this cheerful little woman who was looking dapper in a deep purple shift dress.

She greeted me warmly and offered to take me down the terminal to Starbucks for an early breakfast, since, after all, "We are going on vacation together so we should get to know each other!"

Rich didn't bother acknowledging us until she had her say. It didn't strike me as rudeness, more that he knew trying to get in a word too soon would be awkward. He shook Jim's hand, then mine, then asked his wife to bring him a scone and a black coffee. Jim put in his request for a black coffee, totally missing my telepathic pleas that he not allow this bundle of sunshine to melt me with her radiation. I gave up and allowed Betty to tow me to the nearest coffee shop.

"I wish I had your brains, hun," she chuckled. "Imagine getting ready for a transatlantic flight and not thinking about being comfortable."

"At least you look fabulous," I returned, as elicited.

Her backhanded compliment was as classy as they came, but the joke was on her: I grew up in Texas, where we invented being nasty while sounding like sweet tea tastes. She ordered for us—apparently I wanted a tall, non-fat latte and a slice of pumpkin bread—and picked a table near the counter where our drinks would appear.

"So how long have you and Jim been together?"

"Like, working together?" I asked.

"No, dear," she tittered. "Dating."

"Oh." I took a long draught of latte, hating it, and said, "I'll tell you when we start."

She winked broadly at me. "If you say so. Have you ever been to Poland before?"

It was like being deposed. She fired off questions, never stopping to think, seeming to lead somewhere and then shooting off on a tangent when I thought we were reaching a conclusion. I was never more thankful to feel a knock at the back door than I was sitting there with her.

I excused myself happily with, "Pardon me, Betty, I gotta go drop the kids off at the pool. Thanks for breakfast."

I made my escape, not returning to the coffee shop when I was done but retreating to the relative safety of the hard plastic chair next to Jim. Betty had already returned as well and was fussily pawing through her carryon-sized purse.

As I sat down, Jim whispered almost inaudibly, "Drop the kids off at the pool'?"

"It's called an artful euphemism, look it up."

"I can't take you anywhere."

"And yet, you do."

After the priority passengers boarded what looked like a completely full flight, Jim and I hopped into line with the other first class passengers. I congratulated myself for not looking back at the Beauchamps to see if Betty looked sour about being relegated to the main cabin. I knew I really ought to give her a chance to grow on me, even though she'd obviously allowed her husband to convince her to artlessly interrogate me.

I settled into my spacious window seat with a sigh of contentment, leaning back to see if I could catch a few zees while everyone else boarded. The latte foiled me, and I remained wide awake until right before we landed in New York for our first layover.

▼

I finally fell asleep about 30,000 feet above where the *Titanic* sank, drastically reducing my jetlag when we deplaned in London at

6:20 a.m. local time. Our flight from London to Kraków was delayed by an hour, more than doubling the time we had to spend uncomfortably close to the last place I'd encountered Marcel.

Even if Jim was comfortable in his belief that Marcel wasn't sending people to kill Luke and me, I didn't want to be within a thousand miles of the London-dwelling Frenchman. Luke had preceded us to Kraków two days earlier and had reported that all was well, but he had connected through Madrid instead of London.

We took the opportunity to eat a real meal at the airport, where I once again embarrassed Jim by ordering a Bloody Mary after everyone else at the table ordered coffee. I actually hadn't intended to poke at him that time and was remorseful for about two seconds before Beauchamp changed his order to a Bloody Mary as well. Jim followed suit gratefully. When the waitress looked at Betty, she requested extra cream and sugar with her coffee.

We made it to Kraków at noon and checked in to our hotel, the Bonerowski Palace. Our rooms were mercifully separated by two floors and the entire length of the hotel, about as far apart as any two rooms there. They had been paid for by the Polish government, a cherry on top of our free tickets to the exhibit. Luke's room, underwritten by Jim rather than the Polish government, was even farther away in a different hotel about three kilometers to the south. If all went to plan, we wouldn't see him until Saturday night, May 1, when the private symposium at the museum was to be held.

I was looking forward to the symposium more than the exhibit itself. Not only would I be among the first people outside of Poland to see the Raphael returned to its rightful place, but I'd have the added pleasure of making faces at Jim while he delivered a short presentation on the recovery of the painting. I'd already heard it a dozen times while he rehearsed. It focused on the FBI Art Crime Team's work and skated adroitly over specifics of the actual recovery of the Raphael. The task of giving this presentation had originally fallen on Beauchamp, who was quick to delegate, insisting no one wanted to look at him for 15 minutes.

▼

At Jim's suggestion, I was wearing neither the conservative navy blue dress nor the revealing, backless, royal blue number I'd only bought because I looked so stinking good in it. I was wearing the middle option, a perfect balance of refined and sexy with a long-sleeved, off-the-shoulder lace bodice and a floor-length satin skirt, all in a jewel-tone teal. It brushed the floor as I walked, concealing the simple, gold ballet flats I'd chosen for comfort.

Between the dress and the fancy to-do and waking up in an actual palace this morning, I felt like a princess. How quickly I succumbed to the charms of Europe that my home country simply couldn't compete with. It didn't help that Jim looked like royalty in his black tuxedo complete with the first actual, real-life, silver cufflinks I'd ever seen.

It was going to be a long evening. First we were having dinner with the Museum Director and a dozen other important people and their plus ones at a restaurant near the museum. This group included the Art Historian from Italy, Isabella Franco, who had certified the Raphael's authenticity. I was chomping at the bit to meet her. After dinner was the symposium in the museum's lecture hall, and after that we'd be attending a mixer for the next-lowest tier of VIPs.

The Polish government and the museum were really milking this, and I couldn't blame them. They'd scheduled a photo shoot with the Raphael for Sunday, followed by a private opening that night. The exhibit would officially open to the public on Monday, May 3. The whole affair had probably been planned for decades in anticipation of the lost Raphael's triumphant return.

Our six-person dinner table was filled entirely by English-speakers, none of whom was Isabella Franco. I had looked her up before we left and spotted her a couple tables away, garnering an understandable amount of attention.

Jim had to pinch my leg to tear my attention away from her to the occupants of our own table, the Beauchamps and a couple from California, Mark and Alex Anders, who had donated over half of the money the museum spent putting on this whole show. They had a tenuous connection outside of their wallets: Alex' grandfather had been one of the Monuments Men who recovered so many of the other artworks looted from around Europe by the Third Reich. Alex herself didn't give a fig about art, but once Mark found out I was an Art Historian by education, if not by trade, he talked my ear off about it for the entire dinner.

I barely got six bites in around all the conversation, but I wasn't that hungry anyway. My stomach was filled with caterpillars exploding into butterflies at random intervals. For once I'd been informed of Jim's plan before he executed it, and I found myself feeling nostalgic for the blissful ignorance I'd become accustomed to.

Mark finally shut up when dessert arrived, and I took my chance. Dismissing myself in a rush, I headed over to Isabella Franco and introduced myself. She was in her late 60s, even taller than me and rangy, with pixie-short black hair and thick-framed eyeglasses. She was an Italian to the core, dressed all in black and looking like she woke up ready for her close up. Her plus one, her husband, was nowhere in sight, so she patted the empty seat next to her.

"Your Italian is very good," she said graciously, "but let's speak English. I need the practice. You're with the Federal Bureau of Investigation?"

"That's right. My boss is the one who recovered the painting," I lied with grinding regret.

"And he brought you as his guest?" she asked, half-turning to fix me with one large hazel eye.

I couldn't help but laugh at her dubiousness. "He knows I studied Art History. Poor guy didn't know who else to bring. Am I lucky, or what?"

"Extremely. I am positively *dying* to know where he found it, and *how.*"

"I expect everyone here feels the same way."

"You can't give me a clue? No, I guess you can't. I sent off some samples from the cleaning, to see if that would narrow down the location at all, and they got 'lost'," she bemoaned, making air quotes around the last word. "Now I guess I'll never know. But between you and me," she said, her voice dropping to a whisper as she leaned toward me, "I heard the Polish Ambassador to Chile is the one who brought it into the country. Now what do you think of that?"

"Lots of Nazis fled to South America," I offered noncommittally. "Um—was it damaged, at all?"

"No more than you'd expect after being privately held for over seven decades. Whoever had it took very good care of it."

"Thank God." And Martín, the aged caretaker of Fernando's estate who'd done such an incredible job looking after the priceless painting for decades upon decades.

"So tell me, how does one go from studying Art History to working at the FBI?" Isabella asked.

I explained in brief, leaving out all of the gory details, and quickly steered her into telling her own story. She was, after all, living the life I'd turned down when I chose the FBI over pursuing an advanced degree in Art History. We chatted for so long that Jim had to come over and peel me away so we could walk to the museum for the symposium.

Night had fallen over Kraków, and the air was exactly the right temperature to make me feel cozy and content in my coat. A short walk brought us to the museum, where Jim spotted a tall, hulking man selling roses in the vast square before the museum's front doors. Jim waved the Beauchamps on and made a beeline for the man with the roses.

"Nice disguise," Jim said wryly as Luke picked out a fat white rose and handed it to me.

"That'll be five bucks for the rose and fifty for the unsolicited feedback."

"Seriously?" Jim asked.

"Why do you think I'm selling roses, dude? I'm running low on cash. What are you, on a budget?"

Scoffing, Jim nevertheless passed him a wad of bills and asked quietly, "Did Ingrid get you into the museum?"

I was distracted by a mental image of Ingrid Breker, the BKA agent who'd handled me during the operation in Berlin last year, meeting Luke in a dark alley somewhere. I puffed out a laugh, which Luke echoed as though he knew what I was thinking.

He confirmed, "Yeah, as a waiter for your swanky little to-do after the symposium. I've already gone through an orientation and even have an ID badge. So far, so good."

"Anything noteworthy aside from that?" Jim asked.

"No. They gave us a break after we finished setting up, so I've been out here for an hour, clocking everyone going into the museum. No cloaked assassins, at least none going through the front door. One of the other waiters looks pretty sketchy, but it's probably just the lazy eye…"

Jim actually poked him in the chest. "You better be taking this seriously."

Switching abruptly from English to French, Luke said, "Ha, always!"

He angled away from us to address another couple that had come silently up behind us. The man asked for a pink rose in stilted but effective French.

Jim pulled me away, but I turned back and grinned at Luke

to let him know I, at least, appreciated his lightheartedness. Jim was muttering to himself.

"Oh, lighten up," I chided. "Are you nervous about your speech?"

"Do I seem like the kind of person who's afraid of public speaking?"

"No…"

"I'm nervous that anyone who wants to collect the price on your head has about one square mile to look for you for the rest of the night."

"That's bleak… Thanks for the rose, by the way."

He gave me half a smile. "Anytime."

Jim's pace quickened, and as I hurried to keep up with his long-legged stride, I turned to catch a last glimpse of Luke hawking his roses in the square. Even from a distance, his body language conveyed a calm assurance that I couldn't quite convince myself to feel.

17

Saturday, May 1, 2021

The crowd from dinner had grown in size to about 150 people, filling the little lecture hall to standing room only. Jim and I had reserved seats on the fifth row next to the Beauchamps, but since Jim was speaking, he continued past our seats to the row of chairs off to stage left. The farther from me he got, the more anxious I felt.

"That's lovely," Betty said, holding out her hand for my rose as though she were required to inspect it. "From Jim?"

"Yep," I said coolly, glancing over her head at her husband. "Just between you and me, I think he's trying to close the deal."

Beauchamp shook his head silently while Betty responded, "Oh—well, who can blame him? You look absolutely stunning."

"Thanks, you look very beautiful yourself. Purple is a great color on you. Actually, I think the rose matches you better than it does me. Why don't you keep it?"

The unexpected gesture seemed to confuse her. She smiled

warmly and accepted the gift, leaving me in peace to gaze around at the other people in the lecture hall. I couldn't have said why I was expecting to see a familiar face, but of course everyone else in the hall who I didn't recognize from dinner was a perfect stranger to me.

I knew somewhere on the front row sat two Polish Holocaust survivors and one woman, now in her 80s, who fought in the Polish Resistance when she was barely a teenager. I spotted three white heads bobbing low in the front and thought that might be them. I deeply regretted not having the chance to learn more than a few words in Polish.

There were four speakers, all allotted various amounts of time, three of whom would likely go over. Jim had timed his presentation down to the second, and I'd have believed the moon landing was faked before I would believe he'd err by a single second in either direction.

The first to speak was the director of the museum, Zofia Korsak, who took care of all the required pleasantries: She thanked everyone for this and that, talked about the history of the museum, teased the story of the Raphael's theft, and introduced the next three speakers. On headphones provided by the museum, I and a handful of others listened to a woman translating Korsak into English in real time.

She spoke for about five minutes. Next up was Isabella Franco, who took us all on the journey the painting had undertaken from its creation in the early sixteenth century to its removal to the Wawel Castle in January 1945 by Hans Frank. She ended her lecture with a delightfully pointed aside to Jim that we were all extremely curious to know what happened after that. This woman was not going to accept "it's classified" for long.

The last five minutes had been granted to the Curator of the Europeum, the museum's European art collection, who had overseen the restoration, installation, and exhibit design; but first, it was Jim's turn to speak. I crossed and re-crossed my legs as he walked to the podium, realizing *I* was nervous.

What if Jim forgot his speech? What if he locked his knees and passed out? What if he got heckled? What if he went off script and told a joke no one laughed at?

Betty picked up on my discomfort and patted my knee. "Don't worry, dear, he'll do fine."

Isabella Franco had used a slideshow projected behind her, but Jim didn't have any slides. The screen went blank as he started to speak, and I could almost hear every eye in the room turning to stare at his face. I tuned him out almost immediately, focusing instead on the other people in the room. Were they listening? Was the translator getting it right, or was the perfectly rehearsed and carefully worded presentation getting lost in translation?

The minutes ticked by in spite of my anxiety. Near the end of Jim's talk, I was ripped away from my own thoughts as the tone of his voice shifted. I zeroed back in on him and realized he was indeed going off script. My heart jumped into my throat.

Jim was saying, "Before I give up the floor, I wanted to let you all in on a very well-kept secret about the recovery of this incredible piece of history."

I could tell who was listening in English as half the audience leaned eagerly forward. A second later, the half listening to translators on headphones followed. A reporter on the front row who'd been looking a little sleepy perked up and nudged the photographer sitting next to her. My gaze moved back to Jim, and I realized he was staring right at me. He waggled his finger at me, and 150 faces turned toward me. I shrank into my seat, ears buzzing as my face began to put off heat.

"Anna, come on. I have to do it."

Like this?

The only thought I hated more than getting out of my seat in that moment was leaving Jim hanging up there. I shuffled down the row, bumping into people's knees and getting stunned glances in return for my mumbled apologies. I stood next to Jim, staring at him for a few seconds before I had the fortitude to turn and face the lecture hall.

Don't lock your knees.

Beauchamp's face stood out clearly, drawing my eye. He was frowning so deeply he looked like a caricature of himself.

"This is going to get a little mawkish," Jim informed the crowd, "but bear with me:

"In nineteen ninety-seven, a little girl in Texas watched a documentary with her parents about the Nazis looting the cultural heritage of Europe, based in part on the nineteen ninety-four book *The Rape of Europa*. Raphael's *Portrait of a Young Man* featured prominently, part of a shrinking number of artworks that remained missing over the years while the little girl grew up and got a bachelor's degree in Art History. In twenty sixteen she did what she'd wanted to do for almost twenty years and joined the Federal Bureau of Investigation."

I turned to look at Jim again, not believing what I was hearing, what he was about to do. A camera flashed from the front row, shaking me out of it before I could even begin to wonder why.

"She joined because she wanted to be a part of the team that continues to this day to scour the globe for lost and stolen works of art. She joined because of the Raphael, and earlier this year…" Jim paused for dramatic effect, looking straight at Beauchamp to confess, "*She* found it."

The oxygen level in the room seemed to plummet as everyone sucked in a breath in two successive moments. The camera flashed again, and I wiped one hand quickly across my face.

"I wanted you all to know who really recovered this painting. Don't ask her where, and don't ask her how. She risked her life to do it, and it wouldn't be here without her. So please show your appreciation to Anna Bowman for being the brave, tenacious, unstoppable person she is."

I jerked in surprise as people started clapping. I couldn't stand it, literally or figuratively; my knees were shaking. I mumbled something unintelligible to Jim, then walked as slowly as I could force myself to behind the stage and out of the lecture hall through a side door.

I found myself in the large, open room where the mixer would be starting soon. For now it was empty except for a few waiters milling around and a sound guy trying to make the background music work. I found a high table off to the side of the room where the lights were still off and rested my elbows on it, burying my face in my hands. I nearly screamed as a hand came to rest gently on my shoulder.

"I understand if you want to hit me now," Jim said softly, his hand sliding to my lower back. "I knew you'd hate that, but I couldn't stand there and take the credit."

"You said you were going to tell Beauchamp, not the whole world!" I moaned.

"Eh, six of one."

His verbal shrug, his total relaxation in the wake of what he'd done, was too much for me.

"*You* found it," I argued, still covering my face. "You talked your way into the house, you realized what it was when Fernando showed it to you. You *do* deserve the credit. All I did was carry it out of the house."

"What if you had never joined the FBI and applied for agent, and I'd never seen your file?"

"Someone else would've—"

"No. No one else could have done what you did. You're not some pawn in all of this. I know you think you are, but you aren't. You're everything…"

I made an inarticulate noise, and he pried my hands away from my face.

"I'm sorry I embarrassed you."

"Embarrassed me? Jim, you're going to get fired for this! Or worse. You lied—you lied to the FBI! And instead of privately letting Beauchamp know like a *sane* person would, you just confessed before God and everyone!"

He smiled serenely. "I've talked my way out of worse. Only Rich knows I lied, he'll understand."

I sniffed, hoping he was right. "How did you know that?

About the documentary when I was a kid?"

"When we were in Chile, Luke said you told him that painting was the reason you joined the FBI. I had to tell your dad what happened to get him to cooperate. He told me the whole story. And he's off the hook, now. He doesn't have to lie to the FBI about you being in Berlin. It's a win-win."

"And me?"

"You lied because I forced you to. That's what you're going to tell Rich."

A third person joined us, eerily silent for someone so big. In a crisp, white waiter's uniform, Luke looked like an Imperial Stormtrooper in his parade best. I wondered how they found a shirt, jacket, and slacks big enough for him on such short notice.

"What's going on?" he asked. "What happened?"

"Jim just told everyone I found the Raphael."

"Oh. Wow. You, uh… you want a scotch?" he asked, directing the question to Jim with something like reverence.

Jim laughed. "Please."

"Me, too," I croaked.

Luke left to secure the drinks, but we weren't alone for more than a heartbeat before Beauchamp appeared, slapping Jim heartily on the shoulder. His wife was nowhere in sight.

"Well, James, my boy, that was incredibly stupid."

I was slightly relieved by the smile in his voice.

"As noble impulses tend to be. But it had to be done," Jim sighed.

"I don't like being lied to."

"I am sorry about that."

"We're going to have to alter your report a bit, huh?"

I couldn't believe it, but Beauchamp hardly seemed to care. Maybe Dom's description of their relationship was less of an exaggeration than I'd believed; it seemed Jim really could do no wrong. Luke, on the other hand, seemed to have judged Beauchamp prematurely. As well as he was taking the news of Jim's perfidy, his reaction so far struck me as genuine surprise.

Now that one half of Jim's plan was done, all that was left for me to do was hang around Kraków and see if anyone tried to murder me.

I spotted Luke coming our way with a tray bearing two tumblers half full of amber liquid. I left Jim and Beauchamp to their discussion and headed him off, worried Beauchamp would recognize Luke. When I got back to the table, Beauchamp was plodding away from it.

"Rich volunteered for damage control," Jim explained. "They're going to open the doors in about two minutes. Sorry, but… even with Rich running interference, you're going to get a lot of attention."

"At least you made me cry, you butthole. Is my mascara smeared?"

He cupped my cheek, wiping his thumb once under my right eye. "A little bit. It looks kind of nice that way, though. Poignant."

I couldn't contain myself any longer. I pulled him toward me and kissed him, only breaking away when I heard the main doors open. Korsak was power-walking well ahead of the rest of the crowd and made a beeline for me, saying in English, "We must talk, we must talk—You, Camposanto, come too."

She beckoned a young woman over who I guessed was the translator, waving away a couple more people who tried to follow. Through the translator, Korsak thanked me for recovering the painting and said I'd been bumped up to fourth in line to view it, right after the Holocaust survivors and the resistance fighter. I shook my head, praying the translator was accurately conveying the vehemence of my desire not to receive that particular honor. The Director seemed to get the message.

"I understand, you were not expecting this," she said through the translator, shooting Jim a look saturated with disapproval. "I will have my assistant make arrangements to meet with you about the reward. Thank you again, from the bottom of my heart."

"The reward?" I asked Jim when they'd gone, before anyone else could swoop in. "Is she serious?"

I'd never seen a man so pleased with himself. "Why wouldn't she be?"

I drained my scotch, passed the empty tumbler to Jim, and turned to face the first person who had pressed through the invisible barrier around us: Isabella Franco. She winked at me, shook my hand firmly, and, since she was conversant in Polish, she remained by my side to translate as needed.

Jim hovered behind me, catching about half smiles and half puzzled disapproval. When the reporter and her cameraman worked their way up to me, Jim decided it was time to shut this down. He asked Isabella to explain that I was tired and couldn't answer any more questions, and he pulled me back to the out-of-the-way table where Beauchamp and his wife were waiting. The former fixed me with a beady glare.

"Don't start making plans for that hundred million dollar reward."

"I wasn't—" I started to answer.

"Because that money belongs to the U.S. government, for whom Jim here was working when *he* found the painting. That's a matter of official record."

"An official record no one in the Polish government will ever see," Jim shot back rancorously. "I'll tell them Anna found it, and who's going to argue?"

"Then you better grab an application for the Polish FBI while you're here—"

"Stop!" I cried. "I'm not fighting Uncle Sam over money. There's only one way for that to end. I don't even want that money. I can't even *fathom* that much money." Beauchamp looked appeased, until I added, "And the U.S. government shouldn't take it either. What is that, like half of Poland's GDP?"

"Not even close," Beauchamp said, clearly offended on behalf of the Polish.

"Well. Still." I started to take a drink, realized my tumbler was empty, and grabbed Jim's. I finished it off and said, "You two can fisty-cuff over it to your hearts' content, but no one's giving me a cent because I won't take it."

"I'm going to get us refills," Jim said wearily. I watched him go, praying to God he hadn't been planning on retiring with that money.

"You better slow down, Anna," Betty said gently. "This

thing lasts another hour and you're already pretty unsteady on your feet."

"Wouldn't say no to a bottle of water," I mumbled. She whisked away to go find one, leaving me and Beauchamp alone. I knew what he was going to ask before he asked it, otherwise I might have been surprised into telling the truth.

"As long as we're all being honest, I'm gonna ask you one more time: You and Jim?"

"Ugh," I rolled my head back as though his question had been a physical blow. "You are *obsessed* with that."

His hand covered mine on the table. I blinked slowly at it.

"If you're really trying to get somewhere, darlin', Jim's not the one you want to be bothering with."

I was already too tipsy to modulate my reaction even a tiny bit. I whipped my hand out from underneath his so quickly I almost elbowed a waiter behind me. Instead of punching Beauchamp square in the nose as I was inclined to, I marched away, past Jim who was on his way back with our drinks and back through the door into the lecture hall. One look at the dark, now empty space changed my mind. This wasn't where I wanted to be.

I'd waited patiently, I'd come all this way, and I wanted to see the Raphael already.

18

Saturday, May 1 to
Sunday, May 2, 2021

As I climbed the stairs to reach the doors that would take me back to the museum's entrance hall, I heard the other door open behind and below me. I paused at the top of the amphitheater to see who it was, and Jim appeared around the edge of the stage.

"You okay?"

"Beauchamp came onto me," I said casually, as though my skin weren't still crawling. "I'm going to go see if I can find the Raphael. I need to calm down."

He didn't seem the least bit surprised by my news, and the anger I'd expected was either well hidden or nonexistent. He only said, "Okay. Wait there a sec, I'll see if Luke can go with you. I don't want you wandering around alone."

I started to argue, then thought better of it. I leaned against the door, drumming my fingers on it, for a few minutes while my bodyguard was located. I guessed Luke was avoiding Jim and the Beauchamps' table like the plague since I'd tipped him off earlier.

I was getting bored and considering letting him catch up to me when someone knocked on the door I was leaning against. I yelped in surprise, eliciting a chuckle that I could hear through the door. Luke opened it from the outside.

"Sorry, couldn't resist. Jim said something about wandering around an empty museum at night like you're actually trying to bump into a hitman?"

"Yeah, that sounds like him."

We made our way into the first exhibit, not finding the museum as dark and deserted as I'd hoped. We weren't the only people milling around, and security guards were pacing and shadowing as though this were any other day. About half the lights had been turned off, giving the interior the enticing, forbidden feel of a lock-in.

We followed the signs to the Raphael exhibit and were soon turned away from the open gallery doorway by a security guard. As Luke and I turned to go, another guard joined the first and said something to him in Polish, too quickly and quietly for me to pick out a single word. They called us back; that I understood.

The second guard asked me something and I shrugged, reeling off one of a handful of phrases I'd memorized: "Sorry, we don't speak Polish." He looked frustrated, and I asked hopefully, "Deutsche?"

He held up his thumb and index finger about an inch apart, making a face that clearly said, "Yes, but only a little." In broken

German he asked, "You're the woman who found the Raphael?" At my nod, he grinned and ushered us both inside, saying, "Don't tell anyone."

"Sweet," Luke breathed. "You really do always get your way."

"Ha! Not always."

I related the brief conversation with Beauchamp that had forced me to flee from the mixer, and Luke's reaction was much more gratifying than Jim's.

He bristled, eagerly clenching and unclenching his fists, and said, "That dirty old—You should've slugged him. That's disgusting. You didn't even throw your drink in his face?"

"I didn't have one."

"Too bad. I'll be sure to make him a gin and tonic and bleach when we get back."

I scoffed. "Wouldn't that kill him?"

"Yeah, well… no comment."

We stopped in front of the Raphael and fell silent. My eyes roved hungrily over the familiar face, the implied textures, the soothing palette of blues, browns, and whites.

Luke waited a whole minute before asking, "So? How does it feel?"

My mouth twisted into an awkward grimace, and I found myself admitting, "I feel awful. We just jumped the line in front of Holocaust survivors."

After thinking this over for a few seconds, Luke mumbled, "Let's get out of here."

Luke escorted me back toward the mixer, letting the silence marinate for a few seconds before asking, "So my Rich theory is dead in the water, huh?"

"I'm convinced of his innocence… in at least one regard," I added sourly.

Luke argued, "But the server in Maryland…"

"Maybe David gave you bad info," I guessed. "Or someone gave *him* bad info."

"Why?"

"Heck if I know."

Before we went inside, I found my hotel room key and pressed it into his hand.

He chuckled. "You're drunk with power…"

"It's not like that," I chided. "I want you to have it just in case. We're in the Bonerowski Palace, room three ten."

"All right, all right."

I watched him walk away, took a deep breath, and plunged back inside to find Jim. No one looked twice at me, for which I was thankful. People had clustered together in threes and fours, getting tipsy and waiting for their turns to take a sneak peek at the Raphael. The viewing was supposed to start in five minutes, and I could already see the director coaxing the aged guests of honor from their chairs near the door.

I passed a table where the couple from California was standing as the husband asked, "Where the heck is that waiter with our drinks?" To which his wife replied wearily, "Don't be a pill, Mark."

I stifled a laugh, sidestepped a child running amok and a man who was walking through the crowd with his face an inch from his phone. When I finally reached the right table, Jim wasn't there. Instead, the Beauchamps were chatting with Isabella Franco and her husband.

"Where did Jim go?" I asked the table at large, not bothering to try to sound polite. Betty raised her eyebrows delicately.

"I think he is speaking to the Europeum curator," Isabella answered, eyeing me with concern.

Those hazel eyes, serious and striking, made me think of Jim, and I wondered if they could be related. Jim seemed to be related to everyone.

Isabella turned to scan the crowd and pointed to the opposite corner. "Over there." In Italian, to the exclusion of the Beauchamps, she asked, "Are you all right?"

I forced a smile. "Yes, I'm fine. Just tired."

"Here," she said, pushing a tumbler into my hands. "This one is yours. I think James ordered it for you."

"Thanks."

I didn't realize how tired I was until I admitted it to Isabella. I almost spilled the drink she'd handed me about nine times on the way across the room, but I managed to make it to Jim without scotch splashed across the front of my dress. I sidled up to him, and he gave me a quick sidelong glance.

He started to casually slide an arm around my waist, catching himself halfway through the move and looking at his wristwatch instead. I held in a giggle as best as I could, trying to distract myself with my drink; but it had been neglected for too long and the ice had melted, watering it down and distending its normal, peaty aroma into something vaguely nutty and not at all appealing. I took an experimental sip and surreptitiously spat it back into the glass.

The absence of Jim's touch was only more aggravating for how close I'd come to feeling it. I swirled my unwanted drink and forced myself to tune in to the conversation. The Europeum curator spoke English, but he was joined by his wife, who did not. She was speaking through a translator who appeared to be their son, and I was trying to pick up as much Polish as I could via the back-and-forth. I had hoped it would be easy, but my ears were dialed in to the romance languages.

The translator noticed me peering at him and began to stammer awkwardly. That was the first thing I picked up: the curator's wife asking her son in Polish if he was feeling all right.

I hurried to explain, "Sorry, I was trying to understand you. I'm trying to learn Polish."

That got me wedged into the conversation, and the next few minutes flew by, but I could sense Jim getting antsy next to me. He looked at his watch again, and the curator asked with slight frostiness, "Are we keeping you from something, Mister Camposanto?"

Jim barely missed a beat, smoothly lying, "We've got an early tee time tomorrow morning. Sorry, I'm still a little jet lagged. Ready to go, Anna?"

I nodded compliantly. "Yep, I'm bushed."

"Excuse us," Jim said, flashing the curator's wife a charming smile and shaking the other men's hands. The door to the lecture hall was the closest escape, and Jim allowed me to lead the way toward it, sidestepping the reporter again with murmured apologies.

Once we were alone, I discarded my unwanted scotch on the podium, wrapped my arms around Jim's neck, and kissed him until the insistent, roiling heat inside me subsided enough for us to split for the hotel.

Without the benefit of a couple dozen other people walking around us as we'd had on the way from the restaurant, the darkened streets of Kraków didn't seem quite as benign. I had a little bit of trouble keeping up with Jim, who was walking so fast that I could tell he was thinking along the same lines. His pace cut a twenty-minute walk to fifteen, and we were both slightly winded when we finally got to the room. I met Jim's gaze and let out a shaky laugh.

"It felt like someone was chasing us, didn't it?" I asked lightly, trying to make it a joke. He forced a chuckle.

"It did. Just a sec, I need to call Luke." Catching my hopeful grin, he added, "Settle down, this is a business call. I'm not sharing you tonight."

While he held a brief, muted conversation with Luke, I ducked into the bathroom to wriggle out of my dress and change into something more comfortable. As I returned the dress to its hanger in the closet, I could feel Jim's gaze raking over me as he gave Luke instructions for tomorrow. It was a quick conversation.

As exhausted as we both were, Jim and I fell together the moment he hung up and didn't break apart until I yawned my way out of a kiss. He laughed at me, yawned himself, and said, "I guess that means it's bed time."

After a quick trip to the bathroom to wash the makeup off my face, I returned to find Jim sound asleep. I burrowed under the covers next to him and faced the door, my body prickling with a vague sense of dread rather than the heavy contentment that usually followed Jim's undivided attention.

There was definitely some kind of danger out there, and I was beginning to think this trip had been a colossally stupid risk. I thought I may be too freaked out to sleep, but as soon as my body heat warmed the air trapped around me by the blanket, I was out.

▼

We walked to the nearest café for breakfast the next morning, and by the time I saw the Beauchamps were already there, it was too late. Betty waved us over, and Jim was too well-bred to ignore her. I, however, am not well-bred. I plopped down and said nothing until the waiter arrived to take my order: eggs benedict and a Bloody Mary.

"Heck of a night," I replied to Betty's automatic, silent disapproval. This woman was not taking the hint that her opinion meant nothing to me.

"Did you fall ill, dear?" she asked kindly enough. "You disappeared on us."

I enjoyed Beauchamp's stiffened posture for half a second before answering, "Sorry about that. I run out of steam quick in large crowds."

Since no one seemed inclined to bother me with conversation after that, I nursed my Bloody Mary in peace and let my thoughts wander. The shapeless dread from last night had coalesced into the sort of nightmare I rarely had to endure, lacking that glittery veneer of obvious non-reality and instead presenting itself to me as cold, hard fact. The scene had been sharply defined by every one of my senses, bound by time and logic and the laws of physics in a way normal dreams shouldn't be:

I was in the back seat of Marcel's Dodge Challenger Demon, the supercharged engine grumbling as we drove slowly down Central Avenue in Albuquerque. Luke was behind the wheel while Jim pointed out various sights like a surly tour guide. A news van passed us on the left, and we all saw a man lean out of the back window, menacing us with a machine pistol of the sort generally reserved for shoot-'em-up action films. I drew my own weapon and almost had time to put my sights on the gunman before one shot cracked off. In the same moment the sound assaulted my ears, Luke jerked once and then was still, the Challenger accelerating with a dragon roar that finally, mercifully, broke through the barrier of sleep and sent me lurching back to reality.

Even now, knowing it wasn't real, every cell in my body was screaming at me to borrow Jim's phone, call Luke, and confirm he was alive and well, but I couldn't do it. The immediate certainty that he'd been killed had roused something else in me, something I didn't like and couldn't face: Before the horror had settled in, I'd felt distinct and overpowering relief. Relief that Luke had been killed instead of Jim. I was so ashamed I wanted to cry, all over a stupid nightmare.

I sucked down the last of my Bloody Mary with a rude slurping noise that nearly made me miss a question directed at me by Betty.

"—and Anna, did you hear about that poor little girl from last night? Oh, it was the worst thing."

Oh, good, verbal window-licking. There had only been one child at the mixer last night, so I knew who Betty was talking about. I had no idea who she belonged to, but I'd seen her tottering around in her cute little velvet dress, maybe about four years old, getting underfoot and eliciting constant chuckles and 'aaaaaw's.

"No, what happened?" I supplied.

"Apparently she got into someone's discarded drink and got awfully sick. They had to take her away in an *ambulance*. Her parents were beside themselves, of course."

I frowned. "She got sick from drinking alcohol?"

"I guess so. I'm sure it doesn't take much for a little thing like that."

"Will she be okay?"

"I think so, but I'd like to get my hands on whoever left their drink lying around like that. So irresponsible."

Vividly recalling the moment I'd abandoned my watered-down scotch in the lecture hall, I exchanged a look with Jim.

He said hastily, "Her parents should've kept a closer eye on her."

"Right. And didn't the invitation say 'adults only'?" I chimed in, feeling miserable. Betty pursed her lips but didn't respond.

Breakfast dragged on for an hour and a half, my three companions chatting and carrying on together as if they liked each other or something. Betty even suggested visiting some of the sights of Kraków as a foursome. The suggestion made me want to sob. Jim read my mind, or possibly my face, and made up some excuse about needing to catch up on emails.

The Beauchamps headed for a salt mine tourist attraction outside the city while Jim and I walked back to the hotel. It was a totally silent walk, and if I hadn't been so hopelessly absorbed in my own dour thoughts, I might have noticed that Jim was just as distracted. I eventually did notice when I caught his reflection in the mirrored walls of the elevator.

"Bee in your bonnet?" I asked lifelessly.

"The little girl."

I sighed, the return to the subject of the near-disaster only further dampening my spirits. "It was probably my drink, wasn't it?"

"Maybe. Unless she's allergic to alcohol, the whole thing sounds more like poisoning."

I stared up at him, lost for words.

"Why didn't you drink it?" he pressed.

"It was watered down. It smelled off." My eyes slid out of focus, settling around Jim's navel but not really seeing anything. "It smelled like… almonds."

19
Sunday, May 2, 2021

Jim gave no answer, instead whipping out his cell phone and thumbing impatiently away at the screen. He couldn't get a signal until we left the elevator, frog-marching me by the elbow toward the relative safety of our room while he called the hospital and bullied his way through half a dozen receptionists, nurses, and doctors to make sure the right person got the information: Check for cyanide poisoning.

An hour passed in tense silence while we waited for a return call. Jim had given them more than enough cause to act, but it turned out an astute medical intern at the hospital had already made the connection when the girl's symptoms began to deviate from those of standard alcohol poisoning. She was already receiving the proper treatment and was going to be fine.

The whole ordeal left me winded, sitting on the edge of the bed and staring blankly at the door while I processed the facts.

At some point during the evening, someone had doctored

my scotch—not Jim's, just mine—into a deadly cocktail that only uncharacteristic pickiness had prevented me drinking. The girl had probably ingested a sip, no more, before discarding the unappetizing beverage; I might have knocked back the whole glass without a second thought. If I had, the clever intern at the hospital wouldn't have been able to confirm cyanide poisoning until my autopsy was finished.

While Jim paced back and forth in front of the window, once more conferring with Luke via phone, I made a list in my head: the knife-wielding hobo in Albuquerque, the gunman in Washington, the poisoner in Kraków. Should I add the gunman at the DFW Airport, the one and only Philip Levin? Was I missing something that obvious?

I listed a little to the right as Jim sat next to me, compressing the springs of the mattress. He put an arm around my shoulders.

"We better go home, huh?" he asked softly, as though worried a loud noise might set me off.

"Why?"

"Anna, someone tried to kill you…"

"Once in Poland, three times in the U.S."

"Anna."

Mentally I added the shootout at the warehouse in Houston, amending, "Four times in the U.S."

"Four?"

"This is Philip, Jim. It's not Paolo or Marcel. It's Philip."

"Does it matter?"

I turned to him, disbelieving. "Of course it matters! We have to stop him! We have to—" I fumed, struggling for words.

Jim respectfully waited, his hand constricting around my shoulder. "We have to win this. We got the Raphael, we won your game. Now we have to do this. This one is mine. You can't take this from me. What if he goes after my family?"

He was silent for so long I was afraid he'd ask me to articulate that a little more coherently. Instead he said, "Luke's on his way. We should all three talk about this. We don't know who's behind this. For all we know, cyanide is Marcel's go-to."

I shook my head. "If Marcel wanted me dead, I'd be dead."

Luke arrived within the hour, and once I was planted on the bed with him next to me and Jim on my other side, I felt calmer. Jim filled Luke in on what he'd missed, eliciting the same question Jim had asked:

"Four times?" Luke parroted.

With a longsuffering sigh, I counted out, "First the TIC tried to kill me at the warehouse in Houston, then Philip tried to shoot me in Dallas, then the vagrant in Albuquerque tried to shank me, then the guy on the Metro—"

"Hold up," Jim interrupted. "Shank you? The guy in Albuquerque had a knife?"

I nodded, mildly chagrinned now for omitting that detail. "I took the knife from him. Kinda left that part out earlier."

"Anna," Jim moaned.

"So," I insisted, eager to move on. "With the poisoner, that makes five times total. Assuming they're all related, some sloppy idiot seems to be getting pretty desperate."

"And you think it's Philip?" Luke asked. "Even my guy in Cleveland?"

"He's better than we are at finding you," Jim put in, sounding halfway convinced. "God only knows how."

"Philip could've killed Anna and me in Colorado," Luke reminded us. "What changed between then and Dallas?"

We fell silent, no one willing to throw out a guess until Jim ventured, "Had to be whoever is pulling his strings."

"Duh," Luke muttered.

Jim's retort was cut off by a knock on the door that made all three of us jump. I giggled nervously while Luke tucked himself without comment into the closet and Jim moved toward the door. He peered through the peep hole, glanced around the room once, then opened the door to admit Beauchamp. The visit to the salt mines didn't seem to have improved his mood.

"Good, you're both here," he said gruffly, as though unaware that this was my room, too. "You've heard about the kid, I assume."

A cold hand gripped my heart and I demanded, "What happened? Is she still okay?"

"Sure she is. I meant the cyanide. Potassium cyanide, to be exact. I just got off the horn with the detective who got the case. Speaks lousy English, but I think he told me they're rounding up all the staff from the catering company. He wants to talk to both of you, as well."

I met Jim's eyes, looking away quickly as he asked, "Why us?"

"Because they found the drink. It was a scotch. I told him you were both drinking scotch all night." He eyed me with unsubtle accusation. "Someone trying to off you, Miss Bowman?"

I shrugged. "Marchand, I assume."

"And you're not too fussed about it, huh?"

"I'm shaking in my boots."

Narrowing, his eyes darted to the unmade bed and back to me. "I'm heading to the police station now. Why don't you two join me?"

It wasn't a request. Jim and I got ourselves together quickly, reacting to Beauchamp's obvious impatience. We mutually hesitated at the door.

"What?" Beauchamp snapped.

Jim asked, "How long will we be gone?"

"Why, got somewhere to be?"

When neither of us had an answer for that, we were eagerly hustled away. I trailed my fingertips across the closet door as I left, by way of a goodbye to Luke.

Wishing I could read Jim's mind, I trotted along next to him for the five-minute walk to Kraków Police Headquarters and wondered what sorts of lies I was about to tell now.

Leaving Beauchamp in the lobby, a young officer ushered Jim and me into the detective's office, where he was already seated behind an exaggeratedly disorganized desk. Jim and I settled into chairs side-by-side and sat in awkward silence while a translator was rustled up.

While we waited, I tried out some Polish by asking, "What's your name?" I may have accidentally asked, "What is your name doing here?" but he got the picture.

The detective smirked, correcting my grammar before replying, "Hagen." His first name was left to our imaginations.

My attempt at establishing rapport having fizzled, I was

content to study him in the silence that followed. He was as bald as a doorknob, though not a day over 35, and even seated seemed a good six inches shorter than my five feet, nine inches. Probably to compensate for this, he was what the kids call 'jacked,' lean muscles threatening to burst various seams on his charcoal grey suit every time he inhaled. My guess was he'd been promoted from SWAT less than a year ago.

He let me gaze for a solid minute before saying in a flat, bored monotone, "I speak English."

"So why do we need a translator?" Jim asked.

"Policy." Hagen's gaze flicked upward at something behind us, in the doorway. "Marz. Thank you for coming."

The sentiment seemed ceremonial at best. He didn't smile as the young, raven-headed woman closed the office door, leaned against the window sill, and nodded politely and Jim and me.

"Please forgive his churlishness," she said in unaccented English. "He staunchly refuses to disabuse himself of the notion that his English is superlative."

I barked a laugh at this, catching a deep, suspicious scowl on Hagen's face before he could rearrange it. Jim began tapping his foot audibly while Hagen and Marz held a brief, quiet, rather waspy sidebar in Polish. I was hoping the show would last a little longer so I could pick up some Polish insults, but Jim was not as interested in the exchange.

"Can we move on?" he asked courteously enough.

I couldn't help but comment, "Your English is amazing."

"Thank you," Marz said modestly. "I grew up in Connecticut."

"Yes, she is very special," Hagen concluded, nearly making me laugh out loud again. Either they needed to get a room, or they already had. Hagen proceeded hurriedly, before anyone else could interrupt, to fire off a rapid sentence in Polish that might have been a question.

Marz helpfully supplied, "He wants your names, titles, and a good phone number and email address for you both. Let's pretend he said please."

We proceeded in this manner, Hagen asking questions that carried the tone of demands for information and Marz translating and softening them up for us. I let Jim do most of the talking, and he walked the detective through the whole night up until we left the mixer. I supplied details where Jim's path and mine had deviated.

Neither of us implied even a passing familiarity with Luke, referring to him only as, "that huge waiter with a French accent." Though we hadn't had time to confer, Jim and I knew instinctively that any attempt to gloss over Luke's existence would only raise eyebrows. I was thankful Beauchamp wasn't in the room, because I credited him with at least enough wits to conjure up Luke's name from no more information than "huge" and "French."

Unsurprisingly, Hagen asked through Marz, "Do you know anything about this French waiter? He is one of two people from the catering company who we still haven't been able to track down."

"I only spoke to him to order drinks," Jim lied blithely. "Who's the other one you can't find?"

"The one we want to talk to the most. The bartender."

He solicited a few more details, gave Jim a business card in case we remembered anything else, and then let us go, having warmed up enough from our cooperation to shake both our hands and even give Marz a tight nod as she followed us from his office.

I was exhausted by the interview, but Beauchamp wasn't done with us yet. He goaded us straight from the police station to a restaurant for lunch, where he proceeded over beer and perogies to coax out the minor detail that Jim and I were 99% sure the potassium cyanide had my name on it.

Beauchamp didn't bother asking why we'd omitted this not-so small detail from our conversation with Hagen. If we'd told Hagen I was the target, the detective would have asked how we knew and who we thought was behind it, which would have ended in yet another Polish government official getting stonewalled by "it's classified." Something told me Hagen would have been more than willing to start an international incident to get to the bottom of the little girl's poisoning. No doubt inferring all this, Beauchamp didn't question us, but he didn't look too pleased with us, either.

"I'll have Mary set up a meeting with David," Jim offered in response to Beauchamp's tightly crossed arms and stony expression.

Mary, of the famed British counter-intelligence and security service MI5, had crossed my path ever so briefly last year and seemed like a capable woman.

"Maybe David can confirm whether Marcel had anything to do with this," Jim said.

"Still think it's you they're after?" Beauchamp demanded of Jim.

"Evidently I was mistaken."

"You'll want to keep a closer eye on your operative," Beauchamp said, forcing a disdainful huff of air through his nose. It was more than I could tolerate.

"You're the one who told me to stay away from Jim!" I hissed.

"He needs to learn how to delegate," Beauchamp shot back.

Lip curling, I said, "Oh yeah, you'd like that wouldn't you."

Beauchamp took a fortifying drink of beer, his face reddening. "Look, I'm sorry about that. Gin can make a man say and do stupid things. I'd appreciate it if you didn't tell Betty."

"*I'd* appreciate it if you told me what you two had cooked up for Albuquerque," I countered.

"Who told you we had anything cooked up?" he asked, while Jim gave his full attention to a flock of birds passing overhead. "You weren't supposed to tell her anything, Jim."

"I didn't."

"I don't believe you."

"Just tell me," I whined.

"Can't you take no for an answer?" Beauchamp snarled.

"Can *you?*"

"Just tell her, Rich," Jim sighed. "It's not that interesting anyway."

"Fine." After draining his pint glass, Beauchamp explained, "Barbato's been acting cagey ever since you two got back from Argentina. We think he smells a rat. Jim and I agreed David's message prompting you to go to New Mexico was a little too convenient. Then the very morning you're supposed to fly to Albuquerque, together, who should call but Paolo, demanding Jim go to Italy immediately."

"I don't get it," I admitted.

"Suddenly so humble," Beauchamp chuckled. "Young lady, the biggest obstacle to Paolo offing my boy Jim here is a woman who's stuck to him like glue and can kill people with her bare hands. Get it?"

"No, I mean yes, but wait—I thought Jim wasn't the one Paolo was going after? If it's even Paolo…"

"We know that now," Beauchamp said.

"So you wanted us to stick together so I could… protect Jim?" Beauchamp nodded, and I exploded, "Why'd you tell me to leave him alone, then? You idiot!"

"Anna!" Jim admonished.

"You know, I think I'd die of shock if you ever did anything but the exact opposite of what you're told to do," Beauchamp said. Standing, he dropped some bills on the table and concluded, "Try not to do anything stupid."

"Have I ever?" Jim asked, confused.

"Wasn't talking to you."

"Say 'hi' to Betty for me," I spat as Beauchamp walked away.

After a moment of thick silence, Jim smiled at me and said, "I think he's warming up to you."

20

Sunday, May 2, 2021

Jim and I finished our beers and walked back to the Bonerowski Palace. I was eager to run everything by Luke, not to mention warn him the police were looking for him; so when we walked into the room and saw the closet gaping open, clearly unoccupied, my shoulders slumped in disappointment.

Jim checked the bathroom and announced, "Not here. The door was locked, wasn't it?"

"Yes, I watched you unlock it just now. But I gave Luke my key last night."

Frowning, Jim picked up his phone and made a call. I listened to his side of the conversation while my tired brain amplified disappointment into anxiety.

"Where'd you go? … No, everything's fine, but the Kraków Police are looking for you… Obviously… Leave a false trail, have Ingrid flesh it out… Yeah, that would make sense." Jim listened for about half a minute, then glanced up at me and answered a question I didn't hear, "I won't."

"What?" I mouthed.

"Okay. Good luck. Bye."

"Where'd he go?" I demanded as Jim pocketed his phone.

"Back to his hotel. Said he wanted to check something before the opening tomorrow. Now that he knows the police are looking for him, he'll have to leave town. He'll make it look like he went to London, and Ingrid will… What?"

"He asked you something about me, didn't he?"

Jim hesitated, badly lying, "He wanted me to tell you bye. He'll catch up to us back in Arlington."

"Yeah. Okay." I sat down on the bed, looked around the room, and asked, "What now? How do we find him?"

"Luke?"

"No, the bartender."

Jim checked his watch. "We've got about five hours until we have to be at the museum again. I suppose we could snoop around a little, though that seems risky given the target on your back."

"Quit taunting me," I mumbled. "Jerk."

He sat down next to me and looped an arm around my waist, asking gently, "Isn't one assassination attempt enough? I thought you'd be ready to go home now."

"We don't know anything we didn't know before."

"It doesn't look like we're going to catch anyone red-handed, either. We might have better luck interrogating the guy from the Metro."

"The local fuzz will let us know when he's ready to talk." I stood and paced away, drawn to the dresses hanging in the closet

Luke had vacated. As I thumbed through them, I thought aloud, "What if they get desperate and… I don't know… bomb the museum with me in it?"

"Poland does have law enforcement and intelligence agencies, you know."

"I *know.*"

"And, ironically, they're getting a lot of help from the BKA."

I granted him an unwilling laugh. "So you're saying we don't need to worry about a terrorist attack."

"No more than usual."

"And I'm saying I'm not willing to go home with my tail tucked between my legs." I pulled the backless, royal blue dress from its hanger and held it up to my body, turning this way and that in front of a long mirror by the door. "If I'm being perfectly honest, I've been privately fanaticizing about this since I was a little girl."

"That's not even a little bit surprising."

"Then you're not going to drag me home kicking and screaming?"

"I think not." He came to stand behind me and rested his chin on my shoulder. "I doubt we'll have any more luck than the police."

"We didn't tell them everything, though. We know who the poison was meant for, and we have a short list of people who could be responsible." I turned to face him. "Did Luke say what he was checking at his hotel?"

Again he hesitated before answering, "No, he didn't."

"Why are you lying to me? And why are you doing such a lousy job of it?"

Not ready to admit defeat, Jim merely shook his head and retreated to the other side of the room. He hacked out a text message, sent it, and pocketed his phone again before finally saying, "Because I'm still figuring out what to do."

"About?"

So quietly I barely made it out, he mumbled, "Rich."

"Oh…" Assuming he was referring to Beauchamp's clumsy come on last night, I babbled, "It's really not that big a deal. I think he was just drunk. I mean it's no excuse, but it's not like he—"

"Not that. He still hasn't asked me what you were doing in Argentina."

"Oh. Huh?"

"That was the whole point. Ditching your passport, grabbing Dude. He wasn't supposed to know you were there, or why. So now that he knows, why hasn't he asked yet? By now he must have figured out I lied about the passport so he wouldn't know where you really were."

"Maybe he's waiting for you to fess up. He really doesn't seem that upset about it."

"That's the problem. He should be."

"So what's that got to do with Luke?"

"He's been busy. He left a notebook in his hotel room, and he told me where to find it. He was keeping track of everyone— the other catering staff, the museum employees, the guests, even you and me… and Rich. He didn't want me to tell you, because he knew you'd—"

"We have to go get it! Now!"

"—want to go get it," he sighed.

"Well why not? It could help us figure out who did it!"

"It's not safe, Anna. The police will find it, if they haven't already. If we get caught there—"

"You're just afraid of what we'll find in it," I accused.

"If Luke had seen anything that would make him suspect Beauchamp, he'd have already told me. He said nothing stood out to him, but the cops might find it handy. I agreed."

"So what are you trying to figure out? Whether to tell Beauchamp about it?"

"Get there already," Jim said, giving me a sad smile.

"You know if you tell Beauchamp Luke was here in Kraków, and he still doesn't ask any questions, that Luke might have been right. Beauchamp might be…"

"I still don't think he is."

"So tell him about Luke's notebook."

Jim stood up. "Let's see what's in it first."

▼

We took a cab to Luke's hotel, a converted college dormitory near the Vistula River. Though it was no palace, he certainly hadn't been slumming it in the clean, quiet neighborhood with its easy access to walking paths along the river. Jim directed the driver past the hotel to a park on the river bank, giving us a chance to survey the situation before deciding to approach on foot.

There were no police or police vehicles visible near the hotel, but that didn't mean the coast was clear. Hand-in-hand, we walked a roundabout route from the river to the hotel, making a full loop and coming at it from the east again. We let ourselves into the deserted lobby and headed up the staircase to the third floor.

"Getting nervous?" Jim asked, his hand tightening briefly around mine.

"We'd have a hard time explaining to Hagen what we're doing here."

"Then let's hope he's not here yet."

We turned a corner and both spotted Luke's room immediately, thanks to the yellow caution tape forming an X across the door and the official-looking sticker slapped over the doorknob.

"Or he's already come and gone," I moaned.

Jim pulled me back around the corner.

"It's fine," he said, his expression and tone disagreeing. "There was nothing sensitive in there. Assuming Luke didn't leave behind the key to our hotel room..."

"They're gonna read the notebook and think Luke had something to do with the poisoning!"

"He didn't. It's fine," he repeated. "As long as he didn't get himself arrested."

I groaned but couldn't think of any other response. Jim tugged me by the hand back toward the staircase, but the sound of footsteps carrying several people up the stairs caused him to divert toward the elevator. We scrambled inside and flattened ourselves against the wall as the doors eased shut. Just before they closed, I saw the backs of three uniformed officers heading for—I assumed—Luke's room. I sighed my relief as the elevator began to descend.

After several deep breaths, I whispered, "That was stupid."

"I guess Rich was right," Jim replied, laughing nervously.

"About what?"

He didn't get a chance to answer before the doors opened again on the ground floor lobby. Standing directly in front of the doors, arms crossed and sleeves ready to burst at their seams, was a stone-faced Detective Hagen.

"Mister Camposanto. Miss Bowman. Come with me."

21

Sunday, May 2, 2021

Jim and I had no choice but to follow Hagen as he turned and marched away. He led us out of the hotel, waving away a couple officers who attempted to tag along, and headed west. For the entire walk from the hotel to the riverfront, Hagen said nothing. Short as the walk was, I was writhing with nerves by the time he stopped and turned about to face us. He didn't cross his arms again, but his expression was grave.

"I'd like you to tell me what you were doing in that hotel. Now."

His English, though heavily accented, was better than Beauchamp or Marz had led us to believe. Since he was speaking more to Jim than to me, I knew better than to open my mouth and blunder in; Jim was frowning, but he didn't look worried.

Jim said, "You told us you were looking for that waiter. Did you really think we wouldn't investigate?"

"How did you find out where he was staying?" Hagen asked.

"I can't tell you that."

"Yes, you can. You can tell me why you lied about knowing him, too. Did you think we wouldn't question the other people at the museum? You were seen together, in the Raphael exhibit," he said, casting a glare at me before his stony gaze flicked back up to Jim. "So you *can* tell me. You can tell me here while we all enjoy the sunshine and fresh air, or you can tell me at headquarters after I throw you both in separate rooms and let you spend a day thinking about how you want this to end."

Jim peered down at him, guessing, "You know that'll never happen."

"You are not above our laws. Do *not* presume to—"

"You found a notebook in his room, right? Have you looked through it yet?"

I gaped at Jim, so startled I failed to hide my reaction. Hagen's response was less dramatic.

He crossed his meaty arms again and snapped, "You were looking for it?"

"Yes."

"Why?"

"I can't tell—"

"You *can* tell me and you *will.* A four-year-old girl nearly lost her life because of something you and your people have not seen fit to share with us, and you will *not* leave this country until—"

"No we will leave this country, tomorrow, with or without your permission. You might not get all the answers you want, but we can help you if you loosen up."

Surprise flashed across Hagen's face, but he mastered it quickly. With a touch less aggression, he asked, "How can you help?"

"We know who he was and why he was here. He's not your guy. We don't know where he went. He kept track of everyone at that event, and that notebook is far more use to us than it is to you." Jim let that sink in for a few seconds, then added, "You can have the poisoner when we track him down. We just want to know who put him up to it."

"How generous."

"It's better than nothing," Jim argued, but the tail end of his words was lost in a squawk of sound from Hagen's radio.

The detective held a terse discussion with someone on the other end, speaking so quickly I couldn't make out a single word. He finished the conversation and smiled in a way I definitely didn't like.

"We'll have to continue this negotiation later, I'm afraid. They've just picked him up."

Heart sinking, I asked, "Who?"

"The bartender." Hagen studied me for a second before asking, "This other man, the one with the notebook. Who is he to you?"

"No one who would try to kill me, that's for sure," I answered coldly.

Nodding, he offered, "Come back to the station with me. You can make a copy of this notebook, but don't think I'm out of questions for you."

"Fine," I said, prompting Hagen to stomp away, back toward the hotel. I fell into step beside him, but as Jim took my hand to follow, Hagen stopped again.

"No, Mister Camposanto, not you. I'm sure you have much more important business to attend. Miss Bowman will accompany me back to the station, and you may collect her later today."

I expected Jim to protest vociferously, but he only asked, "Can I at least get a ride back?"

"I'm sure you can find a taxi. Or walk—it's a beautiful day. Miss Bowman?"

"Jim…"

"It'll be fine," he soothed, squeezing my hand before releasing it. "Just don't say anything I wouldn't say."

"What are you gonna do?"

With a hooded glance at Hagen, he said simply, "Important business."

I glared at Jim, but he was unsympathetic. With a heavy feeling, I let Hagen shepherd me away while Jim whipped out his cell phone and made a call. I tried to fortify myself with thoughts of Jim's apparent if puzzling faith in me, but something about the waves of smug satisfaction wafting over me from Hagen's direction made that unhelpful.

The surly detective didn't speak until we'd climbed into his unmarked Kia Venga and set off down the road.

"How do you know this man?" he asked.

Though he'd made a respectable attempt to sound friendly, I'd already decided how to answer any questions he posed.

"I can't tell you that."

"What is his real name?"

"Can't say."

"Why was he keeping track of the people at the event last night?"

"I can't—" I stopped myself, considered for a moment, and said, "He wanted to make sure it was safe. For me."

Somewhere, Jim's ears must have been burning, but I couldn't see a way out of this without telling Hagen I was the intended target. Why else would Jim and I have gotten involved?

"Evidently it wasn't," Hagen returned. "Does this have anything to do with the Raphael painting?"

"I don't know," I said. That was God's honest truth, and Hagen seemed to recognize it.

"Okay. You assume the poisoner wasn't acting alone. Why?"

"I—we—have enemies. And that's all I'm going to say about that."

"Then why come here? Why put yourself at risk?"

I turned toward his stony profile to answer, "I want to know which enemy it is."

The briefest of smiles pulled at the corner of his mouth. "I would, too."

To my surprise and relief, Hagen was out of questions after that. He allowed me to enjoy the rest of the ride in peace and quiet, then escorted me into police headquarters. He ordered me to wait by a Xerox machine for him to check the notebook from Luke's hotel room out of evidence so I could make a copy of it.

He returned with a composition notebook in a large plastic bag, two pairs of nitrile gloves, and an especially dour expression. He put on one pair of gloves, passed me the other, and then opened the evidence bag and withdrew the notebook. I could see fingerprint powder adhering to several of what I had to assume were Luke's fingerprints on the cover.

"Put those on. Don't handle the notebook anymore than necessary. Don't disturb the prints. I will wait while you make your copies."

He stood silent and impassive while I made copies of the first six pages of the notebook.

Luke had created a column for each person whose movements he'd decided to track, using the notebook's horizontal lines for times in 15-minute increments. He'd kept tabs on 26 different people from Wednesday evening to last night, most of them described rather than named. Any words were in French, but I had no doubt Hagen would rustle up a translator for anything he couldn't discern through context clues.

After those first few pages, the notebook was blank but for a crystal clear set of four fingerprints on the second-to-last page. If the prints had returned a match to Luke or one of his aliases already, Hagen didn't volunteer that information. The last page had been ripped out, only an irregular strip of torn paper left behind.

When I was finished, Hagen opened the evidence bag so I could drop the notebook back into it. He then took the copies I'd made and flipped through them, scrutinizing each page for who knew what. When he deemed them acceptable, he traded me the copies for my nitrile gloves.

"Miss Bowman, I strongly recommend you allow one of my colleagues to escort you back to your hotel."

"Sure. Fine. Uh—thanks."

"You're welcome."

He turned on his heel and walked away, and I wasn't quite sure what to do until a female officer sidled up to me. She looked so young I almost laughed out loud.

"I take back to hotel?" she asked, unsmiling. Handpicked by Hagen for the task. I simply nodded.

▼

My stomach was starting to wonder about dinner when Jim finally came back to the hotel room. Laying diagonally across the bed, papers fanned out before me, I'd been pouring over Luke's notes for the better part of three hours. I'd jotted down my own notes on a scrap of hotel stationary and was coming to some rather alarming conclusions, so absorbed by my task that I forgot to worry about Jim at all.

"Oh good, there you are," I mumbled, barely glancing up from my work. "I need you to look at this."

"Okay. Have fun with Detective Charming?"

"No. Where've you been?"

"Lots of places." He waited until I'd looked unwillingly up from my notes to ask, "Are you mad at me for leaving you to fend for yourself?"

"I should be, but no. I got a copy."

He sat next to me, careful not to upset my nest of paper, and asked, "What have you found?"

"Luke's notes aren't detailed enough to rule anyone out definitively. He was minding me, not my drink, so of course the bartender is still the strongest suspect. But look at this."

I showed Jim my notes, and he cooperatively scanned over them for a couple seconds before sighing, "Why don't you give me the condensed version?"

"The Beauchamps and Isabella Franco were alone with my drink while Luke and I were looking at the Raphael. The same drink that I left on the podium later."

"How could that be in Luke's notes?"

"It wasn't. I remembered it myself. But look—" I pointed with my pen "—before Luke found us in the mixer, he clocked Beauchamp talking on the phone outside the lecture hall. It was right after you and I left, while the last speaker was still talking."

"What does that prove?"

"By itself, nothing. But when Luke got to the mixer, he noticed the bartender talking on his phone, too. It was only a few seconds after he saw Beauchamp."

"So what, they were talking to each other? Rich was telling the bartender to pull some potassium cyanide out of thin air and poison your next scotch?"

"Don't be so testy or I won't tell you the worst part."

"What's the worst part?"

"Remember when he and Betty went to the salt mine yesterday? He must have sent Betty off somewhere alone. He wasn't at the mine." I pointed to a section of Luke's photocopied notes that I'd circled several times. "This is Beauchamp from the time we left breakfast—Luke must have been nearby—until Luke got to the hotel. See 'W' and 'NW' in Beauchamp's column?"

"Mhm," Jim supplied, somehow infusing the tone with sarcasm.

"At first I thought it meant west and northwest, but then I realized there's no column for Betty. Luke doesn't even know her name. It means 'wife' and 'no wife.' See? Betty was with Beauchamp at breakfast with us, and not with him here."

I circled the time again, wishing Jim would stop being so obtuse and see what I saw.

"Jim, he was alone, in the lobby, talking on his phone again when Luke got here. And before that, about forty minutes after you and I got back from breakfast, he was alone—"

"Rich didn't have time to get to the salt mine and back," Jim finally concluded.

"I'm just saying, it's not nothing. You should ask Beauchamp who he was calling and why he lied to us."

"This is ridiculous. You've spent all afternoon trying to prove the conclusion you've already decided to prove."

"Well! What have you done?"

"I tried and failed to reach Mary. Spent some time at the hospital trying to get information about the poison, see if they've figured out the source. Nothing useful there. I talked to Ingrid. She said Luke's on a flight from Amsterdam to Miami tomorrow morning, and another from Vienna to Saint Paul tomorrow afternoon. She doesn't know which one he'll take. He tried to convince her to send him to London for real, but he wouldn't tell her why."

"Call him and ask."

"I tried. Straight to voicemail. You better get ready. We're supposed to be at the museum in an hour."

I blinked at him, my mind going blank. "The museum?"

"For the photos before the opening. Remember?"

"Oh, crap!" I leapt to my feet and dashed to the bathroom.

22

Sunday, May 2, 2021

I shrugged into my royal blue dress, already late for the photo shoot at the museum. I never wanted to see a curling iron or lipstick again for as long as I lived. Jim had it a little easier, working diligently on a fine double Windsor knot in his matching tie while I appraised myself in the mirror. His eyes darted to me automatically, returning to his tie and then snapping back to me.

I studied myself in the mirror with detached interest, trying to ignore the hungry expression on Jim's face that was heating me up from the inside out. The dress was admittedly pretty light in the fabric department, spaghetti straps and a plunging V-neck leaving a lot of my upper body uncovered, thin straps crossing my otherwise bare back. The floor-length hem was opened by a slit halfway up my left thigh. I pictured walking around in this sexy little number among the fine people, and my face in the mirror twisted in distaste.

"I can't believe I even brought this one," I said. "I look like a hooker."

"You've obviously never seen a real hooker."

"I should wear the navy one."

I reached for my zipper and started to work it down, but Jim caught my hand in a gentle grip and pulled it away.

"Do you like how you look?"

"Well… yeah."

As he slowly zipped me back up, he whispered, "Me, too. Besides." He kissed me on the check and said, "I don't have time to change ties. We're already late."

At least I got to hide myself in a coat. The Kraków night was chilly, temperatures hovering in the low 50s as we power-walked on the now familiar path from the Bonerowski Palace to the National Museum. At the coat room, I experienced a fleeting sensation of terror as I handed over my coat and watched the attendant's eyes sweep over me.

As Jim took my arm and led me toward the exhibit where the photo shoot was being staged, I realized it wasn't the stupid dress that had me on edge. Jim's confession at the symposium would've circulated widely by now. If his goal had been to bring all of Europe's paid assassins down on our heads, he'd done a fine job of it. I was exactly where I was expected to be, and my would-be killers, whoever they were, were running out of chances to bag me. I suddenly wished formal wear consisted of combat fatigues, boots, Kevlar, a sturdy helmet, and many weapons. Jim stopped me a few yards from the exhibit entrance.

"You're shaking," he whispered. "You look amazing. I'm

trying to think of a joke about Germany invading Poland again."

"*I'm* trying not to think about which one of the people in this room has been trying to kill me," I whispered back.

The temporary exhibit was crowded with additional Raphaels and paintings by other Renaissance masters, as well as other recovered paintings on loan from museums from Saint Petersburg to Los Angeles. All were arranged with great care around the prodigal masterwork.

We both studied the people visible inside: Richard and Betty, the Francos, some museum staff, the Holocaust survivors and the resistance fighter, two white-clad waiters serving drinks and snacks respectively, and an unfamiliar man I assumed was the photographer. A teenaged boy who might have been the photographer's assistant was arranging three chairs in front of the Raphael, presumably for the octogenarian Poles. It wasn't exactly a menacing scene.

"We don't know much about Isabella Franco or her husband," Jim murmured.

I hated to even acknowledge his suspicion, but I answered honestly, "She's the one who gave me the scotch. She said you'd ordered it for me."

Jim said, "I don't believe I did."

The photographer spotted us and waved us inside.

"I wish Luke were here," I breathed.

As we neared the group clustered around the Raphael, the waiters converged on us. Jim and I declined the refreshments. Since we were the last to arrive, the photographer immediately began ordering us into various arrangements in front of the painting.

The only people who didn't have to constantly rearrange themselves were the three aged guests of honor, though they were eventually invited to move their chairs to the side so the photographer could capture me, Isabella Franco, and the museum director Zofia Korsak as a trio. Once that was done, Korsak was dismissed and Isabella and I stood to either side of the Raphael.

Then it was my turn to stand there all alone, an honor foisted upon me by Jim's confession that first night. By then my face hurt from smiling, and my cheek muscles were beginning to twitch. Perhaps noting that my smile had mutated into a grimace, the photographer asked me to look serious instead. After one more, then one more, then just one more, he was done with me.

Jim and Beauchamp had disappeared the moment the photographer dismissed them. Though I knew I needed to find them, I stood behind the photographer and waited for Isabella to have her turn. When she was done, I grabbed two flutes of champagne and intercepted her on the way out the door.

"How about a toast—to Raffaello Sanzio da Urbino?" I invited in her native tongue, holding one glass out to her.

Though she smiled warmly, she didn't take the glass. "Sorry, I am bursting. I'll be right back."

I watched her go, wondering if her willingness to leave me alone with her drink meant what I wanted it to mean—that she had no reason not to trust me, and vice versa. In any case, I didn't trust any drink I didn't pour myself, so I set both glasses down on the nearest table and left in search of Jim and Beauchamp.

Passing the main entrance, I saw a pair of guards with metal detector wands letting VIPs inside for the private opening. Their arrival meant I had one and a half final hours of rarified company to endure, unless something dramatic happened. Halfway hoping something *would* happen so I could be done with this relentless hobnobbing, I waved at the couple from California and continued into a darkened hallway.

I had no idea where they'd gone, so I let my feet do the thinking and ended up back at the double doors to the lecture hall. No light seeped from under the doors, but they were unlocked, so I went inside.

The perimeter of the room was dotted with yellow emergency lights, their glow barely penetrating the darkness. At the bottom of the room, to stage right, a strip of brightness hinted at a closed door with a light on behind it. I walked down the stairs and began to hear voices through the door.

Beauchamp was saying, "… par for the course with you. What really grinds my gears is you thinking I wouldn't figure it out."

"If I hadn't told you she was there, you wouldn't have," Jim responded. He sounded calm, almost amused, so I didn't rush to his aid. I stood outside the door and continued eavesdropping as Beauchamp fired back.

"I saw Jackson at the airport. Uh huh, not so smug now, are you? The size of that boy—good Lord, Jim—how could I not notice him popping up all over Kraków?"

"Well, he's an assassin, not a spy."

"Then who's he here to assassinate? Don't lie to me again."

"No one. He wanted to make sure Anna was safe."

"And who was he there to assassinate in Argentina?"

Jim was silent. I held my breath, waiting for someone to say something, anything. Knowing Jim's mind was whirring while Beauchamp waited, I realized an interruption was exactly what Jim needed in that moment.

I opened the door and feigned surprise at seeing them both there, Jim leaning against a filing cabinet and Beauchamp occupying a ratty old chair on the opposite side of the room. It appeared to be an unused office, a small and rather depressing space smelling of dust and mildew.

"There you are," I said, keeping my tone neutral. "What's going on?"

"Jim was just about to tell me why he threw away your passport in Miami and dragged your dog all the way down to Argentina with you a few weeks before one of the people on Paolo Barbato's hit list just happened to die of acute lead poisoning."

23

Sunday, May 2, 2021

I absorbed Beauchamp's diatribe with a blank expression, all my energy focused on not looking at Jim. I could have sworn I could hear crickets chirping somewhere nearby.

When I failed to answer, Jim asked, "When did you put it together?"

"After I spotted Jackson hanging around at breakfast, I decided to give your dad a call, Anna. He still thought he was supposed to tell me you were in Berlin, so I invited him to look up the news out of Poland. He wasn't exactly what I'd call contrite, but at least he quit lying to me."

"He told you about Dude," I guessed.

"Right in one, young lady." Beauchamp turned to Jim, scowling. "I didn't get where I am by being an imbecile, you know. You took the dog down there so Jackson could follow his GPS tag right to the Sernas' place, didn't you?"

Jim said nothing.

"You got your cousins killed. The list of Barber descendants grows ever shorter. I hope you're satisfied."

"Hey!" I stepped between Jim and Beauchamp, facing the latter, and defended, "He didn't mean for that to happen! Don't you talk to him like that!"

Quietly, Jim confessed, "Marisol isn't dead."

Beauchamp's eyes widened. "I'll be. Is anything in your report true?"

"Nothing of import."

Still forming a feeble barrier between the two men, I looked from one to the other, waiting for someone to speak. They were both staring at the floor between their feet.

At length Beauchamp asked, "What happened to her?"

"I don't know," Jim admitted.

"Why'd you keep me in the dark about this?"

"Either you'd have stopped me from doing it, or you'd be complicit. Easy decision."

"Horse spit." Beauchamp shook his head, glaring at me to demand, "He didn't mean for it to happen, huh? That's why he sent a known assassin an engraved invitation to go down there and find two people the Director of the Bureau himself couldn't find?"

"That's why I was there," I whispered. "I was supposed to…" I looked to Jim, not sure whether I should go on.

Jim said, "She knew what the Raphael was the moment she laid eyes on it. I knew she'd try to trade it for their lives."

"So what really happened? How'd Fernando end up dead?"

Seeing that Jim wasn't going to supply the answer, I said, "There was a firefight. I didn't get a chance to intervene before

Fernando got shot, and I wouldn't have even if there had been. He was a psychotic murderer. And I didn't know the plan," I added sadly.

For a long minute, the room was utterly silent. I stepped backward, closer to Jim, and Beauchamp began to shake with silent laughter. Eventually a hoarse chuckle slipped out, and he shook his head again. I sensed he was still putting the pieces together, realizing how long Jim had been planning the recovery of the Raphael.

"Jim. I mean this the nicest way possible. You are one sick puppy, you know that?"

"I had the best of intentions."

"Yeah well, so did Oppenheimer. So." Beauchamp leaned back and put his hands behind his head, looking us over with a jaundiced eye. "What am I going to do with you two?"

"Same thing we're doing," Jim suggested. "Sitting around waiting to see who tries to kill Anna."

"Any suspects floating to the top of the list?" he asked.

"Besides you? Not really."

Beauchamp laughed again, not holding back this time. He threw another glance my way. "If I were you, I'd put some distance between myself and James Machiavelli here."

"More reverse psychology?" I shot back.

"Nope, more like friendly advice. And since I know you'll ignore it, I'll save what's left of my breath. You're not much use as bait stuffed in here with us, so I reckon you'd better get back to the soiree, young lady."

I didn't move. "What's going to happen to Jim?"

"Heck if I know. He'll probably have my job some day."

Beauchamp led the way out of the room, Jim flicking off the light and shutting the door behind us. We made our way up the stairs through murky darkness, toward the doors I'd left cracked open. Once back on the main entrance level, Jim and I slowed to let Beauchamp get far enough ahead that we could hold a quick, whispered conversation.

"So that's it?" I asked. "You're seriously getting away with this?"

"Seems so."

"I don't believe it."

"You'd rather I get fired?"

"No, but a three-month suspension without pay would teach you a lesson."

"You think so?"

He pulled me to a stop and looked me over. Oblivious that we'd fallen behind, Beauchamp disappeared around a corner.

The moment our boss was out of sight, Jim ran one long finger down my neckline, whispering, "*I think, if we were stranded on a desert island, I'd want you to wear this dress.*"

"Nice segue."

"Thanks for sticking up for me."

He kissed me, reaching around me to run one finger down my back. He smiled against my lips as his touch made me shiver.

"You want to do this right in the middle of the National Museum?" I sighed.

"Kind of, but let's not. We've narrowly avoided causing enough international incidents already."

Nevertheless, his hand stayed on my bare skin for a few more seconds before I forced myself to twist away. I dragged him back to the exhibit, where the party was now in full swing.

The number of guests and waiters had multiplied, bodies spilling out of the relatively small Raphael exhibit and into the hall where tables full of canapes and drinks lined the walls. The lights were dimmed, soft music lilted from speakers hidden somewhere near the ceiling, and all the men and women dressed in their black-tie best made such a pretty picture that I stopped to survey the scene with delight.

"I think this is the fanciest shindig I've ever been to," I said happily.

"It's no hoe-down hootenanny," Jim quipped.

"Only hillbillies are allowed to say that."

"Sorry. Hey—isn't that our friend Hagen?"

I looked in the direction Jim was gazing and saw a man who, from the back, sure looked like the surly detective. He was weaving through the crowd toward the exhibit, and when I spotted four uniformed police officers and Marz trailing him, I knew Jim was right.

"What are they doing here?" I asked.

We hurried to catch up, reaching the doorway to the exhibit right as someone turned down the music. Hagen was talking quietly with Marz while the uniformed officers spread out around the room. They were looking for someone.

Zofia Korsak appeared between Marz and Hagen to ask something in Polish, her tone and expression conveying obvious indignation. She either asked, "What are you doing?" or "Why are you here?"

Hagen responded simply by pointing, and Jim and I followed his outstretched arm to two of the officers who had moved slowly and carefully astride one of the waiters. The man, realizing every gaze in the room was directed at him, slowly lowered the bottle of champagne he was holding and froze like a deer in headlights for two heartbeats.

Then he looked directly at me.

It happened so fast, I only had time to grab Jim's arm.

A small handgun appeared in the waiter's free hand and rose toward me. Someone screamed. The two officers saw the weapon and moved to tackle the waiter, but Isabella Franco was faster. Standing directly behind the man, she stooped to swipe the champagne bottle from his other hand and broke it over his head before he could even get a shot off.

The man crumpled to the ground and was lost under a pile of Kraków police officers. Marz darted forward and stepped on the gun that had fallen from his hand when Isabella clocked him.

A booming voice rose over the bedlam that erupted, crying, "Mia coraggiosa e bellissima moglie!"

It was Isabella Franco's husband, who then grabbed her and kissed her.

Somewhat reviving, I forced a laugh and told Jim, "*Now* it's a hootenanny."

24

Monday, May 3, 2021

With stops in Frankfurt, London, and Charlotte, our return trip to Washington put us back home late Monday night. The opening day of the Raphael exhibit had long since ended, as had the short and not-so-illustrious career of my would-be assassin.

Once Hagen and his team had discovered the man had used a fake name and stolen PESEL (Polish social security) number to gain employment at the catering company, they'd searched his hotel and located not only the cyanide but photos of Jim, Beauchamp, and yours truly. He wasn't exactly a criminal mastermind, but he was smart enough to hide or destroy any hint of who had hired him to do the dirty deed. That was all according to Hagen, who passed the information along to Jim before we boarded our flight home. Beauchamp and his wife had stayed behind in Poland for a couple of days so the former could attend to official business that didn't concern Jim and me. We assumed that meant the reward money.

Luke hadn't called or texted, and my many attempts to reach him during our layover in London were fruitless. Even Jim was beginning to show signs of concern for Luke, which he studiously attempted to disguise. On top of being dog tired, I was haunted by those precious few moments I'd spent with Luke in front of the Raphael. The harder I tried not to, the more I despaired over how long I'd have to wait to see either of them again.

On the positive side, seeing Dude again and the shot of pure joy it sent through both of us was the best I'd felt in months. Jetlag vanished in a flash, and I considered taking him on a nighttime run. Dude had been enjoying Ashley's care a little too much, if the size of him was any clue.

"You're getting chonky," I scolded as I administered emergency belly rubs. "Time for a diet, huh?"

He huffed, rolled to his feet, and trotted off to seek out less judgmental attention from Jim. I followed at a slight distance, thinking I could use a little attention myself, and found Dude sitting squarely in front of Jim's closed bedroom door.

Dude's head tilted from side to side as he eavesdropped on what sounded like yet another phone call going on inside, but why Jim felt he had to shut himself in the bedroom for it was beyond me. I pressed my ear to the door and joined in Dude's spying.

"… don't know what to tell you, we haven't heard from him. Obviously we're looking—no, she would tell me." His voice was slightly closer when he said tersely, "Because I know."

I shook off an unpleasant moment of hesitation and knocked on the door. It opened right away to reveal Jim with his phone to one ear, currently on the listening end of the call. He rolled his eyes at me and waved me in, Dude right on my heels. Jim had already dumped the contents of his suitcases on the bed and appeared to have been in the middle of unpacking when he got the call.

"You know what, Paolo, she's right here. Why don't you ask her?"

"Paolo?" I asked at a whisper, unheard by Jim as he put the phone on speaker and held it out between us.

"You're on speaker," Jim said courteously, his manner so casual and disinterested that I was trying to figure out if this was *the* Paolo Barbato or some other Paolo whose phone calls were a source of annoyance for Jim.

A deep, slightly quavering voice broke through my frantic mental gymnastics. In unhurried Italian it asked, "Am I speaking to Anna Bowman?"

"Paolo, please," Jim snapped. He didn't like being linguistically pushed out of a discussion.

Defensive on Jim's behalf, I answered in English, "Yes, this is Anna. I want Jim to hear what you're asking me."

"Very well. It's nice to finally meet you, Anna. I hope my nephew hasn't been telling stories on me."

"Don't worry, he doesn't tell me crap."

"Charming… I was only wondering if you'd heard from Mister Jackson lately."

"Luke? No, why?"

"He missed an appointment with me. Now I can't seem to reach him."

"That's unfortunate."

Jim pitched in eagerly, "I was just telling Paolo we lost track of Luke in Albuquerque back in April. He seems to think Luke may have reached out to you on the sly."

Not sure how to respond to this blatant falsehood, I said slowly, "Uh… oh."

"You haven't heard from him?" Paolo pressed, as though I might spill some choice beans right then and there. Did he simply want to hear me lie?

"It's like Jim said," I sighed, far too tired to play this game or even inquire about the rules. "What was the appointment about?"

"A financial matter."

"You were going to pay him for killing Fernando and Marisol?" I asked, earning myself a smack on the arm from Jim. "What?" I mouthed. Didn't we all know that was the deal?

"I'm not sure what you mean," Paolo lied with compelling ease.

I was half tempted to start trying to convince him. Jim saved me with an unsubtle change of subject. "If either of us hears from him, we'll let you know. Okay?"

The line was quiet for so long that Jim shook the phone to wake up the screen, trying to see if Paolo had hung up. He was still on.

"You were there, weren't you, Anna?" he asked, voice tightly coiled with suppressed excitement. I shivered involuntarily.

"Where?"

"In Argentina."

"I—" I stammered, searching Jim's expression for some

clue as to what I should say. He seemed calm enough, which I interpreted as a signal that I didn't need to obfuscate. The cat was out of the bag now anyway. "Yes, I was there."

"Did you see it? Can you confirm the job was done?"

I scowled, letting him hear the disgust in my voice. "I'm not going to talk about that."

Undaunted, he asked, "Did Jackson kill both of them?"

Locking eyes with Jim, I said firmly, "Yes."

He was again silent for several seconds. Then, "You're a liar. You both are."

"Screw you," I spat automatically. Jim glared at me, but he spared me another whack on the arm.

"Paolo," he said, his tone nearly pleading, "If Anna says they're gone, they're gone. What more do you need, their severed heads?"

I balked, but Paolo said only, "You will be hearing from me."

With that threat hanging in the air, the call disconnected. Jim tossed his phone on the bed and fixed me with a searching look.

"You haven't heard from Luke, have you?"

"Jim!"

"I had to ask."

"What difference would it make if I had? Marisol isn't dead, and eventually Paolo's gonna find out. Sounds like he already has. So what?"

"He doesn't trust me anymore. I don't like where this is going…"

Supremely disinterested, I scoffed, "Well, you wanted the Raphael." As if I hadn't wanted it a thousand times more.

Jim said, "Once upon a time, I had an actual job to do. I wanted to throw the book at Levin. I wanted it as badly as I wanted this."

So he wouldn't see my expression, I wandered over to the bed and started matching up clean, unused socks from the pile of clothes Jim had dumped there. Perhaps too nonchalantly, I asked, "You don't anymore?"

"I was actually starting to get comfortable with the idea of retirement."

I rounded on him. "You have to be joking. You're forty-two!"

"It's not like I need the money."

"You selfish jerk."

He was anything but abashed. "Hey, I'm not saying I don't owe you Levin at least, but I'm tired of this. Aren't you?"

I returned to folding socks, remarking haughtily, "I'm never going to retire."

"Guess that explains why you thumbed your nose at a hundred million dollars."

We'd had no choice but to let Beauchamp handle the meeting with the museum director regarding the reward for the Raphael. Without Jim there to protect the interests in which I wasn't remotely interested, neither of us had any doubt the prize would be going to the U.S. government. I privately suspected the government would blow the whole wad on one superfluous traffic circle, or something along those lines, but I knew trying to stake my claim would only cause trouble.

"Enough," I breathed, tossing him a t-shirt that needed folding. "Just help me deal with this mess so we can go to bed."

"How about I shove this whole pile on the floor so we can go to bed right now?"

"Tempting, but I need a shower first." I dropped the socks I'd sorted onto the top of the heap and headed for the bathroom.

While I scrubbed away the interminable travel day, I thought about Paolo's phone call and the way it had shifted how I felt about being home.

Never mind that I still technically lived on Dupont Circle. Jim's home was my home now. At least half my stuff was here, and I had no reason to drag Dude back to an apartment when he'd gotten used to Jim's back yard. Still, I intended to hold on to my little one bedroom, if only to maintain the comfortable illusion of independence for as long as I could. In the meantime, I was happy to let Jim slather on the charm if he thought it would convince me to officially change my address one millisecond sooner than I wanted to.

But Paolo's threat kept cutting through my comfortable, homey thoughts.

You will be hearing from me.

Whether "you" referred to me, Jim, or both of us, the reality was the same. We weren't out of the woods yet, and with someone as elusive and powerful as Paolo, getting on his bad side meant we may never be.

25

Tuesday, May 4 to
Saturday, May 29, 2021

Tuesday morning almost started when Jim's 5:30 alarm woke me up, but Jim shut off the alarm and rolled over to pull me against him.

"Let's skip work today," he sighed.

"I couldn't go to work if I wanted to. I'm suspended, remember?"

He fell back asleep without responding, and I was right behind him.

When I came to again, light was beginning to creep in through the curtains, and Dude was whining at the foot of the bed. I let him out, went to the bathroom, let him back in, and burrowed under the covers and right back into Jim's arms.

Half-asleep, he buried his face in my neck, and whispered, "So… Are you an alley cat or a house cat?"

"I'm a person."

"You know what I mean…"

I considered how to answer while Jim's lips distracted me, clouding my judgment.

"Well… Beauchamp pretty much said I'm your bodyguard now."

"So romantic," he agreed.

"And my stuff is here…"

"It is."

"So… I'll think about it," I concluded.

With a frustrated moan, Jim kissed me, and then he mumbled, "I think I'll take this up with your boss."

"You're my boss," I said.

"I meant Dude."

▼

Jim didn't go back to work until Friday, when Beauchamp returned to work as well. Since I had eight more weeks to sit in time out and think about what I'd done, I made myself comfortable at Jim's house and whiled away several days trying to figure out how I was going to while away the coming weeks.

Meanwhile, Jim was up to his elbows again in some scheme with Beauchamp that I wasn't cleared to know about. He was generally gone when I woke up, not to return before six or seven in the evening most days.

While persistent radio silence from Luke infused every moment with ever-growing tension, three weeks passed at a crawl. At my behest, Jim called Luke daily, then weekly, with no response. He only stopped on May 26 when a very cranky woman with an Australian accent called him back and informed him she had no idea who Luke was, he had the wrong number, and he better stop calling before she went "mad as a gumtree full of galahs."

Calm as ever, Jim had thought to ask the woman when she got her phone number. That was how we learned Luke had disconnected his number—the one Ingrid had given him—sometime between May 2 and May 10. Ingrid, who hadn't heard from him since May 2 either, could offer no assistance. Luke was back in the wind, for reasons we could only guess.

That Friday, while waiting for Jim to come home, I decided to cook an elaborate Italian dinner in honor of his heritage and my deep-seated need for occasionally consuming my own body weight in pasta. I was industriously chopping vegetables when Jim got home at 7:30, and together we cooked a palatable meal, drank wine, slipped chunks of mozzarella to Dude while we each thought the other wasn't looking, and made out right there in the kitchen while the chicken parmesan was baking.

Of course our moment of normalcy couldn't even last one whole evening.

While I was cleaning up and Jim was feeding Dude, the alarm went off. One moment I was humming to myself and listening to Jim give Dude his dinnertime commands, and the next the air around me was pulsing with a deafening series of mechanical screams and Dude's earsplitting howls of response.

A little bit wine drunk, I sighed, checked the clock on the oven (10:45), shut off the water, and pressed my hands over my ears. So much for the fight-or-flight response.

Within seconds, Jim had silenced the alarm. Moments later, Dude howled himself out. I lowered my hands, looked around, and saw them both in the living room. Dude had his nose pressed against the glass in the back door, but Jim's attention was on the TV. He'd changed the input to CCTV, all sixteen camera feeds from around the house displayed in a grid. While he scanned these half-heartedly, his phone rang and he went through the rigmarole of convincing the alarm company that he was James Camposanto and there didn't appear to be a real emergency.

I plopped down on the sofa and joined his scrutiny of the cameras. Dude's reaction forced my thoughts to Luke, way back to that night in the cabin in Colorado when Luke had left a duck feather on my welcome mat to scare me away. Now it was Luke's hulking figure I sought on the eerie, monotone night vision camera feeds; but I saw nothing out of place, and neither did Jim. Eventually even Dude dropped his guard and curled up on the sofa with a dramatic huff. Jim and I left the kitchen cleanup for tomorrow and went to bed.

Thanks to the wine, I had to get up in the wee hours of the morning to visit the facilities. As much as I'd like to deny it, I suffer from a juvenile fear of the dark that only surfaces during nighttime bathroom breaks. I blamed my parents for letting me watch *Pitch Black* at the tender young age of 13. Still in denial even as the threatening darkness hugged me, I tiptoed to the bathroom and was heading back toward the bed when I heard a low growl somewhere to my left.

Rationally, I knew it was Dude, who would sooner marry a

cat than growl at me with any malicious intent. Even so, I felt goosebumps rising all over my skin in reaction to the sound, my heartbeat suddenly audible, my windpipe constricting unhelpfully.

I moved toward the growling, which was coming from the far corner of the bedroom. I saw Dude's silhouette, a blacker blackness than the rest of the room, stationed in front of an east-facing window. I stood next to him and looked out the window, as though my weak human eyes were going to see what the source of his problem was. Even with the help of a nearly full moon, all I saw was grass, some trees, and a darker strip of black denoting the back fence.

Dude growled again, exhorting me to look closer. I quickly tired of the exercise and began to shiver in the powerful air conditioning, yearning to slide back into bed next to Jim's warm body. Dude's grumbling rose in volume, almost as though he'd read my thoughts.

"Cut it out, Dude," I whispered. "There's nothing out there."

But I was wrong. Movement near the back fence caught my eye, and once I knew where to look, I was finally able to see the back gate swinging open with each gust of wind.

Staring wouldn't make the scene any clearer, so I crept out to the living room, Dude close on my heels, and found the switch for the back porch lights. Turning those on didn't help much—Jim's back yard was so deep the back fence was still lost in shadow. I considered letting Dude out to roust whatever, if anything, was out there. Maybe give Luke a nice healthy scare if this were his idea of a joke. Wisdom got the better of me, and I returned to the bedroom to wake Jim.

Shaking him by the shoulder until he groaned awake, I whispered, "I think I know what set off the alarm."

"Hng?"

"Someone opened your back gate. It's windy now. Dude saw it swinging and freaked out."

Underscoring my words was a sharp, angry bark from Dude, who was still at the back door. That helped rouse Jim, who returned to the TV to go over the security camera feeds again. Aided by night vision, Jim and I quickly spotted what Dude must have noticed already. Not only was the back gate swinging open in the wind, but on the outside of the gate at about eye level was a pale white rectangle, like a "Beware of Dog" sign but smaller, and blank. We stared at the screen, puzzled, while the white rectangle flashed in and out of sight with the wind.

"What the heck is that?" I finally asked.

"It almost looks like a piece of paper," Jim mused, stepping closer to the TV. "We should wait until it's light out to go see."

I certainly wasn't in a hurry to duck outside with a flashlight, so I curled up on the sofa with Jim and Dude and settled in to await the dawn. The glow of the TV with its array of camera feeds kept us awake for a while, but Dude was the first to fall asleep on watch, followed shortly by Jim. I managed to stay awake until after five, but the moment I shut my eyes to give them a break from the screen, I was out.

▼

After I fell asleep, the wind gave way to a light rain, and I woke up to the soothing pitter patter of raindrops on the roof. For several minutes I lay with my eyes closed, savoring the peaceful music of rain and the rise and fall of Jim's chest under my head.

Then I remembered why we'd fallen asleep on the sofa, and what Jim had surmised about the object on the fence. If it were a piece of paper, leaving it exposed to the rain was a bad idea. What if it was a message from Luke?

I struggled to my feet, shrugged into one of Jim's raincoats, and headed outside without a second thought. In the pale light of a blustery, overcast Saturday morning, the menace I'd felt last night was only a vague memory; and with Dude trotting along next to me, alert but calm, I knew whatever danger had visited us was gone now.

My feet were half-frozen from the damp grass by the time I reached the back gate. Now that the wind had died down, it sat closed, but I could plainly see the simple latch resting open. Worse than that, the padlock with which it was usually secured was lying in the grass just inside the fence line. One glance told me it had been cut off.

"This doesn't smell like Luke," I commented to Dude, who perked up at Luke's name and looked around with eagerness that nearly broke my heart.

I opened the gate and saw at once that Jim was right. A piece of paper—an envelope—was hanging inside a plastic bag that had been nailed to the gate. I ripped it off, shut and latched the gate, and used the edge of the plastic bag to pick up the broken padlock. Thanks to the bag, the envelope seemed dry, but I couldn't see any writing on either side of it.

"Curiouser and curiouser," I whispered.

I heard the back door open and glanced up to see Jim on his way across the yard.

His body language warned me he was upset before he called, "Rich is on his way over. He said he has bad news."

26

Saturday, May 29, 2021

Shaking from head to toe, I followed Jim into the kitchen and laid the plastic bag and broken padlock on the center island. For a moment we both stared down at the strange offering, then Jim pulled his dripping rain coat off of me and hung it up by the back door.

"I'll go get you a towel. Please don't open it yet."

His deathbed tone only made me tremble harder.

Something happened to Luke. It has to be Luke.

The appearance of this innocent white envelope and Beauchamp's mysterious "bad news" had to be related, and those two things had to be connected to Luke's absence. There was simply no other explanation my mind was willing to consider.

Jim reappeared and handed me a towel, which I used to squeeze the water out of my damp hair. As requested, I hadn't opened the plastic bag. I had no desire to.

"I'll make some coffee," I croaked.

"We have to see what it says," Jim argued.

"What if it's full of anthrax?" I shot back.

I turned away from him, seeking the solace of coffee, and Jim ignored my question to ask his own.

"Why open the gate if they were going to nail it to the outside? But then I guess we might never have noticed it. So why not nail it to the inside? Why cut the padlock off? You'd have to be inside the fence to reach it. None of this makes any sense."

"Dude could have gotten out," I said.

"What's that?"

"Dude could have gotten out, and we'd have found this when we went looking for him. Whoever it was could have been scared off by the alarm."

When he didn't answer, I was forced to turn back to him to see what his silence meant. His hands were pressed to the counter on either side of the plastic bag.

"I'm opening it."

I didn't argue, but I retreated with Dude to the other side of the kitchen. Jim used a kitchen knife to cut a slit in the bottom of the bag just large enough for the envelope to slide out, and then he did the same to the envelope. Out of the white envelope slipped another envelope, this one bearing the red, white, and blue edges of an international mail piece. I couldn't help myself; I crept back to the counter to take a closer look.

Jim flipped it over to the address side, and I noticed several things at once. What I'd taken for blue around the edges was actually green. The envelope was already open, cut across the top with a letter opener or knife. The stamp was from Colombia, the postmark and return address were from Barranquilla, and the recipient address was a post office box in Florence, Italy. The names on both addresses meant nothing to me.

"Firenze," Jim read aloud. "That's Florence, right?"

"Someone mailed this from Barranquilla, Colombia to Florence," I confirmed.

"So how did it end up here?"

Since the obvious answer was that someone had hand delivered it, I assumed he was asking how the letter had gotten from Italy to the United States. The outer envelope was completely blank.

I shrugged and asked, "Anything in it?"

Jim peeked inside, then grabbed the barest edge of whatever was inside, pulled it out, and laid it face up on the counter.

It was a greeting card. Not exactly what I'd expected, if anything. The card was in Spanish, a cheerful "¡Buenos!" splashed across the front, failing to arouse any suspicion or fear. Jim tipped it open.

Inside the card was a black and white photograph I'd seen before, in the closet of Fernando and Marisol's grandmother's room in Argentina: Etta and Regina Barber. Paolo Barbato's aunts, two people who'd ended up in the crosshairs of a family feud long after this photo was taken.

I flipped the photograph over, saw the word "Regina," and set the photograph aside. Underneath it on the inside of the card, someone had written only, "Thinking of you." Despite the fact that the card had traveled from Colombia to Italy, the message was written in English. I studied the lines of ink, my brain about a mile behind the rest of me.

"Someone must have sent this to Paolo," Jim said. "Someone connected to Lira? That's his mother there on the right. Regina."

The word brought my mind and body back together, and I stared at Jim. "This photo was in Argentina. I found it there. Not a copy, this exact print. It said 'Regina' on the back."

"Regina and Etta probably both had a copy," he said, not even convincing himself.

"So Regina's would have said 'Etta' on the back," I argued.

Jim tapped the photo, demanding, "You're saying Marisol sent this to Paolo? How would she even know where to send it?"

"Beats me. But she's thinking of him, from Barranquilla, Colombia apparently," I mumbled.

Jim added, "And Paolo is thinking of us."

The doorbell rang, and Jim and I both jumped halfway out of our skin.

"It's just Rich," Jim laughed.

I wasn't cheered by the news. "It's something to do with Luke, I know it is," I moaned.

"I'll finish the coffee. You might want to get dressed," he said gently.

I looked down and realized I was still wearing pajamas. "Yeah. Okay. Be right back."

Hoping Beauchamp would deliver his news quickly and be on his way, I took my time getting dressed and returned to the kitchen almost a quarter hour later. Beauchamp and Jim were bent over the kitchen counter, nearly head-to-head as they studied the greeting card and its many layers of wrapping.

Jim slid a steaming cup of coffee toward me when I sidled up on the far side of the counter.

"It's not Luke," he said, allowing my heart to start beating again.

"David Marchand is dead," Beauchamp said. "Met found him in a trunk at Heathrow a few hours ago. Two to the back of the head."

I stared at the oily surface of my coffee, a rushing sound in my ears nearly blocking out Beauchamp's voice as he plowed ahead with the news he'd obviously already shared with Jim.

"It happened a while ago. State of the body, they figure… a month? Maybe less. It's been warm in London."

My stomach heaved, but I didn't vomit. There was nothing in there, anyway.

"As for his handler, Mary, she's missing. I got the call about David from her boss. Marcel's place outside London is empty, cleaned out, but we're still waiting on word from Lyon whether he's there."

"Luke," I rasped, my voice barely audible. I tried again. "Luke has a house in London. Did they—"

"Searched. Empty," Beauchamp grunted. When neither Jim nor I said anything for several seconds, he asked, "You two think Marisol Serna sent this to Barbato?"

Jim nodded. "I need to go back through the camera footage to see who put it there and when. We're guessing the alarm scared them off. Probably someone hired one-off for the delivery."

I pictured David stuffed into a trunk, his eyes reduced to empty black voids, inspectors from the Met pinching their noses in distaste as they surveyed the scene. Cold air whirled around me, and I had to grip the edge of the countertop to stay on my feet.

Luke and David had been close. How close, I'd never thought to ask. Luke didn't seem the type to melt down in tears at such news. He would be enraged. Did he already know?

"Luke must have found out, or suspected," I said. "That was why he wanted to go to London."

"The real question is where you two are gonna go," Beauchamp said.

"Us? Go? Where? Why?"

Jim explained, "Until we figure out what's going on, it's not safe here. David, the letter, Luke… They may all be connected, they may not be, but none of it is good for us."

"Clearly Barbato knows Marisol survived," Beauchamp added.

We already knew Paolo would find out, somehow, that Marisol had survived. I hadn't realized until that moment how personally offended he was going to be about it. His message was only half clear to me: Marisol had taken the photo from the house in Argentina. She'd mailed it to Paolo to taunt him, to let him know she was alive and knew who was responsible for her brother's death. But why had Paolo forwarded the card and the photo to Jim and me? He wanted us to know he knew we were lying about Marisol, but that couldn't be the whole reason.

Hadn't he said we'd be hearing from him?

My chief concern was what Paolo intended to do now that he had confirmation Jim and I had lied to him. For years he'd been hunting down scions of his unscrupulous family, and for years Jim had escaped the fate suffered by Marisol's parents, Francisco Lira, and Fernando Serna.

Had Paolo moved Jim to the other side of the board?

27

Monday, June 7, 2021

An explosion of sound ripped me from sleep. Nothing around me made sense.

The sound became real before anything else. Dude's enraged barks and growls were filling the interior of the car in which I'd fallen asleep, and his fury was causing the whole car to shake as he tried to get at something outside.

I sat up, letting my confusion and frustration out in one pathetic whimper that I would never have let another human hear. Waking up in a Toyota Echo on the side of a highway in rural Louisiana, just as dawn was breaking through the haze rising from a nearby pond, could have been at least halfway pleasant—without the barking.

"Dude," I moaned. "There better be a *dinosaur* out there!"

I gasped when I spotted what had drawn Dude's ire. A massive alligator lay in the thick grass about twenty feet from the car. It almost seemed to be smiling ironically as its beady black eyes evaluated my dog either as a threat or a snack.

"Okay, that's basically a dinosaur," I allowed.

The creature was so still, I might have missed it if not for Dude's warning. I chuckled, the sound entirely lost in Dude's continued objections. Last night I'd fallen asleep, trusty Glock 29 in hand, smiling to myself at the "Beware of Alligators" sign between the rest area and the pond. Evidently it wasn't supposed to be funny.

I had to pee and suspected Dude did too, but I started up the little Echo and got back on the highway without even stretching my legs. I knew I'd find another rest area or a truck stop in a few miles, and perhaps it would be clear of primordial apex predators.

As I drove north along the peaceful, deserted I-49 corridor through walls of emerald green under a steely gray sky, I hit Play on the CD player. Lesson eight of Polish for Beginners issued from the speakers, distracting me from my woes... for about twelve seconds.

So much had happened in the week or so since receiving Paolo's barely veiled threat that I couldn't quite wrap my head around it.

The first thing I'd done was break my lease at my apartment on Dupont Circle and move to Jim's house in Arlington. This minor victory for Jim was actually for Dom's sake. Jim would be taking an extended absence from work, so he and Beauchamp read Dom in on everything. Now that she knew about Barbato, she was in enough danger without the added risk of me living right next door to her. I officially changed my address, and that was that.

A few days later, a courier had arrived at Jim's house—our house—with a gift from Beauchamp: cash, fake IDs, credit cards, two cell phones, and keys for my Echo and a Chevy Blazer for Jim. Our bug-out supplies. We bundled Dude and our luggage into Jim's car and drove to the parking garage at the Vienna-Fairfax Metro station where our incognito rides awaited. Waiting for them had been pure torture, and we hit the road less than an hour after the courier departed.

As Jim had said, until we figured out what was going on, home wasn't safe. Going to work wasn't safe. Being where anyone with an internet search engine could track us down wasn't safe. Being apart wasn't safe either, but Jim was as adamant about splitting up now as he'd been about staying together when I went to Albuquerque. He had something to do, and he'd been so stingy with the details I knew it was dangerous. I thought I also knew where this mysterious "something" was, and it took all my self control to keep my tiny little wheels pointed north instead of continuing west.

Jim promised he'd find me at my final destination, but he couldn't tell me when. Without knowing how much danger he was really in, I didn't even know how much to worry. I settled on a lot.

Mine and Dude's road trip to my home town of Manchester, Texas, should have taken about nineteen hours. I'd stretched it into three full days of circuitous routes, backtracking, and sitting in motel rooms watching my car through the window to see if anyone was sniffing around. I didn't think anyone was following me—at least I hadn't noticed anyone—but I was heading to the most obvious destination imaginable, so it didn't hurt to be careful.

My fuel-efficient clown car got me to Manchester around noon on Monday. I wove through the familiar old town in my unfamiliar car and finally pulled into a parking place at the Manchester Church of Christ at 12:15. I had less time than I'd hoped before my mom arrived to facilitate the Bible study she'd been running since 2012.

I rolled down the windows and turned off the car. Within seconds I was sweating and Dude was panting. The unmoving, ninety-degree air and high humidity made me feel like I'd been swaddled in cling wrap. I got out of the Echo, gave Dude some water, and walked him once around the small church, noting the handful of cars in the parking lot.

Not much had changed since the last time I was there; I could remember who drove which car and when they'd bought it, with a handful of exceptions. I had nothing in my mental Rolodex for the older model, white Bronco parked in a far shady corner with a sun shade thrown up, but one unknown car did not a crisis make.

My mom wasn't due until 12:30, so I walked Dude around the church a few more times. The third time we passed the Bronco, I noticed the windows were rolled down, which they hadn't been before. That meant the owner was inside, probably watching me case the joint and deciding whether he should call the cops. Luckily, my mom showed up five minutes early and spotted us, and I forgot about the Bronco in favor of worrying why she wasn't even a little bit surprised to see me.

Dude was overjoyed to see her, so I let him off his leash and let him bound up to her. I caught a smile as she scratched his ears, but it disappeared as she looked up at me.

"I was wondering whose car that was," was all she said before she let us into the church.

The cling wrap sensation vanished as soon as I followed her into the air conditioned foyer—or maybe it was my normally cheerful mother's subzero demeanor.

She locked the church doors behind us and said, "You can make the tea and lemonade while you tell me what the heck this is about."

It was so unlike my mother to use even this benign profanity that I stared at her for a good ten seconds before I was able to reply, "Sure, I still know my way around Jesus' kitchen."

"Don't you get smart with me," she snapped. She turned and marched away toward said kitchen, Dude heeling her and me scampering in their wake like a five-year-old.

All the neutral platitudes I'd been planning to cover (How's Dad? How are the girls? How was DC?) died on my lips. We were just going to have to get right down to business. While I set about boiling water for the tea and filling up a pitcher for the lemonade, she handled the cookies, crackers, and charcuterie service.

"I owe you a lot of answers," I sighed over the sound of the kettle clicking away on the stove. "And apologies."

She softened ever so slightly, eyes fixed on the cheese slices she was arranging. My stomach growled audibly.

"Help yourself if you're hungry," she offered.

"Thanks." I made a cheese-sausage-cracker stack and con-templated it while I spoke. "Did Dad tell you about Poland?"

"He did. We read some news stories." She broke a cracker in half and tossed it to Dude, reaching for a new one. "I trust you enjoyed your time abroad."

"Not really. Jim dragged me down to Argentina at gunpoint. Then he left me there to fend for himself. At least I had Dude, but Jim only brought him along so the hitman could find us."

She placed a few more cheese slices and then stopped mid-movement, perhaps realizing the import of what I'd said.

"You shouldn't be telling me this."

"That's the thing. I'm not supposed to, but I don't care any-more. You and Dad and the girls have been through enough. Jim said I could spill the beans to you, and that's good enough for me."

"Well if *Jim* said it was okay," she said, heavy on the sarcasm and still avoiding my gaze. I clicked my tongue impatiently.

"He's a good man. Okay, I mean, not really *good*, but he's—"

"Do you have any idea what it did to the girls? When we came back to the house and Dude was just *gone?* Can you even try to understand what that was like for them?"

To my horror, I realized she was starting to tear up as she spoke. I watched her jerky, violent movements for a few seconds, not knowing what to say. The truth was, I'd been so wrapped up in my own life, I'd hardly given their ordeal a thought.

"They adore him, Annie. They absolutely adore this dog. Think he hung the moon. Ellie used to wake us up every other night scared about something—monsters, burglars, aliens, Lord only knows where she gets the imagination—but Dude started sleeping in her room and she was fine. Not anymore of course. Oh, no…"

I could see her building up a head of steam, but I couldn't think of a way to derail her.

"That was trauma what he did to them. Real trauma. Maybe not the end of the world, maybe they'll get over it, but—my gosh, *I* was in pieces for weeks. Even your dad shed a few tears. But those girls… They'll remember that for the rest of their lives, you mark my words. What an awful thing to do. Unconscionable. I hope *Jim* had a darn good reason for doing it, but it sure doesn't sound like it."

She gave me the in, and I took it. "He did. I promise."

"So tell me. And make it quick. My study group starts at one."

"Okay…"

I took a deep breath. Since I'd practiced and perfected an ultra-condensed tale of the last two years on the drive here, I was able to get it all out in one breath.

"Jim recruited me to recover a stolen painting from his cousins and wanted me to keep them from getting killed by his uncle but it didn't really work and now someone is trying to kill *me* and we're not sure who because so many people have gotten involved so we're going into hiding until we figure it out and I need your help."

After a good stretch of silence, my mom asked, "Why did he take Dude?"

"Dude has a subcutaneous GPS transmitter. I had it implanted when I got him, because I was afraid someone might steal him. The man who was hired to kill Jim's cousins used it to find us."

She met my eyes, asking in a low voice, "Do you really think that answers my question, or is that all you're going to tell me?"

"You said to be quick, and it took Jim like an hour to explain it to me…"

"Can I tell your father what you told me?"

"Yes, but only him."

She pursed her lips, thinking, and said, "I'm no spy, but I don't think the town you grew up in is much of a place to hide out."

"We're not staying here. We're going—well, it's the last place I'd ever be caught dead in."

"Oklahoma?"

I nodded.

"You must be pretty desperate… How can we help?"

"You still have the RV I got in the divorce, right?" She nodded. I sighed with relief and asked, "Y'all feel like taking an extended vacation?"

28

Monday, June 7 to
Tuesday, June 8, 2021

Dude and I left the church a few minutes later. I automatically glanced toward the far, shady corner of the parking lot, looking for that white Bronco. It was gone. Worry needled at me, but I forced my thoughts away from it again.

My mother had agreed to my scheme, and she had promised to talk my dad into it. She was the only person who could. I had every reason to be relieved. Not only would Dude and I, and eventually Jim, be safe and hopefully impossible to find, but my family would be safer too.

Since I'd hatched the plan myself with almost no input from Jim, I was honestly surprised he'd agreed to it. My parents would take Emma and Ellie in my old RV on a vacation to a campground in Oklahoma. I'd meet them there in the Echo, and they'd take my car somewhere I didn't care to know while I stayed in Oklahoma and waited for Jim. With the RV as our temporary home and mode of conveyance, we'd be able to move around as needed without leaving any kind of trail in our wake.

Aaron had bought the RV on a whim almost ten years ago, and his inherent laziness was what made that exact RV the one I needed. He'd actually talked his parents into buying it, then slowly paid them back for it over a few years. When we divorced, the judge gave me the RV. I didn't want it, so I'd given it to my parents. No one had ever bothered changing the title, so it was still registered to Julia Oakley, Aaron's mother, who dutifully renewed the registration each year as a favor to my mom.

Feeling very clever, I headed north again for the K River Campground in Moyers, Oklahoma. Though the campground, so named for its location on the Kiamichi River, was only an hour from my parents' house, it might as well have been Jupiter.

As we crossed the Red River, I flipped off the "Welcome to Oklahoma" sign per tradition and told Dude, "Don't let me die here, buddy."

I made it to the campground a little after 2:30 and took Dude inside the office, where one woman was sitting behind a counter surrounded by Oklahoma souvenirs, sports drinks, and sunscreen. She glanced up at me, then down at Dude, and a smile stretched across her face.

"Now that's a dawg," she said in greeting. "What cin I do fer yew? Checkin in?"

"I hope so. I don't have a reservation, but I need an RV pad for a week, maybe more."

"Mm mm mm," she hummed. She moved over to an ancient PC and jiggled the mouse. "Just about booked up fer the holiday, but I think I cin git yew somethin 'til—yep, I've got one RV pad left. Yew cin only have it 'til July first at the weekly rate, though. Three hunnerd even. That awright?"

"That's perfect. If I can pay in cash."

"Cash is king," she answered. "But government-issued photo IDs are queen, I'm afraid."

I slid my mom's driver's license and $500 across the counter, mentally crossing my fingers. Only a fool would mistake me for a 5'4" brunette born in 1961, but then again a $200 tip probably didn't come her way every day.

Her eyebrows rose slowly as she counted out the crisp, one-hundred dollar bills. They rose higher as she began copying the information from my mom's ID into her register. I let out a slow breath as she dropped three of the bills into her till and pocketed the other two.

"Well awrighty, Missus Bowman. You're at lot twenty-four, right up again' the river. I'm Donna. Yew jist let me know if yew need anythin. Enjoy yer stay."

"Thanks!"

I fled, Dude right behind me, before she could change her mind. In the Echo, I wended my way through the shady but crowded campground to a choice, back-in RV pad. The lot she'd given me was in the rear, fairly isolated from the other campsites, and I could see the river a stone's throw through the trees. It looked like a beautiful spot to wait for my parents and nieces to arrive, until I turned off the car and stepped outside into the sauna.

"Ick," I groused. I let Dude out, and he headed straight toward the water.

With no way to check in with my parents or Jim, who had strictly forbidden any calls except in the direst of emergencies, I was resigned to grabbing a bottle of water and bag of stolen Bible study snacks my mother had given me, wandering down to the river where Dude had already waded in neck deep, and waiting.

I could see people enjoying the slow moving water, perched on inflatable tubes and rafts and nursing their beers and vibrant sunburns. I watched a gaggle of college-age kids drift past, riddled with envy, until one guy waved an arm in my direction. Assuming he'd mistaken me for someone else, I waved him off, hoping my gesture wasn't mistaken for rudeness. Dude stood still and watched the group until they floated out of sight around a bend in the river.

I ate the cheese and crackers, drank the water, gave the meat to Dude, and stretched out in the grass in the shade of a tree that was probably crawling with spiders. I tried not to think about it.

At some point I was lulled to sleep by the still, hot air and gentle rhythm of the river. When I came to, sleep muddled and out of sorts thanks to the cramp in my lower back, I looked around for Dude. He was nowhere to be seen.

I made my way back up to the RV pad, not bothering to call out for Dude. I could see the RV parked next to the Echo, and I knew he was inside enjoying the cool air and a reunion with my nieces. I didn't want to intrude, and some part of me shied away even from greeting the girls and my dad. They'd be gone again soon, so why bother?

I shook off the surly impulse and knocked on the RV's door.

While barking and assorted bedlam erupted inside, I gazed

around the campground. The noise level had picked up, vaca-tioners and long term residents enjoying al fresco dinners scent-ed with the heady perfume of citronella, hot dogs, and beer while generators cranked out cool air. Most of the RV pads and tent campsites I could see were occupied, fireflies blinking on the outskirts of the little holiday city as the sunlight began to fade. I'd slept longer than I should have.

The RV door opened to reveal my dad, and to my everlast-ing relief, he was smiling.

"There's sleeping beauty. Come in here and cool down."

▼

Maybe it wasn't wise, but I was glad my family stuck around long enough to share dinner and catch up. They'd left in the Echo after nightfall, acting secretive about their destination until Emma had sleepily enquired if her cousins would still be awake when they arrived. I inferred they were headed to my mother's ancestral home in Arkansas, but I didn't ask.

I woke up Tuesday morning to the sound of strangers' chil-dren screaming in rambunctious delight. Dude wasn't barking at them, so it was a slightly better morning than last.

Loneliness settled over me like a stifling blanket, but I threw it off and climbed out of bed to let Dude out and clean up the mess from dinner last night. My parents had filled the RV with supplies before driving it up here, and I was all set on food, wa-ter, and even my favorite wine for several days.

It was clear my parents hadn't gotten much use out of the RV, if any. I stood in the center of the living-kitchen-dining area and surveyed the scene in the dim light of a new day.

Vividly I recalled the day Aaron brought it home: the shiny exterior, the new car smell, our giddy plans to go camping every weekend, our first night in it. The sharp, hot pain of cracked cartilage when he'd broken my nose in the tiny kitchenette after I found his stash of empty vodka bottles under the sink. Inwardly I recoiled, but outwardly I was fine. Knowing I wouldn't trade even my current cluster of a life for that one was deeply fortifying.

I let Dude outside and walked around the exterior. No doubt my father had already thoroughly inspected the thing to ensure it was safe and functional, but I had nothing better to do. The old RV was in better repair than I'd dared hope, but it was still a dismal place to call home for any length of time. Roughly thirty feet long, it slept four (none comfortably) and at one time boasted a respectable sixteen miles per gallon.

I couldn't guess how long I'd be waiting here, alone and bored, but at least I had Dude. I got dressed and took him on a walk around the campsite, garnering a few waves and hollered greetings from the friendlier campers. Most of them seemed more interested in Dude than me, which was just as well.

When I got back to the RV, I saw a dark gray SUV parked where the Echo had been. My reflexive irritation vanished as I realized it was a Chevy Blazer—the same Blazer Jim had left Virginia in—and my heart catapulted itself into my throat.

"Jim," I breathed. I almost broke into tears; he was here already, and he was safe.

Dude sprinted toward the Blazer, tail wagging madly. Someone was moving around inside. The windows were tinted so dark I couldn't make out details, but I could plainly see the bulky silhouette of someone way too big to be Jim.

29

Tuesday, June 8, 2021

Dude started barking, and I ducked behind the rear of the RV, heart pounding.

But they were happy barks—joyous, even. A car door opened, then closed. I left my hiding spot in time to see Dude, tail a-wag, following a hulking male figure. He was rounding the front fender of the RV, probably looking for the door. I darted around the other side and caught him coming back toward me.

"Luke."

I rushed him, leaping all the way off the ground and letting him catch me with an 'oof' of surprise. Dude danced around Luke's feet, whining and barking.

"You stupid butthead," I moaned, squeezing him with all four limbs. "You scared me!"

Breathless, he laughed and said, "Sorry. Jim wouldn't let me call and warn you."

"He's not with you?"

His arms loosened enough for me to slither down to land on my feet before constricting again.

"It's good to see you too," he said, slightly indignant.

I wriggled out of his embrace to demand, "Where's Jim? Why are you driving his car? Is he okay?"

"It's a long story. Can we talk inside? It's stupid hot out here."

"Yeah, okay, we—" I looked around. "Where'd Dude go?"

"Uh… He was right behind me."

A perfectly timed yelp of terror ended our brief search. I jogged around the tangle of live oaks demarcating the RV pad and spotted Dude tiptoeing toward a picnic table, tail sweeping back and forth tentatively. A family of five sat frozen, wide eyed, gripping their breakfast burritos for dear life as they watched Dude approach. I called him back and he came, though quite reluctantly.

"I'm so sorry, he must've slipped his leash. He's completely harmless, I promise."

I retreated into the RV with Dude, Luke close behind. Before I could round on Luke and ream him out for disappearing, he scooped me into another hug and lifted me right off the floor.

"I'm so sorry, baby. I didn't have time to say goodbye."

"I figured. Just tell me what happened, and how you ended up with Jim's car. You must have seen him…"

Luke didn't answer right away. He put me down, edged into the kitchen, and began rifling through the fridge in search of food. He finally launched into an explanation as he pulled items out and placed them next to the little stove.

"I got a message from David. He said he was in trouble, so I booked it. But he was already—By the time I got the message, it was already too late. I just wanted to figure out what happened."

"Did you go to London?"

"No." He found a beer and cracked it open, taking an unhappy swig before spitting out, "France. They have a house in Lyon. I went there to find Marcel, to ask him what happened, but no one was there. I couldn't find out anything. I couldn't *do* anything."

He glared at the stack of sandwich makings he'd assembled, and I desperately tried to think of something to say.

"I nearly got caught trying to get back to the States. Took a while, obviously. I wasn't thinking straight. I was so… David didn't deserve to die like that. I don't even know who did it or why."

"But how did you find out? Beauchamp said they only found his—found him a week or so ago."

"I didn't. I knew something had happened, but I let myself hope he'd turn up. Maybe needed help… I don't know. I think I knew when I couldn't get ahold of him that it was gonna be bad news."

I stopped trying to think of a response and instead examined my own feelings about David's murder. I'd barely known him, but I liked him. If I did shed any tears, they were tears of fear, not grief. How had David borne the weight of his last moments, knowing what was about to happen? How would I? Shock and sadness had mutated into a perplexed fascination that someone could vanish from existence so abruptly and unceremoniously. Any leftover sadness was for Luke. I decided to take the conversation in a different direction.

"Jim?"

"Oh, right." He forced a laugh. "He's fine. I finally got back into the country through Laredo yesterday morning, and I called him. He was in Houston, so I hitched a ride there."

"I *knew* it!" I gasped. "That jerk—Why, why was he there? What was he doing?"

"He told me all about it in great detail, believe it or not."

I kicked out at his shin and missed, mumbling, "Not."

"Yeah. He told me about David, at least. Told me to take his car and come up here to meet you, so that's what I did."

"Did he at least fill you in about why we left Arlington?"

"The card you think Marisol sent to Paolo?"

"Yeah. And?"

He shrugged. "I knew she'd be a problem. I don't see why Paolo'd go after you, but I'm glad you're not sitting around at home waiting to find out."

"We should wait until Jim gets here to talk about this," I said, making it an answer rather than a question. "When will he be here?"

"He didn't say. You want a sandwich? Beer?"

"It's eight o'clock in the morning. I want a shower." And I wanted to know that Jim was okay, but I kept that to myself.

"Me, too. Room for two in there?" he asked, tipping his beer toward the RV's bathroom.

I shook my head. "Not even for one."

"Whatever, I'll make it work."

I escaped to the isolation of the campsite showers, which were situated in the center of the grounds and luckily devoid of any human presence but my own. There were plenty of granddaddy long legs, but they weren't so bad as spiders went. I sidestepped a cluster near the door, chose a stall without any dangling spectators, and settled in for a long shower.

So Jim *had* gone to Houston. I couldn't say what had tipped me off, but I'd known from the moment he told me we'd be leaving Arlington separately. Since Beauchamp was the one who provided our bug-out vehicles—two, not one—I knew he was in on it. I felt betrayed, furious. After all that hooey about me being the last line of defense against anyone who wanted to hurt Jim—or whatever line Beauchamp had fed me—he'd gone to the hotbed of the Tres Islas Cartel in the U.S. and sent me into hiding alone. Jim could have asked Luke to stick around to watch his back, but he'd sent Luke packing. Like *I* was the one who needed a bodyguard.

As though he didn't know better.

I finished up in the shower, got dressed, and flip-flopped over to the campground office. The June day was already heating up, and I could only think of one way to survive it without going stir-crazy inside the RV.

"Mornin, Evelyn," the manager greeted as soon as I walked in, using the name on my mother's ID. Whether she wanted to demonstrate continued compliance or remind me I had a co-conspirator to keep happy, I wasn't in the mood to figure out.

"Good morning, Donna. You sell swimsuits here?"

"Oh yeah. Back over there by the freezer. Towels, inflatables, water socks—yew name it."

The prices were as astonishing as the selection was meager,

but I didn't care about that, either. I just wanted to get in the river. I grabbed a swimsuit for me, swim trunks for Luke, two towels, two innertubes, and two pairs of water socks. At the front counter, I tossed in a tube of sunscreen and a six-pack of beer.

"Headed out to the river?" Donna asked as she added up the purchases on a hand-held calculator.

"Yep. Any tips?"

"Hm." She paused her calculating, looked me over, and grabbed a sun hat from a nearby rack. "This one's on me. You look like a burner, not a tanner."

"Thanks."

"What about Mister Bowman? He got a hat?"

"He does. What tipped you off? The swim trunks?"

She gave a modest shrug. "Saw an ol' Chevy come in this mornin, never left. That and the trunks, one and one makes two."

I suppressed a smile. Not much seemed to get past her, for which I was grateful. I watched her add up the last of the items and pulled another bundle of bills from my pocket, rounding it up to the nearest hundred and adding another for good measure. I hoped Jim and his half of the cash got here sooner than later.

Donna accepted the wad of bills with a bright smile and left me with, "If yew float all the way down to two seventy-one in Antlers, there's a fella drives an ol' school bus'll bring yew back up'ere. Works fer tips all summer."

"We'll do that. Thanks again, Donna."

▼

Luke and I spent all day on the river, distracting one another from our woebegone reality as best we could. Sunburned and dehydrated, we dragged our wet towels and deflated innertubes onto the bus in Antlers, Oklahoma and rode back up to the campground in Moyers. It was dark when we got back, but even without the sun, the still air under the campground's massive pine trees was sultry and hot.

We'd left Dude in the RV with the AC running, having agreed the heat and humidity were too much for him. While I took quick, cold shower in the RV, Luke took him on a walk around the campground and then took his turn in the shower. After a meal of grilled cheese and about a gallon of water, I was ready to sleep for a long, long time.

I helped myself to one of Luke's enormous t-shirts as a nightgown, then crawled into bed with a good book in my hands and a good boy warming my feet. Luke stayed up, claiming he wasn't tired; but he'd been on the run for a while. Sleep must have felt like a luxury reserved for the normal people around us. Someone had to keep watch.

Unburdened by Luke's pragmatism, I fell asleep quickly, eased back into wakefulness by the light Luke turned on when he came into the bedroom. I lay still with my eyes closed, listening as he coaxed Dude off the bed and closed the flimsy bedroom door, shutting Dude out. I sat up, but darkness had closed back in, leaving the air around me as black as pitch. I sensed Luke still standing between the bed and the door.

"What'd you kick him out for?" I asked quietly.

"He's not going to like this."

"Oh yeah?" I rose to my knees and scooted to the edge of the bed, feeling for him with my right hand outstretched. My fingers brushed his chest, and he caught my hand, pulling me forward roughly. His whole body seemed to hum with urgency as he kissed me, one hand twisted into my hair, the other gripping my waist.

He took me from zero to sixty that fast, before I realized how starved for him I'd been. I bit his neck, offering no objection while he grabbed at me. The grip of his huge hands was as painful as it was pleasurable, but those wires had been crossed long ago.

"Do you know how long it's been since I had you all to myself?" he moaned, squeezing each part of me as though taking inventory.

"Berlin, I guess."

"You guess. Must be nice, always getting your way."

"It is."

"Let me try it out."

He pushed me backward onto the bed, where I bounced once against my discarded paperback. The book's spine dug uncomfortably into my own as Luke climbed on top of me. The simple pleasure of his weight squishing me into the bed pushed back against the alarm bells his manhandling had set off. I wasn't sure if we were fighting or making out, but I knew I was outmatched either way, so I just held on for dear life and enjoyed it until the inevitable moment came.

Luke tried to take his t-shirt back, and I pressed both hands into his chest, gasping, "Easy, tiger."

"No," he groaned. "Not easy."

"We're not doing this."

"Why does he get to have all the fun?" Luke complained, a faint whine in his voice making me want to smack him.

"He and I aren't doing this, either," I said.

"Seriously?" He climbed off of me and switched on one of the nightlights over the bed. "I don't want to call you a liar, but… come on."

"Ask him," I challenged. "Unless you want to sleep on that tiny couch, you better behave."

He scoffed. "Behave? Maybe I do want to sleep on the couch."

"Fine," I huffed. I got under the covers, turned off the light, and muttered, "But let Dude back in."

He opened the door so Dude could resume his post at my feet. Rather than sentencing himself to an uncomfortable night on a too-shirt couch, he settled down next to me, on top of the covers.

"You're a tough nut to crack," he whispered admonishingly.

"Thanks."

He fell asleep within minutes. With Luke next to me and Dude filling the room with quiet, doggy snores, I laid awake thinking about Luke, and Jim, and what the heck we were all doing until the shaded windows on either side of the bed began to glow in outline, signaling the arrival of dawn.

30

Wednesday, June 9 to
Thursday, June 10, 2021

I finally fell asleep around six and was dead to the world for a solid five hours. When I came to, my first thought was of Dude, who'd presumably been stuffed in the RV for half a day. I staggered out of bed and left the bedroom to find the main cabin of the RV empty. Belatedly I turned around to scan the bed for Luke, who was also gone.

They weren't hard to spot once I'd peeked outside: From parts unknown Luke had gotten his hands on a four-foot-tall, portable metal fence that he'd secured around an ameba-shaped parcel of grass between the RV and the privacy hedge to the west. While Dude rolled around in the grass, Luke was comfortably reposed on a lawn chair, drinking coffee and reading a book in a facsimile of urbanity that wasn't fooling me for a second. I got dressed, snagged my own cup of instant coffee, and went outside to join them.

"How in the world?" I asked, gesturing at the fence.

"Bought them off that family next door, couldn't fit them in their truck. These too," he grinned, grabbing another lawn chair that was leaning against the RV and setting it up for me. "Take a load off."

"Thanks," I said. Sinking down into the chair, I creaked this way and that to get comfortable and gazed around at the bucolic little campground. "Do you feel safe here?"

"Safe enough. How can anyone find us here?"

"I don't know. It seemed like a good idea at the time, but we're still so close to my parents. It's starting to feel a bit obvious."

"Relax. We have to be somewhere."

"Seems like we're never that hard to find," I mused, feeling argumentative in the face of his placid dismissal.

Luke ignored me, pointedly flipping a page in his book. I scanned the cover and realized it was the one I'd fallen asleep reading last night.

"That's mine," I griped. "What am I supposed to read?"

He flashed me a hooded glance, his expression carefully neutral. "You're just spoiling for a fight, aren't you?"

"I'm hungry."

I was also tingling with an ever-growing sense of dread and impatience, a combination of fear for Jim and anxiety at how boring the foreseeable future would be. I stood, restless, and paced around the enclosure once.

"Aren't you hungry?" I pressed.

"Nope."

"I'm gonna go scramble some eggs."

I flounced back into the RV and did exactly that, annoyed now not only at Luke but at myself for being so neurotic. All we had to do was sit tight and wait for Jim; what was so hard about that? We'd done everything right, and the only way for anyone to know where we were now would be if they'd followed one of us or somehow deduced that my parents knew and gotten it out of them. Neither possibility seemed likely. Either we'd have noticed that we were being followed, or my parents would've warned me about the incoming threat.

Assuming this imaginary interrogator had left them alive…

What the heck was wrong with me?

I made bacon and toast too and carted two plates piled high with breakfast goodness outside to share with Luke, who changed his mind about being hungry once he smelled my offering. Having brokered an uneasy peace, I resolved to hang onto it for dear life no matter how infuriatingly calm Luke insisted on being. For all I knew, he was intentionally acting like Jim to mess with me, to stave off his own boredom.

▼

We kept ourselves busy the same way we had in Colorado. There wasn't enough room in the RV for jujitsu, but we managed daily Krav Maga lessons in the living room-slash-kitchen before setting out to explore what nature had to offer within walking distance of the campground.

Each time we left, I Sharpied a cartoon explanation onto a

strip of duct tape on the RV's door in case Jim showed up: Two stick figures and a dog in the river when we went swimming, a pair of hiking boots when we went for a long walk, a fish when we went fishing. Really high-level OPSEC kind of stuff. It never mattered. Jim was never there when we returned.

Afternoons were for showering and avoiding the heat within the air conditioned shelter of the RV, and evenings were for increasingly creative dinners constructed from our dwindling rations.

Thursday afternoon, Luke drew the short straw and went grocery shopping, leaving me with Dude and the last of our wine. My resolve not to pump alcohol into my grumbling, empty tummy lasted until the heroine of my current paperback helped herself to a glass of chardonnay, at which point I decided it would be rude to let her drink alone.

I was pouring myself a refill when someone knocked on the door. Dude gave one perfunctory woof and returned to his catnap, his lack of concern calming me. I opened the door, wineglass in hand, and an inarticulate sound of mingled joy and surprise popped out of me. I almost dropped my glass.

There stood a petite, freckled brunette with a white envelope clutched in one hand and a look of barely contained giddiness on her face.

"Emily!" I squeaked.

She stood a cautious yard from the RV, but at my greeting she bounded up the stairs and locked her arms around me. I had to abandon my wine glass on the counter to reciprocate. Pleasant surprise dissolved into a whirlwind of other feelings as

I crushed my older sister against me.

We embraced until Dude, curious and probably annoyed at being ignored, nosed his way past me in the doorway and sniffed tentatively at Emily's leg. She yelped in surprise and stepped back.

"That's a *heckuva* big dog! Holy crap."

Her voice was thick with emotion, and she laughed off her alarm at the sight of Dude and crept back up to him with her hand outstretched. He licked it once and tried to squeeze past me to greet her properly, but I grabbed his collar.

"Come inside, already. Don't worry, he doesn't jump anymore."

She slipped past us and stood in the middle of the RV, gazing around with satisfaction. Where I favored our dad—red-headed, brown-eyed, tall, and broad-shouldered with a sturdy, low center of gravity—Emily was the spitting image of my mother at 36, which meant she didn't look a day over 26 and had only seen triple digits on the bathroom scale when she was pregnant. I'd always envied her elven good looks and was surprised they'd managed to weather the storm her life had been. Her straight brown hair grew past her shoulder blades, a thick fringe of bangs concealing a forehead that I'd once savagely (in the heat of a long-forgotten argument) accused of being a fivehead. Her dark blue eyes studied me as I studied her.

She grinned at me, breaking the stand-off, and asked, "So how's it going, FBI Barbie?"

I felt a pang of irritation, not at her, but at our parents. "When did you get out? Mom and Dad didn't say anything to me!"

"Just yesterday. I got home and the house was empty, so I

called Mom's cell and they said they were in Arkansas. Dad let me stay in the house one night, but he told me not to get comfortable. This is yours, I guess," she said with a shrug, passing me the envelope and politely not commenting on the name written on it. Annie Oakley.

I hadn't used my married name in years, and only my parents were allowed to call me Annie now; but at that moment I didn't care who sent the envelope, why Emily had it, or what was in it. I set it down next to my wine.

I asked Emily, "Do you want some merlot before I polish it off?"

"I'd literally kill a man for some hooch right now."

I emptied the last of the bottle into a second glass and passed it to her, still dazed.

My diminutive big sister made my hellraising ways seem like a toddler's temper tantrum by comparison. Last I'd heard, her three-year sentence had been padded with two more for possession of contraband, assaulting another inmate, and screwing a guard who ended up with a pink slip. She must have been released on parole, or maybe to ease overcrowding at the prison. No way was it because of good behavior.

Emily had the element of surprise down to an art; no one had ever, even once, looked at that cherubic face and anticipated the delinquent madhattery of which she was capable. I admired her deeply while lamenting some of her poorer life choices. Chief among them was her involvement with the man whose criminal enterprise had resulted in her doing prison time and my parents wrangling full custody of their two daughters.

I assumed he was still safely behind bars, but it never hurt to ask: "Any idea where Joey ended up?"

"Colorado," she announced blithely. I blinked at her, confused, and she added, "He got transferred to a prison up there last year. He called me and tried to tell me he was there for his protection or something, but he probably got swapped for some other career criminal who liked to break the law in multiple states."

"Hope he stays there."

"Me too. He'll kill me if he ever gets out."

I perked up at this casual announcement and demanded, "Why? What's he got against you?"

"Didn't you know I testified against him?"

"No!"

All the rest of my questions were cut off by another single bark from Dude, which preceded the door opening to admit Luke and two armfuls of plastic bags. He stopped on the threshold, looking from Emily to me with picture-perfect, silent bewilderment.

Emily shocked me by asking sharply, "Who the heck are you?"

Luke hefted all the bags onto the counter before shooting back, "Who are *you?*"

This was going well. Though privately I believed it couldn't have been more obvious that Emily was my sister, I said, "This is my big sister, Emily. Emily, this is my… Luke."

"Oh," he said, leaving it at that.

She took a leisurely sip of wine. "Nice to meet you, Luke." She didn't mean it. I was perplexed at their baseless hostility until Luke spoke again.

"Guess you and Anna went to the same driving school," he commented churlishly.

"Do you two know each other?" I asked.

"This moron just about sideswiped me turning out of the Chevron!" Emily accused, glaring at him.

"I was turning right, I had the right of way! And you're supposed to turn into the first available lane, not kamikaze across three lanes of traffic at once!"

"Oh, step off!"

"Unbelievable," I moaned.

"Sorry," Luke sighed, avoiding both our upturned gazes. "Nice to meet you, Emily. Anna, a word?"

I followed him outside, turning as I closed the door to see Emily shooting Dude an apprehensive side-eye that he returned with uncanny symmetry. Luke crossed his arms and stared at me, waiting for an explanation.

I went on the defense. "I can't help it if my mom blabs. I told her to only tell my dad."

"What's she doing here?"

"I'm assuming she needs a roof, since she just got out of prison and my parents won't let her stay at the house."

"Why not?"

"They can be such fascists…"

"Anna, why not?"

I growled, "She's trouble with a capital T. Always has been. But she's my sister and I'm not sending her packing!"

"Jim will. Just you wait."

"He won't either."

His face fell and he mumbled, "I was just getting used to it being the two of us. This isn't fair."

"Don't be like that," I begged, tugging at his sleeve.

"Yeah, yeah, she's your sister. She's a crap driver."

"She's been in prison, give her a break."

"I will if she does."

I led the way back into the RV and helped Luke unload the groceries while Emily watched us with polite interest. At length she asked, "How do you know Anna?"

"Tinder," Luke grunted.

"Dang. I need a phone."

"That's not true," I said, disregarding Luke's warning glare. "I met him on a job. He's a hitman."

"Why would you tell her that?" Luke groaned.

With a satisfied smirk, Emily said, "We don't lie to each other. Get used to it."

Luke grabbed a beer from the newly replenished stock, took a fortifying drink, and fired back, "Why were you in prison?"

"Drug stuff."

"You better not drag that crap in here," he threatened.

She shivered in counterfeit fear. "So scary. You're the boss, John Wick."

Luke had the good grace to cook dinner for three that night—shredded chicken tacos and home fries that tasted like they'd been air dropped straight from heaven. The uncommonly good fare softened Emily, and under my watchful eye she attempted a less antagonistic round of conversation.

"Where'd you learn to cook like this?" she asked.

"My dad was a chef."

I knew she wanted to ask if he'd learned how to kill people from his dad, too. Instead she nodded and said calmly, "Makes sense."

"Did you get to talk to the girls?" I asked Emily, sidetracking her before the effort of playing nice became too much. She happily gushed about them for a while, and then it was my turn to explain what was going on.

Our mom hadn't given her much more than my location and a stern warning not to tell anyone else, so she was understandably curious. There was no question of feeding her some cover story. She'd told it true: We didn't lie to each other. I told her about everything from Houston to Poland, with one outstanding exception; but that was only because I wasn't ready to tell Luke.

She never formally asked for permission to stay with us, but I hadn't been expecting it. While Luke got ready for bed, I helped her make up the loft above the cab, the better to maintain the high ground over Dude. She was never a fan of dogs big enough to maul her to death. She watched from above while I fed Dude, then I got ready for bed myself and ducked into the bedroom.

I found Luke covered to the nose in blankets, pretending to be asleep. Fantastic.

31

Friday, June 11, 2021

Through a haze of restless sleep, I felt warmth on my face and opened my eyes. Light crept into the bedroom through gaps in the shades, and the ritual shift change from crickets to song-birds was underway outside.

Luke pressed his lips to my ear and breathed, "Good morning."

"Is it?"

"Sorry for that. I wasn't quite ready for Anna two-point-oh."

"No one ever is." I turned over to face him. Since the question had kept me up for two nights straight, I decided to put it to Luke. "Why don't you tell me what you and Jim are up to?"

"Together? Nothing. Our last collaboration didn't go well for me."

"That's such a lie. Ever since that night in Albuquerque, you've both been acting like… like you don't even care that I'm in… *ugh*… in love with you both."

"I was cool with it way before he was."

"Neither of you is cool with it!" I argued. "I don't like mind games."

"You seem to like this well enough," he shot back. He kissed me, laughing when I immediately grabbed onto him. "Yeah, you're really having a hard time with it, aren't you?"

"You're so mean."

He kissed me again, pinning me to the bed, and pretty much behaved himself while the interior of the room slowly brightened.

We were running out of these moments. My sister was asleep twenty feet away, and pretty soon (barring some calamity) Jim would make an appearance as well. The RV would be at capacity, though it already was if we counted Dude, and everything would be more complicated. I could feel it through his hands, his lips, his every movement. We were nearing the end, the final struggle of this exhausting saga, and the odds of our friendship remaining unchanged on the other side were so slim as to be nonexistent.

Or maybe I was being melodramatic. Luke fell back asleep after I had to gently tell him off again, leaving me jazzed and ready to start the day. I got dressed and left the bedroom to find Emily still asleep in the loft, Dude sitting patiently by the door waiting to go out. My gaze moved from him to the white envelope, on the counter right where I'd left it after Emily gave it to me. I'd forgotten all about it.

I let Dude out, then picked up the envelope to read the name again. Who would address something to Annie Oakley, if they wanted it to reach me? There was no Annie Oakley anymore. The letter hadn't been mailed; my former name was the only thing on the outside of the generic, letter-sized envelope. I used a kitchen knife to slice it open.

Inside was a single piece of cheap, white printer paper folded in thirds. I heard Dude whining outside and scratching at the door, but I ignored him and unfolded the paper.

The handwritten words stared up at me, turning the quiet hum of curiosity into a keening whine.

Dude barked, I jumped, and Emily stirred.

"Where am I?" she murmured.

"Oklahoma," I whispered back, still staring at the paper.

"Eeeeew," Emily moaned.

I reached over to let Dude inside. Emily waited until he'd curled up on the couch before she hopped down from the loft. On her way to the bathroom, she bent to read the message aloud.

"'Tell Jim I kept my promise'? What does that mean?"

She waited two seconds in vain for my answer, then *tsk'd* and continued into the bathroom.

"You found this at the house?" I called after her.

Through the thin door, she answered, "No, at the front office when I got here."

I grabbed the letter and the envelope and threw myself out the door. Somehow Dude slithered out before the door shut behind me, and together we jogged across the campground toward the office. For the first time, I found the door closed and locked. I knocked on it, then hammered on it, then realized it wasn't even seven o'clock. The sign on the door said the office opened at 9:00.

"Crap," I breathed. I walked back to the RV, mind whirring.

Luke was still asleep and Emily had gone back to bed, so I mixed up some instant coffee and went back outside to sit with Dude and think.

Once 9:00 rolled around, I'd be right back at the office to ask Donna who dropped off the letter and how she came to give it to Emily. Until then, all I could do was guess. Someone who knew Jim, knew my old name, and knew where I was staying had taken the trouble to leave me a cryptic, practically meaningless message but hadn't bothered to come say hi.

But the message wasn't for me, it was for Jim. Someone had made a promise to him and wanted me to verify it had been kept. How could I, if I didn't even know what the promise was?

A light flicked on in the kitchen. Emily, tousle-haired and half-awake, was at the kitchen sink fetching a glass of water. She spotted me and ambled outside, stretching like a cartoon character right outside the door.

"Surprisingly comfy," she rated the loft bed, claiming the second lawn chair next to me. "Thanks for letting me stay. I didn't want to be pathetic, but I honestly have nowhere to go."

Happy to be distracted, I eyed the ten-year-old Malibu she'd parked next to the Blazer. I couldn't help but wonder how she'd gotten her hands on a car so quickly after her release from prison. I decided I didn't want to know. Instead I asked, "How'd you get out of prison? I thought you had one more year."

"Parole," she said vaguely. "It was overcrowded and I'm non-violent. It didn't happen a moment too soon. I was about to go bananas in there."

"You're already bananas."

"Hey, speaking of bananas, you'll never guess who I bumped into in there."

"You're right."

"Grace! I guess she burned down a Taco Bell. Crazy, huh?"

I thumbed through my few memories of Grace and concluded, "Not for her."

"She asked about you," Emily added with a grin.

I dodged it with, "So what are you planning to do?"

"I was thinking about heading to Dallas, try to find work there. Technically I'm supposed to stay in Texas."

"Close enough, huh? Just stay with us. Luke will warm up."

"After what you told me last night, I think I'd just get in the way. And no offense, but this Jim dude sounds like a real killjoy."

Dude perked up, staring at Emily until he realized we weren't addressing him; or perhaps he'd reacted to Jim's name. He laid back down with a defeated sigh.

"Don't worry about Jim. I've got him wrapped around my little finger," I whispered, throwing her a wink. She peered at me with exaggerated suspicion.

"Both of them?"

"Oh yeah. As long as I can make it work."

She was not impressed. "That's sneaky, Sis."

"Oh no," I said in a rush, eager to defend my last shred of honor. "They know about each other. It's not like I'm messing around."

"You're kidding me."

"It was their idea. I figured, 'Hey, why not make the most of it?' and so I am." My forced cockiness receded somewhat under her glare and I appended, "I can't give either one of them up. I'm really stuck."

"Between a rock and a hard place, huh? Bless your heart."

I regaled her with few stories of Luke and Jim that had us both giggling like idiots until we heard the two kids at the adjacent campsite waking up and decided to tone it down a little. Neither of us missed the slight jostling of the RV as Luke finally got out of bed and ducked into the bathroom. I was watching Emily's face for some clue about which way she was leaning, stay or go, when a curiously wistful expression clouded it.

"What?" I prompted.

"He reminds me of Joey a little bit. I think that's why I don't like him."

Baffled, I reviewed my mental image of her degenerate baby daddy. It bore no resemblance to Luke whatsoever, aside from the fact that both were male humans. I twisted my mouth to hold in my protests, hoping she'd elaborate.

"I mean they look nothing alike," she granted. "It's his aura, I guess."

"Luke's not some scumbag."

"You sure?"

"Ew. Don't do that," I growled.

"I bet he's violent."

"He's a hitman."

"Whatever. Let's not talk about this. What do y'all do for fun, besides smashing?"

"We're not smashing," I sighed, almost literally sick of defending myself. I went on, "There's not a whole lot do for fun. We're supposed to be laying low."

"I think I'll hang around until Count Chocula shows up," she said firmly. "Then I'll split for the big D."

"It's Camposanto," I mumbled. She raised her eyebrows, and I added primly, "It's Italian, not Romanian."

She burst into laughter, the contagious sort that soon had me sputtering. We both knew it wasn't that funny; that's just what sisters do. I polished off my coffee and, still shaking with laughter, snagged her water glass and carried it inside for a refill.

Luke had emerged from the bathroom and was toweling off his wet hair. "Hot water lasted two whole minutes," he said. "So how long is *she* gonna hang around?"

"Until Jim gets here. Are you going to be nice to her?"

"Cut that out."

I took that as a yes, then slid the envelope across the counter with the folded letter on top. "Emily brought that from the front office when she got here. I haven't had a chance to ask Donna about it."

He scanned the brief message, swore, and read the name on the envelope. "Annie Oakley?"

"I married him for the schtick."

"I thought you registered here under your mom's name."

"I did."

"Well how are you—"

I cut him off with, "I don't understand this any better than you do. Just looping you in. Maybe Jim will get it."

Leaving Luke inside to make breakfast, I returned to my

chair next to Emily and checked the time. Still almost an hour until I could question Donna. I rose to my feet again.

"Where are you going?" Emily asked.

With all the authority of a nosy kid sister, I informed her, "I need to check out your car and other supplies to make sure they'll get you to Dallas."

While Emily watched, I checked the pressure in all four tires, checked the oil level, made sure all the lights worked, and tested the windshield wipers. That was pretty much all I knew about cars, so I called it good. The Malibu was in decent shape, but it was missing something fairly important.

"It's got no plates," I said, pointing to the rear bumper as though she needed proof. "How'd you get your hands on a car, anyway?"

"Long story," she dodged. I crossed my arms and let her stew in it until she went on. "So this meth head I was locked up with got out on the same day, and her boyfriend picked us both up. We stopped at this crack house in the middle of nowhere and they said they were only going to be inside for fifteen minutes. I waited thirty minutes and then booked it. They probably still don't know it's gone."

"For crap's sake, Emily…"

"Well, what was I supposed to do? Walk?"

"What happens when you get pulled over for not having a license plate?"

"I'll figure that out later."

"Where did Methany's boyfriend get it? Is there anything in the glove box?"

I didn't wait for her answer before ducking into the passenger side and popping open the glove compartment. Among the typical contents—gum, old receipts, user's manual, broken flashlight—I found a cracked glass pipe, a lighter, a bag of you-know-what, and an expired insurance card. I pocketed the card and laid the more interesting items on the passenger seat for Emily to see.

"I didn't know that was in there," she mumbled.

"You know Jim's a LEO, right?"

"So what, I'm a Pisces."

"A law enforcement officer!"

"Oh. So then don't tell him. I'll get rid of it. I should've known those tweakers would leave me with something like this."

I gave a truncated sigh, distracted by the wild impulse to laugh. "Emily, they didn't leave you with this, you stole it."

"Whatever. Jeez, you're being such a fascist right now. Want to dial it back a notch or two?"

"I'm sorry, but this is the last thing we need right now."

She said nothing, merely contemplating the drug paraphernalia in strained silence, so I pulled out the insurance card to see what I could glean from it. Somehow I didn't believe Chantel Johnson of Paris, Texas, was either the driver or his girlfriend. The six-month policy had expired eighteen months ago, so the card was useless. I tossed it back in the glove box, gathered up the other items, and gruffly ordered Emily to chuck them in the dumpster behind the showers. I ducked back inside to wash my hands.

"Hungry?" Luke asked, studying my stony profile from his post in front of the stove.

Even the smell of bacon and eggs couldn't brighten my mood at the moment. I filled him in on the drug bust and was annoyed to find him laughing silently when I finished.

"How is this funny?" I demanded.

"You weren't kidding about the trouble. Guess you got all the brains, huh?"

"She's not stupid!" I defended, rounding on him. "She just has terrible judgment. And you have to admit, there wasn't much else she could have done in the situation."

"Jim's gonna have an aneurysm."

"Jim's not gonna hear about it," I snarled.

He dismissed me with a laugh. Emily chose that moment to appear, retreating immediately to the bathroom to wash her hands. When she emerged, I saw the look of sullen determination on her face and knew what she was going to say.

"I should probably go. Thanks for letting me stay the night."

I talked her out of it with visions of routine traffic stops, arrests, and jail, aided unexpectedly by an offering of breakfast food from Luke. An hour later, he was setting out again in the Blazer with a list of clothing and personal care items Emily needed. I was surprised at his helpfulness but decided not to question it. I had an appointment to keep.

Leaving Emily with Dude, I marched back to the office and found Donna refilling a vending machine out front.

"Met yer sister yesterday," she said, not looking up from her task.

"Who gave you that envelope?" I'd meant to sound polite and curious, but the question came out like an accusation.

She pushed a few more bottles of water into the machine, closed it up, locked it, and finally turned to face me. "Local kid, Danny. Known 'im all 'is life."

"Well… who gave it to him?"

"No idea. But whoever it was told Danny the Annie Oakley thing was an inside joke. Said it was fer Anna Bowman. I didn't think of it again 'til that little woman came in yesterday and asked fer Anna Bowman. Evelyn'd be yer mother, then?"

"I wish you'd stop figuring stuff out," I sighed.

"I wish cars'd stop pilin up achyer lot, but we can't all git what we want."

"My sis—the latest one will be gone soon. Listen, I'm sorry to be rude, but that letter freaked me out. I'd love a heads up if anyone else comes in here asking for Anna Bowman."

"Which is you."

I nodded.

"I can do that. Got a cell phone?"

"Yeah." I gave her the number. "Thanks, Donna. I mean it."

"Some kinda trouble looking fer yew?"

"No more than usual."

32

Saturday, June 12, 2021

The real world, or at least what passed for it lately, returned with Jim on Saturday morning.

I was the only one awake. I'd picked my way through the dark campground before sunrise to wash the smoke smell out of my hair from last night's campfire, taken Dude for a quick walk, and settled into a chair in his makeshift yard to drink coffee while I waited for my companions to stir.

The campground was hopping as soon as the sun was out, a steady stream of weekenders tramping past with inflatable tubes, beach balls, coolers, and kayaks to enjoy the nearby river. I watched them with detached interest, barely registering any surprise when a Kia nosed into the scant space behind the RV. Dude and I both stood up as Jim got out of the car, and I left Dude inside the enclosure while I dashed out to greet him.

My anxiety about Jim had been safely compartmentalized until the exact moment when his arms wound around me. I buried my face in his shoulder and breathed through a surge of emotion. It took a while. Dude barked, throwing in a few whines to let us know how much he'd missed Jim, too.

I gave Jim one last squeeze and was alarmed to feel him wince slightly, a sharp intake of air preceding a breathy, self-deprecating laugh. "Easy, kiddo," he chided.

I stared up at him, one hand pressing lightly against the ribs on his left side. "What happened? Are you okay?"

"I'm fine. You should see the other guy." He kissed me and said, "Let's get inside first. I'm starving."

"Oh, uh, wait—" I stammered, backing up as he started toward the RV. "There's something I have to tell you first."

His eyes darted to the Malibu, then back to me. "What."

"Um… remember how I have a sister?"

"… Are you serious?"

"Look, my mom sent her here, and she doesn't have anywhere else to go. She said she'd split anyway once you got here, but I'm pretty sure that car is stolen and if she gets pulled over she'll end up right back in prison—"

"Whoa, whoa, whoa," he soothed. He gripped me by the shoulders. "Breathe, Anna. I'm in no shape to kick anyone to the curb right now."

"You're not mad?"

"No, I'm pretty mad. But at your mom, not you. I assume you told her to keep her mouth shut." I nodded. "Fine. We'll deal with it. You're not going to like my news, either, so let's call it even for now. Can I please get a bite to eat?"

Relieved, I ushered him inside and allowed Dude to follow.

While they greeted each other, I rustled up some pancakes. We made sufficient noise to rouse Luke, though Emily remained steadfastly asleep through it all. Luke emerged from the bedroom, rubbing his face to wake himself up.

I hid a smile as Luke shook Jim's hand in an almost halfway friendly way and said quietly (the better not to disturb Emily), "Hey, man. What kept you?"

"You're not going to believe it," Jim assured him.

Luke took over the cooking, I made coffee, and Jim sat rather stiffly on the couch while he brought us up to speed at a respectfully library-appropriate volume.

"The day after we found the card, I got a call from someone claiming to be Thomas Holladay."

He paused to let that sink in, perhaps expecting some theatrics or arguments from me; but since Luke's revelation about Tommy in New Mexico, I'd become comfortable with the possibility, even the likelihood that he was alive.

Jim cast me a puzzled glance and went on. "I agreed to meet him in Houston, but he wouldn't say what he wanted. He said he'd only talk to you, so I let him believe you were coming with me. We agreed on a meeting place and time, and I told Rich. He said not—"

"Not to tell me, yeah," I finished. I wasn't angry, or surprised. I just wanted Jim to go on.

"He was supposed to make contact the night I got to Houston, the fifth, but he didn't show up until the next morning. By then I was packing, about to check out. He must've been waiting until I opened the door, because he pushed his way inside and held me at gunpoint, demanding to know where you were. Thanks," he interrupted himself, accepting a cup of coffee from Luke. "I hadn't been expecting Holladay, but it was really him. He got too close, I grabbed the gun, which turned out not to be loaded, and we got into a minor kerfuffle. The little punk almost broke my ribs, but a few knocks to the head cooled him down."

"You're *proud* of yourself," I hissed, making it an accusation. Now I knew how he'd felt listening to the tale of my hobo fight.

"The kid is half my age, of course I'm proud of myself. We're not all prize fighters like you."

Luke snorted, I glared at him, and Jim pushed through the needless interruption.

"Anyway, it gave me a chance to draw and convince him to sit down. He calmed down but refused to answer any questions until he saw you, Anna. He asked if you were in Mexico with Luke."

I started correcting him before his words could make sense. "*New* Mex—What?" I squeaked. "How'd he know Luke was in Mexico?"

"No one knew where I was," Luke added. "No one."

"He refused to say. He kept insisting he had to talk to you. In person. I decided to let him go."

Another "What!" popped out of me, provoking an enraged groan from the loft.

Quietly, Jim argued, "What was I supposed to do? Arrest him? For what?"

Luke flipped a pancake and reeled off, "Aggravated assault, threatening you with deadly force, lying to a federal agent, sprinkle on some obstruction of justice, resisting arrest, maybe see if he jumped through all the required legal hoops to get that weapon…"

"All right, I get it. But marching into the Houston field office with an undercover operative who's supposed to be dead? Great way to keep a low profile."

"What's the deal with this guy, anyway?" Luke demanded. "Whose side is he on?"

I whispered, "Nobody knows. That's the deal with him."

Jim said, "All we really know is that he wants to talk to Anna."

"Why did you stay in Houston so long?" I asked.

"Because I told Tommy to wait. I said if he could wait a week, I'd take him to you, if you agreed to it. He was supposed to come back last night, but he never did, so I came here."

While I mulled all this over, Luke asked, "He driving a white Bronco by any chance?"

I perked up, an image of that exact car flashing through my mind twice—once in the church parking lot a few days ago, and again nearly a year ago, on the dirt road that led to the cabin in Hesperus, Colorado where Luke and I met. Why the memory chose that moment to resurface, I couldn't say. I must have made an odd sound, because both men turned to look at me with matching expressions of concern.

"You've noticed it too, haven't you?" Luke asked.

I shook my head, knowing I'd missed something. "Where have *you* seen it?"

"Everywhere. At Walmart both times, following the bus when we came back from the river."

"Did he follow you from Houston?" Jim asked.

Shaking his head, Luke insisted, "I never saw it until I got here."

"Oh, my God," I breathed. "He was waiting for me. He was already in Manchester when I got there to talk to my mom."

"Yes, he left in a white Bronco," Jim answered somewhat redundantly. "I should've come straight here. He could've done whatever he wanted…"

"And he's been lurking around this whole time," Luke added.

"But he hasn't done anything," I concluded.

Luke passed around plates of pancakes, and we ate in silence, a miserable pause in the conversation while we all ruminated on how thoroughly we'd been hoodwinked. I was afraid to deepen the embarrassment by mentioning the sighting in Colorado, but I had to have out with it.

"I saw it in Hesperus, too. Shortly after I got to the cabin." Prompted by no more than their expectant stares, I briefly related the tale. "Might not have been him, though," I ended lamely.

"This is exactly like Philip turning up in Colorado," Jim said. "We never figured out how he found Luke. Tommy shouldn't have been able to find you."

I groaned, "Dang it… I have to talk to Tommy, don't I?"

"I'm not telling you one way or the other," Jim said. I saw his lips move and heard the words, but my brain refused to accept it.

"You're leaving it up to me?" I demanded. "Who are you and what've you done with Jim?"

"I would never ask this of you," he said, so seriously that I couldn't think of a response. Out of the corner of my eye, I saw Luke shift impatiently.

"Wasn't he your partner? Don't you want to see him? I mean, jeez, you thought he was dead. None of this makes any sense."

I felt Jim's gaze searing my flesh. He asked, "You haven't told Luke?"

"It hasn't come up," I whispered.

Luke protested, "Yes it has. It came up in Chile, and you told me to drop it."

Something must have passed between them, but I missed it because my eyes were glued to the floor between my feet. I could feel my ears turning red. Luke's voice was soft when he spoke again.

"Forget it," he said. His hand came to rest on my back, so heavy my posture collapsed a tiny bit. "Just forget I asked."

I was happy to oblige.

"You haven't told him *what?*"

We all jerked in surprise and turned toward the loft, from which the voice had exploded.

Having confessed to her eavesdropping, an unrepentant Emily climbed down from the loft and fixed Jim and then Luke with a very sisterly glare indeed. They took the hint, retreating outside so Emily and I could talk in private.

Hot tears were already leaking out of me, angering me. It wasn't crying time, it was planning time. Emily covered my clasped hands with her own.

"This is so humiliating," I groaned. I felt the question in a twitch of her hands and added, "Not telling him. I'm embarrassed because I thought I was over this. It happened so long ago."

"What happened, and why should you get over it?"

I shrugged.

"Will you tell me what he did? I want to make sure I hate him exactly the right amount."

Knowing Emily had already guessed how my story would end made it easier to start. Until then, the only people I'd told were Jim and Philip, and I hadn't gone into detail for them; why would I? I kept the story short anyway, so Luke and Jim had only been outside a few minutes when I was finished. I felt better but worse, lighter but smaller. Emily's hand pressed into my back was keeping me calm, but I was afraid what would happen when she took it away.

"I should've told Luke. I have no idea why I didn't. Jim was the first person I told, then I had to tell Philip, and that seemed like enough."

"Can't help you there," she said kindly. "Want me to let them back in?"

"Sure."

She planted one on my forehead and intoned, "Love you, Sis. Please kick his butt for me."

She opened the door to admit the banished men and shared a fleeting, indecipherable look with Luke. He crossed his arms, looked down at me, and said simply, "I want to meet this guy."

"What do you want, Anna?" Jim asked.

"I want to talk to him. I've got a million questions for him."

33

Saturday, June 12, 2021

Jim had not been idle in Houston. Holed up in a cheap motel room waiting in vain for Tommy, in self-imposed isolation, he'd spent the last week committing everything he knew to paper. This was no simple list or narrative report. It was a map.

From his suitcase he pulled a stack of paper, which he began assembling on the kitchen table. Emily drifted off to take a shower, mumbling something about getting ready to go. Luke took Dude on a walk, and I sat down on the couch and watched Jim work.

When he was done, the entire surface of the kitchen table was a patchwork of Post-It notes and sheets of yellow paper torn from a legal pad, some of which had been stuck together with cellophane tape, others piled on top or on the bench seat in discrete piles of unknown category.

After studying his work in silent fascination for twenty minutes, I asked Jim, "So what's on the cafeteria menu at the CIA?"

"Is that a joke I'm supposed to get?"

"This is crazy. Can I approach, is it safe?"

He waved an inviting arm toward the table, grumbling, "Laugh all you want, but this is going to help."

I leaned over the table, careful not to let the trailing ends of my hair disturb any of the papers. I was looking at a dumbed-down map of the world, names and dates, events and questions grouped together by geographic commonalities.

Jim had placed Luke, Marcel, Giles, X David, Mary from MI5, and even Alice, my former roommate, in London; Ingrid was in Berlin; my would-be assassin was in Kraków, dubbed Dr. Cyanide; Paolo and Emilio Barbato were in Sardinia. The Eastern Hemisphere was reduced to those four locations.

Meanwhile, Jim had positioned himself with my neighbor, Dominique, and our boss, Beauchamp, around Washington, DC. Dom was in the center, Beauchamp was above her in what I assumed was Maryland, and Jim was below in Virginia.

Next to Dom was Harry Dowd, the man DC Metro Police had identified and indicted for trying to kill me back in April. Dowd had so far been mum on the topic of for whom he was working. In Cleveland, X Luke Killer was all alone.

Down south in Georgia was FR, denoting Marcel's U.S. base of operations for Frères Enterprises in Atlanta; and my parents and Emily were to the west in Manchester above a cluster of characters in Houston: X Lira, Tommy, and Philip. Farther west, in Albuquerque, was Stabby Hobo. Ernest and Doreen Perkins, who owned the cabin where I'd met Luke, held down the fort in Hesperus, Colorado.

The TIC was across the gulf in Colombia; and at the very bottom, X Etta, X Fernando, Marisol, and Raphael were in Argentina. Jim had certainly been channeling me when he'd categorized the Raphael painting as an actual person.

All the names had been written on individual, yellow sticky notes. On blue notes, he'd penned significant events with specific dates and stuck them as close as possible to where they'd taken place.

Between "12/7/1945: house fire" in Georgia and "6/5/2021: Holladay" in Houston, Jim had made note of perhaps two hundred dates, some of them difficult to understand because of their brevity. It took me several minutes to figure out that "12/27/2020: Italians" referred to the meeting between Marcel and Paolo's associates in London to which I'd been invited with such interesting consequences. I didn't know how Jim had been able to remember all this and realized that he must have a copy of our report to Beauchamp squirreled away somewhere.

Equally baffling was "12/29/2020: Chkpnt Charlie" in Berlin. I remembered the event, if he wanted to call it that, quite clearly, but what I couldn't figure out was why it mattered enough to take up space on his carefully ordered map.

Jim watched me study his work, probably resisting the urge to explain it all. He waited until I'd given up and plopped down on the couch before saying, "We should've been looking at this in three dimensions all along. I'd prefer it if your sister didn't get involved."

"She said she'd leave when you got here," I said, nodding in agreement.

"What have you told her?"

"Everything."

He nodded, distracted, then stopped to stare at me in disbelief. "Everything?"

"Everything."

"Why, Anna…"

"She's my sister!"

"To the FBI she's a career criminal who couldn't get a security clearance to save her life. Do you make a habit of sharing classified information with people just because they're related to you?"

"Oh, screw you," I growled.

"Yeah, screw you."

Emily's voice came through the door, and then she did. Judging by the look on her face, she'd heard quite enough to be insulted. Jim was far from repentant.

"She shouldn't have told you anything," he said calmly. "Which she already knew when she told you."

"*She's* sitting right there," Emily shot back, pointing at me.

"She said you were leaving. Where are you going?"

I knew perfectly well Jim had referred to me in the third person again to make Emily mad, but she didn't take the bait. She plopped down on the couch next to me and reverted to an attitude of serene compliance she'd perfected long ago, in dealing with our father.

"I'm going to Dallas to find work, but first I have to check in with my parole officer to make sure I don't have to stay in Red River County. Harriet Gronager. Would you like her phone number?"

Jim wasn't snowed, responding only, "We're not in Red River County."

"What do you want her to do, sleep in her car!" I cried.

"No, I want her to stay with us."

I met Emily's eyes, confirming she was as surprised as I was. She asked, "Why?"

"Tommy found Anna in Texas, and we don't know how. He's been hanging around since Luke got here, maybe even sooner if he followed Anna here. We have to assume he knows you're here, too. If you leave, he may follow you and try to get information out of you, or worse. And thanks to Anna, you've got plenty of information he might want."

"He won't follow her. He wants to talk to me," I argued weakly.

"It's obvious he can find you or Luke again whenever he feels like it."

"So wait… I'm in some kind of danger now?" Emily asked.

Churlishly, Jim answered, "Welcome to Anna's orbit."

"Oh don't you act like any of this is my fault!" I yelled.

Emily jumped to her feet, announcing, "You two are a bit much. I think I'll go find Luke."

Jim waited until the door closed behind her to ask me, "We are?"

His sincere confusion made me laugh, anger evaporating. "No one likes to listen to couples argue. It's unseemly."

"You shouldn't have told her anything, Anna."

"Well I did, and I'm sorry if she's in danger because of it, but I'm not sorry she's staying with us. What are you gonna do about it?"

Suppressing a smile, he threatened, "How about I knock some sense into you?"

"You can try."

He pulled me off the couch and shoved me toward the bedroom, trying to hide a wince of pain. Fearing he had a cracked rib or worse, I pressed my hands into his chest before he could throw me down on the bed.

"Are you hurt, or are you injured?"

He yanked me forward by the waistband of my jeans and kissed me, mumbling against my lips, "Not hurt enough to waste a few minutes of privacy."

Jim and I spent a good forty-five minutes locked in the bedroom, carefully getting reacquainted without exacerbating his bruised ribs, and emerged to find the RV still empty. Luke and Emily were outside with Dude, chatting in voices too low to hear. They looked serious, and I was tempted to eavesdrop until Emily spotted me through the window and waved me outside. Jim followed, grabbing us each a bottle of water. Emily winked broadly at him as he sat down on the bottom step.

"Don't do that," I sighed. Since we only had two chairs, I sat cross-legged in the grass, one eye on the ground in case anything tried to sneak up on me on eight legs.

"Why not?" she grinned. "I'm impressed. What are you, like forty-five?"

"Forty-two," Jim corrected placidly, adding with the barest hint of a smile, "and injured."

"You ought to spread some of this wealth around," Emily lamented, pointedly addressing the comment to Jim instead of me. "It's really not fair."

"Shut up, you filthy commie," I snapped.

I wasn't sure what she was up to, but I knew I didn't like it. She started to answer back, but I aimed a kick at her shin which she easily dodged. Jim cleared his throat to call us to order.

"Let's get something straight now. Holladay knows where we are, and he's not going away. Are we staying?"

Since he was looking at me, I answered for Luke and Emily, "Yeah."

"All right. He's keeping his distance for a reason, so someone's going to have to find that Bronco and give him a way to contact us so we can give him the all clear."

"I can do it," Emily was quick to volunteer.

Luke said, "He's already contacted us." In the face of my confusion, he added, "The letter. It had to be him."

"What letter?" Jim asked.

While Luke explained, I gazed around the quiet campground, kicking myself for not figuring it out sooner. The Bronco, the letter… What else had I missed?

"What do you think he wants?" I asked, once Luke was finished.

"Your guess is as good as mine," Jim said. "After we found out he might be alive, I tried to figure out where he went after that night last February. Rich hired the same PI who helped us find Luke. There was no trace of him in Houston, not by his name or the alias he was using then. If he's done any mischief since then he's managed to make it look like someone else." He stared at the grass between his feet, a pained look crossing his face. "I have to admit, this one caught me totally by surprise. I don't like feeling like things are getting out of my control."

"No one does," I soothed. "At least you whooped him."

He granted me a half smile and lamented, "We can't even tell Rich what's going on. No contact until this is over, unless it's a life-or-death emergency. He was very clear about that. Does anyone have a theory about how Holladay's doing this? It can be crazy, impossible, asinine, I don't care, I want to hear it."

A comically long pause followed while we all glanced at one another in uneasy ignorance. Finally I noticed Emily wriggling in her chair, obviously holding her tongue. She had no idea what was going on here, so I assumed she didn't really believe Jim wanted her two cents. Jim noticed, too.

"Just spit it out," he sighed.

"Well, it has to be some kind of GPS, right? You spies ought to be able to figure that much out."

"Dude has GPS," I answered. Jim frowned to himself but didn't say anything.

I thought back over the months of work Jim and his team had been through to track Luke from Houston to Colorado, the bewilderment that Philip had followed so close on my heels, Philip's own admission that he'd expected to find Luke, not me. Dude's GPS wouldn't have led to Luke at his motel in Houston, or more recently in Cleveland.

I could tell Jim was following the same train of thought. He stared at Emily for a while, not really seeing her, and then turned to Luke.

"You really have nothing to say?"

I was surprised to find Luke looking—What was that? Guilt? Apprehension? He met Jim's eyes briefly but decided to direct his answer at me. "I have been wondering what those guys were doing at my motel in Houston. It wasn't even in TIC territory."

"Who got there first?" Jim asked.

"I did."

"Had you been followed before that? What about after?"

"I always got away clean, until Houston."

I said, "Come on, you two. This is absurd."

"What else could it be?" Emily asked, defending her theory.

We bandied back and forth for a while, most of the arguments provided by Luke and me. I didn't want to accept such a simple answer. He, plainly, didn't want to be tagged like some kind of sea creature. In the end, though, GPS (or something along those lines) was the only thing that made sense. We had no choice but to accept it and move on to the next conundrum: Where, and in what form, was this theoretical tracking device?

We ruled out a subcutaneous transmitter, since there was never an opportunity to plant one or a mark on Luke to indicate injection. Also because that was simply beyond credulity.

It had to be something on Luke, something he wore or carried. The problem was, Luke was even more of a nomad than I was. He owned nothing, picking up and discarding possessions for mere weeks or months at a time.

Lost in thought, I rested my palms in the grass and immediately felt something crawling across my left hand. I twitched it, annoyed, not wanting to be distracted by a spider right now. My watch didn't budge, a sure sign my wrist was swollen and I needed to let the wristband out a bit, so I took it off and studied the slight indentation left behind on my skin.

The funny thing was, it didn't just hit me like a bolt of lightning; it hit all four of us at the exact same time. I was staring at my watch, the watch I slept in, bathed in, swam in, and only removed on the rarest of occasions, and suddenly I realized everyone else was staring at it, too. Emily finally pointed at it, leaving the question unspoken.

"No," Luke said firmly. "She wasn't with me."

I said, "You never take your watch off, either."

34

Saturday, June 12 to
Sunday, June 13, 2021

All eyes moved to Luke's left wrist. A bark of laughter shot out of me. There was no way, no *way* it could be that simple. Jim articulated the question first.

"Where'd you get it?"

"I'd rather not say."

"Say it anyway!"

"Lira. Took it off him after I killed him, okay? What does a dead guy need a watch for?"

"Let me see it."

Luke wordlessly removed the heavy watch and passed it to Emily, who passed it to Jim. He studied it for a moment, then took out his phone. I recognized his Googling face.

After a minute Jim said, "This model comes with an optional anti-theft device. It's worth ten thousand dollars, so I'm guessing most people take them up on it."

Emily sputtered, "Ten thousand dollars?"

"I just thought it was a nice watch," Luke mumbled, clearly miserable.

"Makes sense," I said.

I turned to Jim, expecting some more follow up questions, but his eyes had slid out of focus, and he was staring sightlessly at the watch resting across his palm. This was what I looked like, I assumed, when suspended at the apogee of a leap of intuition. I waited with bated breath for him to land.

Finally, "We never did figure out why Philip didn't blow your cover, Anna. Or kill you both."

For Emily's sake, I explained, "When I met Luke, I told him I was hiding from my ex-husband, Philip, who was really my boss. He caught up to us and parroted my cover story to Luke."

"Thanks for that," she said.

"He spooked you, and you changed your plans. You went to London. To Marcel," Jim finished, to Luke.

"You're saying that was the whole point?" Luke asked.

"It may have been."

"And once he knew I was still looking for Luke, he tried to kill me," I said.

"So it's been about Marcel this whole time?" Luke asked, skeptical.

Jim shook his head. "Not Marcel. Paolo."

"Paolo is Jim's uncle," I said in an aside to Emily.

She shook her head. "Don't waste your breath, I'm completely lost."

"You know what, I am too," I admitted.

Luke said, "Same here."

Jim said, "I need to think," and stood, climbing into the RV and shutting the door behind him. Seconds later we saw him disappear into the bedroom and heard the door shut.

"I thought we were helping," Emily pouted.

"We were," I said. "But I for one need a break. What's for lunch?"

The three of us put the whole thing out of our minds as best we could, cobbling together a meal of sandwiches, chips, and store-bought potato salad that we enjoyed outside to keep from disturbing Jim. While we ate, we talked in hushed tones about anything but business. Luke and Emily left in search of the infamous white Bronco, and Jim emerged from the bedroom to sit down at the kitchen table and pour over his map.

I desperately wanted to join him and get some clue about what he was thinking, but I didn't want to interrupt. Instead I took Dude on a circuit of the campground, then veered off down the narrow footpath that led to the river. My walk turned into a jog, then a slow, steady run. Dude kept pace easily, not questioning my impromptu flight.

Any minute now I'd plunge through a spider web and look down to find the erstwhile homeowner clinging to my torso, but I had to take the risk. After all the skulking around and hiding, running through the woods alone with nothing but Dude for protection was like a shot of pure adrenaline. I felt like I could run all day.

By my estimate we followed the river for a good two miles before turning around and heading back. By then the temperature had risen to a stuffy 90-ish degrees, and I was drenched in sweat. I worried about Dude in his thick fur coat, but an occasional dip in the river seemed to cool him down enough to enjoy the excursion. We got back to the campground around 4:00 to find Luke and Emily building a campfire to grill hamburgers for dinner.

They'd located the Bronco across the street from Walmart, but Tommy wasn't around. All they could do was write Jim's phone number on a piece of paper, stick it under a windshield wiper, and hope Tommy got the message.

I conscripted Emily into helping me give Dude a bath at the dog wash station, then left him with Luke while we showered off in the campground bathroom. It was too hot for a fire, but we sat around it anyway, finally giving in to the urge to prognosticate about what had Jim so lost in thought.

Fireflies were blinking on the periphery of our campfire, darkness fully descended, by the time Jim rejoined us. He looked exhausted, and none of us had the heart to ask him what he'd been thinking about. He didn't volunteer it, either. He merely passed Luke back his watch, grabbed a half-eaten bag of chips, and sat down in the grass in front of me, leaning on my legs. I ran a hand through his hair, wishing I could open up his head and see what was going on in his brain.

Jim's phone rang, and we all held our breath and listened on tenterhooks to his side of the call.

"Camposanto. Yes… That's right… You already know, don't you? … Lot twenty-four… I guess you'll find out when you get here."

He hung up, then stood up.

"He'll be here tomorrow at six p.m. I'm going to bed."

▼

I slept in Sunday morning, surfacing well after the sun rose. I kept my eyes closed, estimating by the heat and light in the bedroom that it was at least nine o'clock. Muted voices were in the room with me, both Jim's and Luke's. I couldn't make out what they were saying, so I enjoyed the harmony created by their voices.

Both spoke in a typical baritone register, but Luke's voice was a little bit gravelly next to Jim's silky, seductive tones. They sounded earnest and anxious, but about what in particular I could only guess. With my language infatuation, their subtly different dialects became a source of fascination: Jim's words were clipped neatly around the edges, each syllable distinct; Luke's words blended together, listing toward such bastardizations as "gonna" and "dunno." He tended to omit the subject of any given sentence, especially when angry or hurried, while Jim occasionally chopped up his sentences for effect, each word chosen so carefully.

I felt like I could listen to them forever, freed of the distraction of knowing what they were actually talking about. I heard my name, then Emily's. When I heard "Holladay," I tuned in enough to deduce they were gaming out tonight's meeting.

A hand closed gently over my ankle: Luke's hand, a gesture

I'd come to regard as a plea when he was distressed or about to make a demand of some sort.

By holding my breath, I was able to pick up the thread of the conversation.

Jim was saying, "… don't think he's planning on hurting her. He could've attacked before you or I got here. He's after something else."

"What if you're wrong?"

"We'll deal with it."

"I want to be close by," Luke said.

"That's fine with me, but I don't want him to see you."

"He'll know where I am, anyway."

"He'll know where your Rolex is," Jim corrected. "If he follows that instead, we'll have a better idea what he wants."

"Hope he wants to start something. I'm gonna kill him anyway, might as well be in self-defense."

"Don't tell me that," Jim sighed. "I'll have to testify under oath about this someday."

"Whatever, it's all hearsay."

"Do not kill him. If there's a link back to Philip, he's all we've got."

"Tell me what he did to her. I want to hear it. Emily won't tell me anything."

So quietly I barely heard, Jim replied, "You'll have to ask her. But I wish you wouldn't."

"Whatever."

They fell silent, and soon enough I could feel two pairs of eyes on me. The moment was brief, ended by Jim asking, "So are we in agreement?"

"Yeah."

"All right then, get lost."

"Make me," Luke taunted, a smile in his voice.

"You're as bad as she is."

Their volume had risen steadily, concern for my continued sleep evidently waning. Luke's grip tightened a bit, and he said my name a couple of times. I made a show of waking up, turning over and smiling sleepily at the two of them sitting there.

"Good morning." I looked from one to the other, asking, "Anyone have a quarter?"

Luke was good enough to laugh at my crass attempt at humor, but Jim wasn't amused. He stood up, sighing, "It's too early for this crap."

I thought our discussion was reasonably quiet, but before Jim could take his leave, a sharp series of knocks on the bedroom door preceded my sister calling, "When you've finished with your debauchery, some chick named Donna is at the door and wants to talk to you!"

The bed shook with Luke's laughter, but otherwise he ignored her. Since Jim was already up, he answered the summons. Luke and I sat there, both pretending not to listen, while a conversation ensued at the door.

"What's the problem?" Jim asked, not entirely friendly.

"Would yew be Mister Bowman, then?" Donna sounded downright jovial by comparison, this being just another day in the life for her.

"Sure."

"Well, I see yew've got three vehicles parked in this pad now, plus the RV. Seems like every time I go by there's a new car here. The limit is actually two, I'm afraid."

"We weren't aware of that."

"Ah. Well, I waited to come by until the space next t'yew opened up this morning. I can put it under yer reservation. It's a tent pad, thirty-five dollars per month or five dollars a night. Up t'yew."

"I think we can manage that. Thirty-five, you said?"

"Make it thirty, on account'a yer being so understanding about it." I imagined money changing hands, and Donna's crestfallen expression at the exactly $30 Jim had probably given her. Slightly less jovial, she said, "I appreciate it. Yew folks have a nice day."

"Hold on—Can I ask you a couple of quick questions?"

"Well, sure."

"There's a parking lot up front for visitors, right? Have you seen a white Bronco up there lately?"

"Don't think so. That the big, boxy one OJ drove?"

"That's the one."

"I'll keep an eye out for it. Friend of yours?"

"Not really."

She laughed, perhaps not taking him seriously. "Well, visitors don't alus park there. They're s'posed to, since this's all fer overnight only. I reckin yer Bronco might've driven in and out without me noticing. But I'll keep an eye out."

The door closed, only to open again to the sound of jangling keys as Emily and Jim both went outside to move their cars.

Emily returned first, announcing herself by banging on the bedroom door again and yelling, "If you're done defiling my sister, how about some breakfast?"

"Yeah, yeah," Luke called back, apparently comfortable in the role of cook. He got dressed, too, and soon I was alone in the bedroom, staring up at the ceiling and wishing I could be catapulted twenty-four hours into the future.

35

Sunday, June 13, 2021

At 5:00, Emily and Luke, with Dude, drove off in the Malibu and the Blazer. Their instructions were to leave the Blazer at Walmart with the Rolex in the glove box, then park a few spots away and wait for a sighting of the infamous Bronco. Luke had the gun Jim had wrestled away from Tommy—a beat up little Taurus .380—as well as my burner phone, from which he would text Jim to let us know if Tommy appeared or if anyone else descended on the Blazer.

Dude was with them for his safety, not theirs. On the off chance Tommy's real intention were to track me down and start spraying lead around, I wanted Dude as far away from the X as possible. I wanted Jim far away from it, too, but he'd hear none of it.

Come to think of it, I also wanted to be far away, but that would hardly accomplish anything.

Jim and I waited in the RV at the kitchen table, over which

he'd tossed a beach towel to hide his map. After a good quarter hour of strained silence, I asked, "Why does he want to talk to me, anyway?"

"Maybe he wants to apologize."

"Har, har."

"I don't know, Anna," he sighed.

"How did he look?"

"He seemed thinner than his picture from when he started at the FBI. He's aged quickly."

"Still shaving his head?"

"I don't know, he had a hat on."

I began plucking at a loose thread in the beach towel, musing, "He's just normal?"

"Seemed that way to me."

I lapsed back into silence. Jim moved aside the portion of beach towel that was covering the western hemisphere of his mystery map and began studying it. I couldn't tell if he was bored or onto something. Eventually his left hand covered my right hand and peeled it away from my left, with which I'd started nervously picking at my cuticles.

He seemed to be focused on either Texas or Colombia, but from my angle (roughly at the North Pole) it was hard to say for sure. The map wasn't at all to scale, but I figured he already knew that. I read his notes upside down as best as I could, noting my name was nowhere in evidence.

"Am I not on the map?"

"Couldn't decide where to put you. You're everywhere."

"Arlington, obviously."

Other than his grip on my hand tightening, he gave no response. I switched between studying him and staring uselessly at the map for a few minutes, then stretched out and rested along the bench seat with my head in his lap. I must have dozed off, because the next thing I knew, his phone was buzzing and my watch read 5:57.

"Hello?" Jim listened to the caller, the volume too low for me to make anything out. I assumed it was Luke, but after a moment he said, "Thank you, Donna," and hung up. "That was the manager," he explained. "He just pulled in. He's headed our way on foot."

I sat up slowly and rubbed my face, trying to wake up. Where my earlier anxiety had gone, I had no idea. All I felt was impatience to get this over with and move on to the next step. Whatever we intended to do with what Tommy told us, I sensed the sooner we did it, the greater our chances of success. Then again, if he was only here to get information out of us, we were all going to be sadly disappointed.

Jim went outside to head Tommy off, and I remained at the kitchen table. Conscientiously I covered the map back up, then I sat there and argued with myself.

It probably wasn't really Tommy.

But Jim wouldn't have told me so unless he was sure.

But the Tommy I knew never could have talked his way out of the mess I'd left him in.

But the Tommy I knew never would've—

The door opened and in he walked, settling my brief waffling back-and-forth. Jim was close behind, gruffly ordering

Tommy onto the couch. He sat without comment or complaint, hunching forward with his elbows on his knees, his hands tightly interwoven. Either he was nervous, or Jim had already told him exactly what to do with his hands. I assumed the latter. Jim slid onto the kitchen bench next to me, one arm along the back of the bench behind me.

Six feet apart, we studied each other in dumbfounded silence. Jim's assessment that he'd lost weight and 'aged' wasn't at all true. To my eyes, he might as well have been frozen in time from February 15 of last year until this exact moment. The only difference was his hair, which he'd allowed to grow back out to its normal length. Tommy Holladay still looked too young, too baby-faced, to have done what I knew he'd done.

He didn't seem up to meeting my eyes for more than a split second at a time, but I could see his gaze take in what little of me the kitchen table didn't block from his view.

"You look like you're doing good," he said.

As though he'd been waiting for Tommy to speak first, Jim said, "Here's how this is going to go: I ask questions, you answer them, and then you leave. Got it?"

"I came here to talk to Anna, not you."

"You could've done that all last week," Jim argued. "You've been here, haven't you?"

His answer went to me. "I didn't want to scare you. He said to stay away, so I stayed away. Give me some credit."

"That's the only reason we're still here," Jim said.

They glared at each other until I said, "Jim's not going to leave me alone with you. Sorry. Whatever you have to say, he's going to hear it."

Tommy glanced toward the back of the RV and asked, "Where's Jackson?"

"You tell us," Jim said. "That's question number one."

Tommy frowned, confused, and I added, "Tell us how you've been tracking him."

"I have no idea. He's just a dot on a map."

"You better have real answers for the rest of my questions, or you and I are going to have a problem," Jim growled.

"Are you insinuating we don't already have a problem?"

Jim gave no sign Tommy's sarcasm had annoyed him, but I could feel his patience slipping away with unusual haste. I put a hand on his knee. "Jim. I think Tommy and I should talk alone."

"No."

"I think it would be better."

"I don't care."

"Please."

His snort of impatience was perfect, probably genuine. He climbed to his feet and waited until Tommy looked up at him to say, "You've got five minutes."

It was pretty hard to slam the RV door, but Jim managed it. I let the silence following his departure deepen for thirty seconds, counting them off in my head. Just because we'd choreographed that whole Good Cop/Bad Cop display didn't mean I was comfortable with the result. A lot could happen in five minutes.

"So what did you want to tell me?" I finally asked.

"Everything. A lot more than five minutes' worth. Why don't you ask me what you want to know."

That was a tall order. What *did* I want to know?

I thought back to those months Tommy and I lived together in Houston while we prepared to infiltrate the Tres Islas Cartel; the change that had come over my partner after the new year, when training was over; the wedge our boss, Philip Levin, had driven between us; the assault that left me reeling. I'd had ample opportunity to ask about all that before Tommy and I went to that warehouse on February 15, but I hadn't; and then I'd survived and gone about my life, assuming I could find my own answers.

Remembering how narrowly I'd escaped after Francisco Lira clued us in that our identities had been uncovered, I marveled again that Tommy had made it out alive. After thinking all this over for a few seconds, I settled on, "What happened that night, after I left?"

I didn't have to tell him what night I meant. He said, "I was still coming around when they got through the door."

His words took me right back to the warehouse, to the room in which we'd been locked. Tommy lying senseless on the floor, unable to climb out with me because I'd choked him out. In self defense.

Tommy went on, "There were three of them, all armed, so I didn't see much reason to put up a fight. They dragged me into another office where Lira was waiting and sat on me. I could hear the gun shots outside. Eventually they stopped, and three other guys showed up. Lira said they got you. I didn't believe him. The six grunts left us alone.

"Lira had a lot of questions for me. I don't remember what I told him. You rang my bell pretty good… I think my speech was a little slurred, because he had trouble understanding me. He didn't torture me or anything. He didn't even seem that mad. I don't know how long he worked on me, but eventually he got fed up and left me alone. A few minutes later, I heard more shots. They were quiet, three shots one after the other. Sounded like the next office over. Lira didn't come back after that."

I couldn't help but picture Luke, target acquired, one in the chest and two in the head. No fuss no muss. He had no idea what he'd walked into, me struggling through the cold water below, Tommy dazed and abandoned in the next office. In my mind's eye, Luke took a few seconds to relieve Lira of his $10,000 Rolex before slipping away as silently as he'd entered.

He'd return to his motel, job well done, and go a solid sixteen months without any idea how special his new watch was.

[illegible]

36

Sunday, June 13, 2021

"Are you listening?" Tommy asked, exasperated.

"Yes."

"Okay. I finally realized I wasn't even tied up and started trying to get away. That's when they found Lira's body. I heard them next door yelling and carrying on, and then one of them came and grabbed me and dragged me over there. Lira was dead, shot a few times. I tried to tell them what I'd heard, but they didn't understand me. From the way they were coming at me, I figured out they thought *I'd* killed him. I thought they were going to tear me apart, but one of them had the bright idea to call their boss.

"He talked to her for a few minutes, then gave the phone to me. She spoke English and asked me what had happened. I stuck with our cover story and acted like I had no idea why they'd tried to kill us. I told the truth about the three shots I'd heard—honestly, I thought it might've been you who killed Lira, but I didn't tell her that.

"I guess she believed me, because she asked me to give the phone back to the first guy and must have told him not to kill me. They patted me down, didn't find anything, and the first guy stayed on the phone with this woman for a while. I'd give my left arm to know what they were saying.

"Anyway, after he hung up, they made me help them throw Lira's body in the river. Seemed kind of harsh, you know? But that's what we did. Then three of them tossed me in the back of an Impala, and we drove across town to a crummy little motel a few miles north of downtown. I tried asking what we were doing, but I might as well have saved my breath. Whatever they were looking for there, they didn't find it. We turned around and went right back to the warehouse."

He paused, shifting his grip so that his right thumb lay over his left, then shifting it back again as though that arrangement were too uncomfortable. It wasn't lost on me that Tommy's story had just dovetailed perfectly with Luke's.

"Well?" I prompted.

"It gets weird from here. I'm about ninety percent sure you're not going to believe me."

"Try me."

He swallowed. "Back at the warehouse… the three guys they left behind were dead. We found one at the door, and the other two in the office where Lira had been. They were all looking around, guns out, totally ignoring me, so I started to slip away. Out the back, through the loading bay.

"I was about halfway there when he came out of nowhere and shot the last three dead. None of them got a shot off. I guess after he killed Lira, he stuck around for a while. Lots of places to hide in that warehouse."

My mouth opened, and only Jim's timely appearance prevented me saying the dumbest thing I'd said in a while.

Tommy glanced at his watch, protesting, "I've got a minute and a half left!"

"Write your congressman. You okay, Anna?"

"Yeah, I'm good," I said, not taking my eyes off Tommy. He didn't look like he was inclined to continue his tale with Jim standing there. "We need five more minutes."

"Fine."

Once Jim was gone again and Tommy had finished glaring indignantly at the door, he went on.

"And he said, 'Wow, you're alive. How about that.' Those exact words. If I'd had a gun right then, I'd have shot him in the face."

The trailing end of his sentence was buried in a rush of sound that seemed to come from inside my head. For a full ten seconds I believed it, I believed Luke knew Tommy and had been keeping it from Jim and me this whole time; and then my head cleared, and I understood: Tommy wasn't talking about Luke. I'd missed something. Again.

"Anna, it was Philip. He set us up, and I can prove it."

He let that sink in, the result of which was me standing up and forcing out, "Hold that thought. Jim!"

Jim was inside within one second. How much he'd overheard, I had no idea. He stepped between me and Tommy, asking, "What happened?"

"Nothing." I wrapped one hand around Jim's arm and asked Tommy, "Can you give us a couple of minutes?"

"What, wait outside?"

"Please."

Tommy stood with a longsuffering sigh and left, pursued by Jim's command, "Don't go too far!"

Once we were alone, I let go of Jim's arm and sank back into my seat. After a summary retelling of Tommy's story, I concluded, "He claims he witnessed Philip gunning down the last of the TIC guys. He thinks Philip killed Lira, too."

Jim took about two milliseconds to draw the conclusion, "He wants us to protect him in exchange for evidence against Philip."

"Seems so. But why now, after all this time?"

"What's he been doing?"

"I don't know, we didn't get that far. I'm hoping he'll talk to both of us so I don't have to play telephone with this information dump."

Jim's response was to lean backward, craning his neck to see through the window in the door. He stood like that for a few seconds, then whispered, "He's on his phone. I don't like this. He asked where Jackson was. I'd bet the farm he's tracking that GPS signal on his phone somehow. Maybe he wants all three of us, together."

"That's a nice thought," I mumbled.

Jim opened the door and asked Tommy to come back in. Once we'd all arranged ourselves as before, Jim said simply, "You need to talk to both of us."

Tommy acquiesced immediately with a shrug. Sullen once more, he waited for a question.

"Why did you flip out on me that night?" I asked, thinking of Tommy's wild accusations right before the bullets started flying.

"I really did think Lira was the asset and you were working for the cartel. Up until I saw Philip, I thought you were the one who shot him."

"Why would you believe that?"

"Because you were with *him*," Tommy insisted, waving a hand at Jim. "Philip showed me all these travel records, passport pages with stamps in and out of Colombia every year, credit card charges, bank accounts, a boat—all these trips and assets that Camposanto never reported. He even said Lira's mom was a distant relation and that he was in contact with another one in Argentina. I bought it all, okay? I trusted him."

Offended on Jim's behalf, I cried, "That was all Philip's activity!" Except for the distant relations, but I didn't think Tommy needed to know that. "You should have trusted *me.*"

"I know that now. Why do you think I'm here?"

"Did you track Luke from Poland to Mexico?" Jim interjected. At Tommy's nod, he pressed, "Why?"

"I knew Anna would be with one of you. When I found you alone, I knew Jackson was either with her or going to her."

"How'd you know I was coming here?" I asked.

Tommy shifted fussily, confessing, "It didn't take a detective. I knew you'd go to your parents eventually, but I couldn't hang around their house without attracting attention. I decided to chill in the church parking lot, thinking maybe I could strike up a conversation with your mom and figure out where you were. Then you showed up. First stroke of good luck I've had in… I don't even know."

Clearly not buying it, Jim challenged, "There's more than one church in Manchester."

"Only one Church of Christ," Tommy countered. "You forget I know Anna just as well as you do."

Jim shot me an irritated look, asking, "Aren't they all churches of Christ?"

"It's complicated," I said.

"Why did you go to such lengths to beat Luke here?" Jim asked, dismissing my silly, protestant quibbles. "You told me you'd leave Anna alone."

"I did."

"Why?" Jim repeated, tensing. I could feel his mounting anger through his body pressed against mine. "Or maybe I should ask, what convinced you to stick to our deal?"

Meeting my eyes, Tommy answered, "I didn't want to scare you. I took one look at you and realized if I surprised you, you'd kill me."

"Smartest decision you've ever made," I snarled.

"I know you hate me, and you'll never trust me again. I'm not asking you to forget about what happened. Philip's been jerking me around for nearly two years, and I'm done. He's bad news. If he finds out I've come to you, I'm toast."

"He's in prison," Jim spat.

"He's bad news wherever he is."

▼

In another hour of questioning, Tommy filled in the contours of the story he came to tell me. After the warehouse debacle, Tommy and Philip were the last men standing. Philip hadn't left Tommy in suspense about why he'd spared his life: Tommy had a new undercover job, this time with Francisco Lira's boss, the woman Tommy had spoken to on the phone that night.

If Tommy didn't want to do it, he had the option of taking the fall for Houston instead. Tommy chose door number one. Instead of heading home to rest and recover, Tommy received a different fake identity, a white Bronco, and a GPS tracker.

Throughout his tale, Tommy never mentioned Lira's watch, and neither did Jim or I. From Tommy's perspective, the blinking red dot on a map, identified later as Luke Jackson, international assassin, had been arranged somehow by Philip, and no questions needed to be asked.

Tommy tracked the dot to Colorado but found he couldn't get within a mile of his quarry without attracting attention. The area was too remote, every human a rarity protected by leagues of open space in every direction. Philip told him to stay put, make sure Jackson did so as well, and wait for further instructions.

At that point in the story, we were forced to take a break by a phone call from Luke at 7:00 on the dot. He and Emily had seen nothing suspicious, were sick of looking at the people of Walmart, and wanted the all clear to return to the RV. Jim asked them to stay away until 8:00, refused to say why, and ended the call with Luke so brusquely that I fully expected the two of them to show up in due course, demanding to know what was going on. Tommy got back to his tale of woe.

It was during his stint in rural southwest Colorado that he began to take stock of his situation and ask himself what was really going on. Philip hadn't told him anything about Luke, not even a name, merely requiring him to conduct surveillance and allowing him to believe the blinking red dot had nothing to do with the catastrophe in Houston (a misconception Jim and I would happily have allowed to persist, if subsequent events hadn't interceded).

Not long after I arrived in Colorado to find Luke, Philip contacted Tommy and told him to leave the area. The white Bronco I'd spied was Tommy after all, heading south on Philip's instructions to the Albuquerque Sunport. Tommy flew to Miami and regularly apprised Philip of the dot's location until contact abruptly ceased on September 4, 2020—the day Philip met me at the DFW Airport, tried to ice me, and ended up in federal custody.

Given the circumstances, namely that Philip entered the secure area of an airport with a firearm and an intent to murder, I was surprised to learn Philip hadn't tipped Tommy off to the possibility that he'd be on his own for the next… forever. It all smacked of a last-minute, poorly-conceived, deliberate sacrifice. I kept these thoughts to myself, eager for some privacy with Jim.

In the absence of Philip feeding him lines, Tommy had done the only thing that made sense: He laid low, kept an eye on the red dot, and tried to figure out what happened to Philip. He reasoned that if Philip had been killed, he could finally go home and start to sort out what had happened to me and why we'd been betrayed in Houston.

Around December of last year, he discovered Philip was in prison awaiting trial for attempted murder, among other things, and he stumbled across an online article about the shooting that included fuzzy surveillance video footage of the event. He recognized me in the video and set off on his own to track me down and find out what was going on.

Months passed. All Tommy knew about me was what Philip had told him: I was working with Camposanto, and I hadn't been killed in Houston. The break Tommy needed came in the form of my face blipping onto the screen ever so briefly every time the Raphael exhibit in Kraków appeared on the news. As Jim had so kindly informed the entire world that I found the painting, the rest of the pieces fell into place all on their own.

It turned out that pesky red dot had been in Kraków at the exact same time I was. Before that, it was in Argentina, then Chile, then the United States. It spent some time in a swanky suburb of Arlington, Virginia, called Ashton Heights, so Tommy headed that way to investigate while the dot was safely out of the way in France.

There I was, and there Jim was, bold as brass, living what appeared to be a normal life in Virginia while Tommy had been stuck in Miami living under an alias and wondering what was going on. He'd decided it was high time to risk Philip's ire and re-establish contact with me.

▼

Jim and I listened to all of this without comment or question, though Jim took thorough notes. Only when Tommy was finished did Jim flip through his notes and ask a few questions.

"Why did you keep checking on the GPS tracker if you didn't think it had any connection to Anna?" Jim asked.

Sullen, Tommy answered, "Out of habit. Boredom. What else was I supposed to do?"

"What can you tell us about the woman you spoke to the night Lira was killed?"

"She sounded old. She spoke English without an accent."

"Have you left the country at all since February last year?"

"No. My passport expired."

"Did Philip confess to killing Francisco Lira?"

"No."

"Where, when, and how did you learn the identity of the red dot?"

"I don't remember. Philip must have told me at some point while I was in Miami."

Jim was out of questions after that. I couldn't think of a single thing to ask, and the closer we got to eight o'clock, the more distracted I was by hunger and Luke and Emily's imminent arrival.

37

Sunday, June 13, 2021

We left Tommy in the RV with a stern admonition to stay on the couch and not touch anything. Luke, Emily, and Dude appeared in the Malibu and parked at the adjacent tent site, and we intercepted them a few yards from the RV. I crouched down next to Dude and wrapped my arms around him, receiving a few licks and the inexpressible comfort of his warm, fluffy presence. A glance at Emily told me she was brimming with questions, but she simply rested a hand on my shoulder and said nothing.

"He in there?" Luke asked, eyeing the RV as though trying to see through its walls.

"Yes," Jim said, quickly sidestepping as Luke tried to get around him. "I'm not done with him. Cool your jets. Did you leave the Blazer at Walmart?"

Luke nodded. "No one looked twice at it. What do you mean you're not done with him? You've been in there forever, what is he, holding out?"

"He was very forthcoming," Jim said through gritted teeth, the exact source of his frustration not immediately apparent to me. "We've got a lot to talk about now, in private. But we're not getting rid of him anytime soon."

While we conferred, the sky darkened prematurely and the wind picked up. I thought the chill in my bones was a personal problem, but Emily shivered and I saw goosebumps rising on her arm. The temperature had dropped rapidly since Tommy's arrival. I glanced up, and a fat raindrop landed squarely between my eyes.

Jim decided to stick Tommy in the Kia and asked Emily to keep an eye on him from inside the RV. She agreed, and I huddled between her and Luke while Jim rousted Tommy out of the RV. No one but a blind man could have missed the way Tommy looked at Luke as he passed us. I saw recognition, dislike, and—most unnerving of all—triumph.

Luke was not impressed, throwing Tommy an emphatic middle finger before herding Emily and me toward the RV.

Once we were all settled accordingly, it was raining in earnest and the outside air was crackling with energy. Between the thunder and the thunk of raindrops, Jim had to raise his voice nearly to a shout to fill Luke in. Jim gave him the short version.

"He connected us to you with the GPS tracker when we were all in Kraków, but he doesn't seem to know that's how they found your motel in Houston. He's being cagey about how he knows your name, and either he genuinely doesn't know you killed Lira, or that's what he wants us to believe.

"To hear him tell it, he's been working for the FBI, albeit

under duress, by tracking you for Francisco Lira's boss all this time." Turning to me, Jim added, "I think he was lying about leaving the country. He said his passport was expired, but he was using an alias. I'm willing to bet he's got a fake passport, and that he's used it."

"To go where?" Luke asked.

"I've got a hunch," Jim said with a shrug. A chill crept through me, a familiar warning that Jim was withholding something. He went on, "But that kid's as mad as a hatter. If more than half of what he told us turns out to be true, I'll die of shock."

"How're we going to figure out the difference?" I grumbled.

"More importantly, how are y'all letting unstable lunatics like this work undercover with my sister?" Emily put in.

"The point was getting Anna into the operation," Jim sighed. "Tommy was an afterthought. He and Anna both passed routine psychological exams, and nothing further was required. Sometimes people fall apart. And he's got something in common with over half the serial killers the FBI's profiled."

Jim was looking at me, waiting for me to finish the thought. I wasn't really in the mood for a pop quiz, but I thought about it anyway and concluded, "One too many cracks on the head, I guess. So I broke him?" I asked, recalling when I'd delivered two such knocks on the noggin myself.

Jim shook his head. "You didn't break him. Neither did I. Whatever was wrong was wrong well before he attacked you. But like you said the day it happened, it seemed like he'd had a personality transplant. I think the real break must have happened between the time you started training and when you returned to Houston after the new year. Maybe that was when Philip convinced him I was a cartel asset. We may never know, though. He would never admit to it."

"This is some weapons-grade baloney," Luke muttered, scanning Jim's handwritten notes. "There's a lot of time unaccounted for when he claimed to be hiding in Miami."

Jim said, "From his description of the woman he spoke to, I'm thinking Regina Lira née Barber. Tommy said one of very few things that we can actually corroborate: He showed up at your motel in Houston. Regina must've known about the watch. She might've bought it for Francisco, so she'd know about the anti-theft device. Whatever Tommy's been using to track the GPS signal, he got it from Philip. That's our link between Levin and the TIC. We need it."

"Well, the Rolex is still at Walmart," Luke pointed out. "Tell him to prove he can really track me that way, and out comes the GPS tracker. Maybe we can convince him the transmitter is in the Blazer, keep the watch as our little secret for now."

Jim peered at Luke and muttered, "That's actually clever."

"Imagine that."

"Uh, guys," Emily broke in urgently. "He's talking to someone on the phone now."

A deafening snap of thunder followed her words, making us all jump. Dude, who'd been lying by the door, leapt into my lap, expressing his opinion of the noise by whimpering piteously.

Jim and Luke moved in unison toward the window to watch Tommy, and Emily scooted a little closer to me, both of us waiting silently. A low, rumbling growl settled in Dude's chest as the storm's intensity jumped that invisible line between Oklahoma in June and Tornado Alley in June.

"He hung up," Luke announced, pulling my phone from his pocket. He checked something and amended, "Or maybe he lost service. I did."

Jim and Emily checked their own phones and confirmed the campground had gone dark. Luke tossed me my phone, which I pocketed.

"Maybe a cell tower went down," I ventured.

"Good," Jim said. "If he is talking to Regina Lira, it can't be good news for us." He turned to me and asked, "How are you doing?"

I knew he wasn't concerned about my mental state. He was about to ask me to do something I wouldn't like. I sighed, "Well enough, all things considered."

"Well enough to go talk to him?"

Emily jumped to my defense, crying, "You can't ask her to do that!"

"He's asked her to do worse," Luke muttered darkly.

"What does that mean?" Emily asked me.

At that point I was feeling like a little alone time with Tommy might be a welcome relief from the three of them. At least Jim wasn't wasting all our time by coddling me. I gave Dude one last squeeze and stood.

"What do you want me to talk to him about?" I asked.

"It doesn't matter. We're stuck with him, and we all know the pretext: He wants protection. I want to know the real reason. You're the only one of us he's ever trusted."

"And you want me to get him to trust me again?"

Jim didn't have to answer. Emily spat, "You're a piece of work, Jim."

"That's been established," he said.

I left the RV to get away from their bickering. The three-second trip to the Kia left me soaked through, and I swear I could taste the ozone crackling in the air. The sky above was a sickly, poisonous green. We were in the grip of what my mother called a Lightning Death Storm. It was the last stop before an actual tornado.

I was less worried about a tornado than I was about the scrawny kid sitting alone in Jim's Kia. Nevertheless, I tapped on the passenger side window and gestured for him to unlock the doors and let me in. He complied after only a brief hesitation, and I slid into the passenger seat. The thrum of raindrops on the little car was deafening.

"So." Tommy said. He stared straight ahead, arms crossed.

"They don't trust you. But I'm guessing you weren't counting on that."

"Do they believe me? Do you?"

"I believe you," I said, leaving the first question unanswered. "I wish you'd done the same for me, when I told you about Philip. Houston might have turned out differently."

He finally turned to face me, rage burning in his eyes. "You left me for dead."

Flatly, I responded, "Sorry." We both knew I wasn't.

Seeing that he'd failed to strike fear or even regret, Tommy huffed and turned back to the windshield. "So, you and Camposanto, huh?"

"What about me and Camposanto?"

"He's in love with you. I can tell." When I didn't respond, he volunteered, "I was too, back when we first started working together. I thought you were the sexiest woman I'd ever met."

"I really don't want to hear this."

"What happened in Houston—"

"Stop. Luke will twist your head off like a chicken if I ask him to."

"Well, what did you come out here to talk about, then?"

On impulse, I lied, "Jim wanted me to ask you what you want."

"What I want?"

"For Philip. The information you're giving us."

"I don't want anything. I only want to be safe."

"You think I don't know circular reasoning when I hear it? You didn't come to us for protection for coming to us."

I let the challenge hang in the air, watching his stony profile for signs of mental movement. We all knew there was someone calling the shots from way over Philip's head. A vague suspicion that it was Francisco Lira's mother, another scion of the troubled Barber clan, wasn't enough. I wanted to hear him say it.

Stubbornly, Tommy muttered, "He'll find out what I've done, and he won't care why I did it. Prison bars aren't going to save me."

"You think Jim will?"

"I think he'd do anything for you."

Well, he was right about that, but I was missing the part where I had any reason in the world to see to it that Tommy was kept safe from Philip and the TIC. Rather than pressing my luck by asking about that, I said, "I'm starving. You?"

"I could eat."

I made an executive decision to take Tommy back to the RV with me. Though we interrupted a discussion between Luke and Jim, the latter allowed Tommy to stay while the former whipped up a feast of what he insisted was the only appropriate food to eat for dinner in a thunderstorm: grilled cheese and tomato soup. No one challenged his authority on the matter.

While Luke cooked and Emily bravely attempted casual conversation with Tommy, Jim dragged me into the bedroom and closed the door behind us. He sat on the bed to peer searchingly up at me.

"Say the word, and I'll send him packing," he said in a low voice.

Disregarding the offer, I said, "I almost got him to admit he's in contact with Regina. Or someone. He claims he's afraid of Philip, but even he knows it's not true."

"Anna, tell me you're okay."

"Quit handling me," I hissed. "What difference does it make if I'm okay? When has that *ever* made a difference to you?"

Looking like I'd slapped him, Jim wisely declined to answer.

"I am *not* afraid of Tommy, and I care just as much as you do about seeing this through. Is that good enough?" I watched his expression shift, a smile tugging at his lips, and snapped, "What?"

"I'm thinking about the power dynamic here. I'm wondering if the others see it the way I see it."

"That explains nothing."

"You know, the first time I saw you, you scared the crap out of me."

Frowning, I asked, "At the party at your house?"

"No."

I sat down next to him and said, "This better be good."

"It was right after I had them pull you out of the running for agent. I mean right after, that afternoon. It was a fluke. For once I went to the gym instead of the pool—"

"At the FBI? Why?"

"Don't laugh. Rich called me stringy. It got under my skin. I went to the gym to pump some iron."

"James Camposanto," I giggled, pressing my hand over my mouth to avoid making it sound too much like we were canoodling. Once the giggles died down, I whispered, "I had no idea you were so vain."

"Neither did I. I assume you recall that afternoon clearly."

"Sure. I was beside myself. You saw me at the gym?"

He nodded. "I walked in and saw a handful of guys all watching something, which turned out to be an unbelievably sexy redhead raining down absolute hell on a heavy bag in the corner. When I realized who you were and why you were so mad, I turned around and ran for my life."

"That's a great story. What does it have to do with this mythical 'power dynamic'?"

"Seeing how angry your sister is about what I've put you through. What she must think of me…"

"She made herself very clear on that point."

From left field, he hit me with, "Do you think I've abused my position to coerce you into a relationship?"

I burst out laughing again, and that time Jim was the one who clapped a hand over my mouth. He seemed satisfied by my response, moving his hand so I could say, "You couldn't coerce me into an armchair."

"I know. I know that, but I still think about it a lot. You know it's wrong."

"It feels right to me."

"And there has been significant coercion…"

"Not like that." I pushed him backward and straddled him, thinking all of a sudden that a little coercion was an excellent idea. "If it assuages your guilt, rest assured I don't give a crap about the psychology of it all."

I kissed him, smiling against his lips as his hands found me. Before we could really get going, someone pounded on the flimsy bedroom door.

We stopped and listened, and after a moment we heard Emily breathe through the doorframe, "If you two are in there playing doctor, I'm going to *murder* you." She raised her voice to add, "Dinner is ready."

As soon as Jim and I emerged, Luke headed for the door, announcing his intention to go get the Blazer and asking Emily to take him in the Kia. She happily obliged, leaving Jim and me alone with Tommy.

I ate my grilled cheese at the slowest pace I could manage, choosing in the awkward silence unleashed by their departure to stare at Dude.

He was sitting about a yard from Tommy, watching him eat. At first I thought he was begging, but something in his rigid posture told me he was seriously considering tearing Tommy's throat open. Tommy was making the smallest movements possible. I basked in his quiet terror until my grilled cheese was gone, then beckoned Dude over to me.

"I don't think he likes me," Tommy mumbled.

"He's an excellent judge of character," Jim said.

38

Sunday, June 13, 2021

The rain had all but ceased when Luke and Emily returned nearly an hour later. The silence in the RV had become so oppressive by that point, even Tommy seemed glad to see them. It was impossible not to notice the watch now gracing Luke's wrist, but I did my best not to stare at it as he sat across the kitchen table from Tommy and said, "Time to show us how you've been tracking me."

I saw Tommy's eyes dart down to Luke's wrist before he drew his phone from his pocket, but he made no mention of the GPS transmitter's presumed location.

"It's just an app," Tommy mumbled, swiping at his phone and passing it to Luke. I leaned over Luke's shoulder to study the screen.

It was about like I'd pictured: A little red dot was blinking slowly over a map of Southern Oklahoma. I zoomed in. Google pinpointed the K River Campground a hair to the northwest of the dot. I shoulder-surfed while Luke explored Tommy's settings and looked for other red dots, but Luke's was the only one on the globe.

Without prompting, Tommy explained, "The transmitter has a code. If you know that, you can track it with the app. It has a password, too, but some of them don't. Philip gave me the phone and told me the code and password in case I had to re-load it."

"So anyone with the code and the password can track it with this app?" I asked.

"I assume so."

"It's got to be in the Blazer," Luke concluded. He was surprisingly bad at lying, but I didn't think Tommy noticed. I couldn't help but wonder why Regina Lira hadn't changed the password, though. Maybe she couldn't, or maybe she didn't see the need.

I shared a prolonged look with Jim, deciding he was wondering the exact same thing. He seemed pleased about it for some unknowable, Jimly reason.

"So take it for a drive and see if the dot moves," Emily said. I could tell they'd rehearsed this, but my sister was a spectacular liar compared to Luke. I almost believed the transmitter *was* in the Blazer.

Jim saw fit to launch a proverbial torpedo into the conversation, saying, "But you didn't have the Blazer in Hesperus, did you?"

Though Luke's expression clearly bespoke his desire to punch Jim in the face, he only shrugged and shook his head.

I was happy to believe Tommy's subsequent honesty was the exact response Jim had been angling for.

"Guys, I know it's the watch, okay? It was at Walmart, now it's here and this guy's suddenly got bling? I'm not an idiot."

"Is there any way to muffle the signal?" Jim asked.

"How should I know?"

"Wrap it in aluminum foil," Emily suggested.

"That won't work," Jim said dismissively.

"We can at least try," I shot back.

Emily did the honors, carefully forming an aluminum foil pouch and slipping the watch inside. She folded over the opening like an envelope and, for good measure, wrapped the whole thing in another layer of foil. Luke watched Tommy's phone all the while, venting a gusty sigh of defeat after about a minute.

"It's still blinking," Luke said.

"Try moving it," Tommy suggested.

So Emily grabbed the pouch, hopped in the Blazer, and took off. We all waited in puzzled silence while she was gone, and sure enough that pesky dot never moved a millimeter. She returned about ten minutes later, describing the route she'd taken, but it didn't matter. The app thought the watch had never left the RV.

"Ha!" Emily laughed, grinning triumphantly at Jim. "The townie wins again."

"I don't know how your parents survived you two," Jim sighed.

"This better not be some kind of trick," Luke told Tommy. "That dot could be pointed at you, for all we know."

"How did I know you were in Mexico, then, huh?" he fired back.

"Dumb luck."

"There's enough of that going around," Tommy scoffed.

"Shut up."

"Both of you shut up," Jim snapped. "We've all had a long day. Chill out." He waited, giving us a chance to refuse to do so. When no one spoke, he continued, "I think for safety's sake, we should move the girls—" Emily and I snarled in unison, forcing him to correct himself. "—Anna and Emily out of the RV. If this watch is a target, we don't all need to hang out within five feet of it."

Various expressions of assent issued from all of us, even Tommy. I certainly wasn't too liberated to accept sexism when it worked in my favor.

Jim called Donna and explained in his implacable way why we needed to rent a cabin immediately and couldn't wait until morning. I told Jim to sweeten the deal with the promise of some cold hard cash, and Donna offered us a cabin across the campground from our RV pad. It was even pet friendly.

Though it felt a bit like a break up, I was excited to put some room between myself and Tommy's baleful presence. Jim brought over the papers he'd laid out on the RV's kitchen table and rearranged them on the table next to the cabin's token armchair, the better to keep his work away from Tommy. I sat on the bed and watched him arrange everything, and Emily took a lightning-fast shower and departed for the RV to make sure Luke didn't decide to murder Tommy. So much for the separation of the sexes.

Though it was late and I was beyond tired, I grudgingly approached the table to take a fresh look at Jim's notes. He was studying them again, looking troubled.

I asked, "Are you ever going to tell us what you thought of the other night? Something about Paolo?"

"Maybe. I'm not sure it's really anything… and not to be rude, but I don't need a bunch of random guesses and wild theories flying at me to confuse the issue."

"I didn't realize we were such a burden," I grumbled.

"Do this for me: Look over my notes from talking to Tommy and tell me which parts you think are true. Get Emily to help. Obviously Luke and I can't discuss it in front of Tommy. Are you listening?"

My gaze snapped back to meet his, having drifted across his face to alight dreamily on his temples. Was I so enamored with Jim's ever more numerous grey hairs because I was—according to him—personally responsible for them? He seemed to hear my wandering thoughts and was on the verge of laughing at me, but he caught himself. He wrapped one arm around my shoulders and planted a very chaste kiss on my temple.

He whispered, "We probably shouldn't test your sister's patience any more."

"Hnnng."

He left me alone with his notes, which I poured over again, hardly noticing when Emily came in and started meandering around the tiny cabin doing who knew what. On the sticky note bearing his own name, Jim had added "/Anna & Dude," which made my tummy do a goofy little somersault.

After setting up the map in its new location, Jim had placed a bottle cap above my parents, which I assumed marked our location in Moyers, Oklahoma. The map really wasn't to scale.

I read through all the names again, then crossed my eyes slightly and tried to only pick out the names with an 'X', which it didn't take a genius to interpret. They were people who'd died—most of them violently. That didn't cause any flashes of intuition, not that I'd expected it to.

Again my gaze was drawn to "12/29/2020: Chkpnt Charlie" in Berlin. Jim had taken me to see Checkpoint Charlie before meeting Ingrid, merely for the sake of interest, and he'd captured the attention of some drunk passerby when he'd tried to kiss me. Did he think the drunk guy was significant? The inebriate was the only material difference between that occasion and the point later in the night, when Jim had pushed me up against a wall and…

"Bedtime, young lady," Emily proclaimed, her voice seeming to cut through time and space to Berlin, to which my mind (and other parts) had absconded. I shook my head, not in answer but to clear out those thoughts and feelings.

Cuddled up together in the cabin's queen sized bed while the rain raged on, we did as Jim instructed and studied his notes for traces of honesty. When we finally called it a night around 1:00 a.m., Emily had penned a list of questions and observations for Jim's review:

- Tommy didn't see who shot Lira. Had no idea it was
   Luke, so he decided it was Philip. Might be a big fat

lie.

- Someone called the boss (Regina?), and that's how they discovered the watch was missing and tracked Luke down.
- So if Philip was supposed to have killed Lira, y did his mom send Philip after Anna/revenge? Hasty. Makes no sense. They know it wasn't Philip.
- He has to remember what Lira asked him?!
- Bet the part where he's getting 2nd thots in CO is true.
- If Tommy left with TIC guys to go to motel, why didn't we see him on the security camera like we saw Luke? Why didn't we see Philip?

39

Monday, June 14, 2021

While I would have preferred to wake up as an Anna sandwich with Luke and Jim as the bread, waking up next to my sister was nice, too. I felt safe with her, even if it were an illusion. Add in Dude curled up between our feet at the end of the bed, and I was quite satisfied with the arrangement.

I had been unpleasantly surprised by Emily's reaction to learning of my situationship with Jim and Luke. Of all the weird, illegal, and downright self-destructive things she'd done, it was a bit rich for her to act morally superior now. Without moving my inert, obscenely comfortable body, I scoffed quietly at her attitude. She was just jealous.

She was also, apparently, not in bed. At my quiet scoff, she asked from the vicinity of the kitchen, "What's funny?"

"Holy moly," I laughed, sitting up to marvel at her. "You're awake? Before me?"

"I couldn't stop thinking about these notes. I want to talk

to Jim."

"You're really invested in this, aren't you?" To her wordless, distracted noise of agreement, I answered, "Well, I'm glad you're here. You see things differently."

"Nowhere else I'd rather be."

"You and Luke are getting along nicely, don't you think?"

"Yeah, he'd be a real catch if you could stop emotionally waterboarding him for five minutes."

"Wo-o-w. Tell me how you really feel, Ems."

"It's not fair, okay? You obviously love Jim, though God himself only knows why. You're dragging Luke behind you because you can't let go."

"Excuse me, this whole arrangement was their idea," I defended, my voice rising a full octave.

"Yeah, but you don't know what the real arrangement is."

I stared at her, willing her to look at me and explain, but she was gazing resolutely at Jim's notes and refused to meet my eyes. Finally I slipped out of bed and snapped, "I think I'll go enjoy a nice, judgment-free shower."

"I'll still be judging you," she called after my retreating figure. Always had to have the last word.

All my warm, sisterly feelings thus dispensed with, I raced through the shower and departed in frosty silence for the RV. On the way there, I passed Luke, whose automatic smile of greeting faltered when he saw my expression.

"What's eating you?" he asked.

Brushing past him, I said, "You were warned. We don't keep secrets from each other."

He must have understood my meaning, because when I turned back at the RV door, I saw him knocking on the door to the cabin, his body language conveying obvious anger. Good, Emily was in trouble, too.

I let myself into the RV, managing not to wake Tommy, who was sleeping in the loft. Jim was still in bed, reading the paperback I'd finished days ago and looking very mature indeed with a pair of reading glasses perched on his nose. He whipped them off as soon as I opened the door.

"I didn't know you wore glasses," I said, softly shutting the door behind me.

"Surprise. What's wrong?"

"Tell me what you and Luke decided in Albuquerque."

"… Is it not obvious?"

"The truth, please. Luke told Emily something. Something about an arrangement."

He vented a burst of anger in a quick, forceful sigh, then composed himself. After a few moments to deliberate, he asked, "You know how to play chicken, right?"

"Yeah…"

"That's what we were doing. That was the arrangement."

"I don't understand," I lied, now wishing I hadn't even asked.

"We both figured whoever held out the longest would win it all. First one to ask you to choose would get a bus ticket."

"Stop mixing metaphors, you're making no sense."

"Don't stand there and lie to me and act like you don't understand what I'm telling you."

"Don't be so mean."

He stood up, came around the bed, and got right in my face. Clad only in a pair of boxer briefs, he achieved that unlikely mix of sexuality and aggression that always set me back on my heels. At this distance, his ten-inch height advantage was at its most pronounced. I stared at his clavicle, cowed for the moment.

"*I'm* mean?" he demanded in a low voice. He walked back his tone a bit, tugging on a lock of my hair. "I thought you liked that."

"Stop it."

"Look at me."

"Jim…"

He tilted my chin up, putting a lot of effort into being gentle about it. Once I'd unwillingly met his eyes, he whispered, "Are you mine?" I nodded, and he pressed, "Say it."

"You really are piece of work, James Camposanto," I breathed, the fondness in my voice somewhat undermining the insult.

He smiled. "Close enough." To his credit, he didn't try to close the deal with Tommy sleeping mere feet away. Instead, he kissed me and said, "Let me get dressed, then we can go talk to Luke and Emily. You looked over my notes, right?"

I nodded. "As ordered."

"Good."

Leaving Tommy asleep in the RV (but taking the keys with us), we walked over to the cabin to find Luke and Emily hunched over the kitchen table, studying Jim's map of notes. Without looking up, Luke said, "There was a back way out of the warehouse. Thought you knew."

I recalled the loading bay at the back of the warehouse, which Tommy mentioned yesterday, but Luke's statement didn't have much impact. Jim and I looked at each other and shrugged.

"Apropos of…?" Jim asked.

"Their notes asked why we didn't see Tommy leave with the TIC guys on their way to the motel. They must have left out the back way."

He tapped a piece of paper on the table, inducing Jim and me to take a closer look.

"Here's the gravel road around back of the warehouses. There's a road that runs from the gravel road to the next pier over, where I left my car. There's a big cottonwood right where the ruts leave the gravel road. That's where I hid while the lead was flying."

"If you knew about the back entrance, why'd you come and go through the front door?" Jim asked.

"No one guarding it," he shrugged. "They were all around back. Guess they figured no one would be dumb enough to knock on the front door."

"Except Tommy and me," I groused.

Jim said, "We didn't know about the other road. How did you know?"

"Reconnoitering, bro."

Jim looked up at the ceiling as though it might hold more clues. He sighed again. "It doesn't matter. It's interesting, sure, but it doesn't help us prove or disprove Tommy's story."

We all stared at the hand-drawn map, waiting for more revelations to leap out at us. Idly, Luke flipped back to the page with Emily's notes and read through them. Whatever occurred to him, he voiced it only by saying, "I think it's time to beat the truth out of Holladay."

"Second," Emily said.

"This is not a democracy," Jim gritted.

"Well, consider this a military coup," Luke said, standing up and seeming to inflate a little as Jim rounded on him. "I'm going to have a talk with him."

"I'm asking you to wait."

"Why did you let him know we knew the transmitter was in the watch?" Luke demanded. "You're up to something, and I know for a fact the rest of us aren't going to like it."

"You're the one who took the watch," Jim replied, unruffled, as he flipped the map over to look at the notes Emily had written. While Luke was still struggling to reply, Jim pointed to something and asked Emily, "What do you mean by 'hasty'?"

"Anna said it didn't seem well thought out, the way Philip came at her at the airport. Public, tight security, innocent bystanders…"

I nodded, adding, "I always felt like it wasn't meant to succeed, or he was meant to get arrested or killed."

"Maybe Regina wanted to take you both out of the equation at once," Luke suggested.

"But not Tommy," I said.

"How's that?"

"Well, if she gave Philip the code and password for the watch, then cut him loose, why didn't she change the password? She had to have known he gave it to Tommy."

After a protracted silence, Jim said only, "Huh."

Something darted before my mind's eye, like a tiny bird, a flash of intuition too fleeting to understand. Jim saw the absent look on my face and fell silent, letting me think. I reviewed the last few seconds of conversation, then said slowly, "Suppose… suppose something happened. Between Regina and Philip. A break. She traded out Philip for Tommy."

"To what end?" Jim asked. "Philip was ideally placed at the FBI, and Tommy's completely burned. He's one layer of red tape away from being officially dead."

I shook my head. "I have no idea. But you know what happened around the same time, right?"

It was my turn to let Jim think. He got there faster than I would have. "Luke got his next assignment from Marcel. Fernando and Mari."

"Regina's niece and nephew," I supplied.

He asked, "So she punishes Philip? How is that Philip's fault, when Marcel and Paolo are the ones picking targets? And how would she even know about that?"

I admitted, "I don't know. It's half an idea. One quarter."

Luke reminded us of his presence by pressing, "Tommy can answer that."

Stubbornly, Jim said, "He will. Not yet."

For a moment it looked as though Luke would relent, but in a heartbeat he'd turned and headed for the door, Jim close on his heels.

40

Monday, June 14, 2021

Emily and I remained rooted to the spot. We each knew the other had no interest in getting in the middle of Jim and Luke's spat. I privately hoped Luke would prevail, by dint of physical superiority if all else failed, but I worried how far Jim would go to argue the point.

A rustle of paper told me Emily had flipped back to the map and was trying to absorb what she could from it, no doubt warring with a characteristic desire to ignore things she didn't understand. My gaze was fixed on the door, all senses straining to pick up some clue about what was happening on the other side of it.

At length, she asked, "So, are they gonna fight, or what?"

"Jim and Luke? Probably not. Jim won't even fight me." I scanned the map, then met her eyes. She looked either worried or excited. It was hard to tell with Emily. "Do you want to go check on them?"

"Yep."

We left Dude inside and stepped out into the sauna. By my guess it was approximately 200 degrees outside at 11,000% humidity, and it wasn't even noon. I made an involuntary noise of disgust as my pores immediately unleashed moisture all over my body.

Jim and Luke were at a standstill about halfway between the RV and the cabin, on the shoulder of the gravel road that encircled the campground. Even from a distance I could see there was nothing to worry about. They were having a heated discussion, not a wrestling match. Emily and I lagged back, half-hidden behind a tree, and watched them. They didn't appear to be reaching any sort of agreement.

I looked past them and focused on the RV, from which I knew Tommy could see the same thing Emily and I saw, if he cared to look through the windshield. In the same moment I realized this, I saw the RV door open. Tommy slipped out, walked behind the RV, and disappeared. Emily saw it too.

"Now where the heck is he going?" she asked.

"I'll find out. Lock the door and stay in there with Dude. Just in case."

Emily hurried back to the cabin, and I cut into the woods on a course that would put me in Tommy's path, assuming he didn't turn left or right. I made it all the way to the river without spotting him and stood on the bank of the swollen and muddy waterway. While I was trying to decide what to do next, some instinct warned me to turn around.

There in the shadows of the overhanging trees was Tommy, apparently alone. I fought back an urge to run away and wondered how long he'd been standing there. I cleared my throat.

"What's up?" I asked, trying to sound nonchalant.

"I saw Jackson and Camposanto arguing. It's bad news for me, isn't it?"

"Are you taking off?" I challenged.

"Am I safe here, or not?"

"Look, we know you're not telling us everything. You'd be in a better position if you told the truth."

"You told me you believed me."

"Jim changed my mind," I fibbed, happy to throw Jim under the bus. "He's always right."

"I told you everything you need to know. You're calling me a liar."

I felt a brief stab of panic. I didn't like the look in Tommy's eyes one little bit. If he came at me again, I'd have to kill him, and then where would we be?

We both turned at the same time toward a rustling sound in the trees. Dude emerged from the brush, threw a meaningful look at Tommy, and then sat down on my feet. Emily must have let him out, knowing he'd come find me. I made a mental note to ream her out for leaving herself vulnerable.

Tommy took in Dude's steady, confident stare, and his pre-attack posture relaxed.

Trying to sound kind, I said, "Come back to the RV. I won't let Luke hurt you, I promise."

"So he does want to beat the crap out of me."

"They all know what you did to me, Tommy. At a word from Jim, they'd get in line."

"I should never have come here…"

"It's a bit late for second thoughts. Let's go."

With Tommy in the lead, Dude in the middle, and me bringing up the rear, we tramped back through the woods to the RV and found Jim and Luke in a state of mutual but restrained panic. Luke made a beeline for Tommy immediately, and I stepped between them.

"He came to us for protection, Luke. Leave him alone."

"At least let me take his phone. We all know he's been talking to—someone."

I turned to Tommy and held out my hand. "He's right."

Fuming, Tommy fished out his phone and slapped it into my hand. At the *smack* of plastic on my palm, Dude took a step toward Tommy and issued a low bark of warning.

"It's okay, Dude," I cooed. I passed the phone to Luke, who handed it to Jim in a surprising display of deference.

"So I guess I'm your prisoner now, huh?" Tommy asked.

Jim opened the door to the RV and waved him inside. "Beats Guantanamo Bay."

I left Dude at the RV-slash-prison and rushed back to the cabin to let Emily know everyone was okay. She was sitting at the kitchen table, nose-to-notes again, and jerked her head up when I walked in. Forgetting to yell at her for letting Dude out, I flashed her a thumbs up, and she relaxed a bit.

Sliding her hands into her hair, she groaned, "What I wouldn't give for an edible right now."

"Ah… How about some coffee instead?"

"That's literally the opposite. But okay."

I busied myself with the coffee and pictured the notes Emily was pouring over. Last night, she'd been the one to posit that Regina Lira had sent Philip after me. To her, that point was beyond argument, but Jim didn't seem convinced. I thought I knew why: If Luke being instructed to target her niece and nephew was what set her off, how did she even know? Why hadn't she made a move to protect them?

My brain skipped like an old record as the coffee pot farted out a burst of steam. My bullet train of thought derailed, and I gave up on the thinking for a while and contented myself to sip coffee and answer Emily's questions while she familiarized herself with Jim's map.

"He is… thorough," she mused, peeling up a sticky note that was covered in tiny writing that continued onto the note underneath it.

"You don't know the half of it."

"You mad?"

She came out of nowhere, deliberately catching me off guard, and I blurted, "At Luke and Jim? No. Was Luke mad at you for telling me?"

"Not really. I could tell he wanted to be, but he was more… resigned. He's kinda cute when he's pretending not to be mad."

A clap of thunder saved me from thinking of an answer to that. Instead I sighed, "Here we go again."

"Getting started early today," Emily remarked without interest. I agreed.

It was barely 3:30, and generally the inclement weather didn't start until around dusk. Like me, Emily wasn't going to waste any anxiety until we heard tornado sirens. We went back to our study, and the hours slipped by without drawing much notice. At the very moment I checked my watch again and saw 6:48, someone knocked on the door. Emily was first to her feet to answer it.

As soon as she opened the door, Dude bounded inside and dove under the kitchen table, sticking his nose between my knees. I had to throw my arms over the table to keep Jim's notes from scattering in the rush of wind from outside. Only then did I realize the storm was getting awfully violent.

Jim, Luke, and Tommy filed inside, and Emily required Luke's help to get the door shut against the gale.

"We figured it was safer in here, in case there's a tornado," Luke explained. "We battened down the hatches in the RV and found this."

He nodded at Jim, who held up two, full handles of cheap scotch whiskey. I laughed out loud. "That's got to be a decade old. Aaron switched to vodka a long time ago. Must have forgotten he hid it in the RV."

Nodding sagely, Emily added, "He was like a squirrel, except with cheap booze."

Seeing that neither Emily nor I was objecting to their intrusion, Jim went about finding five glasses and distributing the rotgut. He even offered Tommy a glass, nodding curtly at Tommy's mumbled, "Thanks."

I took an experimental sip and waited for the traditional whiskey spasm to rack my body before coughing, "Beats a hard kick to the face."

"That's the spirit. Cheers," Jim said before tipping back his glass and emptying it in one swallow. He shuddered, poured himself a refill, and joined me at the table in the seat Emily had vacated.

As soon as he sat down, I leaned toward him and pointed at Emily's notes to ask at a whisper, "What do you think about Regina being the one who sent Philip after me?"

Without hesitation, he said, "I'd come to the same conclusion."

"And you kept this to yourself because…?"

"Obviously, to see if anyone else did."

"Nice to know you're treating this like a middle school science fair experiment."

"We can't afford to rush this, Anna," he said in an aggravatingly stern tone. I felt my internal temperature rising, but I kept my voice low enough to exclude eavesdroppers.

"Don't you talk down to me," I snapped. "I'll rush if I want to. I'll rush harder."

I could've sworn he started to smile but hurriedly quelled the reaction.

"Do what you want," he dismissed.

After another hit of cheap whiskey, I asked, "Anything else you're keeping up your sleeve?"

"The answer to that will never be no."

"What are you two whispering about over there?" Luke called from the kitchen, where he and Emily seemed to be in the middle of a discussion centered around a box of brownie mix.

I responded with an unsubtle glance at Tommy, who was

skulking in a chair by the door, and Luke accepted that as an answer. He and Emily whipped up a batch of brownies, and then Emily found a deck of cards and decreed that we would play Spades. She'd chosen a four-player game that precluded the necessity of inviting our unhappy guest to play, and no one mentioned it.

As I drank and played, severely handicapped by having Luke as a partner (he really was a terrible liar), I began to be aware of a sensation of longing that was growing in strength in direct proportion to the wildness of the storm outside. After a whiff of Jim's hair gel, I groaned out loud and realized I was mad as a March hare. The whiskey wasn't helping.

"Uh… you okay, Sis?" Emily asked.

I caught a look as it passed between Luke and Jim, and that only made it worse. I stood up with every intention of dashing to the RV and hoping Luke or Jim (I honestly didn't care which) followed, but I didn't get any farther before multiple cell phones erupted into an earsplitting chorus of emergency screeches.

Emily and I checked the alerts on our phones and silenced them. Jim did the same with his own phone, asking the table at large, "Which is worse, a warning or a watch?"

We all fell silent, unconsciously straining our ears while we tried to remember. Far in the distance, so quiet I could bare-ly make it out, a tornado siren droned urgently. Jim and Emily didn't seem to hear it, but one look at Luke told me he did.

"What do we do?" Luke asked.

Before anyone could answer, three things happened at the exact same time: Jim pulled Tommy's phone from his pocket, the emergency tone blared again, and Tommy jumped to his feet.

"Sit down, Holladay!" Luke ordered, almost drowning out Jim's slightly whiskey-befuddled complaint that he couldn't shut off the alert on Tommy's phone. The screech erupted again, and that time we all realized it was coming from Tommy.

"He has another phone!" Emily cried.

Tommy ripped open the cabin door, which was nearly torn from its hinges as rain and gale-force winds rushed greedily inside. Dude, no longer able to control his panic, jumped to his feet and ran into the bathroom, tripping Luke on the way as he lunged forward to stop Tommy. Already on my feet, I was closest to the door and followed without a thought as Tommy threw himself into the driving rain.

41

Monday, June 14, 2021

I could feel the rumble coming through the ground now, like a hundred freight trains in the distance, a living sound that seemed to reach out and grab me. Through the rain, I could see the sky had again taken on a green tint. Lighting flashed at irregular intervals, thunder rolling together and bowing before the onslaught barreling down on the campground.

Looking around for some sign of Tommy, I got my first sight of the funnel cloud beyond the alfalfa field across the highway. It hadn't touched down yet, so it was still a milky white color untainted by the mud and debris soon to be caught up in it. Whipping erratically like the tail of some enormous beast, it stood out clearly against the gray-green sky and charcoal clouds. Every time it snapped downward, it was closer to the ground.

Distracted by this taunting dance, I forgot why I was standing outside getting soaked to the bone and lashed with twigs and leaves. Then someone crashed into me from behind and I heard

Jim's voice, thin underneath the hammering rain.

"Get back inside, I'll deal with him!"

With a dragon roar, the funnel cloud met the ground. When I looked again, the spinning wall had turned muddy grey and had doubled in width. I turned to answer Jim and found myself standing alone, which gave me a moment's pause. Had he already taken off in pursuit of Tommy, or had he been plucked off the ground by a freak finger of wind?

I set off at a jog in the direction I'd last spotted Tommy and soon collided with something solid again. This time it was a tree, and I pressed myself against it and tried to get my bearings. I saw Emily's Malibu, which forced me to adjust my perception so rapidly it made me sea sick: I thought I'd been running north, but I'd gone straight west, and not very far.

As soon as I realized this, I saw the driver's side door standing open and Tommy crouched on the ground next to the car, his head and arms under the steering column. He was hot-wiring Emily's car.

I looked around, didn't see Jim or Luke or anyone else at all, and experienced one of those sudden bursts of inspiration that always, *always* get me in trouble. Tommy clearly didn't see me, so I walked around to the back of the car and tried the trunk release. The trunk popped open, the sound completely lost in the storm. I curled up inside and closed the door behind me.

Why? Because no matter what Tommy was up to, it was information, and information was what we needed. I heard the engine roll to life and a faint snap as the driver's door closed. Then we were moving.

I pulled out my phone and turned off emergency alerts. I silenced it and texted Jim to let him know where I was, then I shared my location with his phone. As soon as I was done, he responded to my text with words so predicable I nearly gave myself away by laughing out loud.

"Ever heard of impulse control?"

Glad he was okay, I chose to read the loving subtext behind his words and texted back, "Just ride it out. By the time the storm's over, we'll know where Tommy really wants to be. Give Dude a hug from me."

No answer. I opened Google Maps and watched our progress as Tommy navigated out of the campground and onto the highway. He headed south, and within 15 minutes the roar of the tornado had faded to a whisper behind us. Gradually even the rain let up, and all I could hear was the rush of the road passing beneath us.

▼

It took two and a half hours to get to DFW Airport, where I watched on Google Maps as Tommy weaved through the airport and stopped the car in long-term parking. I hadn't received any more texts from Jim, but I knew he was watching our progress too and was working out what to do. Ideally he'd gotten everyone into the Blazer and set off after us, but who knew? Maybe the tornado had ripped through the cabin and killed them all.

I winced, banishing the unhelpfully macabre thought. On the bright side of things, I was soaking wet and utterly miserable in the cramped coffin of the Malibu's trunk.

Tommy got out and shut the door behind him, leaving me dithering. Jump out now and confront him, or try to see where he was going? I chose the latter, tugging at the emergency trunk release when I hoped he was far enough away. I helped myself to the contents of a plastic bag Emily had either lazily or negligently left in the back seat: an unopened package of cheap underwear, two plain white t-shirts, and a pair of athletic leggings.

I grabbed an old backpack from the trunk and filled it with the clothes, a discarded hairbrush I prayed was my sister's, and her bundle of hotel toiletries. I couldn't believe my sister's sloppiness had netted me so many handy items, when I'd spent so much of my life decrying it.

Feeling self-conscious in my soggy clothes and generally disheveled appearance, I reached the air-conditioned haven of the airport's interior and scanned the crowd for Tommy. I spotted him ducking into a men's restroom and decided I had time to go into the women's side to clean myself up. Something told me I wouldn't get far looking like I swam to the airport.

When I came back out in my clean clothes and partially blow-dried hair, Tommy was near the front of a line at the American Airlines counter, nervously scanning the crowd while he waited his turn. I stepped behind a concrete pillar as his gaze swept in my direction.

I gave him a few minutes, then joined the queue as Tommy was power walking away. I thought I spotted a boarding pass in his hand. My phone buzzed, and I eagerly read the text from Jim.

"Airport?"

I texted back, "Yes, he bought a ticket. Everyone ok?"

"We're fine. Where to?"

"No idea. Following."

"Please don't follow him onto a plane. Wait for me."

"I'll stall him."

By the time I reached the front of the line, I'd abandoned any hope of getting information out of the ticketing agent and simply bought a ticket to Houston, gambling that I could get through security and then change my ticket to wherever Tommy was going.

Several hundred dollars later, I was in line at the security checkpoint. I had no idea if my latest fake ID was good enough to get me through airport security, but I had to try. If Tommy were leaving the United States, I was out of luck. Beauchamp's last gift had not included passports.

My harried state and falsified driver's license didn't raise any TSA eyebrows. I set off on a loop of the central concourse, hoping I'd see Tommy before he saw me, but there the luck of the Irish ran out. He'd planted himself at the first gate with a good view of the passengers exiting security, and I didn't notice him until he'd jumped to his feet and started toward the exit.

I caught up to him, grabbed his sleeve, and jerked him to a stop. "Tommy, stop. Look at me."

"Leave me alone."

"Obviously I'm not going to do that."

He twisted out of my grip but turned around, snarling,

"You don't understand."

"Duh. Why do you think I followed you?"

"Don't you know when to give up?"

"I'll let you know when the urge takes me. Why don't you let me buy you a drink, or do you have a flight to catch?"

Tellingly, his gaze flicked behind me, not toward the gate where he'd been sitting but toward the opposite arm of the concourse. I'd already read the sign and knew the international flights all departed from that side. Crap.

Taking a wild leap of faith, I asked, "What's in Colombia?"

His eyes widened, confirming my suspicion. "Regina," he said, leaving it at that.

Inwardly I crowed, forcing my expression to remain politely curious. "Regrouping?"

"She told me to find out what you know, then get out. I could tell Jackson suspected something. He was going to get it out of me one way or another. I don't want to go back to her."

"So don't."

"I thought I might be safe with you. You said you believed me."

Sensing the truth was about to be mine at last, I pressed, "Can we please sit down somewhere? I'm dehydrated and hungry and a little sick from that cheap whiskey."

He relented, meaning either his flight didn't leave for a while or he was toying with the idea of letting it leave without him. I scanned the departures board as we walked toward a restaurant and saw that the next flight to Colombia (Bogotá) departed in seven hours.

I asked for a booth in the far corner of the restaurant, we ordered drinks, and while we waited for them we stared at each other. He seemed to be deflating before my very eyes, dreading the arrival of his beer as much as I longed for my iced tea. When it arrived, I sucked down half of it and gave myself a serious brain freeze before diving in.

"You've been communicating with Regina this whole time?" I asked.

"Yes."

"I did believe you, you know. Jim was the one who saw through your lies."

"How?"

"He's smarter than both of us put together," I assured him. "You want him on your side. Trust me."

"That's why I lied. No way any of you are gonna trust me now. No way."

"Let's set the bar a little lower than that. Tell me the truth, and we can work something out. I mean, we're talking about the FBI here. They can take care of you."

"Why start now?"

"Okay… fair enough. *We* can take care of you. We may not like or trust each other, but sometimes it's enough to need each other. Take Luke and me. When we met, I thought there was a pretty good chance he'd try to kill me. I thought he might've killed *you*. We got along okay."

I sucked my iced tea dry while he pondered this, and the waitress ambled over to offer a refill. I demurred, asking for a martini instead. Her appearance seemed to remind Tommy he had a beer in front of him, and he took a few fortifying gulps.

His next words were directed at the salt shaker.

"It happened like I said, from when you left the warehouse to when Philip sent me to Miami to when I went to Virginia to find you. It's just that I knew it was a lie from day one. I knew what Philip had me doing wasn't part of an FBI operation. I knew he was—but I guess you already knew I was lying about all that."

"Why did you take the back road when you left the warehouse?"

Again he displayed shock at how much I'd already guessed, asking, "You knew about that?"

"We worked it out, Sherlock style."

"They didn't say why. Or, I don't know, maybe they did. It was all Spanish. The guy in the passenger seat, the one in charge, he called her again when we got to the motel and didn't find anything. We went back, and they tied me to the same chair where Lira'd interrogated me. I fell asleep, and when I woke up, he was there. Philip. He untied me, put me back in the Impala, and we left. He told me they were all dead. Regina told him to kill them all. He stuffed their bodies in crates and left them in the warehouse."

42

Monday, June 14, 2021

Again the waitress reappeared. I saw her glance between Tommy and me, sensing and mimicking our tension. Rather than prying, she wisely left us alone. I sipped at my martini, trying to make it last.

"Lira was her son," Tommy went on. "They let him get killed, so I guess they had to go, too. Philip drove me back to our duplex, lying the entire way. He said Regina Lira was the asset, not Francisco. He said I'd assumed it was Francisco because I didn't know of any other Liras. He said I had to help them track down the guy who'd killed her son. He made me pack some stuff and stuck me in a motel to 'await further instructions.' That was the last time I ever saw him."

"So you've known all along that it was Luke who killed Francisco, not Philip."

"I—" he stammered, knocking back an uncomfortable-looking draught of beer. I sipped at my own martini while he recovered from his dismay. Apparently I wasn't supposed to know that. "I didn't know until recently."

I shook my head, growing angry again. "You knew immediately that it wasn't Philip. Why would Regina have him mop everything up if he was the one who killed her son?"

"Okay, I lied about that. I didn't think you all knew about Regina."

"Don't you sit there and try to make this a two-way exchange of information. You came in with lies and made everyone mad and now you're still playing some kind of game."

He looked furious, refusing to answer, so I backtracked.

"How'd you know Philip was lying about the operation?"

Tommy thought for a moment, then said, "I guess because he killed those guys. Maybe because he said I couldn't go back to DC. I don't really know how I knew, but I knew. And I knew everything he'd said about you and Camposanto was a lie, too.

"But what could I do? I thought you were dead, I didn't know why I wasn't dead too, and I had nowhere to go. I hung out at the motel in Houston until a package arrived. It was March twenty-second. Cash, ID, keys, the typical stuff. The main thing was the phone. One little note, that was it as far as instructions: 'Call me,' and a phone number.

"He told me to drive to Colorado where this dot was blinking, check out the area, stay with it if it moved, but otherwise keep my distance. Of course I knew it had to be the person who'd killed Lira. I kind of wondered if it was you, if you were alive, but I was too scared to get close and find out.

"Couple months go by, and he tells me to leave. Go to Miami. I didn't know why I was there. Philip wouldn't tell me anything, and as far as I could tell I was supposed to just sit there and make sure the God Dot didn't move. So I did.

"Around the beginning of September, I stopped hearing from Philip and started talking directly to Regina instead. She'd call randomly and ask questions. Who is this Camposanto guy? Do you have a passport? Have you heard from Anna? Had I seen you in Colorado?

"That's what got me thinking. Why'd she think you were in Colorado? I really started to think the red dot was you. I started watching it again. London, Germany, Argentina, Poland… that dot got around. But when it was in London, you were in Dallas nearly getting shot by Philip. When I saw you on the news and realized you were in Kraków with the dot, I knew it wasn't a coincidence.

"I decided to sack up and ask Regina what was going on. She'd always been pretty nice to me, so I figured it couldn't hurt to ask. The next time she called, I asked who the GPS device was tracking, and she actually told me. It was the man who'd killed her son, his name was Luke Jackson, and she wanted to know who he was working for. She said he killed her nephew, too, and if we couldn't stop him he'd kill her and her niece, too. She told me to—"

"Hold the phone!" I squeaked. "Her niece is with her?"

Tommy looked shiftier than ever as he mumbled, "I guess so. Is that important?"

"Extremely! They're in Colombia?"

"As far as I know."

I paused to gather my thoughts, polishing off my martini in the meantime. Tommy seemed to be in no hurry to continue now that he'd divulged something germane.

I thought of the card that had set all this in motion, the unsubtle message from Marisol (presumably) to Paolo letting him know she knew he'd signed her death warrant. That was how I'd taken it, anyway, and Jim and Beauchamp had agreed.

How did Marisol and Regina know Paolo was behind her brother's death, and when did she find out? If Regina's goal was really to find out who was sending Luke after her family, it seemed unlikely she'd been forewarned of Luke's next target as early as September if she hadn't known from where that information was coming.

"I'm confused," I voiced.

"Why is the niece important?"

"She's not, really. I—the family connection in general is important. Has Regina ever mentioned any other family? In Colombia, elsewhere, anyone at all?"

"No."

I closed my eyes, thinking, *Give trust, get trust.* I knew Jim would blow his stack when he found out I'd revealed this, but it felt like the right move. "Tommy… Jim is her nephew, too."

"That can't be right."

"I'm telling you. Great nephew, if we're being technical. Her brother's son, Jim's uncle, is the one who's been sending Luke after the rest of his family."

"Why?"

I shook my head. "It's a long story. But once she knew Jim's name, it wouldn't have taken Regina long to work it out. I think she found out about Paolo, the uncle. I think she's been getting inside info from someone in Jim's office."

"You lost me."

"I lost me, too. What did she tell you to do?" He gave me a blank look, and I prompted, "Before I interrupted you, you were about to tell me what Regina told you to do after she told you about Luke."

His eyes slid out of focus, then zeroed back in. "Oh yeah. She told me to go to Arlington and figure out what you were up to. She gave me Jim's address, and I knew the dot—Luke—had been there before. I was on the way when I realized how close the dot was to me. I called the only Camposanto listed in Arlington, Virginia, and you know the rest."

"How are you supposed to get to Colombia?"

He reached in his jacket pocket and pulled out a United States passport. He held it up for my inspection and I noted the name (Martin Vanover) and other identifiers while he explained, "Regina sent this to me. She said if I needed to run for it, to come to her. And, well… here we are."

I was dying to snatch the passport out of his hand and flip through the visa pages, but I forced my way past the impulse. Tommy watched my internal struggle, giving me time.

At length he asked, "What do we do now?"

"We go back to the car, call Jim, and figure out how to get out of the middle of this family feud."

To my surprise, he offered no objection to this. I paid for our drinks and then called Jim, who was already nearly to the airport. He told me to find a hotel and text him the address. I did as instructed, securing a suite at one of the nicer airport hotels.

Jim's texted reply was bewildering. "When I get there, play along. Delete this text."

I did as instructed, then hopped on an airport shuttle with Tommy and checked in to our hotel. I was white-knuckling my way through being alone in a hotel room with him when the sound of his phone ringing nearly made me scream. He shot a hooded glance at me, then answered it.

"Hello? Yeah, I'm still at the airport… My flight doesn't leave for a few hours still… Not much, do you want to know now or wait 'til I get there? … Yeah, they were about to turn on me, I had to cut and run… Don't think so… Okay, I'll call you when I land. Bye." He set the phone down gingerly, as though worried it might object, and shot another glance my way. "She knows where Luke is, so I'm sure she knows where I am. She probably knows I lied."

"She's tracking him, too?"

"Why wouldn't she?"

"Right."

We both straightened up as someone knocked on the door. Tommy looked stricken, on the verge of panic.

"I'll get it," I sighed.

I looked through the peephole to make sure it was really Jim. It was, but his expression gave me pause. He was either exceptionally angry or so deep in thought he might not notice if I didn't open the door at all. I did anyway, stepping back as he took two long strides past me into the room.

As the door slowly eased shut, Luke, Emily, and Dude were nowhere in evidence. Reacting to the danger implied by Jim's body language, Tommy unwisely sprang to his feet.

Jim drew his gun, pointing it at Tommy's chest. "Sit down."

Tommy silently complied. Jim holstered his weapon and rounded on me, hissing, "You little *idiot*, what were you thinking?"

43

Monday, June 14, 2021

I couldn't remember thinking anything. I stared at Jim, and he stared at me. Belatedly I remembered I was supposed to be playing along, but I didn't know what game we were playing.

He gave up on waiting for me to speak and snapped, "You crossed a line with this one, Bowman. I am done with you."

I blinked at him, torn between confusion and laughter. All I could think to say was, "Bowman? Seriously?"

"You act without thinking, you are constantly putting yourself and everyone else at risk, you are incapable of remorse, you've almost screwed everything up more times than I can even count. What I wouldn't give to send you packing right now."

I pointed behind myself, at Tommy, and argued, "I got the whole story, *Camposanto*. The real story. If we'd done it your way, he'd be long gone by now."

"Congratulations. I'm thrilled. Great job. And what if he'd driven straight to some TIC hideout and delivered you on a silver platter? Did you think of that, by any chance?"

"He didn't know I was in the car!"

"Something tells me he would've figured it out!"

"Well he didn't!" I held back further argument and waited, silently begging Jim to find a way to feed me some lines on the sly.

"I'm not going to be the only person who gives a crap what happens to you anymore," he shot back, as though that excused or explained anything.

Tommy finally found his voice and said, somewhat feebly, "Lay off her."

"You shut up," Jim hurled toward him before rounding on me again. "Out in the hall. Now."

I led the way, pressing my back against the wall a few feet from the door and flinching in spite of myself as Jim's hands cupped my face.

Frantically, he whispered, "I was nervous. I think I oversold it. Did I oversell it?"

"I don't know what you're selling, but you just scared the crap out of me," I breathed.

"Sorry. Look, we don't have time to argue about this, okay? I need you to make Tommy think you want to stay here."

"Where? This hotel?"

He shook his head once. "I have to call Paolo. He'll want us to bring Tommy to him."

"That doesn't—*agh*—Where's Emily?"

"They're on the way to Manchester. Your parents are coming home. Luke and Emily will meet them there with Dude."

"Then where are *we* going?"

"I don't have time to explain. Just tell me if you can do it."

"I can do it."

He shot me a worried look but didn't argue. Instead he led the way into the room, loudly ordering Tommy, "Tell me this so-called real story, and don't lie to me again, kid."

Tommy launched into the story he'd already told me. I listened inattentively, wondering how I was going to make him believe I wanted to stay in Texas. I imagined having dinner with my parents, nieces, sister, and Luke, Dude camped underneath the table waiting for someone to drop a scrap of food, and suddenly tears were queuing up behind my eyes. Once the idyllic image sprang to mind, my entire body strained toward it. This might be an easy sell after all.

Tommy finished talking, and silence fell around us like a collapsing tent. After an intolerable few seconds of this, Jim asked, "What were you going to tell Regina?"

"Everything. I don't owe you people anything."

"What do you owe Regina?"

"Screw you."

"Anna," Jim snapped, making me twitch. "Call another Uber—we're going to the airport."

I shook my head, hating this. I wasn't an actress, I didn't know my lines, and I didn't know how much was riding on my debut performance. I decided to keep it simple and said, "Get your own Uber. I'm going home."

"Did you not hear me? This isn't up to you. Uber. Now."

"You can't force me to come with you!"

A look from Jim, a flash of sincere frustration, warned me it was time to start acquiescing. The problem was, I wasn't playing a part. Jim could be forgiven for assuming I'd want to tag along no matter what, but for once he was wrong.

I wanted to go home, and I didn't even understand why.

Jim didn't give me another chance to argue the point. Putting his phone to one ear, he pointedly ignored my gaze and waited for someone to pick up on the other end.

"It's me," he said, throwing a menace-laden glance my way as though to discourage eavesdropping. "I did get your message. Do you still want me to come, or would you prefer to throw another tantrum? … Because I have someone here I think you'll want to talk to… Florence? Why? … It'll take some time… Fine. All right."

Without bothering to confirm he'd just called Paolo Barbato and offered up Tommy as an olive branch, Jim hung up and immediately made another call.

"Rich, we need our passports."

Thanks for reading! If you enjoyed *Bigger Fish*, please take a couple minutes to leave a review or rating wherever you found it. Reviews help readers decide whether to buy my books, and every single review helps so much—even the bad ones!

Want to be the first to know when new stories come out? You can sign up for my mailing list on my website, akweller.com. You'll get my occasional newsletter, and you'll receive a link to download a free short story.

▼

About the Author

AK Weller was born and raised in Texas, moved to New Mexico, and now lives in Montana with her husband, four cats, and three dogs. She mostly enjoyed brief careers as a technical writer, private investigator, social worker, and pet sitter before finding her calling as a semi-employed writer. AK writes mysteries and thrillers while running her own graphic design business. Her favorite books to read over and over again were written by JRR Tolkien, Stieg Larsson, Sue Grafton, Michael Crichton, and JK Rowling.

▼

Also available from AK Weller

The Anna Bowman Thrillers: a 5-Book Thriller Epic

<u>Book 1: Enemy Closer</u>

On the run from her ex-husband, a powerful federal agent, Abigail takes shelter in a cabin in rural southwest Colorado with her trusty German Shepherd, Dude. When she learns someone else has been using the cabin to hide out too, she'll find herself stuck with a shady, surprise roommate for the summer. While they figure out how to get along, they'll learn their stories were intertwined long before they met. *Enemy Closer* is a suspense thriller that allows you to experience each new piece of information along with the characters right to the end, when you realize everything you thought you knew was a lie. A deeper story has only just begun to unfold.

<u>Book 2: House on Fire</u>

Thanks to her boss, shady FBI Agent Jim Camposanto, Analyst Anna Bowman finds herself the target of two different international criminal cabals. With no obvious way out of the mess she's just beginning to understand, she'll have to drag the truth out of her secretive boss and a hitman who just can't seem to shake her. Will Anna ever get to relax and feel safe with her beloved German Shepherd, Dude, or will she become addicted to Camposanto's dangerous games? Anna Bowman's misadventures continue in *House on Fire*.

Book 3: Bigger Fish

Home from her unlikely triumph in Argentina, Anna thinks her life is getting back to normal until a surprise visit from David March—and sets her on a collision course with Luke Jackson once again. With a little help from two people straight out of Anna's past, they'll unravel a mystery that takes them out of the frying pan and into the fire.

Book 4: No Port in a Storm

After unraveling a murderous family feud, FBI castoffs Anna and Jim travel to Italy to deliver a final peace offering. Amidst their fraught romance, they find no shortage of ways to make new trouble. While fostering unlikely friendships against an idyllic Mediterranean backdrop, they provoke dangerous enemies closer to home. Emily, Luke, and Dude were supposed to be safe in Texas, but suddenly they're in the crosshairs again. As tensions escalate, Jim's clever schemes are put to the test. When generations of hostility erupt into all-out war, will Jim's cunning save them, or will Anna's fighting spirit be their only way out?

▼

Coming soon from AK Weller

<u>2.15.2020</u>

In the prequel to *Enemy Closer*, Anna Bowman escapes her boring hometown and joins the FBI. After a few years as a quiet but efficient cog in the machine, she tries to achieve her childhood dream of becoming an FBI Agent, only to be rejected and bewildered. Ensnared instead in the intrigues of Agent James Camposanto, Anna will embark on an unexpected assignment in Houston, Texas with her protégé, Thomas Holladay. What really happened on February 15, 2020, in Houston, and how in the world did a divorced art historian from Manchester, Texas end up there?

<u>Friday the 14th</u>

Anna Bowman and her older sister, Emily, just wanted a fun night out to celebrate Anna's twenty-fifth birthday. While enjoying some much-needed time away from their significant others, the sisters accidentally pick up a new friend at a casino in Oklahoma. When a tongue-in-cheek plan to burn down each other's houses and collect the insurance money falls into the wrong hands, Anna and Emily will have to band together to stop an arsonist… if they decide they want to. Find out who's left standing on *Friday the 14th*.

<u>A Last Time for Everything</u>

A Last Time for Everything tells the tragic and unbelievable origin story of 17-year-old Anna Bowman and the events that set her on the path to joining the FBI.

Sam Walsh, PI Mysteries

<u>Prequel - Tiger by the Tail</u>

Private Investigator Samantha Walsh has been in denial about her true identity for 25 years. When a terrifying figure from her past explodes back into her life, Sam will have to decide how much she's willing to sacrifice to stop running from her father's killers in *Tiger by the Tail.*

<u>#1 - Sam vs. the Black Hat</u>

Newly independent PI Sam Walsh needs clients, and she can't afford to be picky. When her old boss sends a prospective client her way, Sam takes the case - a classic cheating spouse - against her better judgment. Caught between a dishonest client and a dangerous, shadowy foe, Sam will either solve her first case or die trying. Sue Grafton's iconic Kinsey Millhone is catapulted into twenty-first century Texas suburbia in book one of the Sam Walsh, PI Mysteries.

Underworld: A Short Suspense Thriller

Underworld follows mystery woman Seffy Nix as she moves into a 140-year-old mansion that seems to be haunted by a slovenly, inconsiderate ghost bent on distracting her from the mission that brought her to small-town Helena, Montana.

The Beast and the Books: A Short Monster Story

All alone one night, Rodney is clearing out a storage unit. His biggest problem is his wife's massive book collection, at least until the lights go out and he realizes he's not alone. Something is living deep in the bowels of the storage facility, and it's about to make a break for freedom. Unfortunately for Rodney, he's right in the creature's path.

Anywhere But Home: A Memoir

A short memoir about budding author AK Weller's increasingly nonsensical attempts to fill a void in her life caused by an abusive relationship. From Oklahoma to Texas to Colorado, she hops from one distraction to another until she realizes the answer to her problem is starting over.

<u>The Institute: A Short Story</u>

High school junior Miguel thought getting an underage drinking charge would derail his life at New Mexico Military Institute in Roswell, but when his new friends draw him into their world of pranks and mischief, he'll discover there's a lot more going on at NMMI than he ever imagined. Will Miguel maintain his hard-won GPA and graduate with a diploma that will open doors for him to wherever he wants to go, all while learning how to mix a little fun into his busy life? Will his new friends have his back when things start to get spooky?

▼

Keep turning for a sneak peak at the next chapter of Anna's story: *No Port in a Storm*.

1

Friday, June 18 to
Saturday, June 19, 2021

There is no rest for the wicked. My body was starved for sleep, my heart aching for a few hours of numbness, but my brain hummed and snapped like a bug zapper on a Louisiana summer night. *You can't close your eyes!* it sang. *You're in Florence. You speak Italian. Your window is open. Everyone else is asleep. You're only on the second floor. Climb out.*

Run.

"Well that's idiotic on its face," I whispered to the dark ceiling above where I lay.

An answer floated under my door in sotto voce Italian.

"Ho fame. Non ho mangiato tutto il giorno. C'è del cibo in casa?"

Translation: One of the men outside my door was hungry.

"Perché me lo chiedi? Non lo so. Vai in cucina e scoprilo. E portami del vino."

The other man wanted wine.

At least two other people weren't asleep, then—the two most likely to take umbrage to me climbing out my window and disappearing into the sultry Mediterranean night. I listened to the two men bickering, smiling to myself at the banality of their argument. After a minute or so, one set of feet clumped down the stairs in search of food and wine. Silence reigned until my inner voice chimed back in.

You love wine. Don't you want some wine right now? And some cheese? Cheese, Anna!

My brain had it right that time. I could most definitely go for some wine and cheese. My empty stomach was gurgling, and if I couldn't pass into dreamworld, I could at least numb my senses with alcohol. The problem remained what it had always been: the wickedness.

I climbed out of bed, disturbing no one. My travel companions, Tommy and Jim, had been taken to different rooms. I supposed Tommy was locked in like I was, and that was for the best. No one here trusted him, and God only knew what he'd do if left to his own recognizance. Jim, on the other hand, would be considered trustworthy enough to avoid the indignation of a locked door. All Paolo Barbato had to do was make the demand, and Jim had whisked Tommy and me from Texas to Florence to meet him.

Paolo Barbato and Jim. PB&J. It was worthy of being carved into a tree with a heart around it.

Tiptoeing to the window, I eased it open as far as it would go and leaned out over Via Riscoli. Though midnight approached, people were still out and about, mostly tourists by the look of them. Directly below me, a leggy blonde was sitting on the hood of a black Maserati, posing for a cameraman across the street. She kept shaking back her luxurious mane of curls, annoyed at the tourists wandering fecklessly between her and the camera.

I watched her for a while, then looked up over the city toward the Basilica di San Lorenzo. The floodlights illuminating its façade had been shut off, and I could barely make it out. Disappointed, I propped my elbow on the windowsill and rested my chin in my hand, not realizing what a poignant pose I'd struck until a waspy voice below caught my attention.

"Do you want to join us, lady?"

I peered down again at the Maserati model and saw her upturned face scowling at me. Her offer appeared to be sarcastic. The camera across the street was pointing up at me, which explained her verbal attack.

"Scusa," I mumbled.

I leaned back and shut the window, drowning out the woman's angry chattering as she berated her wayward cameraman. Glancing down at myself, I confirmed I was mostly decent in a silk camisole and pajama shorts. Another overpriced item I'd bought for this trip, to torture and punish Jim.

Thinking of Jim and why I was torturing him unleashed a wave of anger that cut right through me, heating me. A surprise vacation to Italy was far from the worst thing Jim had done to me, but I didn't want to be here. Not like this, not when we were so close to the finish line. How could he not see that?

I stalked to the door and rapped smartly on it.

From outside, a wary, "Sí?"

"Enzo?" I guessed. I'd known Enzo and Aldo all of an hour, so I was still learning to tell them apart.

"Sí."

In his native Italian, I asked, "Can you let me out? I'm hungry. I'm starving."

I felt his hesitation, which ended in a click as the door unlocked but didn't open. I did the honors, cracking the door to smile out at Enzo. Aldo was still downstairs.

"I heard you two talking," I confessed. "I could really use a glass of wine right now, you know?"

He smiled, revealing a row of straight, white teeth. I took a moment to study him more closely: dark eyes, nearly black to match his short-cropped hair that was beginning to curl at the ends, a straight, Roman nose, full lips, clean-shaven. He wasn't attractive per se, but individually his features were quite becoming.

A nasty little gremlin which had recently taken up residence where my soul used to be suggested an efficient and fun way to punish Jim. I smiled back.

"I won't cause any trouble," I whispered.

"Paolo told me to watch out for you. He said you're dangerous."

Paolo Barbato thought *I* was dangerous? That was high praise, coming from the mysterious mafioso whose Hatfield-and-McCoy-style vendetta had set all this in motion.

"Do I look dangerous to you?" I asked, opening the door all

the way so he could make a proper risk assessment. The insubstantial pajamas, the long, red hair, the toned limbs, the breasts that weren't quite as perky as they were ten years ago but still held up thank you very much, all were supposed to be driving Jim crazy with hopeless longing. I wasn't above using them in a more roundabout way.

Enzo took his time studying me from head to toe before concluding, "Yes."

"What do you think I'll do? Try to leave? I want to meet Paolo."

Relenting with a sigh, he waved me out of the room. "Come downstairs. I'm sure we can find something to eat, if Aldo has left us anything."

I followed him down the stairs and through the darkened house to a kitchen at the back. Aldo was indeed within, standing by the island at the center of a small, homey kitchen and stacking together slices of tomato, mozzarella, and bread. He wasn't alone.

Leaning against the stove was James Camposanto, the very Jim I wished to torment. Tall and thin with salt-and-pepper hair and serious gray eyes that ordinarily drove me bananas with longing, the sight of him was currently a source of bitter irritation. He was sipping at a large glass of red wine and watching Aldo with detached interest, at least until Enzo and I appeared in the doorway.

"What are you doing up?" Jim asked me.

Neither Enzo nor Aldo understood his English question, but neither could mistake his hostility. They shared a glance, and Aldo forced a laugh.

Switching to English and a decidedly less seductive tone, I shot back, "What do you care?"

"Make me one of those," Enzo said before Jim could reply, gesturing at the massive sandwich Aldo was about to shove into his mouth. With a good natured grumble, Aldo complied. I sidled up next to him and stole a slice each of mozzarella and tomato, then sat down at a stool on the other side of the island to enjoy them.

The Florentine cocina wasn't so different from an ordinary kitchen back home in the States, but one feature kept me firmly grounded in reality: the heat. In Texas, my parents' AC would be cranking out cold air in June, even at night. Here a warm, sticky atmosphere pervaded indoors and out. One could catch a stray breeze outside, but the windowless kitchen was stuffy. I risked a quick glance at Jim to make sure he was wearing the long-sleeved t-shirt and flannel pajama pants I'd picked up especially for him. He was, and his forehead was glistening with sweat.

I smiled sweetly at him when he met my eyes. "Hot in here?"

He shook his head but didn't answer, giving his full attention back to his wine glass. Enzo sat down next to me and asked, "Can you ask him to share?"

He nodded toward the wine bottle at Jim's elbow. I hopped off my seat and fetched three more wine glasses from the cabinet next to Jim's head, ignoring him while I emptied the rest of his Chianti into the first glass, opened a second bottle from the rack behind him, and tipped a healthy measure into the other two glasses. These I took to Enzo and Aldo before returning for my glass.

"Why don't you put some clothes on?" Jim murmured, barely looking at me.

My answer was to return to my stool, facing Enzo with my back to Jim, and proceed to act as though Jim didn't exist.

It wasn't so much that Jim was angry at me. That was nothing new. I did things to make him angry all the time, most recently by leaving him, along with our friend Luke Jackson, my sister Emily, and my dog Dude, in the middle of a tornado in Oklahoma to climb into the trunk of a car and let Tommy unwittingly drive me to the Dallas-Fort Worth airport. It was an impulse, and Jim was quite accustomed to me following those.

If that wasn't the source of his rudeness, my second best guess was that Jim was mirroring my bad attitude, but that hardly made sense. Jim took pride in being the foil to my petty reactiveness, acting like he had ice in his veins, Mister Cool as a Cucumber.

Cucumber. Hng. I let my thoughts wander for a moment, then reeled them back in.

His rank hypocrisy was keeping my vindictiveness alive. Jim had put me through hell, almost two solid years of it, starting with ruining my dream of becoming an FBI agent in July 2019. A few months ago, he'd capped off months of lies and manipulation by tossing me between his cousins and an assassin's bullets, all so I could save his cousins by offering up a priceless, lost Renaissance masterpiece for their lives.

The whole tale is a little more complicated, but the point was simply that, after hearing Jim's full confession, I'd forgiven him. I'd come to a conscious decision, dismissing logic and evidence, to trust him. To *love* him. And there the smug puppet master sat, treating me like a wayward child, some kind of burdensome baggage, when it was his idea to drag me to Italy without even asking if I wanted to come.

"He really doesn't speak Italian?" Enzo asked.

I sensed his disbelief and shrugged. "He doesn't even know what 'Camposanto' means," I said, provoking a laugh from both men.

Jim was far too genteel to let us get to him, giving no sign he'd heard his own name.

Enzo cast a hooded glance at Jim and asked me, "Can you tell him we don't mean any offense? I don't think we're making a great first impression on our cousin."

"Cousin?" I echoed, ignoring the rest.

"Aldo is my brother—well, half-brother—and Paolo is our father. So that would make James a... second cousin? Something like that."

"But you'd never met him until today?"

"Nope."

"Don't waste any time worrying about his feelings," I said. "He doesn't have any."

"Why did you come here with him, if you hate him so much?"

I thought hate was a bit strong, but rather than correcting him, I repeated my earlier lie. "I told you, I want to meet Paolo. Why isn't he coming until tomorrow?"

"He's a little paranoid. Don't worry. He's eager to meet you, too."

That may have been true, but it wasn't the reason Paolo was coming. Neither was Jim. The third member of our party, who was hopefully still locked in his room upstairs, was the real reason Paolo was emerging from wherever he'd been hiding from his family, why he'd ordered Jim to Florence. That would be Tommy Holladay, who'd entered my life two years ago a fresh-faced, eager trainee at the FBI's Organized Crime Unit and left it a violent, angry casualty of an undercover operation in Houston that went pear-shaped in the blink of an eye.

At least I thought he'd left my life. Tommy had turned up last month, alive and not-so well, seeking safe harbor. He'd claimed he was living in fear of Philip Levin, our former boss who'd personally betrayed and sent us to our deaths in Houston. That claim turned out not to be super duper true. Tommy was, in fact, now working for a woman named Regina Lira. Paolo had ordered Regina's son, Francisco, killed that same night in Houston.

Paolo had accepted Tommy as a peace offering from Jim, and here we were to deliver him on a silver platter. I assumed Tommy was lying awake this very moment, wondering if he knew enough about Regina to make himself useful to Paolo, and what would happen if he didn't.

9798991630818